P 6- 8-6

W9-BRL-762

SWEETWATER

Also by Paul Charles

The DI Christy Kennedy Mysteries:
  I Love the Sound of Breaking Glass
  Last Boat to Camden Town
  Fountain of Sorrow
  The Ballad of Sean & Wilko
  I've Heard the Banshee Sing
  The Hissing of the Silent Lonely Room
  The Justice Factory

Other fiction:
  The First of the True Believers

Non-fiction:
  Playing Live (The Complete Guide to)

PAUL CHARLES

SWEETWATER

A DI Christy Kennedy Mystery

BRANDON

First published in 2006 by
Brandon
an imprint of Mount Eagle Publications
Unit 3 Olympia Trading Estate, Coburg Road, London N22 6TZ, England
and Cooleen, Dingle, Co. Kerry, Ireland

www.brandonbooks.com

10 9 8 7 6 5 4 3 2 1

ISBN 0 86322 356 7

Mount Eagle Publications/Sliabh an Fhiolair Teoranta receives support from
the Arts Council/An Chomhairle Ealaíon.

Cover design: www.design-suite.ie
Typesetting by Red Barn Publishing, Skeagh, Skibbereen
Printed in the UK

Dedication and thanks

Special thanks to Steve and the fab Brandon team
and to Andy and Cora.
This one is dedicated to Catherine.

Chapter One

THE JACKET HE once wore still lay on the back of his chair. The lifelines, which marked his most frequent torso movements, were still evident by the creases around the elbows and the back flap of the lifeless garment.

His desk, in his absence, as it had been in his presence, was meticulously laid out. His obsession for tidiness was evident in each and every particle of his six-by-eight-metre corner office. Should he have been present with Kennedy as the Ulster-born, Camden Town-based detective inspector examined the office, and wandered, as Kennedy did, over to the double-aspect set of windows, his sense of tidiness would have been offended by the lone car which spoiled the near uniform rows of empty parking bays in the floodlit forecourt three storeys below.

When the owner of the lonely jacket and deserted office had parked his car, a Silver Jaguar X Type, sixteen hours earlier at 6.55, it had been the lone vehicle in the car park then as well. By the stroke of 9 a.m. (barely) his silver pride and joy had been joined by 107 other vehicles of varying colours and models, and by the time the nearby bells of St Martin's wearily rang out 7 p.m., it was the sole occupant once more.

Kennedy sat behind the desk. It felt strange to sit in someone else's space, particularly when the someone in question had broken the habit of twenty-six years, five months, one week and two days, by disappearing from his office into thin air. The only sign that Riley had ever existed was, in fact, the aforementioned dark blue creased jacket, which swung limply as Kennedy tilted the captain's chair back to a precarious angle to facilitate his search for a key to the locked drawers of the grey metallic desk.

No joy there.

Kennedy, in a funny way, fitted in with the office. Say for instance a stranger were to have visited the office and popped their head around the door, as strangers sometimes tend to do, then the 45-year-old detective would not have looked out of place. Kennedy liked to fit in. Well, it wasn't that he liked to fit in as much as that he didn't like to stand out, as it were. His excuse was that if he blended in, he wouldn't be noticeable, and if he weren't too noticeable, he could easily observe his surroundings.

He was five foot and ten inches high, weighed nearly ten stone—about half a stone under his normal weight—had jet black hair, loosely parted in the middle and which he wore just long enough to be able to tuck it behind his ears. He had clear skin which didn't take to the sun too well but never suffered the dreaded five o'clock shadow. The detective's most striking features were his green eyes, which came fully alive when he broke into a smile. The same smile that he had used on numerous occasions, but rarely intentionally, to diffuse awkward situations.

While on duty, Kennedy tended to favour dark classy clothes, as in jackets and trousers, his concessions to colour being mainly the blue of his shirt, the variety of his sober ties, which he wore more out of choice than duty, and his selection of vividly coloured socks. He loved traditional black leather shoes, the type that start to look and feel great only when you've been wearing and polishing them for several months or maybe even—as with a couple of pairs he could remember—a couple of years.

The over-all package tended to create an air of gentleness rather than the archetypal hostility one tended to expect from the London policeman.

Although Kennedy has spent the majority of his life—twenty-seven years that 27 September, to be exact—living in London, he was still an Ulsterman with the distinctive tones and wry humour of an Ulsterman. He had spent an even larger part of his life, forty-five years at his next birthday, being intrigued by, and absorbed in, the art of detection, which is how he came to be a discreet stranger in that particular tidy office.

He looked around the office. There were no other outward signs of the occupier. The grey felt notice board was neatly adorned with company notices, product posters and rotas. You would think for someone who had reportedly enjoyed a happy trouble-free family life, there would be at least one photograph of the wife, two daughters and the son Kennedy had met in Superintendent Thomas Castle's office two hours previously.

Normally a missing person is not officially a missing person until they've been missing for at least twenty-four hours. Normally though, friends of Superintendent Castle, Kennedy's amicable superior, didn't disappear. Normally Kennedy would not be working on a missing-person's case. But the fact of the matter was that he still wasn't 100 per cent fit, having discovered that no matter how much your mind might want you to jump straight back in the saddle after being injured in the line of duty, your body will have the final say by refusing to do as you bid. So, far from being a burden as an invalid, he was helping out as much as he could around North Bridge House, the home of Camden Town CID.

He suspected that Castle wanted to impress the wife of his friend by putting one of his top men on the case and, truth be told, Kennedy was happy to escape having to deal with all the complaints from local residents up in arms about the recently constructed traffic-calming ramps, the lack of parking facilities or the drug dealers who, having been moved on, were simply decamping to yet another estate.

In his enthusiasm, Castle had nearly gone as far as shooing Kennedy and the remaining members of the Riley family out of his office. It had been the older daughter, Christine, who had sheltered her mother from the near farce by immediately involving Kennedy and the family in conversation.

'Are you from Scotland?'

'Ah—' Kennedy smiled. 'Close . . . I'm actually from Ireland.'

'Oh,' Christine replied immediately. 'You don't sound a bit like Terry Wogan. Does he, Mum?'

Christine, obviously the socialite of the family, seemed happy, even anxious, to start a conversation up out of nothing.

The mother, obviously distracted, muttered, 'Sorry?'

'DI Kennedy here is from Ireland.'

'Oh, that's nice,' the mum replied, trying to force a smile.

'The Corrs are from Ireland, aren't they?' Christine continued, 'Well, at least the girls look like they're from Ireland; the man looks like he could be from Wales.'

The other sister rolled her eyes at Kennedy in an 'Oh she's off on one again' expression.

Kennedy wondered whether Christine took after her mother or her father with that particular trait.

John Riley, according to his wife Sally, was a creature of absolute habit.

That morning, like every other morning excepting Sundays, he rose, with the aid of an alarm set for 5.58. He always rose at 5.58, the wife reported—never six o'clock. He showered, shaved—electric—dressed, kissed his wife on the forehead, 'Right, that's me, darling, talk to you later. Enjoy your sleep.' He quietly closed their bedroom door, crept down the stairs—as his wife turned over and went back to sleep—and slipped out of his house, without breakfast. He was always behind the wheel of his car at 6.35 ready to drive from their home in Glenilla Road, Belsize Park, to his office on Pratt Street in Camden Town, stopping off en route for a copy of the *Times* and a coffee and almond croissant.

Then he went to his office and started his day. On this particular morning, it appears that some time after 11.40—he was spotted by one of his colleagues going to the toilet—he just quite simply disappeared, leaving nothing behind but his jacket.

Chapter Two

I T WAS JUST before lunchtime the following day when Kennedy met Fr
Vincent O'Connor for the first time.

The detective was visiting Sally Riley up in Belsize Park, firstly to
secure some additional background information, and secondly to advise
the family that there had been no overnight news or sightings of John Riley,
husband and father respectively.

'I still half-expect to see John walk up the garden path,' Sally Riley said
as she guided Kennedy through to the conservatory, which overlooked a
spectacular garden. It was a much bigger garden than you would ever imagine in central London. Kennedy was convinced that it must be the biggest
domestic garden in NW1. The lawn was perfectly manicured, and the June
sun threw its light magnificently over the bushes, small trees and numerous types and colours of flowers.

Fr O'Connor, Christine and Sally, all of whom had been enjoying coffee and generous slices of carrot cake, sat around a wicker table, which was
half in the conservatory and half spilling out into the garden. Kennedy
passed on coffee, wine and water, more than happy to settle for the fourth
option, tea. It might have been the tea or it might have been the combination of carrot cake *and* tea, but it hit the spot and hit the spot big time.

Kennedy loved few things more than a cup of hot tea. His preference
was neither too weak nor too strong, flavoured with two sugars, and cooled
and blended with honest-to-goodness milk.

'This is his pride and joy,' Sally began, nodding in the direction of the
garden.

'A credit to the man,' O'Connor added.

'He's always either at work in his office or in his dungarees in the garden,' Christine continued. 'He was here all day Sunday, weeding, trimming
and cutting. I mean to say, I find it incredible really. I can come out into the
garden, and I have to say I'm taking much more enjoyment out of it now

than I did when I lived at home, but to my eyes it would be perfect, and then you'd see Dad come out of his shed dressed in his battered dungarees—'

'When he's working in the garden, you'd swear the man didn't have a penny to his name—' the mother said, interrupting the daughter who continued as flawlessly as Morecambe and Wise routine:

'—nor a care in the world. He'd toil all day, finding things that just needed to be done. Same at night in the summer—if there was any daylight left when he came home, he'd be out here, wouldn't he, Mum?'

'Absolutely, much too much if you ask me,' Sally Riley dutifully replied. 'I suppose the garden is his sanctuary, where he can be alone with his thoughts. I often looked out the window at John diligently going about his work and wondered if he was thinking about his gardening or thinking deep thoughts.'

Mrs Riley paused as if considering whether or not to develop this line of conversation. Eventually she concluded with, 'I always thought that a garden needed attention only in the spring and through the summer, but he'd be busy tending to it the whole year around.'

'Was he under pressure at his work at all?' Kennedy felt obliged to ask.

'You know what?' Sally smiled. 'I can't remember the last time any of us discussed work with him.'

Christine appeared slightly more worried on the second day.

Kennedy could definitely see the logic in that; a whole night and day had now passed without a sighting. This in turn also served to move John Riley's disappearance much further up the serious scale. The mother, on the other hand, seemed much more relaxed. Kennedy couldn't work out whether it was as a result of Valium or of the priest's presence.

Fr Vincent O'Connor definitely had a calming air. He had twinkly, friendly eyes and a mischievous smile, similar to that of flautist James Galway. Unlike Galway though, O'Connor had a face—bulky nose, bushy eyebrows, thin lips and a heavy jaw—that would have been perfect for radio. The priest's large eyes suggested he had nothing to hide—no agenda—and he seemed like someone eager to get to know you, and perhaps, if you were lucky, even become your friend. He had the air of one whose belief came from intelligence and not from blind faith. Kennedy always found this disconcerting. He always felt as though such people were tuned into something he wasn't.

O'Connor's traditional black suit and dog collar did nothing to dampen his spirit.

'Detective Inspector, we know you have to ask Mrs Riley—Sally—some potentially embarrassing questions, and I want you to know she's ready for them,' O'Connor said.

'Yes, but to save you having to ask—no, he hasn't committed suicide, and no, there isn't another woman,' Sally volunteered before O'Connor had a chance to finish.

'I absolutely concur 100 per cent,' Christine chipped in, sounding so unnatural that Kennedy assumed she had said the words only to support her mother. Kennedy positively loved to listen to people, sometimes as much for their manner of speech as for what they were actually saying. Other times, what they didn't say frequently gave just as much away.

'So, is there any other reason either of you can think of that might explain his continued absence?' Kennedy asked.

Sally looked to Fr O'Connor and Christine looked to the floor. Kennedy was happy none of them was looking at him. He felt a sharp pain burn in his stomach. Six months on and he was still experiencing brief twinges. His doctor thought it was a phantom pain brought on by psychological, rather than physical, strain. Kennedy just wished he could transfer the trauma, brief though it was, to his doctor so he could see *exactly* how psychological the pain was.

He had had a few conversations with Dr Taylor about the attacks, and Taylor reckoned it had something to do with the delayed reaction of his body to the incident. In other words, he was suggesting that as Kennedy had been doped up on painkillers since shortly after a run-in with a fugitive, his body was paying the price. That explanation Kennedy could cope with. He could see the sense in that. He resisted the temptation to raise his hand to his stomach to feel the healing wound. Kennedy was happy that O'Connor, Sally and Christine Riley were too preoccupied with their own thoughts to be worried about what he may or may not be feeling.

'It's nothing really,' Christine started, looking at her mum for approval to continue. O'Connor was the one who nodded approval. 'It's just that my mother and father had an argument on Sunday morning.'

Kennedy nodded, as if to sympathise.

'And that's it really—that's all we can think of, isn't it Mum?'

'And even that was something and nothing,' Sally added definitely, giving the appearance of someone not remotely concerned about the argument.

Sally Riley was dressed, Kennedy guessed, in her Sunday best—a light blue, knee-length skirt, with a matching three-quarter length jacket that she had a habit of gathering about her every time she stood up or moved about the house. Her not-quite-so-elegant outfit was completed with white flowing silk blouse and a pair of matching blue-patent leather high-heeled shoes. All her clothes seemed carefully sculpted to minimise the appearance of her weight. Kennedy had noted the previous day, on their first meeting, that whereas the son and the other daughter shared their mother's generous proportions, Christine was slim. Sally Riley's blue-rinse hair had only recently received attention, and her make-up and overall appearance implied that Fr O'Connor's visit was a scheduled one.

'Okay,' Kennedy started, hoping that a clue to the reason for the disappearance was coming, 'what did you both argue about?'

'I'm sorry,' Sally began, sitting up in her creaking seat. 'I don't want to discuss it. All I wish to say on the matter is that it was about something and it was about nothing. It didn't mean anything really. He went out to the garden upset, and by the time he came back in for his lunch, it was all but forgotten. That's John's way. He'd never harbour a grudge. I believe he feels that you can never repair things with words alone, and I discovered pretty early on in our marriage that his preference was just to move on.'

'My mum and dad could never stay angry with each other for very long,' Christine offered, forcing a smile. 'I mean, considering they've been together for over twenty-five years, they get on great.'

'Christine, how many times do I have to tell you that it's not nice to speak about me as if I'm not here?' Sally chastised her daughter.

'Sorry, Mum,' Christine said, rubbing her mum's back, 'I do need to say, Detective Inspector, that Mum hasn't told me or my brother or sister what the argument was about.'

'Nor me,' O'Connor admitted.

'Well, no disrespect, but surely it's nobody's business but John's and mine.'

'Tell me,' Kennedy began, changing tack but not before duly noting that Sally Riley has chosen not to discuss the argument rather than lying about it, 'are you aware of anything at all that might have been troubling Mr Riley?'

'Well, no,' Sally began. 'I mean, financially we're comfortably off, not what you'd call rich. Well, few are these days, thanks to Blair and Brown, but we're okay. We own this house, we have no debts, and we have a nest egg, which we hope will get us through any difficult times and into retirement. Well, it's such an unusual concept, isn't it? You know, saving up for retirement. I mean, how much is enough? How will we ever know until it's too late?'

'What are Mr Riley's interests?' Kennedy asked.

'He loves gardening, he absolutely adores going for walks on Primrose Hill, he seems to like his work, but, I'd have to say, he's not a great holiday man. We go to Italy once a year for three weeks, and he likes the food and the walks a lot, but he loves, even more, to come home. He's not flash—he doesn't splash his money around. His one uncharacteristic folly is his choice of car; his pride and joy is his Jaguar X Type. He loves to read, but he claims he never gets enough time for that particular pastime.'

'What kind of books does he read?' Kennedy asked.

'Classics, biographies and Bill Bryson,' Christine chipped in immediately. 'I'll show you his bookcase if you like. It's in his study.'

'That would be helpful,' Kennedy said.

'We can do that when you're finished with Mum,' Christine offered.

'Actually, I think I have as much as I need for now,' Kennedy said, standing up and happy to do so if only to try to ease the pain in his stomach.

Sally Riley and Fr O'Connor said their goodbyes to Kennedy as Christine led him up to the first floor of the house and took him into a small back room, which offered an even more spectacular view of the garden through a window that seemed out of proportion to the room.

'He loves to sit here,' Christine said, pointing to a well-worn leather chair positioned directly in front of the window. 'He had our builders enlarge this window just so he could sit here and read or look out over the garden.'

Kennedy looked around the room. It was packed with row upon row of books. There was no desk or computer, just walls of books, a wooden floor, a large window with a white roller blind and the leather chair.

'Do you think he's okay?' Christine asked, her concern apparent for the first time.

'Well, so far I have learned nothing to suggest otherwise,' were the carefully chosen words Kennedy used in reply.

'I'll leave you here in peace,' Christine offered helpfully. 'I'll be in the room directly across the hall when you want to leave.'

'Thanks,' the detective replied, his mind now distracted by the numerous rows of hardback books. There was something about book rooms—something that he could never quite put his finger on—that always stopped Kennedy in his tracks.

For all his genuine interest though, Kennedy discovered nothing in Riley's study but books. He couldn't find any drawers, nor was there anything incriminating hidden behind the cushions of the leather chair. He half-heartedly removed a few books from random points in the shelves and flicked them open. He paused at one, not because he had found any evidence therein but because he loved the first page. It was *Seabiscuit* by Laura Hillenbrand. A special acquaintance of Kennedy's, ann rea, had been absolutely raving to Kennedy about this book, and now, after stealing a glimpse at Riley's copy, he resolved to read it as soon as possible. *Goodness,* he thought as he returned the book to its position on the shelves—he had read nearly every book published since his near-death experience, so why not *Seabiscuit* as well?

From the condition of each and every one of Riley's volumes, it was obvious that he loved his books as much as he loved his garden.

Ten minutes later, Kennedy found himself, for the second time in twenty-four hours, sitting in one of John Riley's chairs; this time the Camden Town detective was staring out over the garden and wondering why this man had allowed so little of himself in both of his personal spaces.

Chapter Three

KENNEDY HAD WALKED up to Belsize Park and was three minutes into his return saunter when a car pulled up beside him. Kennedy was caught unawares and automatically looked away.

'Can I give you a lift somewhere?'

He immediately recognised the voice.

'Oh, Father, it's you. Thank you, but I'm happy to walk.'

'No bother, hop in. I'd like to have a chat with you anyway.'

'Thank you,' Kennedy said as he climbed on board the battered, light blue VW Beetle. O'Connor waited until the policeman had fastened his seat belt before pulling away from the kerb. They were close to the England's Lane junction. 'Tell me, Father, did you know John Riley very well?'

'Not at all,' O'Connor replied. 'Sally is a devout supporter, but we rarely see the daughters, son or husband.'

'Oh.'

'It's not unusual in this day and age. The family has grown up, the mother finds herself with more time on her hands than she knows what to do with. Then she finds the church and discovers that we offer quite a few social distractions as well as spiritual ones, you know.'

'There's nothing you could tell me then that might help me with our inquiries?' Kennedy asked.

'Sadly not,' O'Connor replied. He spoke so softly that Kennedy had to concentrate to hear the words above the racket of the engine. It was a disarming but compelling trait. 'I can tell you though that I am not in possession of any information, of a confidential nature, which might be of use to you. You know, as in the confessional type. Even if I were, of course, I could not and would never reveal it to you, but I don't believe I'm breaking any religious vows by telling you that you know everything I do.'

'Right,' Kennedy replied.

'How common an occurrence is this?'

'Well, about 210,000 people are reported missing in the UK each year,' Kennedy said.

'You're kidding, I didn't realise it was anywhere near that number.'

'London alone accounts for just over 24,000 of that figure. The vast majority—I think it's around 70 per cent—turn up within the first seventy-two hours. Girls up to age seventeen are more likely to disappear than boys, but from the age of eighteen onwards, it swings the opposite way. Six people out of every ten who go missing do so intentionally.'

'And what of the 30 per cent who don't show up within the first seventy-two hours? What happens to them?' O'Connor asked, appearing as though he felt he should have known all this information already.

'Well, the greater the time elapsed, the lesser the chance there is of mis-pers (missing persons) being traced.'

'As you remarkably seem to have all of this information on the tip of your tongue, could you then explain to me why, generally speaking, people do go missing?'

'Oh, one of the advantages of being on semi-sick leave is that you actually get a chance to read all the reports which pass over your desk. Let's see,' Kennedy replied, and tried to recall the list in his mind before relaying it aloud. 'As close to an order of popularity as I can remember: family conflict—that's certainly the most common; then debt; illness or accident; anxiety or stress; depression or mental illness; abuse by a member of the family; amnesia; senile dementia or Alzheimer's disease; alcohol or drug abuse; because they feel like it; or abduction by either humans or aliens.'

'I doubt there'd be much of the alien type around here.'

'Oh, I wouldn't be so sure about that. If you'd a few jars too many and you stumbled upon the druids on the top of Primrose Hill on 21 June, you'd be forgiven for believing anything is possible,' Kennedy replied, not feeling at liberty to tell the priest some of the incidents and fears which had been reported to him over the years.

'Yeah,' O'Connor sighed, 'after some of the things I've heard in the confessional box, I can well believe that. Have you any ideas yet about which category John would fit into?'

'Well, some people just simply feel like disappearing—starting anew, you know, wiping the slate clean and starting their lives over again.'

'Ah now, if only we could all have a stab at that.'

'Some people, perhaps like John Riley, have a problem communicating with their family. That's the only thing I've picked up so far. He seems a wee bit distant from his family. When he's not working, he's out in his garden; when he's not out in his garden, he's up in his room reading a book or looking at his garden. He has an argument with his wife and, rather than deal with it, he goes out and works in the garden all day and then comes back in to have his dinner as though nothing has happened. He seems to be a bit of a loner.'

'Yes, Sally does joke about it sometimes, but she doesn't seem concerned about it. Maybe she likes the freedom his need to be alone gives her,' the priest offered.

Kennedy nodded as if to suggest, *I see what you mean,* and said, 'But the problem with the loner route for our guy is the fact that he's outside the age range of males most likely to disappear—twenty-four to thirty years old. But, you know what? These are all just theories. In practice, some people just let things get out of control. It could be something like gambling—you know, trying to find some way of getting themselves out of trouble but ending up so deep in trouble they feel they just can't face the consequences. Stress greatly reduces our ability to deal with problems.

'The other important thing here is that it might not necessarily be a recent problem which drove him to disappear. Loners do tend to let things build up, and he could be harbouring something for the last couple of years, letting whatever it was that was troubling him fester away inside him and just waiting patiently for the opportunity to do a Basil Bond.'

'A Basil Bond?' O'Connor inquired, a smile creeping asymmetrically across his weatherbeaten face.

'Basil Bond was a famous French disappearing artist.'

'Oh.'

Kennedy sighed. 'Sometimes the people who disappear . . . feel that they're doing their survivors a favour by getting out of their lives.'

'Some people are just victims and can never escape it,' O'Connor said, looking off into the distance, way beyond the road ahead of them, before continuing. 'Or as Oscar Wilde believed, "We are each our own devil, and we make this world our hell."'

'Indeed,' Kennedy replied. 'Indeed.'

'Tell me, Inspector Kennedy,' O'Connor said as they pulled up outside North Bridge House, 'I noticed while we were in the Rileys' house that you winced a couple of times, like you seemed short of breath or you were experiencing some discomfort, and you went to hold your stomach—are you okay?'

'A bit of a work wound which comes back to haunt me. I suppose it's a reminder—'

'You mean, as in it's a bit of a reminder of our own mortality?' O'Connor interrupted, as he climbed out of the car to shake Kennedy's hand. 'Aye, such reminders are very necessary, very necessary indeed.'

He passed Kennedy one of his business cards, 'Please keep me posted on this. You're welcome to ring me any time.'

Kennedy waited until the priest had driven off before he stole a glance at the card. All the time he had been wondering what a priest would have on his business card.

O'Connor's was classy and simple and, as well as a Camden Town telephone number, it bore the legend:

Scepticism is the beginning of Faith.
Oscar Wilde

There's always someone to talk to.
Father Vincent Joseph O'Connor

Chapter Four

FIVE AND A half weeks later, there was *still* no sign of John Riley. In the intervening weeks, Kennedy discovered that John Riley had not used any of his credit cards since the day before he disappeared. Nor had he recently written a cheque or made any large withdrawals from his account over the previous dozen years.

As far as Kennedy could ascertain, he had no enemies, no debts, no girlfriends and no boyfriends. There were no sightings on CCTV recordings, and no bodies unaccounted for were found on the Camden streets or dredged up out of Regent's Canal.

There were, however, a few alleged sightings. One was of a man fitting Riley's description sitting in the Princess pub on Gloucester Terrace the Wednesday after the disappearance, eating an Indian meal and drawing attention to himself because he washed it down with seven pints of Guinness. Another sighting was on the Camden Bridge to Richmond overground train, and the third, and final, was in the lobby of the RFH at the time of an Elvis Costello concert. Whereas Christine Riley was a big fan of the artist formerly known as Declan McManus, she was convinced that her father had probably never even heard of him, and she knew for sure that her father had never been to a pop concert in his life.

No, John Riley had well and truly disappeared, and no number of hints from Castle, subtle though they were, would help to find him.

Normally the case would have slipped down the list of priorities because of other cases coming up on the fast track. But as far as Castle was concerned, Kennedy was still officially on sick leave, and so his workload, and that of DS James Irvine, reflected this.

As far as Kennedy was concerned, he felt fine. Yes, there was the odd twinge, but there were no nightmares, no bouts of depression, no listlessness or any such. Kennedy felt that he had his parents to thank for that. When he was growing up, they never made a mountain out of a molehill.

If he fell and cut his knee, they would dust him off, attend to the cut or bruise and send him back out again. If he had a cold or flu, they would look after him, not mollycoddle him, and get him back to school as soon as possible. In short, they taught him not to be preoccupied with recovery. His mother would say that the tearing is always a lot more painful than the sewing, and that referred to all aspects of life.

So, Kennedy was aware of exactly how much damage his body had suffered and he had patiently allowed time to do what it could do best—repair. He didn't feel that he had been careless. He felt it had been something similar to what Formula One racing drivers term a 'racing accident'. It didn't matter how great a driver *you* were, it was the *other* drivers you had to worry about—you had no control over them. In Kennedy's case, if he chose to work in the police force, of course there were times when he would put himself in a position of danger.

If anything, it was the criminal's logic, rather than any personal worries of his own about returning to work, that concerned Kennedy. In all his years in the police force, he still could not fathom how someone, anyone, could use the removal of another life to further his or her own. The only conclusion he kept coming back to was that they were just different creatures from him.

But Kennedy felt he had had enough time to consider the minds of murderers, to go to the cinema, to read, to wander about his house, to go for walks in Regent's Park and Primrose Hill and to listen to the music he loved—he found that when you slowed down and weren't listening to music on the run, the enjoyment factor soared. He even took the occasional trip to Brighton, just to be near the sea. He liked the sea, always had, but still he had resisted the urge to return to his parents' home in Portrush where he could have seen and heard the ocean from his bedroom window.

Why hadn't he gone home?

He wasn't sure really. He figured maybe it might have taken him more time to recover. He figured it might have been seen as a slight on ann rea, who, even though they were on the verge of splitting up before the incident, had shown just how good a friend she was afterwards by decamping to his house and looking after him day and night, night and day.

In this recovery time, they had agreed to put their romantic relationship on hold. Both seemed equally unwilling to spend time and waste energy being preoccupied by it. And as it happened, taking all that crap out of the air enabled them to get on fine. 'Just ducky,' as ann rea had a habit of saying. And that's how they remained, both appearing anxious not to examine whatever it was that had been keeping them from making the final giant leap together emotionally.

The more he got back on his feet, the less she was around his house. The less she was around his house, the more he wanted to get back to doing what he loved—solving puzzles, crime puzzles that is. So, bit by bit, he worked his way back up, and eventually people started seeing him around North Bridge House again. At first, they seemed to react as though they were surprised that he was still alive. He even noticed some of his colleagues, when they thought he wasn't looking, do a little fancy footwork so that they could or would avoid him. But as ever, Desk Sergeant Flynn proved himself to be solid as a rock, salt of the earth and every other cliché you could think of, although none described accurately the fact that he was just a great man with no hidden agendas. Flynn didn't patronise Kennedy—far from it. He was happy to share his duties with Kennedy, and the very fact that Flynn thought that the front desk was the most important and vital part of North Bridge House showed exactly how high in his esteem he held Kennedy.

DS James Irvine, Kennedy's favourite bagman, checked in with Kennedy every morning and every afternoon and even found himself dragged into helping out with the front-desk duties.

One of the main causes of complaint at the front desk came from Camden residents who had recently visited the nearby Somers Town only to find their lives under threat, not from villains of the street but from villains of the air in the shape of seagulls. For those couple of weeks, with the formidable trio of Flynn, Irvine and Kennedy—representing the North and South of Ireland and Scotland—none of the usual Parkway characters (or should that be chancers?) stood a chance, instead receiving the short, swift Celtic shrift.

A few weeks passed, and as Kennedy hadn't collapsed and returned to his sick bed, Superintendent Castle seemed to accept the fact that he just might be ready to come back to work officially. So Kennedy's chores had started to build up again to the point where he was deemed well enough to take responsibility for a missing person.

It wasn't even that he felt that mispers cases were beneath him. No, as he explained to the priest he had met in Riley's home, many serious cases start off with a missing person.

Kennedy was completely intrigued by this one though. Not a single clue, or could that have been not a single clue he had been sharp enough to pick up on?

When people disappear of their own accord, they sometimes leave a few carefully orchestrated clues as to what *might* have happened. Like with the John Stonehouse affair where he reportedly folded all his clothes and left them on the beach before skipping the country.

On the other hand, this John Riley chap appeared just to disappear. Now, Kennedy knew that no one could just magically vanish. Even if Riley had been murdered and buried or given concrete shoes for a swim off Brighton's busy pier, he, or his remains, would still *be* somewhere. The secret with magic was not to follow what the magician wanted you to follow but to study the movements off camera, for therein lay the secret of the illusion.

He had discussed this in detail with Fr Vincent O'Connor over Kennedy's favourite pasta at Trattoria Lucca on Parkway. Even though O'Connor had been the one who had passed on the phone number, he was the one who had made the regular calls to Kennedy at North Bridge House, to check up on the progress of the Riley case. Eventually the telephone calls grew into visits to North Bridge House, where it transpired that Sgt Flynn and Fr O' Connor were well acquainted. Kennedy was not surprised to discover that Flynn was a regular churchgoer, but he was amused by the fact that O'Connor and Flynn had known each other for getting on twenty years. You never know who's going to turn up at any stage in your life. Equally you rarely know where they come from, or who they may, or may not, have known that you already have connections with.

Kennedy did not have many friends in his life. He subscribed to the theory that the majority of people on this earth can count their true friends on the fingers of one hand. Kennedy found that he always struggled beyond the middle finger, no matter in which direction he was counting. So taking this into consideration, he was surprised by the ease with which Fr Vincent O'Connor slipped into his life. Kennedy was not entirely sure why he had made such a strong connection with Fr O'Connor. He was initially prepared to accept that the priest had probably viewed him as a potential flock member, a lone sheep badly in need of a guide back to the comfort and safety of the flock. Kennedy did not fault the priest for that. He wondered if his own enthusiasm for the relationship had anything to do with a deep yearning for there to be something else in his life, in everyone's life for that matter, other than the nothing he believed and, quite possibly, feared.

He also felt that if he had met the priest before he had started his relationship with ann rea, then the friendship with the priest, if that was what it was to become, would not have gone beyond the first couple of meetings. But now that Kennedy and ann rea were no longer seeing each other as much as they once had, he seemed somewhat reluctant to resume his previous solitary existence. This reluctance somewhat amused the detective.

Talking with the priest was never an intellectual chore for Kennedy. Their conversations flowed naturally without any great consideration on Kennedy's part. It reminded him of being at school and college again, where some boys would find friends and they would seem as if they did nothing but walk around talking all the time. Kennedy remembered wondering what these people found to talk about all the time. Surely they must run out of things to talk about? Then, just before the time when he first grew interested in girls, he had found his mate—also called Vincent—and had found himself lost in these marathon conversations. The conversations then were mostly about girls and music, with the feminine topics surprisingly running a poor second. The Fr Vincent O'Connor conversations rarely touched on girls or music. Kennedy was surprised at the priest's lack of interest in music. The priest claimed that all music did for him was to slow down his ability to think.

For all of that, the detective genuinely liked the priest and took to him immediately. The same seemed to be true in reverse. O'Connor, for his part, seemed to have no hidden agenda in that he *wasn't* looking to extend his immediate, and dwindling, flock. The priest and the detective would have a coffee, tea, lunch or dinner at least once a week, and it wasn't long before Kennedy introduced O'Connor to his favourite Italian restaurant.

Over one such meal, they took to discussing Kennedy's theory in depth.

'So, you think we should be looking off camera?' O'Connor said, taking up Kennedy's theme. 'Figuratively speaking, of course.'

'Of course,' Kennedy replied.

'Right,' O'Connor said. 'Help me here. I'm new to all of this, this murder game. I've always held the view that to do murder is most definitely to commit a wrong; one should never do anything that they can't discuss after dinner. But, be that as it may, what exactly is off camera?'

'In the magician's instance, it's what he's doing with his spare hand as his visible hand takes the audience through the trick,' Kennedy said, missing the Wilde quote buried in the priest's question.

'And in our particular instance, you know, John Riley's disappearance?'

'Well, on camera, he's not there, as it were . . .'

'Sorry, on camera he's not there?' O'Connor laughed. 'How on earth did you ever get this far without being found out?'

'But off camera,' Kennedy continued, choosing to ignore him, 'perhaps, say for instance instead of his wife grieving and being concerned as she *appears* on camera, she could be helping him stage his disappearance.'

'And the reason for that would be?'

'Insurance,' Kennedy replied. 'There's a £320,000 policy out on Mr Riley's life. It's not a new policy; it's several years old.'

'Which implies?'

'Either that if she is involved, it's been a long-term plan, or that she, or she and her husband, merely took advantage of the fact that there was an insurance policy already in place,' Kennedy guessed.

'But he—I mean, they—didn't need the money,' O'Connor reasoned.

'That appears to be correct. The firm is in great shape, there are no large debts, and there's no history of gambling.'

'What else do we have off camera?'

'We have the possibility that the son, or one of the daughters, or a combination of the siblings, could be helping him.'

'I doubt that in this family the children would ever side with one parent over the other.'

'Yes, that's the feeling I had too.'

'I notice in our conversations that even though you may already have an idea in your head, you'll still throw up all the options for discussion. Flynn says you do it a lot. Is that for your own benefit or for other people's?'

Kennedy was a little taken back.

'I suppose if you have a theory,' he began, his voice dropping to a whisper, 'for it to work and to help you solve the case, it needs to be a solid theory. My point would be that you shouldn't be scared of considering other people's ideas. Definitely encourage others to say what they think of your ideas. Hopefully the discussions and criticisms will help you see the flaws in a theory. If you can find a way to dismiss certain ideas, in the initial stages of an investigation, well, that, in a way, is invaluable. I believe it's equally important to follow certain leads down a line to their natural conclusion, right or wrong. I think it's fine to be wrong in your own lines of investigation. The important thing is to accept the fact that you were wrong, and work out exactly why you were wrong.'

'That makes sense,' O'Connor began as he finished his pasta—

spaghetti with peas and a creamy pesto sauce, a particular favourite of Kennedy's which O'Connor had initially turned up his nose at only to find it delicious and a good bed for his glass of excellent house red wine. 'So, tell me, what's your theory on this one?'

'Nagh, I'm not there yet.'

'Well, at least tell me where exactly you are with your theory.'

Kennedy blew a long sigh through his lips, 'Okay, between the two of us and to go no further . . .'

Kennedy waited for the priest to acknowledge and accept his condition before he continued: 'I think he's still alive. I think he got to be fifty years old, took a good look at his life and didn't particularly like what he saw. His children had grown and were self-supporting. His wife was comfortable. I don't think there's any love lost there, at least not from her side that I can see. From his side, all that we see is that he'll do anything to be out of her company twenty-four hours a day, seven days a week, forty-nine weeks a year.'

They looked at each other for thirty seconds as Frank, the amicable and humorous owner, cleared away the plates, declaring, 'Don't tell me, just the bill. I'll never get rich with the two of you—no starter, no dessert, just the DI's special. Ah well, I suppose having both of you plonked in the window will be good for business. The father here will attract the righteous while DI Kennedy will dispel Camden Town's, shall we say, less hoity-toity element.'

'There is more that you're not telling me, isn't there?' O'Connor began when Frank had taken away the plates and cutlery in a sweeping movement Paul Daniels, or David Copperfield for that matter, would have been proud of.

'Yes, but that's as much as you'll get this evening.'

'I suppose I should have known.' O'Connor sighed as he wiped imaginary crumbs from his black suit. 'A true magician never gives his secrets away.'

'Something like that.' Kennedy laughed. 'Or maybe they just haven't a clue themselves and are too busy searching for the missing pink elephant.'

Kennedy did indeed have an idea as to how one John Riley had carried out his illusion, but his priority now was similar to that of the magician and the missing ridiculously coloured elephant, in that the detective was preoccupied not with the mechanics of the disappearance, but more with *where* exactly John Riley had disappeared to.

Chapter Five

EVEN THOUGH HE was a priest, Fr Vincent O'Connor had an active social life of his own. Kennedy knew it was stupid to think otherwise, but for some strange reason he had tended to see priests in their black uniform and had not considered their lives beyond that, if indeed he conceded their personal lives existed at all.

Why shouldn't priests have a life? Kennedy remembered asking himself as he walked down Parkway, and who should he bump into but O'Connor, laughing and joking with another similarly aged (mid-forties) man?

It was mid-July, a Saturday afternoon, and all three were jacketless. Kennedy was wearing white chinos, slip-on campers and a blue-check short-sleeved shirt. As he was putting on the shirt, he had remembered ann rea frequently saying, 'Blue suits you, Christy.' Did this mean that he had secretly hoped to meet her while out on his regular bookstore and record-shop trail? The seventy-five-minute-plus dander always took in a pit stop at his favourite spot in Camden Market, the doughnut stall. This particular stall, pitched close to the entrance of Dingwall's dance hall, contained several hundred variously coloured and flavoured doughnuts. Kennedy always, just about, managed to resist the temptation to purchase more than a single doughnut, which he washed down with a great cup of tea from another stall over in the nearby stables.

'Ah, off for your Saturday constitutional?' O'Connor said, smiling and holding out his hand.

'Funny you should say that, but as a matter of fact I am.'

'Mmmh, would you mind telling me whether you are pre-Camden Market or post-Camden Market?' O'Connor continued. He still had his dog collar on with a light grey short-sleeve shirt and black pressed trousers but was minus his black jacket. To Kennedy he looked out of kilter, improperly dressed. A bit like he was playing truant from school.

'Pre-market actually.' Kennedy smiled, remembering that he had told the priest of his traditional and much-loved Saturday routine. 'I've just been to Regent's Book Shop for a browse and picked up the new Alan Bennett.'

'Signed, of course,' O'Connor chipped in, smiling at his companion.

'Of course,' Kennedy continued, proudly patting his Regent's Book-shop trademark blue carrier bag.

'Ah, in that case, would you permit us to accompany you on the next part of your journey, not forgetting that in Camden Lock there's safety in numbers?'

'Not to mention the treat in store at the end of the journey,' Kennedy said. 'Of course, you'd both be very welcome.'

'Harry,' O'Connor said, by way of introduction, 'this is Christy Kennedy, the detective I was telling you about. Christy, I'd like you to meet one of my oldest friends, Harry Ford.'

Kennedy and Ford shook hands. Ford's grip was firm and friendly. His blue eyes caught Kennedy's in a genial smile.

Kennedy's thoughts drifted to O'Connor for a moment. *What was it about this priest?* Kennedy liked the priest, who seemed, in turn, to like him, and now here he was introducing a friend who seemed to share the priest's sincere qualities. Yes, he knew believing that was a big leap of faith, but his instincts rarely let him down. Kennedy figured that his problem was that in the course of his work he rarely came into contact with anyone other than those with criminal intentions. So it was just that every now and then, such as on this occasion, you are allowed to see what goes on in the world outside your window. He wondered whether if he and ann rea had enjoyed the company of a more normal group of people they might perhaps have had a better chance.

He wondered if he had hit on something important here. If he and ann rea had made friends with people like Harry Ford, and the wife the stranger's wedding band suggested, and they had made a connection with them socially, would that have helped them to enjoy a more normal type of relationship? And what was a more normal type of relationship anyway? One that lasted was the only conclusion Kennedy could come up with. His problem was that whenever he and ann rea had been together, whether at the end of a busy day for both of them or at the weekend, he didn't really want to share her with anyone else. Had that been selfish? Had his selfish-ness meant that it now looked like he was going to be deprived of her com-pany anyway? If he had been less selfish with his demands on her time, would he in fact have been more selfish because he might have been able to enjoy more time with her? Such thoughts, which once used to preoccupy him, he was now leaving further and further behind; did this mean he was getting over her?

Harry Ford was good-looking in an old-fashioned movie actor kind of way. That is to say, good-looking in a way that men admired rather than women swooned over . His brown hair was out of fashion in that it was long—long but well kept and even better cut. You couldn't fault any of his looks: eyes, nose and chin were off the peg from the dream shop of good looks. But for all his blessings in that department, he still looked personable—humble even to accepting that good looks weren't anything more than another test God set. Ford appeared to be dressed head to toe in Ralph Lauren. Khaki knee-length shorts—ten years previously one wouldn't have been seen dead walking down Parkway in Camden Town in shorts, no matter the name on the label, but similar shorts were now even available in the classy GB clothes shop located next door to Kennedy's favourite Italian restaurant. Ford was sockless and wore tan moccasins and a starched white T-shirt under a blue patterned Hawaiian shirt, opened the whole way and flowing in the gentle breeze. He was of medium build and height. He carried not an ounce of fat. He looked like someone who kept in shape rather than a fitness fanatic.

'Great to meet you,' Ford started and then stumbled on the name.

'Christy is fine,' Kennedy said.

'Great to meet you, Christy. I've heard so much about you from Vincey,' Ford said in a classic radio presenter voice, somewhere halfway between Johnny Walker and Charlie Gillett, two of the best-sounding voices ever heard on British Radio. 'How long have you lived in London?'

'Oh, I've been here about twenty years.'

'You haven't lost a bit of your Ulster twang,' Ford continued, eventually letting go of Kennedy's hand.

'Oh, I think you need to *want* to lose your accent before you can lose it,' O'Connor chipped in as he, with a discreet opening of his hand in the direction of the pavement, suggested they continue with their journey.

'That's an interesting point, Vincey. Is that your excuse, you know, that you wanted to lose your accent? I mean, when I met you first, you sounded like a bog man, and now you speak nothing but the Queen's English,' Ford teased.

'No, actually it's more basic than that; I was told by my bishop that unless I was able to converse with my flock within the boundaries of a common language they'd at least have a chance of understanding, I'd be as well to return to Ireland where people could at least comprehend me. That's the polite version of his instructions, by the way.'

They took a right into Inverness Street and then a left into Camden High Street, over the bridge which spanned Camden Lock. The ancient lock was now the centre of some heavy and expensive development. With all expensive development came political pay-off. With all political pay-off came voter suffering. In this case, the developers had been putting pressure on their local and national politicians to clear up the area of drug dealers, druggies and other such undesirables. The politicians in turn complained to Kennedy's superior to do something about it. Castle in turn put pressure on Kennedy and his colleagues to clean it up, and Castle, just like the politicians and the developers further up the chain, didn't want to hear that the reason why there were so many undesirables on the streets of Camden Town was that there were fewer police visible on the streets and also that developers in King's Cross were putting similar pressure on their police force to clean their streets.

Druggies and drug dealers can't just disappear—they don't crawl under a stone and die. They have to go somewhere else, and in the case of the King's Cross crowd, nearby Camden Town became the magnet. When Camden Town CID in turn started to get tough, the undesirables would have to move yet somewhere else, until, in a few years time, they would be back to King's Cross again. By that time though, the developers wouldn't be concerned, having made their money and moved on as well.

Kennedy could sense O'Connor's pace quickening as they crossed the bridge. Perhaps one of the clichés about priests was true after all; Kennedy smiled at the recollection that all priests were believed to have a very sweet tooth. A point that was confirmed a couple minutes later when Kennedy directed O'Connor to the doughnut stall and the priest's eyes lit up like that of a five-year-old coming downstairs to discover that *all* the presents he had asked Santa for had been left under the Christmas tree.

Kennedy insisted on paying for the doughnuts. O'Connor encouraged him to go for the bargain half-dozen option and, five minutes later, they were sitting down at a table in the stables part of the market and enjoying their doughnuts and coffee (O'Connor), mineral water (Ford) and tea (Kennedy). Kennedy also insisted on paying for the drinks on the basis that it was his patch. O'Connor scoffed down three doughnuts in the same time

Ford and Kennedy managed one. They both insisted that the priest keep the sixth for 'afters'; they could not have pleased him more if they had offered their respective souls to Christ, Kennedy thought.

Kennedy loved being around the Camden Market on Saturdays. The noise, the multi-coloured stalls, the numerous accents, the mixture of smells—all helped to create individual slices of life continuously going on, all around, with and without you. To Kennedy these were truly intoxicating sights. The scenes were there all the time, but Kennedy realised that all it took was the ability to slow down and enjoy them. He was a habitual people watcher. He loved nothing more than to watch the variety of characters interacting and to imagine what they were saying, doing, thinking, and feeling. And all of this went on to a soundtrack, a cacophony, of sixties soul music, garage music, nu-metal, rap, classic sixties pop music and even classical music, all blaring out of the sound systems in the various stalls. It shouldn't really have worked as a pleasing musical cocktail, but for some strange reason it did.

From what Kennedy could pick up, Ford and O'Connor seemed to be enjoying the experience as much as he was. Now and again, a smiling Rastafarian would make a wise crack about O'Connor's collar. O'Connor always took it with great humour and indeed gave as good as he got. He had time for everyone and seemed to be a magnet for those down on their luck. He would recommend the official food kitchens in the area while resisting the requests for money, knowing that, nine times out of ten, any donations would never be spent on food. Kennedy was saddened by the fact that, nine times out of ten, the requests were delivered in an Irish accent.

They chit-chatted between interruptions about this and that as the market began to wind down and the traders started to pack their wares away in a time-honoured ritual. Just after O'Connor, who was unable to resist the temptation any longer, downed his fourth doughnut, Ford said to Kennedy, 'What are your plans for the rest of evening?'

'Oh,' Kennedy sighed, 'I'll take it easy, maybe hang out, start reading my Alan Bennett book, you know . . .'

'But you've no definite plans?' Ford persisted.

Kennedy hesitated.

'Good, then, you can join Vincey and my family for a bit of supper—nothing fancy.'

'I couldn't possibly . . .' Kennedy started.

'Oh yes you can,' O'Connor said, rubbing his stomach. 'You've treated us to a major feast, so now—'

'But your family . . .' Kennedy protested.

'Vincey dines with us most Saturdays; he'll just have to forego seconds.'

'I *couldn't* possibly,' the priest protested.

'Forego them or eat them?' Ford laughed as he took out his mobile and punched in a number. 'One extra for supper if that's okay?'

Ford smiled as he listened to his mobile.

And that is how, forty minutes later, Christy Kennedy sat down to dinner in a strange house with a strange, but friendly, family and an extremely friendly priest.

Chapter Six

KENNEDY ENJOYED HIS evening with the priest and his friends, the Ford family, in their cosy home. Being a habitual people-watcher, Kennedy was intrigued by what went on behind closed doors—the politics of a functioning family.

The Ford family hadn't stood on ceremony, and the supper was very informal.

The family consisted of Lizabeth Ford, wife and mother; Bernadette, the youngest daughter whom Harry referred to as Babe—her nickname from when she was the baby of the family, but now that she was twelve years old, she chastised her father with 'Da-dee' every time he used it. 'Babe' was selected as her nickname when she was six months old by her mother, who didn't quite mind their third daughter being named after the child's grandmother, Harry's mother Bernadette, but did mind the prospect of her daughter ending up being called Bernie. Lizabeth Ford positively hated the name Bernie. The missing siblings were Von—apparently short for Yvonne, 21 years old and a student, coincidently, at Queen's University, Belfast—and Vycky, a 17-year-old fresher at Manchester University.

Kennedy thought it was amusing that when Harry and Lizabeth were introducing, listing *and* spelling the children's names, they were happy to give out their ages but resisted providing their own. Kennedy pegged Harry to be in his mid-forties and Lizabeth as probably having just crossed the big four–oh barrier. Their house on Church Row in Hampstead was amazing. Kennedy loved the way they had styled it in a mixture of pure American Arts and Crafts and Ralph Lauren, so much so that the Lauren people could have shot *the* perfect brochure within the 400-year-old building.

Bernadette went to her room immediately after dinner. Kennedy marvelled at how keen the modern teenagers were to retreat to the sanctuary of their rooms while, when he was growing up, he went to his bedroom only either to sleep or as a punishment for misbehaving. *What* a difference a generation makes.

Harry and Vincent cleared away the dishes, and then Harry fired up the coffeepot; the wine bottle was nearly empty, but no one favoured opening another. Harry left the room to visit Bernadette while everyone else remained in the kitchen around the severely battle-scarred circular table, chit-chatting away about everything and nothing. Fifteen minutes later, Harry returned chuckling and completed the preparation of the coffee.

'Babe cracks me up every time,' he said as he set out various pieces of delft and cutlery. 'She's a great kid, and I love the way all her questions are three questions away from the actual question she wants to ask.'

'What was it tonight?' a proud mother inquired.

'Well, she was asking how we met.'

'She asked me the same question yesterday.'

'I figured as much. Did she give you her routine about whether you knew it was right because both of us had the experience of several other relationships?'

'Yeah, and . . .' Lizabeth replied, shaking her head sharply to clear the Burgundy blur.

'And that not all relationships had to have been important or even anything other than intellectual or conversational?'

'Yes?' Lizabeth continued, as husband and wife monopolised the conversation.

'And that the relationships could happen, you know,' Harry said now aping his daughter's ultra casual tone, 'any time with any one, really!'

'Oh?' Lizabeth asked. 'And?'

'*And,* what did I think about Zane, Debbie's older brother?'

'But he's eighteen and he's got studs and hair all over his face, and his trousers are always falling off his behind,' Lizabeth spat out in sheer disbelief. 'And what did you say?'

'So Babe's not the only one paying attention to his behind,' Harry jested. 'Actually I said I thought he was cool.'

'But?'

'No buts,' Harry smiled. 'When you're an 18-year-old lad, a 12-year-old girl chasing you is the last thing you need for your street cred. She's infatuated, but there's no need for us to make anything of it. We don't need her to feel that the inevitable disappointment will have had anything to do with whether or not we disapproved.'

Lizabeth looked to O'Connor, obviously seeking support.

'He's right,' O'Connor replied with a mock sigh. 'I hate to admit it, but he's spot on this time.'

'But why did she not mention this to me?' Lizabeth continued.

'Obviously you didn't answer the preliminary questions correctly,' Ford replied as he poured the coffee.

With no tea on offer, Kennedy accepted the coffee, but one sip was enough for him. Even though the trio of friends gushed on and on about the unique blend, it tasted vile, similar to how he imagined soil in hot water would taste.

'How *did* you meet?' Kennedy inquired. Once the question had escaped, Kennedy wondered where it had come from. Was it the wine? Was it the need to contribute to the conversation, his wish to distract the mother from the daughter's oncoming and unstoppable adolescence, or just his need to know how it happened in real life? His need to understand how two people met, got together and lived happily ever after.

'Well, it was thanks to the Four Musketeers, really,' Lizabeth began expansively. 'They met at Reading University. There was the father here—'

'Oh, that was a long, long time ago, before either Harry or I were fathers,' O'Connor replied in a slightly camp manner.

'And Neil, that's Neil Roberts, and Neil's sister—what's her name?' Lizabeth pantomimed searching in space, 'Yes, Alice, that's it—Alice Cain, Cain's her married name. Neil and Alice were very close, even for a brother and sister—and, of course, Harry. They were pretty much inseparable, a self-contained unit if you will. They were confident, but never arrogant. I, on the other hand, was a loner—not by choice; there just wasn't anyone I wanted to hang out with. I thought all my fellow students were nerds or into punk, so the eighties wasn't a great time to be a single girl.'

'Ah, you did okay, Lizzy,' Harry interrupted.

'Oh, not as well as some—say two of the Musketeers, for instance—'

'You *both* did okay,' O'Connor said, interrupting and settling the pretend squabble.

'Anyway, Harry here and myself, well, I think we were the only two people at Reading University who liked Jimmy Stewart, and we both turned up at the film society's screening of *Anatomy of a Murder,* a classic movie and an even better book, but we were the only two people in the audience. We could have either ignored each other and behaved like train spotters or we could have sat together. We chose to sit together.'

'I liked it that she had the courage to go and sit in a cinema by herself just because she loved the movie,' Harry said, refilling everyone's (except Kennedy's) coffee. 'I think the main difference between us was that, say either of us had been the *single* person who showed up for the screening, well, if it had been me, I wouldn't have stayed, but if it had been Lizzy, she wouldn't have cared. She'd have been so happy to see the movie, she wouldn't have noticed that there was no one else there. She's always been the more self-sufficient of the two of us.'

'So the lights went up, we started to chat,' Lizabeth continued, appearing to ignore her husband's compliment, if that's what it was. 'We walked out of the cinema and stopped for a coffee. I loved his energy, his vitality; he looked like he could have hung out with Fonda and Stewart when they were younger—goodness they were so gorgeous . . .'

'Yeah, if she could have pulled the real thing, I wouldn't have stood a chance,' Harry laughed.

'Oh, never knock the attraction of availability, darling,' Lizabeth replied playfully. 'Anyway, we started talking, and we've been talking ever since.'

'A-men to that,' O'Connor said grandly.

'Oh,' Lizabeth added as an afterthought. 'Listen, just in case you're getting the wrong idea about me, Christy—nothing happened for ages. We became friends. He was actually seeing someone else for a time, and he was too much of a gent to be involved in all of that deceit. I never got to hang out with the Four Musketeers, but I had a hunch something was going to happen between Harry and myself at some point and I was in no hurry.'

'And what's become of the other Musketeers?' Kennedy asked.

'Well, Vincey here is one of our best friends, and he sees the other two. He's kind of the social secretary, the worker, you know—the link who puts a lot of energy into keeping us together, I suppose,' Lizabeth replied. 'On top of which, I just love the fact that he comes around here so much. All our neighbours will be jealous as Joseph, as Fr O'Connor always says, because they see him as our leg up to heaven.'

'And where, pray, would the Hampstead heaven be?' O'Connor asked.

'Oh, let's see,' Harry began slowly. 'Probably somewhere like right in the middle of Gainsborough Gardens, with Gap, Next, Liberty's, Fortrum & Mason's, Selfridges, the Ivy, Hatchards and Ralph Lauren forming a central mall. A place where you can eat or drink as much as you like and not have to pay the price, or do the exercise the following morning.'

'What, and no house of worship?' O'Connor tut-tutted.

'I did mention Ralph Lauren, didn't I, Lizzy?'

'Even in your sleep, darling.'

'Yes, that's all we could ever dream of for heaven,' Harry said and drained his coffee.

'Be careful what you wish for, Harry,' O'Connor offered as a mild chastisement.

'Oh, surely it shouldn't concern you, Vincey; sure you don't even believe in heaven in the first place.'

'Sorry?' Kennedy said, the first word which came to his mind. He wasn't sure if he was sorry because he was begging pardon that he hadn't heard Harry Ford correctly or sorry because he couldn't believe that a priest wouldn't believe in heaven.

The thing about friends, particularly friends who have been together for twenty years—at least as far as Kennedy could work out—was that they pretty much knew each other's thoughts on life's big subjects and so probably rarely discussed them any more.

'Aye now, we'll have to leave that particular topic for another occasion,' O'Connor began.

'We certainly will,' Lizabeth interrupted. 'I don't want Babe wandering down here and finding that the only stable man in her life doesn't believe in heaven. She has a way to go before she's ready for that one.'

'Sorry, darling, of course you're right. I shouldn't have brought it up,' Harry said, sliding up beside his wife and cuddling her.

'Oh, you can feel some more sorry if you wish,' Lizabeth said.

'Right, Christy, that's our exit sign—these two canoodling is not a pleasant sight.'

'Particularly for a priest, now—' Harry began.

'Harry!' Lizabeth chastised in a whisper.

'Okay,' Kennedy said, standing up. 'Look, that was excellent; thank you very much for inviting me into your home. I really enjoyed myself.'

'You were very welcome. Next time, bring your . . .' Harry hesitated for a beat before saying, 'partner.'

'Is there someone in your life?' Lizabeth asked.

'That's another even longer and more convoluted story—not quite as complicated as how a priest doesn't believe in heaven, but let's just say the honest answers is . . . I don't know.'

Chapter Seven

'I THINK HE does that a lot,' DS Irvine said, helpfully. The time was the following Monday morning. The location was North Bridge House, the home of Camden Town CID. The listener was Kennedy, and the speaker, Irvine, was discussing Superintendent Thomas Castle.

'Perhaps,' Kennedy agreed, 'but even if it's only a trick, it certainly seems to work. I mean, he's pretty much got an interchangeable team, to the extent that even when he loses a key member, say DC Anne Coles for instance, the team isn't noticeably weakened.'

'Meaning, of course, that we can all be replaced?' Irvine said, more as a statement than a question, but it actually came out sounding more like a question.

'Yes,' Kennedy sighed. 'He's not above—as you've witnessed over the previous few months—replacing me.'

'Aye, but it's not been the same around here without you,' Irvine stated and added, 'Even Castle has discussed your absence with regret on more than a few occasions.'

Kennedy, never one to accept a compliment easily—no matter how subtle—muttered something to the effect that the sooner he was on a 'proper case' again, the better he would feel.

They had been discussing DC Anne Coles, who had recently received her promotion and been transferred to Tooting. She claimed she was happy to venture south of the river for experience, but she hoped to return to Camden Town CID on her next promotion. Kennedy knew that her transfer had been on the cards since she had let her personal feelings get in the way of her work. He was equally aware that her, albeit temporary, bout of unprofessionalism had nearly cost him dearly. Castle had been too subtle and too much of a gentleman to move Coles at the time of the incident. Anyway, with Kennedy on sick leave, there wasn't really an issue that needed addressing. Kennedy wondered if he should take heart from Coles' imminent departure in that it was suggesting his return.

By the time Kennedy finished his conversation with Irvine, he had already spoken with ann rea, who had gathered all the valuable information on the various reunion websites, another angle he wanted to use to try to trace the misper, John Riley. ann rea was very friendly with Kennedy, even to the point of suggesting that as it was August they should perhaps go away for a long weekend, or even a week's holiday together. They could both do with a break, she observed with a smile evident in her voice. He suggested that they discuss it further over dinner. She insisted that they meet that very evening to enjoy their favourite cosy meal in the Engineer on the corner of Gloucester Avenue and Princess Road.

Next, Kennedy made a quick call to O'Connor to see if he knew which college/university Riley had attended. The detective wanted to avoid ringing Sally Riley, because he knew that the minute she heard his voice, she would be filled with equal amounts of expectation and trepidation.

He wondered, if Alexander Graham Bell had known how much grief and sadness his new invention would be responsible for delivering, whether or not he would still have proceeded with it. Perhaps he would have hidden behind the 'don't shoot the messenger' spin. He would probably also have brought it to everyone's attention how much good news his invention also delivered.

He decided to go for a stroll, one of his favourite strolls in fact.

Kennedy, in his recuperating periods, would often go for walks in Regent's Park. He loved the sensation of feeling lost while literally in the centre of one of the busiest cities in the world.

He often stopped at the Honest Sausage on the Broadwalk for a breather. When he admitted this to ann rea, she tittered—à la Frankie Howard—in disbelief. It wasn't that she was a gastronomic snob; it was more the idea of it. Kennedy liked to go for clean honest food, no matter the surroundings, and truth was—at least Kennedy's truth was—that the Honest Sausage's vegetable soup was most definitely second to none!

Yes, the soup was certainly excellent and, in some of his weaker moments, Kennedy had even sampled their superb bacon butty, which was also a treat, particularly when the chef was prepared to accept some hints as to exactly how well the bacon should be cooked.

For Kennedy the compulsive people watcher, the Honest Sausage was one of his favourite spots to indulge in this non-physical sport. The thing about a café in the middle of Regent's Park is that it tends not to be frequented by what you would call regulars, but more by a lot of what you would call out-of-towners.

Kennedy—while pretending to read *The First of the True Believers,* Theodore Hennessey's excellent novel on the Beatles—looked on in shock as one particular gentleman, his flared white trousers betraying his age if not his origins, heaped the contents of sachet after sachet of sugar into his coffee. Kennedy reckoned that the chap must have poured at least an inch and a half of solid sugar into the bottom of his cup. At one point, he transferred his hand from the spoon, mid-stir, to remove some oily hair from his eyes, and the spoon stood upright, entombed, no doubt, in syrupy sugar. Naturally Kennedy thought that the chap must be severely rotting his teeth, not to mention his stomach, but, in a series of mouth-open-wide guffaws, he displayed to his young female companion, and Kennedy, as good a set of molars as the detective had ever witnessed smiling down on him from posters adorning his dentist's surgery's walls.

And there were other equally eccentric characters, all in varying shapes and sizes. The curves were more visible in the summer than the winter, but Kennedy noted that even in this modern day, people seemed to be caring less and less about the shapes of their bodies. He briefly regretted ordering the bacon butty in preference to the wholesome healthy vegetable soup. His next thought though was that he could probably afford to put on a few pounds—at least that's what ann rea was always telling him. He wondered if it really was the case that he needed to gain a few pounds, and also whether she would have told him he could do with losing a few pounds had he been overweight. He wondered if people needed to find a way of looking at themselves through other people's eyes, preferably the eyes of strangers.

To him it was quite simple, really. When you see someone you don't know, the old mind is not scared about being too judgemental. The first thing that springs to your mind might be 'They could do themselves a favour by losing a few stones . . . from each leg!' or, 'How did that mutton ever have the nerve to go out dressed like a lamb?' or any one of numerous variations on those two themes.

Kennedy then thought of John Riley and wondered, as he did several times a day, what exactly he was doing at that exact moment. Such knowledge would be an invaluable, albeit impossible, clue; if Kennedy could just eavesdrop on Riley's life for thirty seconds—that was all the detective would need to kick start the game.

'Wish in one hand and cry in the other and see which one fills first,' Kennedy said to the remnants of his bacon butty.

What was it he was missing?

The only glimmer of light was the single fact that Mrs Riley would still not admit (to anyone it appeared) what the pivotal argument had been about.

Kennedy considered what husbands and wives might argue about. He took out his pen and notebook and started to compile a list:

Other women / other men
Furniture
Decorating
Money
Leaving the top off the toothpaste
Not raising the toilet seat
Control of the remote control for the television
Shopping
Food—eating too much or too little
Drink
Walking the dog
Washing up
No number 13!
Old lovers
Holidays
Being too quiet
Being too noisy
Cars
Politics
Religion
Jobs/work
Children
Who gets to be on top
Gardening
The in-laws
The pub
Drinking partners
Confidants/friends

Cats
Football
Music
Party pieces
Health
Hygiene
Clothes
Arguments

Yep, Kennedy mused as he returned pen to pocket—some couples actually argue about the arguments they were having.

He tried to think what he and ann rea had argued over.

Nothing!

Nothing?

This realisation hit him so hard that he was actually stunned into shock.

Was there really nothing they argued over, he wondered, and checked down through his 36-point list again.

Correct. There was nothing on the list that he and ann rea had ever argued over.

They only ever argued over whether or not they were going to stay together. That was the single point on which they disagreed. They were *simpatico* apart from that single issue.

'Un-be-lievable,' Kennedy muttered louder than he had meant to, so loudly in fact that some of his co-diners in the Honest Sausage stared over at him in annoyance. A couple glared at him as if he were slightly mad and then averted their eyes rather than engage in some kind of social intercourse with a crazy.

Before Kennedy brought the final curtain down on his current thoughts, he considered once more the lives and times of John and Sally Riley. What might it be from their past which could shed some light on his disappearance? What skeletons could either of them have tried to hide: old lovers, new affairs? In these times when everyone has a professional detective service—the internet—at their disposal, they have the ability to track down old college friends by merely typing their names on a keypad. Those unhappy with their current lives and with the experience of years were perhaps now realistic enough no longer to seek perfection. They could now very easily revisit their past, perhaps even picking up unresolved relationships again. Kennedy wondered how many such people realised, to their cost, that second best didn't always mean you had to compromise.

So, did Riley have a woman from his teenage years who for various reasons and commitments hadn't been available to him until recently? Perhaps her spouse had died; perhaps she had only been waiting for her children to move away from home. Had Riley been patient? Had he been waiting for years for the time to be right? Had the time been right at 11.40 the previous Wednesday morning when he had put his long-planned dreams into motion? Or had it been a spur-of-the-moment thing, and had he just headed off unsolicited to follow his heart and pick up the pieces of his life?

That did not make as much sense to Kennedy. It was more likely that Riley and his lover/companion/whatever had both been working on this since they had discovered that each had made their respective romantic mistake but that now they wanted to be together. Or had both, discovering themselves in loveless marriages, gone off looking for something more from their lives and subsequently met by accident? Whatever the circumstances, perhaps they even felt they *owed* it to themselves to make the change.

Kennedy wondered why he was so preoccupied by this approach and less inclined towards the one where Riley had died either by accident or design?

He resolved to do two things.

The first was to check, at the first available moment, the details ann rea had given him for Friends Reunited, to see if Riley was registered with any of the various sites. He could also check out Riley's early school and college classes to see if there were any same-year female classmates registered.

The second thing also concerned ann rea. He decided to use the excuse of their dinner-date to discuss in person the second thing on his mind.

Chapter Eight

THE EVENING WITH ann rea worked out a lot better than Kennedy had planned. It wasn't as if he had had a big plan and that it had been bettered. He just knew that he really needed to see her and felt that when he did, they would get into discussing and talking about the major topic preoccupying them both. All that went out the window the minute they walked in the door of the Engineer.

The usually efficient greeter had messed up with an earlier reservation and she was now totally out of sync with subsequent diners. It eventually worked out in Kennedy and ann rea's favour in that they were offered, and accepted, a table with four seats in a superior position by the front window. They were just settling in and feeling great about it all when Kennedy noticed a well-dressed gent drop his shoulder in disappointment as the greeter, now temporarily out of tables, passed on her bad news. The man, who had been standing with his back turned, scanned the restaurant, desperate to locate a couple of diners who looked like they were finishing their meal. Kennedy recognised the dejected man's features; he knew the face but just couldn't place it at first.

'That's Harry Ford,' Kennedy said, half to himself and half to ann rea. 'The man I was telling you about.'

'The friend of the priest?'

'The very same,' Kennedy replied. 'Look, they were very hospitable to me at the weekend. Would you mind very much if I invited them to join us?'

'I'd mind very much if you didn't, Christy—go now before they leave or something.'

And that was how Harry Ford, his wife Lizabeth, ann rea and Christy Kennedy all came to be dining together in the Engineer on the borders of Primrose Hill on that pleasant August night.

'You're sure this is okay?' Lizabeth asked when the introductions were over and they were all seated.

'Of course,' ann rea replied immediately and sincerely.

'Our pleasure,' Kennedy added by way of agreement and confirmation.

'They were very apologetic,' Harry said, waving out his napkin and placing it on his lap to cover his brown corduroy trousers.

'Yes,' Lizabeth agreed. 'But *saying* "sorry" is so frightfully easy, isn't it?'

'Ah well, not to worry—we're fine now, aren't we?' Harry said to the three of them with a smile warm enough to melt the iceberg that sank the *Titanic*.

'Yes, yes,' Lizabeth agreed, and then added as an afterthought. 'Unless of course we're ruining Christy and Miss rea's romantic dinner.'

Kennedy and ann rea both laughed the comment off. Surprisingly, Kennedy sounded more casual about it than ann rea did.

They settled down to the very important business of ordering their food. Then they discussed O'Connor; they discussed kids, namely Babe Ford; they discussed Seamus Heaney—Lizabeth was a big fan; they discussed music—ann rea was surprised to actually meet two people who would admit to the fact that music wasn't a large part of their lives; they discussed Camden Town, colleges, cars, movies; and then they discussed relationships.

'How did you two meet?' Harry asked just as their desserts arrived.

'We actually met at Heathrow,' ann rea replied as Kennedy was deliberating on how to answer the question.

'I saw her in the book shop at Heathrow, terminal one, for the first time and, well, I—'

'Christy had a habit of allowing his jaw to trail on the ground in those days,' ann rea added, appearing to want to save herself the embarrassment of Kennedy gushing. She told the story of their meeting from her perspective.

'You were on the same plane?' Lizabeth asked, stealing a spoonful of her husband's ice cream.

'Yes, and we were both on the same return flight too. That's when he started talking to me and we discovered we both worked in Camden Town.

'Oh yes,' Harry said, his eyes betraying the fact that something had been bothering him, 'I recognise the name now. You're a journalist; you always have your name in lower case in your by lines. I think that's such a brilliant idea.'

'Yes, but sadly not original,' ann rea sighed. 'I nicked it from the singer k.d. lang, who in turn borrowed it from e.e. cummings. Anyway, then Christy and I bumped into each other in the street a few times, and eventually he asked me out,' ann rea offered as she put her hand affectionately on Kennedy's arm.

'And you've been dating ever since?' Harry asked.

'Ah, now that's another story,' ann rea replied, taking her hand away and concentrating on her fruit platter again.

'Isn't it always?' Lizabeth said, glaring in Harry's direction.

'Yeah, getting started,' Harry offered guardedly. 'That's always the easy bit.'

'Maybe,' Kennedy said. 'Although not at the time.'

'Corr-ect,' Harry continued, and then returned to his original train of thought. 'But making it work; well, that makes the initial meetings seem like kindergarten stuff.'

Harry looked over at his wife, who could have been playing an absolutely blinding hand of poker; she gave nothing away.

'It's like,' Harry said, proceeding hesitantly, 'you have to remember that at one point you both jointly agreed to do this, to be together, and you have to find a way of accepting that as fact and just getting on with it and living your lives together. If you think and talk too much about this stuff, it will invariably drive you mad.'

ann rea stole a 'tell us about it' look at Kennedy as Harry continued seamlessly:

'And then your children come along and you no longer have even a second to think about yourselves. It all becomes about the little people who depend on you 100 per cent for survival. Then you witness your wife coping with the un-copable and you experience such an admiration for her and for what she does that you really do experience true love and you find yourselves becoming a *real* couple—thinking and acting like *a couple* because you are the providers and protectors of these new little people.'

There was silence at their table for a time, interrupted only by the ambient hum of the busy restaurant.

'Listen to us, will you,' Lizabeth said, breaking into a large smile. 'Ma and Pa Ford getting ready for the cocoa, pipe and slippers.'

'Yeah,' Harry joined in. 'She gets the pipe and I always end up with the cocoa.'

They all laughed.

'So Christy, what's this we've been hearing about seagulls attacking humans and pets over your way?' Lizabeth asked.

'Absolutely true,' Kennedy replied.

'Oh come on,' Harry said, stopping mid bite.

'Yes, over in Somers Town hundreds of seagulls have been nesting on the tops of some of the high-rise flats. Come the breeding season, they do what comes natural to them; they're out fighting for food for their newborn chicks, and they've been known to dive-bomb pensioners carrying shopping bags, and dogs and cats with food.'

'But it's okay,' ann rea offered, the beginnings of a grin visible around her mouth. 'I've kitted Christy out in a bowler hat to protect his head during these attacks, and I've also loaned him my pink brolly so that he can fight them off.'

A bit more laughter, this time at Kennedy's expense.

'So you're the journalist with the *Camden News Journal*?' Harry said at the end of his laughing.

'Yes,' ann rea replied, appearing as if she felt she should elaborate but would prefer not to.

'Do you enjoy it?' Harry pressed.

'Yes, I do as a matter of a fact, although for me the writing is not as enjoyable as gathering and discussing all the different stories.'

'Have you thought about writing a novel?' Lizabeth asked.

'I'm not sure I would have the discipline required for that. Come to think of it, I don't think I would enjoy it as much as I enjoy what I do now anyway.'

'Maybe you're waiting for the right subject to come along,' Harry offered.

'Perhaps,' ann rea said, smiling just a little too sweetly. 'There's a photographer I know. He's called Willie Henderson, and I've done some work with him, and his work really is so beautiful and evocative, that I've been trying to encourage him to do a book. I mean, I think his work is *that* good that everyone deserves to see it and, well . . . he says that he'll do a book if I do the words to go with his pictures.'

Kennedy looked like someone who was hearing this information for the first time.

'That seems fair to me,' Lizabeth replied. 'Is that something you'd like to do?'

'Well, the major problem I have is that I think Willie's photographs would go perfectly with Nick Drake's lyrics. I hear Nick Drake's voice and melodies every time I look at the photographs, but we'd never get permission to do that.' ann rea sighed, apparently intentionally avoiding Kennedy's stare. She moved the conversation back up a few gears with: 'I'm afraid you have me at a disadvantage here; I don't know what either of you do.'

'At the moment, I'm the branch manager of a building society.'

Lizabeth staged a chuckle and said, 'Ever since we've been married, Harry has always said that, you know: "At the moment, I'm a branch manager . . ." as if he was about to change his job.'

Harry smiled at Lizabeth in a tolerant yet kind way, the way long-standing couples do when they give off the air of, 'Yes, I am annoyed with you, but I'm not going to rise to the bait.'

Lizabeth smiled back, acknowledging that she'd overstepped a mark.

'Is there something else you'd like to do?' ann rea asked as Kennedy experienced their domestic moment—a potentially embarrassing one— pass harmlessly into the ether.

'Well, here's the thing, I—'

'He's overqualified for his job,' Lizabeth said, helping out. 'Aren't you, darling?'

'It's not so much that. My work is not very taxing, which also means that it is not very rewarding. The only time I can remember having to work late or bring my work home is when I was checking up on a suspected office fraud, but apart from that, it's a doddle. I mean, the salary is excellent, and they gave us the option to buy a bunch of shares when they went public a couple of years ago, which I kinda knew would go well because we'd watched another couple of building societies do the same thing, and sure enough, our share price went through the roof.'

'But not before Harry had poured our savings in; we enjoyed a five-fold increase before he pulled out and reinvested everything elsewhere.'

'So, everything considered, the financial part of the package has been . . . well, just unbelievable really, but I'd love to run my own business now for a while.'

'Even at this stage, in this climate?' Kennedy asked.

'Yes. I think there's never really been a perfect time, but if you're pre-pared to commit to it, think it out properly and put all your energies into your company, it will serve you well.'

'And why haven't you done it so far?' ann rea asked.

'Well, there's always been something I needed—' Harry said, looking at Lizabeth, '—something *we've* needed to do or buy first. A house, a car; there's the cost of the children and then the children's education; holidays; then the circle starts back up again when your children grow up and leave home and they need help with a flat, a car, travel expenses for their year out. There's always something that you desperately need to finance, so you don't want to take a risk. The Coalition & Aylesbury Building Society pays its managers well. The main problem with my job is that I don't really *do* anything.'

'Well if you're the branch manager, you must be doing something, not to mention doing it okay,' ann rea suggested with genuine encouragement.

'Yes, yes,' Harry said quickly, yet in a dismissive way. 'But Christy here solves crimes and you write articles which are published and Lizabeth and her friend Mary run a very successful cottage industry, making and fitting curtains, making cushion covers and re-covering sofas. They've got as much work in as they can physically take. And so the three of you all really enjoy doing what you do and you are all doing something worthwhile. You all create an end-product.'

One by one, they nodded their heads in agreement, ann rea more hesitantly than the others.

'Well, I don't have any of that because, as I've just said, I don't really do anything. Yes, I make lots of telephone calls, I attend numerous conferences and take hundreds of meetings, but I don't actually *do* anything, do I?'

'Okay, so what would you like to do?' ann rea was compelled to ask.

'Well . . .' Harry started shyly, 'I love making furniture. I love working with wood.'

'My father was a carpenter until he retired,' Kennedy said.

'And he supported his family with his chosen trade?' Harry inquired hopefully.

'Why, yes,' Kennedy replied immediately. 'I mean, that's what he did as a job of work. His carpentry financed the family until he retired. He was an amazing man with wood, a real craftsman; but the bottom line was that he worked as a carpenter to earn a living.'

'You see, there's the problem for Harry,' Lizabeth cut in as Harry developed a faraway look in his eyes. 'He's worried that this is only a pipe dream of his.'

'Well, no, not exactly,' Harry replied, clicking back into their conversation again. 'It's just, how do I go about doing it?'

'Well, you obviously make some stuff and just sell it, don't you?' ann rea said innocently.

'But, you see, that's the thing, isn't it? If it's to succeed as a business, then one man making stuff—no matter how much pleasure he may derive from doing so—is not going to make it a successful business. So then you think about staff and the organisation and, before you know it, you've got quite a big set-up in place. So, if your organisation is going to be that big, well, someone is going to have to manage it; someone is going to have to be in charge, right? My worry would be that *I'd* be left to run it and wouldn't have enough time to be a carpenter. Like, I'm sure the people who run these businesses are as frustrated as I am running a building society. But having said that, I've drawn up various business plans over the years for my carpentry company, and I often felt I should just stop thinking about doing it—you know, just take the plunge and *do* it.'

'Harry's dream is to retire to a wee cottage in the Cotswolds. A beautiful cottage with several outhouses he could convert into workshops and he could just drop out. But I have to keep reminding him that he's missed the hippie movement by about forty years.'

'I nearly did it,' Harry admitted with a forlorn look in his eyes. 'About five years ago, I nearly went for it.'

This revelation seemed to shock his wife, because she grew visibly agitated before saying, 'But you were let down, dear, weren't you? Not everyone shared your vision.'

Something in the way Mrs Ford said this made Kennedy think that that she was referring to someone other than herself. He didn't have long to dwell on his thought though, because Harry cut in.

'Yeah, you can't afford to become too hung up on your dreams. You need to leave your dreams in their own special place; otherwise they no longer function as dreams for you.'

He sighed a sigh that signalled that he was nearing the end of this particular part of the conversation. As the four of them dwelt a bit longer on his words, he changed gear, looked at Kennedy and said, 'So, have you any more news on the missing member of Fr O'Connor's flock?'

At this juncture, the conversation fragmented into two separate ones; Harry and Christy in one, and Lizabeth and ann rea in another. As Kennedy went on to inform Ford that there were still absolutely no new developments on the Riley case, Lizabeth, in a conspiratorial whisper, was quizzing ann rea on how much of an inside scoop Kennedy gave her on his cases.

The men discussed the case for a time while the women discussed writing, and the conversations opened up again when Harry was talking about how parenthood and children did tend to ground you.

'There's nothing wrong with having your feet firmly on the ground,' Lizabeth replied with genuine conviction. 'Give me a realist over a dreamer any day of the week.'

'For every dreamer, you need an interpreter,' ann rea added.

'Yeah, even a magician needs an assistant,' Lizabeth said, smiling.

'And in that case, it's the assistants who create most of the magic,' ann rea said.

'Yeah, and it's the magicians who take all the credit,' Lizabeth added, winking at ann rea.

'Ah, now the game's up, Christy. We've been found out, and here I was thinking I'd been getting away with that secret all my life.'

They all laughed at this, some more than others. Kennedy excused himself to answer the call of nature, he said.

When he returned, they chatted for a time before Lizabeth looked at her watch.

'Harry, we'd better ask for the bill . . . the babysitter?'

'Goodness,' Harry said, checking his watch. 'I didn't realise it was so late. Yes, of course.'

'It's okay. We've covered it,' Kennedy said. He dismissed the polite protests with, 'It's okay; it's totally our pleasure.'

Ten minutes later, as Kennedy and ann rea were walking home and Harry and Lizabeth Ford were driving home, both couples discussed issues they felt the other couple was going through. Neither conversation was negative.

'Yes,' ann rea said as she snuggled up close as skin to Kennedy in bed twenty minutes later, 'Mr Harry Ford is definitely a CBM.'

'A CBM?' Kennedy asked in a distracted sort of way, because his mind was definitely elsewhere. He was imagining Harry Ford as a carpenter.

'Oh, yes,' ann rea purred, barely managing to get her last words out. 'Same as you'll be yourself in a few years—Cute But Married.'

Chapter Nine

A S THE DAYS passed, Kennedy could feel himself growing stronger again. He knew that he must be getting better because he was beginning to grow annoyed about not making any progress on the John Riley case.

Kennedy was convinced that Riley was not dead. So far they'd discovered nothing in Riley's past to suggest that he had made any enemies. Occasionally homeless people and itinerants had been known to fall into Regent's Canal or had been found dead lying around the wasteland that bordered the railway line. But managing directors of successful companies rarely ended up in either location unless they were unceremoniously dumped there.

So, in Kennedy's book, John Riley had, for reason or reasons unknown, literally just opted out of his social circle.

Why? And how?

Kennedy had come up with a variety of answers to these two important questions. Sometimes he could even connect the answer to the former with the answer to the latter. Money offers the softest cushion Kennedy was aware of. So, how did someone who appeared as honest as the day was long—and Kennedy's investigation had so far not uncovered any contradictions of this assessment—finance the most successful disappearing act since Harry Houdini?

Kennedy decided to visit Harry Ford and rang him up in his office to make an appointment to see him. This was the third Thursday in July. Since the dinner Kennedy had enjoyed at the Fords, the two men's only meeting had been at the Engineer when the Fords had joined Kennedy and ann rea.

The Coalition & Aylesbury Building Society (CABS) offices were at the bottom end of Camden High Street, just opposite the Camden Palace and not a million miles from the landmark Black Cats Building. Kennedy visibly winced at the memories of what Camden CID had uncovered in there. The CABS was the second large company, following in the footsteps of Sainsbury's, to locate at that end of the High Street. Kennedy was happy about this; it meant that where the big boys had gone, others would soon follow, and the result would be that this part of Camden Town would receive its much-needed development.

Harry Ford's nondescript office was functional as opposed to opulent, and Kennedy felt that Ford looked somewhat out of place in there. From Ford's dress-sense, Kennedy would have pegged him as being more comfortable as an American lawyer in an office with wood-panelled walls, deep rich carpets and subtle lighting.

Ford's office, on the other hand, was at bursting point with piles of files covering most of the available floor space. The only outward sign of individuality was a unique two-tone wooden desk. Ford's own hands had created the desk, and Kennedy was mightily impressed, so much so that he was convinced that Harry Ford, like Kennedy's own father, would have no problem making a living from his craft.

'Thanks for fitting me in at such short notice,' Kennedy said as they shook hands warmly.

'Any distraction from this is welcome,' Harry said, removing a pile of files from the second of only two chairs and inviting Kennedy to rest his weary bones. 'It's always a zoo in here. I'm for ever saying that we need to take a few days and do nothing but tidy the place up, but we're so busy, there's never the time.'

'Well, in this day and age, that's a good thing, isn't it?'

'I suppose so. We're one of the most successful branches and, well, the annual bonus does tend to reflect that,' Ford replied very affably but then moved into a more business-like mood. 'But enough about CABS, Christy. How can I help you today?'

'Right, actually I was wondering how difficult it would be for someone to just walk in here off the street and plonk down, say, three or four hundred quid and open an account.'

'Dead easy. We do it every day. As Bob Hope used to say, "A bank is somewhere that will lend you money, provided of course you can prove that you don't need it." However, if you want to give us money, now that's a different matter altogether. We'll welcome all deposits with open arms.'

'But what if they wanted to do it using another name, a different name from their own?'

'You mean a false name, for instance?'

'For instance.'

'Difficult really, in the last four years—since 9/11 really,' Ford said and considered his words before continuing. 'There's much stricter monitoring on the movement of funds. But if you walked in, and say you'd doctored your electricity bill—you know, photocopied it a couple of times, removed your name and inserted, say, the name you'd like the account to be opened in—well, you just might get away with it.'

'I thought as much, but I'm thinking about before all this recent trouble. I'm thinking back maybe as long as ten or fifteen years.'

'Well, yes, ten years ago, it would have been a lot easier to open a fake account.'

'And because this account would have been running for ten or fifteen years with regular deposits, you wouldn't have been required to make any retrospective checks?'

'An impossibility really. There's just too much current activity for us to focus on such checks; we'd never have the time for that. If, however, our fictitious customer were to remove a large sum from their account in cash, well, then we'd have to raise a flag on that type of activity. Again, similarly, any large cash deposit would be duly noted and mentioned to your boys at the Yard.'

'I see,' Christy said, stalling.

'Is this to do with Vincey's missing man?'

'Yes.'

'Right, I see. You think he might have been planning his disappearance for years and siphoning away some of his funds as a parachute fund, a nest egg of independence?'

'Yes. ann rea tells me the ladies would call it their "running-away fund." I think it's the most likely possibility at this stage.'

'I believe Vincey thinks he's dead.'

'Does he really? There's nothing there to suggest that's the case,' Kennedy replied, surprised by Harry's disclosure. 'Did he give a reason?'

'He just thinks there's no other explanation. If Mr Riley were alive, the very least he'd do would be to contact his family, if even just to let them know that he's still alive.'

'Hmm,' Kennedy mused. He was happy that Fr O'Connor's assertion was not based on fact. 'Well, we'll see. I'm intrigued really. I mean, as long as he's classified as missing, I'm going to have only limited time and resources to spend on it and—'

'And if you weren't recovering, you probably wouldn't have any time at all to spend on it?'

'Well,' Kennedy said, a smile creeping across his face. 'As from this morning's medical, I'm officially better, ready, willing and able to get stuck back in again. So, come Monday morning, I'm not going to be able to get away with late mornings and early afternoons any more. No more skiving.'

'That's great news, Christy,' Ford said, rising up from behind his desk and shaking Kennedy's hand. 'So what you're telling me is that from Monday morning onwards, the dive-bombing herring gulls over in Somers Town will be someone else's problem.'

'Exactly,' Kennedy said, looking around the heaps of files slightly apologetically. 'I can now pass on my bowler hat and brolly to someone else. Look, I'd better leave you to it, but thanks a million for your time.'

'No problem, Christy. Let's get you and ann rea up to the house for dinner—maybe Saturday week?'

'That sounds great. I'll check with ann rea and give you a shout.'

Since Kennedy had risen from the chair, they had been shaking hands and continued to shake hands. Kennedy liked the fact that even though Ford had literally been up to his eyeballs and preoccupied with his workload, he had not made Kennedy feel even slightly uncomfortable.

Ford's energy and warmth had never once been begrudging, and Kennedy resolved to remember this graciousness the next time he felt under pressure at North Bridge House.

Yes, Kennedy liked the man he had known only a matter of weeks. ann rea had also taken to both Harry and Lizabeth Ford, and Kennedy felt confident that she would be available for Saturday week and probably look forward to the dinner engagement as much as he would.

He was not usually a great one for social dining, but he relished the opportunity to get to know Ford better. He wondered if that might have anything to do with the fact that he and ann rea seemed to be moving into a different gear, and an opportunity such as dining with the Fords really took the spotlight away from the intensity of his relationship with her.

Chapter Ten

DAWN IS A sight mostly unseen by the inhabitants of St Martin's Gardens, NW1. Those not fortunate enough to find a bed in Arlington House or sanctuary in one of the numerous doorways of the Camden Town retail sector make the most of the three corners of the gardens. The fourth and possibly the most secluded corner—St Martin's Close, the entrance to the gardens—is generally avoided like the plague, due in no small part to the high concentration of ancient headstones.

Obviously the graveyard, or some kind of burial site at least, gave way to either ecumenical or commercial progress, and the former inhabitants' final testaments were scattered like pages torn from a book and placed, some vertical and some horizontal, along the St Martin's Close and Pratt Street corner of the gardens. The current bunch of regulars was forced, at the very least, to spare a thought for the faithful departed each and every time they entered and departed St Martin's Close.

On moonless nights when the wind was howling through the trees and you could hear a few dogs barking in the distance, the headstones' names, dates and final verses were responsible for more than a fleeting consideration on the ancient dwellers by the current ragtag and bobtail users of the square. Imaginations did tend to run riot after sundown, and even some of the seemingly honest inhabitants were known to arise, take up their beds and walk (permanently).

Mostly though, the Dwellers of the Gardens were casualties of one kind or another and were in their own personal oblivion in the wee small hours. In these cases, their demons rose only when they did.

The body was discovered just after dawn by the dweller known simply as George.

George—he no longer used a second name, claiming he didn't need it any more—was a burly, not-to-be-messed-with, fiery red-haired and bushy-bearded Scot. He'd been using the square for dossing for around eight years and had inherited his patch—to the rear of a large chestnut tree in the Georgina Street meets College Street corner of the gardens—from another older Scot.

In the world of dog eat dog, someone who would guide a novice around the food kitchens, illuminate them in the unwritten rules of life on the street, and teach them the vital rules of keeping themselves to themselves—perhaps, more importantly, encouraging them to keep to themselves—was an invaluable, not to mention an extremely rare, creature. Meeting such a character was as valuable as winning the lottery was to those in the straight world.

George had been a good student, so when his mentor had decided to go on the road again—this time to Scotland, as he correctly predicted, to die—George had been unopposed when he moved across the gardens to the prime pitch. He wasn't by any means the leader of the gardens, because such a person never existed—'Leaders are more for the straight world, and look what a mess they're making of that,' George always said—but he *could* be classified as a respected elder.

Dawn was George's hour. He loved to be up with the birds. He loved to get a start on the day and, as it was August, he did not have to go through the whole rigmarole of packing up and protecting his bedding, such as it was. So, in the dying days of summer, he was usually keen to make his way either to the top of Primrose Hill or into the Rose Garden in Regent's Park to experience sunrise. For George, the real pleasure of his life was to experience the birth of a new day with all its wondrous blues, reds, oranges and greens.

It was not something he did every day though. He claimed he didn't want to spoil himself. On Tuesday, 30 August, he did, however, rise early. He packed and stored his stuff and was making his way to the toilets at Euston Station for his daily wash when he noticed a stranger lying, near enough, in the middle of the square.

He later recalled that he had realised immediately that the body was one of a stranger, because none of the regulars would ever have slept in such an exposed—personal safety and weather-wise—position.

George walked over to investigate. The closer he came to the intruder, the more he realised that the solo sleeper was not one from the streets; his clothes were too swank, much too swank.

A chill went through each of George's 206 bones as he realised that the swank was dead. George had not needed to feel for pulses or other such—

he was no stranger to the look of death, he said, and besides which, no one sleeps with their eyes open.

George continued with his statement:

'His piercing blue eyes were staring up to heaven to a God that had forsaken him. They were just totally devoid of life.'

George had immediately gone to the telephone coin box on Pratt Street and dialled 999 and was waiting (with his back to the body) when the first police patrol car arrived four minutes and forty seconds later for a routine check, by which time all the dwellers had disappeared. The constable radioed in for back-up, which arrived eight minutes later in the shape of DS James Irvine and DC Jenny Lowe.

DS James Irvine examined the body and radioed into North Bridge House for the SOC team. Within another ten minutes, St Martin's Gardens were filled with an ever-growing, efficient team.

By the time Detective Inspector Christy Kennedy arrived at the square, Dr Leonard Taylor had pretty much concluded his initial examination of the body.

DS Irvine greeted Kennedy. 'There's nothing like getting right back up on the horse again, sir.'

'Aye, but I wouldn't wish this on anybody, James. Equally, I have to admit I'm happy to be back at work again, if only so that I can leave behind Castle's vanity cases.'

Kennedy, as ever, was delaying until the last possible moment his personal examination of the body.

He stood about ten yards away from it, and Irvine had George explain, for the fourth time that day, how he had discovered the body and how he had heard nothing unusual during the night.

Kennedy walked to and fro, the fingers of his right hand twitching, as George recounted his tale. Only thirty minutes previously, Kennedy was being served a generous portion of porridge by ann re, who still insisted that he needed building up again, physically speaking. He was surprised by how pleasant the porridge tasted. As a non-breakfast man, he was usually more than happy with a glass of orange juice or water, but equally he realised and accepted that not only were ann rea's intentions good, but they were also necessary.

Unable to delay the inevitable examination any further, he put all thoughts of ann rea, breakfast, porridge and clean teeth out of his mind, and walked the eleven steps necessary to reach the body.

Kennedy fixed his gaze on the tan-leather sensible shoes of the corpse. The detective immediately had a flash that these were the type of shoes he imagined John Riley would wear.

Chapter Eleven

AS KENNEDY CIRCLED the victim, avoiding staring directly at the face, he could feel the memory banks of his brain run their various checks on the look of the body.

The height was average—say five foot nine, or ten, inches; the build was slim, the chest rising up higher from the ground than either the tummy or the waist, which tended to suggest he was fit; the skin, which was showing the final signs of a hot summer, was taut but definitely too young to be John Riley's; the hair was brown, tucked behind his ears and disappeared under the collar of his dark blue blazer; the clothes were Ralph Lauren meets Marks and Sparks; there were slight seepage stains on his deep-blue shirt, betraying his nine, yes . . . one, two, three, four, five, six, seven, eight and nine, stab wounds. The stains tended to suggest that he had been stabbed somewhere else, probably with the shirt removed, and brought here post-death.

Kennedy hunkered down. He used the thumb and forefinger of his right hand to give the corpse some dignity in his final resting place by closing the eyelids. As his skin made contact with the corpse's skin, the electric shock of the coldness made him jolt slightly backwards. Simultaneously his brain successfully concluded its search through the thousands of likenesses stored therein. The reason why his usually effective brain had taken so long in its task was not that it was off peak as a result of his recent illness, but simply that he was, in fact, staring at a relatively new image.

In the split second after he reeled back from the coldness of the corpse and experienced his first glimpse of the piercing blue eyes, he realised that he was staring at the remains of one Mr Harry Ford, a very recent acquaintance and, up to seven seconds ago, a possible future best friend.

Chapter Twelve

KENNEDY'S BRAIN NOW flashed through a sequence of images of Fr Vincent O'Connor, Lizabeth Ford, Babe Ford and ann rea. The images mostly involved Kennedy telling them of this untimely death and comforting them as they were all overcome by emotion. At the same time as Kennedy was registering the loss on a personal level, he was also aware of a certain detachment on his part—detachment in that he had not been overcome with grief and was able to continue to assess the situation with his usual analytical mind.

Dr Leonard Taylor broke into Kennedy's thought process.

'Are you okay, Christy?' Taylor began, hunkering down beside his colleague. 'You've actually turned green.'

'I knew this man,' were the only words Kennedy could find.

Taylor finished what Kennedy had started by closing both of Harry Ford's eyelids.

They hunkered together in silence for a time, each alone with his thoughts.

Kennedy's thoughts were that he was here, staring at Harry Ford, with Dr Taylor so close to him he could actual smell the excess helping of Johnson's Talcum Powder that Taylor had obviously lavished over himself following his morning shower or bath. He wondered for a while if Taylor was a shower or bath man; most probably bath with his ample proportions, Kennedy concluded.

Taylor was the first to rise and he rose awkwardly. Kennedy followed.

'Are you sure?' Taylor asked, appearing more to want to say something than to question Kennedy's ability to recognise his acquaintances.

'Yes, yes, of course.' Kennedy replied deadpan and then asked, 'What can you tell me, Leonard?'

'I'd say he was killed somewhere between 8 p.m. and midnight yesterday evening,' Taylor started, making one of his legendary accurate guesses.

No response from Kennedy.

'As you can see, he was stabbed repeatedly. I'd say the middle stab wound was the fatal one; it's slightly off centre but probably went straight into his heart. His wrists were bound together. I'd guess they were bound in front of him and not behind him.'

Here Taylor demonstrated with his own hands how when your hands are tied together behind your back, they normally, most naturally form an 'X', whereas when they are tied in front of you, it's most naturally wrist to wrist.

'His ankles were also bound together. I'd say he was tethered with tape due to the evident strips of body hair absent from around his wrists and ankles; more than that I cannot tell you at this time.'

'Humph,' Kennedy grunted, not in annoyance but in acceptance, sounding more like Tom Jones than Kenneth Williams.

'Let's let DS Irvine finish his work here, and you and I go and find a good cup of tea,' Taylor suggested as Kennedy continued to stare at the body.

'Good idea,' Kennedy replied. 'You go and scout one out. I just need to absorb the SOC a bit more. We'll get you the body as soon as possible.'

Taylor hobbled off in the direction of the police camp being set up out on Pratt Street.

Kennedy continued to walk around the corpse. As near as he could guess, Ford had been positioned in the centre of the gardens.

Irvine had reliably advised Kennedy that at the time they guesstimated the body was being deposited, there were at least twenty-three people that George knew about in the square. They were talking about sometime after 1.30 a.m. as that was roughly the time when the last of the regulars returned to their patch to bed down for the night.

Both Irvine and Kennedy knew that they were going to have to do their utmost to locate each and every one of those twenty-three people in case one of them had seen something, anything, during that particular dark midnight hour. That was certainly going to be a challenge. It was not as if you could find out their weekend addresses and go knocking on some doors. Kennedy felt that some of last night's inhabitants had now departed the square for good. He also knew that there was a very effective bush telegraph around Camden Town and that if someone had seen something suspicious, Camden Town CID would eventually pick up the information, albeit third or even fourth hand.

All this time, he was slowly walking around the body, studying it, willing it to talk to him by throwing up evidence. For some strange reason, he heard George Harrison's beautiful guitar solo from the Travelling Wilburys' song, 'Congratulations', replaying over and over again in the recesses of his mind.

He focused back in on the clothes again. He noticed a darker patch on the right arm just below the shoulder, somewhere around the position he would have worn three stripes had he been a sergeant in the army. He knelt down again and examined the patch closely. It was definitely a stain, not dark enough in colour to be a blood stain but a stain nonetheless. Kennedy imagined it must be a post-death stain. He believed that Harry Ford was too clothes-conscious to go out knowingly in stained or soiled clothes. He felt the borders of the stain, which was an irregular oval, six inches across at the widest point. He was not sure whether it was cold or damp he was feeling.

DS James Irvine's attention was also drawn to the patch, if only by Kennedy's attention. He was positioned on the other side of the body.

'There's a similar marking on this arm, sir.'

As Kennedy rose to investigate Irvine's discovery, he noticed similar dark patches around the bottom of the each leg of the cream Chinos. This time the marks were distinctly damp to his touch.

'Let's have forensic run a check on these.'

Kennedy was fine now. He was investigating. The body, for him, was no longer a dead person but a piece of valuable evidence in his investigation. This was the only way he could work.

If he allowed himself to think back to the dinner at the Engineer with Ford, his wife and ann rea, and if he were to recall Ford in full flight—funny, articulate, a loving husband and caring father—the impact of his demise would become totally unbearable, particularly if Kennedy were to consider, as he no doubt would, that this vital life had been ended by another human. Kennedy thought back to the recent meeting, where Ford, although apparently under immense pressure of work, had shown himself to be generous and gracious with time for Kennedy to help him on the Riley investigation. He had wondered afterwards if this had been a professional gesture or a signal of friendship; on reflection, he had leaned towards the latter.

Truth was, because of such thoughts, Kennedy could not afford to consider the dead body now lying in the middle of St Martin's Gardens as that of a departed friend. He could not allow himself to sit and wonder how this once-spirited human, this man who shared a passion for his father's trade, carpentry, this man with his plans, dreams, vanities, assets (spiritual and monetary), aspirations, memories and dependants—how this man was now nothing more than a rotting chunk of flesh and bones, growing smellier by the minute.

He knew that he could be effective in his work only if he could detach himself from the sorry state of the body lying before him. He forced himself to consider the body as *a* body of evidence.

'Any vehicle tracks?' he asked Irvine.

'Not even a wheelbarrow,' Irvine replied, walking around both Kennedy and Ford now. 'Hundreds of faint footprints, which means no footprints. Do you think he was carried here by two people?'

'Probably not.' Kennedy sighed, the fingers of his right hand twitching furiously again. 'People rarely murder in twos, besides which it's just as awkward for two people to carry a body as it is for one. A good strong chap could throw this eleven stone over his shoulder and dump him here.'

'Well, he certainly wasn't dragged here,' Irvine offered. 'There are no betraying marks, and we did get here when the scene was still fresh.'

'Okay,' Kennedy agreed and added, 'Also, if you're dragging a body after you, it does tend to draw attention no matter how unlikely the chance is of being spotted. However, if someone has a large bulk thrown over their shoulder, it could be anything—a bag of clothes, wood . . .'

'Could even be a mate they're bringing home from the pub.'

'Exactly.'

At this point, Taylor signalled over to Kennedy from the entrance to the square; he made a large 'T' using his arms.

'Okay,' Kennedy sighed. 'Our esteemed doctor has discovered the vital tea source. I'll leave you to search the body, bag it and see what else we can find around here before we get the body off to Taylor.'

Kennedy walked back towards Taylor, who had disappeared into one of the several police mobile units. Every so often, Kennedy turned to look back at the lifeless body of Harry Ford and saw the progress of DS Irvine as he went from pocket to pocket, bagging the contents carefully.

For some reason, unknown even to himself, Kennedy seemed reluctant to complete his journey. At the last possible moment, instead of climbing the three steps into the wagon, he shouted in to Taylor that he would be with him in a few minutes, and he veered to his right and continued to walk around the perimeter of the gardens.

His first consideration was that the bedroom windows on Bayham Street and Greenland Road afforded a clear view of the St Martin's Gardens. Indeed, he had spotted a face every fifth window or so observing the police at their work. He wondered how much thought the spectators would spare for Harry Ford.

People do tend to distance themselves from death.

Yet, at the same time, the very same people do seem to take some kind of comfort from the fact the Grim Reaper has chosen someone else's door to thump upon, figuratively speaking. Thereby implying, Kennedy supposed, that when the Grim Reaper came visiting, he always had to depart with a prize.

Kennedy dwelt on this thought for the time it took him to walk half the (long) side of the gardens. Could death really just be some form of natural culling process? Could this mean that in any one particular day, in order to keep the earth's population at a predetermined level, so many babies are going to be born and so many people are going to die?

The deaths, just like the births, could either be planned or be accidents. That would be RTAs, domestic accidents, natural disasters, homicide, incurable diseases and people dying peacefully in their sleep.

Why do some people need to die in tragic circumstances while others are allotted a long life before passing away peacefully on a soft mattress in a deep sleep? Has death more to do with those left behind than the actual fatalities themselves? Sometimes death actually galvanises those left behind: lovers, wives, husbands, fathers, mothers, children, friends and colleagues. A death in your circle does tend to force you to consider, to one degree or another, your mortality. For that space of time, as you consider the demise of your loved ones or friends, people do tend to be more considerate of those around them. They do tend to put matters in order, reflect on things and celebrate the life of the faithful departed.

While on the subject of life and, to a greater degree, death, Kennedy wondered why relatives sometimes seem to be hit harder by the death of an 84-year-old than by the death of a middle-aged person. Does this have more to do with the life force of the deceased than the manner of death? Is the death of someone who was 84 and a good person who was healthy in body and mind more of a blow to the survivors because that's what we all aspire to be—a good person, healthy in body and mind? Yet such a death forces us to realise that no matter how good we are, the inevitable Dr Death is always there, lurking around some corner if not the next one.

Kennedy reasoned that humans never ever come to terms with death. His grandfather, for instance, had been 99 years old when he passed away and, right up until the day before he died, he had been still living his life to the full. He had been very much alive, reading a national and a local paper most days of his life, and he could successfully hold a conversation with anyone on numerous subjects. Yet, although he was 99 years old, his death was 'totally unexpected'. One day, his grandfather had been, at least from the outside, full of life and beans. The very next day, the breath had disappeared from his body, shocking and distressing all who knew him.

Kennedy wondered whether death was, as far as the majority of us are concerned, something that happens not so much 'tomorrow' as 'the day *after* tomorrow'.

'So,' Kennedy said in a whisper to the trees as he passed them, 'did the murderer of Harry Ford believe that it didn't matter a fig how they lived their life—they were still going to come to a sad end? Did they accept that no human can change that fact, so, by extension, it doesn't matter how you live your life—you are still going to die?'

He realised he was talking to himself, so he returned to his thoughts, thinking that it was a long leap from the fact that we are all going to die, no matter how we lead our lives, to, 'Okay, so if it doesn't matter what I do, I'm going to be happy to do the things which will make my life easier. I don't need a social conscience and so, in my opinion, I can make the time I have on this earth easier by removing someone. And so be it."

So, whose life could have been made easier by removing the life of one Harry Ford?

Whose indeed?

Kennedy knew that he and his team needed to gather a lot of information before they would be in any position to start considering any such assessments.

In the meantime, as he had now just completed one lap of the gardens, there was the prospect of a life-enriching cup of tea to be enjoyed in the entertaining company of a certain Dr Leonard Taylor.

'I always seem to forget this part of my work,' Kennedy began as Taylor played Mum with the makeshift equipment: a Bunsen burner; a tripod; a wire gauze; a large beaker; two polystyrene cups; a couple of Taylor's endless supply of Tetley tea bags; a wooden thingy (which makes you go 'agh' when the doctor puts it in your mouth) for stirring; five sachets of brown sugar—three for Taylor and two for Kennedy—and a half-pint of milk he had persuaded a constable to go and purchase from the newsagent's around the corner. The same newsagent, in fact, who was fast discovering exactly how sweet were the teeth of Camden Town's CID.

'The getting started, you mean?'

'No,' Kennedy sighed as he took a sip of his tea. 'The fact that mostly what we do starts off with someone losing their life. That seems to be the bit I put out of my mind when I was sitting at home desperate to get back to work again.'

'It is easier when you don't know the victim,' Taylor sympathised.

'Only fractionally,' Kennedy confessed, in what was a rare revelation for him.

Chapter Thirteen

TAYLOR AND KENNEDY knew each other well enough that they were both comfortable about being in each other's company without feeling the need to fill the space with words. Both were lost in their thoughts. Kennedy about the Ford family and his supper with them; and Taylor, Kennedy imagined, about whether the detective was well enough recovered to take on a case such as this, with all its personal implications.

Irvine joined them, ending the silence that had hung between them.

'I thought you might like to see the contents, sir,' Irvine said, with a subtext of: 'Would there by any chance be a spare cup of tea in the pot?' or, in this case, '. . . in the beaker?'

'Did you find anything interesting?' Kennedy asked.

'He had a couple of grand on him, which rules out robbery.'

'Which rules out robbery,' Kennedy agreed, lacking any element of surprise in his tone.

'Why would you want to be wandering around Camden Town with two thousand pounds on your person?' Taylor asked both of them.

'Good question, Doctor,' Kennedy replied, refusing to speculate.

Irvine seemed to note not only the words but also the tone of Kennedy's reply. He certainly knew that his leader liked to deal only in facts, and when he had amassed all the facts possible, and certainly not before then, he would consider the information and start to draw conclusions.

'He also had a credit-card wallet with three credit cards and seven first-class postage stamps; a small leather wallet with his driver's licence in one side and a photo of a woman and a child on the other. The funny thing was that when I removed the licence, I discovered a second photograph underneath of a young woman.'

Irvine fanned the wallet to show the photos, first the family shot and then the solo female shot.

Kennedy recognised Lizabeth and Babe Ford but could not put a name to the girl in the other photo. It was a head, shoulder and hair shot of a teenage girl. The solo girl was breathtakingly beautiful in the sense of classic beauty, more Katharine Hepburn than Sandra Bullock. She wore a warm generous smile, had perfect white teeth, brown eyes, clear skin and no make-up.

Kennedy flicked the photo over. The once white of the paper had browned with the years. The blue fountain pen's smooth writing had also faded. It was, however, clear enough to make out the legend: 'Hello you, love A.' It was dated, 'Nov. 23rd 1978'.

Could this young girl be in some way or other involved in Ford's demise. The fresh-faced youthfulness of the photograph made him doubt this possibility. Then he thought of the classic early black-and-white shots of George Harrison, Brigitte Bardot, Paul McCartney and Marianne Faithful. He realised that he had been studying the shot through his years. When he looked at it again and considered her vitality and the eagerness of her eyes to engage the camera, the photographer, the viewer, the world, he assured himself that his first assertion was still worthy of consideration.

'Love, A.'

Who was 'A'? Perhaps Ann? Annie? Maybe Angela? Angelina? Or maybe even Anthea? Female Christian names starting with the letter 'A' were few and far between. Was that because Kennedy had faltered at Angela at the memory of a bespectacled teenage girlfriend? Then what if the 'A' stood for a nickname. America? The girl in the photograph didn't look American.

Kennedy was about to give the guessing game up as a lost cause when he remembered Ford and O'Connor's university days. He wondered whether the young girl in the photograph was Alice, the member of the Four Musketeers who had melted Ford's heart in 1978.

'There's a set of keys, house and car, one pen, one pencil, two cinema ticket stubs for the delightful E*tre et Avoir* . . .' Irvine continued.

Under his breath, Taylor muttered something about everyone's being 'a Barry Norman', which Irvine didn't hear, so intent was he on his list: '. . . three pounds and seventy pence in loose change, a receipt from WH Smith's for sixteen pounds and thirty pence dated for the previous day at 17.20.'

Kennedy took the bagged receipt from Irvine and read aloud: 'A bar of Cadbury's Whole Nut, a pint of milk, two bottles of mineral water and a pack of Duracell AA batteries, right.' Thinking beyond the list, he continued, 'None of these items were found on his body.'

'Correct,' Irvine replied in his distinctive Connery dialect. 'And finally!' he grandstanded, producing the final evidence bag.

Kennedy examined the contents of the diaphanous bag, keeping it well within Taylor's view.

'What on earth's that?' Taylor asked, putting down his tea and moving closer to Kennedy and the bag to afford himself an even better view.

Kennedy passed the evidence bag over to Taylor, who sat down again on a rather rickety chair and twisted the bag this way and that, examining the contents from every conceivable angle.

'It's a BlackBerry.'

'Right,' Taylor said in an I'm-none-the-wiser tone. 'It doesn't look like the most tempting blackberry I've ever come across.'

Chapter Fourteen

KENNEDY LEFT IRVINE supervising a house-to-house of all the 'indoor' residents of St Martin's Gardens, St Martin's Close and Pratt Street to see if there were witnesses to any nocturnal comings and goings. His next task would be to have his team check Camden's famous—yes, maybe even infamous—late-night bars, cafés and minicab companies and continue their questioning in those particular areas in the hope that it might turn up a single shred of evidence.

Taylor accompanied the remains of Harry Ford back to St Pancras' All Saints Hospital to carry out the crucial autopsy.

In the meantime, Kennedy had to visit Lizabeth Ford to give her the bad news. Needless to say, it was a task he was not looking forward to. He decided to enlist the assistance of DC Dot King, a confident and youthful replacement for the aforementioned DC Anne Coles.

It was King's irreverence that Kennedy admired, and at times her confidence surely bordered on impertinence. More importantly, she was a great driver who was happy to take her lead from Kennedy as to whether they talked or not. Furthermore, when the opportunity presented itself, she always proved to be bursting with ideas and suggestions. Kennedy liked that in a person. Too many people on the CID were so intent on getting it right all the time that they held back from making suggestions until they were absolutely convinced they were correct. In the meantime, the case was usually, hopefully, solved. Kennedy was all for the idea of running theories up the flagpole and seeing how they flew. If they didn't fly, you discovered why and moved on.

The other thing Kennedy liked about King was that she was absolutely in love with the idea of being a detective; it was a true vocation for her and not just a career. On top of that, if that needed topping—and because of the Coles incident, where DC Anne Coles' and his mutual attraction had nearly led to his death, Kennedy felt that perhaps it did need topping—DC

Dot King was 23 years old, had been dating the same boy, 'my Ashley', since they were 17, and planned to wed on her twenty-fifth birthday.

So it was that he and DC King were standing on Lizabeth Ford's doorstep when she answered the bell.

Kennedy spotted all the signs of delayed-reaction shock as and when they happened.

The resident, in this case Mrs Lizabeth Ford, firstly noted the uniform and the first wave of panic set in. This is a mild wave, and sometimes people are not even aware of it themselves, believing it to be a rush of adrenalin from seeing a stranger on their doorstep. A split second later, Ford registered the face of Kennedy, so she relaxed a little. Then she noticed that neither Kennedy nor the uniformed police officer was smiling, so her panic level increased again. She was still in what could be considered a controlled stage of panic.

Next, she spotted pity in their eyes.

Subconsciously she did a head count. Kennedy could see this entire process going on in her eyes. *Harry's at work, Babe's upstairs, Von's over in Belfast and Vycky's up in Manchester, both my parents are in the South of France and both Harry's parents are dead.*

Kennedy noticed the first flicker of self-doubt in her eyes. Although unable to read her thoughts exactly, he knew that something along the following lines was going through her head: *Hang on, Harry wasn't in by the time I'd gone to bed last night, and he was gone by the time I awoke this morning.* (Lizabeth filled in the actual details for Kennedy later that day. It was not unusual for her husband to be the last to bed and the first up.)

Then her mind's eye flashes back to a scene she remembers seeing outside their en-suite bathroom earlier in the morning. Harry Ford showered every single morning—and again in the evening in the summer months; he also changed his underwear and socks every day. She remembers that his pile of dirty clothes was not in its traditional position on the floor just outside the bathroom door. She did not, as normal, have to clear them up and dump them in the linen basket.

Next, Lizabeth—maybe even because neither Kennedy nor King is offering any words of comfort, friendliness or normality—raises her hand to her mouth and opens her eyes to their widest.

She looks to Kennedy, searching his eyes, his body language, for any sign, no matter how small or apparently insignificant, which might convince her that all her assumptions and deductions are incorrect.

All Kennedy has to say for himself is, 'Can we come inside, Lizabeth?'

Lizabeth Ford then pulls herself together, her *foolish* panic attack ebbing. She wipes her flour-covered hands on her apron and says through flour-marked lips, 'Yes, of course. How rude of me. Please come on inside, won't you?'

By now her brief panic attack has subsided and she is totally composed again. Inwardly she is chastising herself for having harboured such foolish and childish thoughts. She is thinking to herself that it has taken her husband only twenty-four years, but at last he has managed to find the linen basket.

Kennedy looks at her. He knows no short cut or easier way to deliver his news.

'Lizabeth, I'm afraid I have some bad news for you . . .'

The words are not necessary, but through the violent storms exploding throughout her head, she hears Kennedy continue: 'It's Harry . . .'

Of course, you idiot, I know it's Harry; it can be no one else but my prime mate.

'I'm afraid he is dead.'

Oh God, I know, I know. If Harry were alive, the police would just have contacted me by phone, or your eyes would have been filled with hope and not pity when I opened the door.

She hears her own voice laugh, a laugh of, *Oh, don't be silly, you've made a mistake. Of course he's not dead, he's my husband, he's Babe's dad.*

The friendly Ulster detective does not return her laugh. DC Dot King moves slowly towards Lizabeth.

Go away, Lizabeth thinks. *Who do you think I am—a helpless old woman? I can look after myself.*

At which point her legs fail her. One minute they are supporting her nine stone, eight pounds and the next they are like jelly and she feels her body collapse in a heap on the floor like a sad rag doll.

At the same time as she experiences flashes in her brain, she loses her eyesight. In actual fact, she does not lose her eyesight but her pupils are so suffused with tears she cannot focus on anything. Simultaneously her brain turns on the waterworks and her nose thinks it's running for England, and even though, by now, she is lying on her hall carpet, she attempts to raise the hem of her apron to wipe her nose. She knows such action is neither a pretty sight nor socially acceptable, but she has company and some sort of decorum is called for.

All of the above happens in a twenty-three-second time span, and Lizabeth, unable to cope with the sheer intensity, not to mention immensity, of feelings, passes out.

Twenty-seven minutes later, with the aid of tender loving care, she comes around again to witness that her doctor and her daughter have joined Kennedy and King. Her daughter, the youngest—Babe—is being the adult and keeping it all together.

Kennedy knows that they are all intent on survival and following some kind of primitive instinct.

Mother and daughter are holding hands.

'I know,' Babe says, more mouthing the words than speaking them.

Her mother hugs her, clinging on as though both their lives depend on it.

Through the sobbing, Kennedy overhears the mother mutter, 'Oh, your poor dad. He was wearing his new jacket for the first time. It didn't bring him much luck though, did it?'

'I know, I know,' Babe whispers, continuing her mantra.

Chapter Fifteen

KENNEDY DEPARTED, LEAVING King in the Ford household. He was a matter of six steps away from the front door when Fr Vincent O'Connor's distinctive VW pulled into the driveway.

The priest looked very distraught and barely had a word for Kennedy, shaking his hand briefly as he passed him on his way straight to the front door of the house.

Kennedy wondered whether the Camden Town bush telegraph was as effective as ever or if Babe Ford had rung the priest. He considered hanging around to catch O'Connor on the way out but decided it was probably better to return to North Bridge House and set the investigation into gear.

He walked back to the police station via Primrose Hill. The beautiful morning had held its promise and was developing into a magnificent day. Some of the grass and many of the leaves on the trees had been scorched by the summer sun, and so the hill, complete with its cloudless blue sky, looked more like it was located in Carmel, California, than the borders of Camden Town, London. Kennedy stood atop the hill for a few minutes. He knew he didn't really have the time for such a luxury, the sort he had been enjoying almost daily while he was recuperating; equally he knew that if he was not of the mind to steal such moments, he would never ever enjoy them again. Such sights were not something you could store up and save for later on.

There was only one other occupant on the hilltop: a bearded man who was sitting on the bench with his legs spread out before him and his arms outstretched on either side, resting on the back of the bench. He was dressed in a blue artists' smock, brown cord trousers and topped and tailed with a cap—similar to the one Dylan wore in his formative years—and a pair of sensible brown leather shoes. This man was so immersed in his spectacular environs that he was totally oblivious to Kennedy.

Kennedy looked to his left to the high-rise block of flats known as Hill View. This was such an ugly building, with absolutely no redeeming features, yet those astute enough to have bought one of the twenty-five flats could savour one of London's most glorious views, not to mention enjoy their cosy little investment. Kennedy wondered if any of the current owners were one of the original two-dozen-plus-one owners or if the properties changed hands frequently. He could not imagine people ever wishing to sell, particular those lucky enough to have selected the upper three or four floors.

He looked to the right and could see all the way down to the London Eye, which broke the skyline like one of Finn Mac Cool's bicycle wheels.

He looked to the centre and saw the Zoo and the trees of Regent's Park, and somewhere to the left of that was North Bridge House, the home of Camden Town CID. He set his sights on his work base and headed off in that direction.

By the time he returned to his office, the forensic department had left a message for him saying that the damp patches on the arms of Harry Ford's jacket and the legs of his trousers showed traces of a water and sugar solution.

'A water and sugar solution,' Irvine said, repeating Kennedy's words half an hour later. 'What's that all about?'

Kennedy had already started to compile information relating to the case for his 'Guinness Is Good for You' green felt notice board. Over the years, he had made his office in North Bridge House his home-from-home, personalising the usual drab surroundings detectives were forced to work in. He was so successful in his endeavours that his office—the top floor, at the Regent's Park end of one of the oldest buildings in the area—looked nothing like the other offices in the police station

Kennedy, like his father, was a carpenter. Unlike his father, though, he was not a master carpenter. He had inherited enough skills to get by, and he had panelled the walls with dark oak wood; he had sanded the floorboards, varnished them up and placed a royal blue carpet at the end of his desk; he had replaced the standard-issue grey metal and pretty board desk with an American Arts and Crafts desk he had picked up 'for a song' or 'four pink Grannies' in Camden Market. Camden Market had also produced two matching—although purchased eight months apart—leather easy chairs; two (different) captain's swivel chairs; a couple of standard lamps; a traditional desk light complete with the original green glass lamp shade; wooden shutters for the tall windows; and the Guinness Is Good for You notice board. The police department came up with an evidence table—Kennedy liked to have an uninterrupted space where he could spread the various bits and pieces that came to light on a case before him; a standard notice board for the police notices and two overhead lamps for the evidence table.

By removing years of wallpaper, plasterboard and wooden studs, Kennedy had discovered a deep recess in one of the dark corners of his office. He had used this precious reclaimed space to build a cupboard, in which he had installed his tea-making paraphernalia. For Kennedy, the magic of this cupboard was that when the door was shut, it blended in with the wall on either side, and the cupboard was totally invisible.

His office, by CID standards, was pretty organised, Kennedy's logic being that, at least for him, it was hard, if not impossible, to enjoy an organised mind when you had a disorganised office-cum-workspace. How could he expect himself to be able to think, let alone solve a crime, when his surroundings were chaotic? Yes, his office was cosier by far than most CID offices, and why not, Kennedy reckoned that he spent the majority of his life in this room. Well, at least that had been the case before he met ann rea.

Camden Town CID—no, make that Superintendent Thomas Castle to be exact—had indulged Kennedy in his little whims, such as the office, possibly because Castle genuinely liked Kennedy, but probably mainly because Kennedy produced results. Kennedy, unlike Castle, was not pre-occupied with these statistics, figuring that you needed to approach a new crime with a clear mind and not take for granted that your success rate was going to guarantee you continued success.

Kennedy's need for a clear mind was another reason why he forced himself to move beyond the fact that he knew, at least to some degree, the victim in this particular murder.

Yes, Kennedy would admit to having had a 'sentimental moment' when he was writing out Harry Ford's bio card. 'Harry Ford, 45 years old, CABS Branch Mgr.' But by the time he was pinning the card to the notice board, the moment had passed and he was concerned simply about getting himself and his team stuck into the case. The other cue cards already written out on his desk were for:

Elizabeth Ford

Babe Ford
Von Ford
Vycky Ford
Fr Vincent O'Connor
Alice Roberts/Cain
Neil Roberts
Sugar Water
Stabbing.

'You're gotten off to a flying start!' Irvine said, apparently mentally reading the information on the cards.

Kennedy ignored the remark, as he tended to do with anything that vaguely resembled a compliment. He was not very good with compliments; he never had been, and didn't know why. He would admit, at least to ann rea, that he did like people to think well of him; it was just that he grew increasingly embarrassed when the same people expressed their admiration in his company.

'Did you turn up anything on the house-to-house?' Kennedy asked.

'No, not a thing so far,' Irvine replied, looking dejected for a second or two. 'I mean, we found the usual wife, house-husband or partner at home with their bedfellows out at work, so we're going to try again tonight at seven o'clock when most will have returned from their work.'

'Ah,' Kennedy began with the air of someone who knew he wasn't about to give a popular command. 'I'd like us to go back to the same houses again and, where possible, find the address of the places of employment of the absentee residents and visit them there.'

A little blood drained from Irvine's face.

'Two reasons really,' Kennedy offered by way of explanation. 'One, we don't have a lot of leads to follow at the moment, and two, I'd like us to talk to them before a day at the office has managed to dull their memory cells a little further.'

'Sorry, sir, you're absolutely right. I'll get on to it myself immediately.'

'No,' Kennedy replied immediately. 'Get DS Gibson and his boys out on the footwork. I need you to get a small team together and accompany me to the Coalition & Aylesbury Building Society offices so we can start to interview Ford's work colleagues.'

'Okay,' Irvine said and turned on his heels to leave Kennedy's office.

'Oh, and you'd better send someone to relieve DC King, who's on compassionate duty up at Ford's house. She's going to be more useful to us at CABS. She's very sharp and picks up on things very quickly,' Kennedy said, proving that even if he did have a hard time accepting compliments himself, he had no problem dishing them out.

'Yes, she's certainly a shinny little button, isn't she?' Irvine agreed as he disappeared down the corridor.

The Coalition & Aylesbury Building Society offices, which were just opposite the Camden Palace, were nothing palatial, but then again neither was the Camden Palace. The overwhelming atmosphere that hit Kennedy the moment he walked into CABS must have been similar, he felt, to that of a ship without a captain. Five days previously, when Kennedy had last visited, the office had been incredibly busy, but at the same time, it appeared to be efficiently run. Now, Kennedy noted, everyone appeared to be just as busy but seemed to be performing in a more directionless manner. The result, Kennedy noted, was that the same team was probably spending twice as much energy accomplishing half the result.

Kennedy and King set about searching Ford's office, the same office that Irvine had had the foresight to secure with a constable earlier that morning.

King had all the files in Ford's office boxed and removed to North Bridge House for inspection by the finance detectives. The object of the exercise was not necessarily to discover any wrongdoing or embezzlement on Harry Ford's part. No, King instinctively knew that statistically speaking, 98 times out of 100, victims tend to be murdered for a reason. The reason invariably fell into one of two groups: A) Domestic (in the majority of cases); and B) Professional. Should this murder prove to fall into the latter category, the details of Ford's professional life, or at least a certain part, could be found in the files scattered around the office.

With these files removed, it was remarkable how much larger Ford's office appeared, so large in fact that Kennedy decided to set up his base in there, but not before he and King had had a good old nose around in the deceased's drawers.

There was a stack of alternating light and dark wood drawers on each side of the unique two-tone wooden desktop. There were three drawers on each side, which grew larger from desktop to floor. The bottom drawers were packed to overflowing with more files. These additional files were added to the consignment waiting for North Bridge House. The top two drawers in each stack contained the usual bric-a-brac that humans seem unconsciously to accumulate.

Kennedy looked into the drawers and was reminded how, like magpies, we are all attracted to 'stuff'—'stuff' which, after we have accumulated it, we don't really know what to do with. We don't really know what it's for; all we know is that we are attracted to this 'stuff', and a lot of us will carry this 'stuff' from office to office, or house to house, and then, when we die, someone will have to go through our 'stuff' and dump, if not all of it, then certainly most of it. More insulting than that is the fact that our survivors will unceremoniously dump most of our 'stuff' without a second thought.

Ford's stuff, at least his office stuff—Kennedy knew from personal experience that there was going to be a stash of home stuff as well—consisted of:

A broken Mickey Mouse watch

Numerous cheap pencils and pens

A cassette of Tanita Tikaram's *Sentimental*

An autographed paperback copy of *The Lonesome Heart Is Angry*

A black dress dickey bow in a plastic box

Several postcards rubber-banded together

Three old penny coins

Ford's personal bank statements

Ford's pay slips

Blank postcards

Two first-class stamps

A small green tray with three marbles

A John Player Navy Cut cigarette tin box with a hinged lid containing various pins, nails, a pen top, a tiny screwdriver and three bones for a shirt collar

A couple of cheque book stubs

Five unattached keys

A Tara Travel document wallet packed with dead tickets and travel itineraries

A file a couple of inches thick containing correspondence with an insurance company, Sure Lock Homes

The postcards were all impersonal, from various UK locations, all with writing that looked very similar to the writing on the rear of the photograph from 'A' that Irvine had discovered hidden behind the driver's licence in Ford's wallet earlier.

Kennedy had a brief read through the Sure Lock Homes file. The policyholder, one Mr Harry Ford, was in dispute with the company over a break-in at his home address. Ford had claimed for the damage caused to his property and for loss of several items from his home. The items included a Dell laptop computer, a portable television, a toaster and a small radio.

'A toaster,' Kennedy said out loud, in disbelief.

'Sorry, sir?' King responded, stopping in her tracks.

'A toaster—ever heard of a tealeaf pinching a toaster: a chrome Dualit toaster.'

'Can't say I have,' King laughed. 'Toasters weren't even mentioned at Hendon, and I'm sure they covered most items and the reasons for their removal at college. I suppose one thing's for certain, sir.'

'What's that?' Kennedy replied, as he started back into the insurance file again.

'Well, that the thief certainly wasn't a drug dealer,' King said, laughing as much to herself as Kennedy. 'I mean, what could be more uncool than having to go around trying to sell a second-hand toaster?'

Her attempt at a joke probably hadn't registered with Kennedy, and if it had, he didn't acknowledge it, so engrossed was he in the file.

Ford was in dispute with Sure Lock Homes over exactly what their liabilities and responsibilities were on his claim.

Kennedy read the loss adjustor's report. Loss adjustors, he felt, were mostly descendants of the Sheriff of Nottingham, because if Robin Hood took from the rich and gave to the poor, loss adjustors helped take from the poor and return it to the rich. If both parties conceded that, in fact, there was a loss, why did it need adjusting? The client never suggested they needed to bring in a payment adjustor at the beginning of the relationship when demanded to fork out the high premiums. If Kennedy had known King better, he would have been discussing the matter with her as they went about their work. He knew it was a potential soapbox moment for him, at least ann rea was always telling him that it was. It was just that as a detective he had seen so many hearts broken when victims had returned home to discover that their houses had been broken into. Sometimes he would witness the same victims even more distressed over the way the insurance companies treated them.

King was content to go about her work silently and efficiently, examining the top drawers of more of Ford's stuff. She discovered:

An address book

A CABS diary marked up with times and dates for various meetings
A telephone book
A couple of half-used chequebooks
A building society (the Halifax) pass book
A Phillips (star) screwdriver
An ordinary screwdriver
A box of Swan Vesta matches
An unused Liberty diary for 1996
A few receipts, mainly for office supplies from Ryman's of Camden High Street
Several CABS envelopes
Three National Westminster Bank £1,000 plastic bags torn open and empty
A Guinness salt cellar
A pair of sunglasses
A Tetley Tea promotional key ring
An envelope addressed to Ford containing a typed letter of thanks, and offer of spiritual support, from Fr Vincent O'Connor

'Nothing here,' King said as she leaned back into Ford's chair and closed the top drawer.

'Hmmm,' Kennedy said quietly. 'There's a lot there; it's just that we need to know what it all means.'

'You mean, we can learn something from everything?' she inquired, her big brown eyes totally focused on Kennedy.

Dot King had an accentless voice, not posh but educated. She always spoke confidently and appeared fearless. She was slight in build, but her thick dark curly hair gave her figure the appearance of at least some substance. Cleverly she had avoided trying to find a way of stuffing her wild mane into her pillbox hat, content enough simply to plonk her regulation hat down on her crown and secure it in place with craftily positioned hair clips.

'Something like that, yes,' Kennedy agreed. 'We just have to study everything, and try to look at it from Harry Ford's perspective. If we manage to do that, there's a greater chance we'll find the significance of some of his stuff. Which in effect means we also require a great memory to retain the images of all this stuff in the hope that, at some time in the future, the penny will drop and something will finally click into place for us.'

'Right,' King said, noting, marking and inwardly digesting his words. 'Shall I bring the first of the staff in to be interviewed?'

'Yes, let's have his secretary in first,' Kennedy replied, moving one of the two chairs from the front of Ford's desk and placing it by the cream wall, where he sat down with the window to his right and the door to his left. This way he wouldn't have to be presumptuous and sit behind Ford's desk. It also meant that he didn't have to sit with his back to the door as Ford's colleagues entered the office for their interviews.

Chapter Sixteen

MISS JILL CODONA was the kind of girl going on to be a woman—even though she was only in her late twenties—who looked better from a distance. That is not to say that she looked awful close up. It's just that when you were close enough to shake her hand, as Kennedy was, you could see exactly how it had all been put together. For someone who had just lost her boss of six years, she appeared remarkably well composed. Kennedy was sure that he even noticed a polite, albeit brief, social smile as she walked towards him. She had jet-black hair done up in an Elvis quiff, complete with the Tony Curtis DA. Her hair was tucked behind her ears with one and a half inch drops of hair perfectly recreating—at least from a distance—Elvis's trademark sideburns. Again from a distance, the hairstyle and slim figure gave one the impression that Miss Codona was tall. She enjoyed what could be best described as Spanish cum gypsy features, with big brown eyes that seemed as if they would look just as happily glad as sad.

She wore a short grey pleated skirt over black opaque tights, which covered her shapely legs. Her clothing was completed by orange and red leatherette high-heeled shoes, a crisp snow-white shirt, a decorative white bra which was particularly noticeable through her shirt because of the contrast of the white and her tan skin. The ensemble was completed by a black woollen waistcoat, which she wore open.

Her make-up, while not betraying any telltale signs of tears, did look either a little bit tired or a little bit overdone. Kennedy could not be sure which. She wore no jewellery around her neck or on her ears or fingers, but she did have a silver bangle on her left wrist and a matching watch on her right.

Considering the overall package created by her look, Kennedy was somewhat taken aback to hear her London accent. It wasn't broad enough to be considered Cockney, but the streets of London shone through loud and clear even on her opening line: 'Goodness, this is a right sorry old mess you have to sort out, isn't it?'

'Yes, it's very sad, isn't it?' King agreed.

'I mean, has anyone told Lizabeth yet? That's his wife, you know.'

'Yes, there's someone there with her now,' Kennedy replied, inviting Miss Codona to sit in front of the desk.

DC King made her way behind the desk and took Ford's chair.

Jill Codona started off again, unprompted.

'It's weird, you know. It's very much like being in limbo land, not that I've ever been in limbo land, of course, but I think you know what I mean.'

Kennedy and King nodded agreement even though neither of them had ever visited the land of perpetual preparation either. Codona smiled what appeared to Kennedy to be an I-won't-tell-on-you-if-you-don't-tell-on-me type smile before continuing: 'Since we heard Mr Ford was dead, no one has really known what to do. I mean, we were all told in no uncertain terms that we couldn't go home, we had to stay put, well, at least until we'd been interviewed by the police. And, well, maybe it's just the image that the police have these days, but I'd say that most of us in the building here are more preoccupied about being interviewed by the police than spending time grieving for Mr Ford.'

'Had you known Harry Ford a long time?'

'I'll tell you something, it's an eye-opener for me, you know, all of this,' Codona offered in reply, completely ignoring King's question.

'Sorry?' King said.

'Well, for instance, our branch manager has just died and no one really knows how. On top of which, there are all of these incredible theories floating around the office, so before anyone can even consider their grief, let alone deal with it, you've got people in here trying to step into Mr Ford's shoes before they've had a chance to cool down. Perhaps some of the pretenders will get a chance to see what it's really like. My grandad always used to say, "Walk a mile in a man's shoes before you criticise him." Mr Ford didn't make a fuss about being the boss here, but I know how hard he worked to make sure we were one of the most successful branches on the chain.'

Jill Codona paused for a brief laugh. Kennedy and King did not interrupt but both broke into gentle smiles.

'Sorry, I was just thinking about that being a very commonly used mixed metaphor, you know surely it should either be "one of the most successful links in the chain" or "one of the most successful branches on the tree", but we always say, don't we, one of the must successful branches on the chain. I suppose I'm just overly aware of what I'm saying this morning because I'm talking to the police. Where was I? Oh yes. Next we received a directive from head office in Aylesbury informing us that no one could leave, even following their police interviews, and that they'd have a deputy branch manager over here by lunchtime.'

'Well, I suppose they have to consider the needs of your customers,' King offered.

'Oh, yes, of course at CABS it's always business as usual . . . but what about Mr Ford? What about us?'

'Are you okay? We can wait,' King offered as Kennedy raised his eyebrows slightly.

'Of course I'm okay,' Jill Codona replied, smoothing out her skirt or at the very least trying to stretch the material a little more towards her knees thirteen inches away.

'Okay,' Kennedy said. Again his voice was so quiet that both King and Codona had to strain to hear him. 'How long have you worked at the building society?'

'I came to work here the minute I left school. We were up on Chalk Farm Road in those days, nowhere near as plush as this. I started off as a receptionist. I did that for eighteen months, and then I was transferred into the typing pool. I was there for about a year, then on the counter for a year and a bit, and then I did their grade "A" examination, followed by an interview, and eventually I received my promotion. Then, just before we moved down here, I became Mr Ford's PA.'

'What was he like to work for?' Kennedy quickly continued.

'Very considerate, no macho stuff—I mention that only because there's a lot of that stuff, flirting and cheating and all of that goes on here, as with most offices, I imagine.' Codona for some reason was addressing only King at this point and staring her straight in the eyes.

There was an embarrassing moment broken by Codona continuing: 'Look, I'm sure you'd love to hear that Harry Ford, a seemingly happily married man, was cheating on his wife with his PA. I completely realise such a scenario would open up your scope a bit for motives, but that wasn't the case. We had a relationship, but it *was* one of boss and employee. Neither of us ever crossed that line; neither even considered it. He wasn't my type for a start. I like boys of my own age, and Mr Ford seemed to go for the more ethereal, intellectual, classic beauties. So because there never was any other agenda, we enjoyed a very healthy working relationship. There was never any cause for office chat about us.'

Another pause for consideration before Codona added, 'That's not to say that on a professional front he was anything less than a magnificent boss. When he was annoyed by your work or attitude, he wasn't afraid of letting you know. But provided you didn't make the same mistake twice, he didn't bear any grudges.'

'How did he get on with the rest of his colleagues here?' Kennedy asked.

'Well,' Jill Codona said, drawing out the word in her apparent consideration, 'I'd have to say he was respected, but he was never interested in being popular. When he needed to pull certain members of the staff up about something, he wasn't scared of doing so, but then the same as in his dealings with me, if they didn't make the same mistake twice, he was well capable of letting bygones go by.'

'Was there ever anything serious?' Kennedy continued in a quiet matter-of-fact voice.

Jill Codona looked first at Kennedy and then at King before saying, 'Well, I suppose that would depend on what exactly you mean by *serious* . . .'

'I was thinking—'

'I think I know what you were thinking,' Jill interrupted. 'I've been thinking about nothing else since I heard the awful news this morning. I've been wracking my brains to try and see if I could think of anyone who might have had a reason for doing this terrible, terrible thing to poor Harry.'

By the end of her reply, Miss Codona's voice was starting to break up.

'And could you think of anyone who might have had a motive?' Kennedy coaxed, his gentle voice comforting and soothing but at the same time effectively probing away.

'Look, I won't tell you any lies . . .' Miss Codona started, seeming very unsure of how she wanted to word her reply. 'I won't speculate, I can only give you facts, and the only facts that keep coming back to the top of my mind are that in April of this year, a man—Frazer McCracken—who thought he was on the fast track to running this company by the time he was thirty was discovered to be guilty of a serious infringement of, shall we say, *financial improprieties*. These discoveries were made by Mr Ford, and as a result of my boss's investigations and subsequent report, Mr

McCracken's employment was terminated. All I can tell you about Mr McCracken is that he's extremely ambitious and he has his own lawyer.'

'What exactly were these "financial improprieties"?' Kennedy asked, his antenna fully extended awaiting all and any new information on this particular wavelength. He noticed that if King had been a bloodhound, and not a novice detective, she would either have pulled the arm out of her handler's socket by this time, or be at least three fields away while her handler was still putting on his scarf.

'I'm sorry to say that you're going to have to get that information from head office. Mr Ford passed over the file to them. I know some but not all of the facts. I think it's probably better if you don't get me to speculate. I'm quite sure you'll hear quite a bit of speculation around here before you leave—you know, about Mr Ford's investigation and report being biased by the fact that he was apparently scared of Mr McCracken taking over the branch manager's job on his way to the top. That's just not true. I was here when it was all happening and you can take my word for it, but I'm sure you'll find all of that out for yourselves over the course of time. Apart from anything else, that was an impossibility. If he succeeded in his endeavours for promotion, it was always going to be on condition that he would be transferred to a different branch.'

King was furiously writing away in her notebook. Her diligence became noticeable only when Codona stopped talking. Ford's PA looked over at King and shyly opened her right hand, which had been closed since she had entered the office for her interview. She removed a folded piece of paper, unfolded its four quarters and passed it over the desk to King.

'I've taken the liberty of including Mr McCracken's last-known address and telephone number.'

Kennedy observed how discreetly Codona had carried out this manoeuvre, and also how King appeared barely able to contain her excitement.

'Were there any disgruntled customers, unhappy they were turned down for a mortgage?' Kennedy continued, happy to move on.

'We give them a mortgage if they've got a pulse these days,' Codona semi-sniggered. 'Because if we don't, you can bet your house on the fact that the next building society up the street will.'

'Any other inter-office stuff we should be aware of?' Kennedy asked.

'No. I mean, he didn't really have any what you would call mates in here. The truth is I suppose that it's difficult when you're the boss, but having said that, even if he hadn't been boss, I know he'd have got on well with most folk. The assistant manager for instance, Denise Goldsmith, who took over Frazer McCracken's position, she and Mr Ford worked well together. I'm talking professionally, of course.'

'Did Mr Ford promote her after the McCracken debacle?' Kennedy continued with the questions while King continued taking notes and Miss Jill Codona continued with the answers:

'No, that would never have been the procedure. All promotions and appointments are on an M3 grade—that is to say, branch managers and assistant branch managers—and are handled by head office, and the promotion is always someone from another branch. Yes, I believe head office does solicit opinions from the branch managers, but it's always the head office that makes the final decision. But as I say, they never promote from within. Just so you're aware of the structure, next up the ladder after M3s is M2s, which is area managers, and then M1s, which are the head office management team.'

'Is that not frustrating for the staff,' Kennedy started, and then seeing that Miss Codona was confused, he added, 'You know, knowing that no matter how hard you work, you are never going to win promotion.'

'No, I mean, yes. Well, look, here's the thing—yes, of course you can win promotion, but if you do, it's always on condition that you move to a different branch.'

'Why on earth is that?' Kennedy asked.

'Oh, I think it's something to do with not wanting the staff getting too friendly with the natives.'

'Oh, I see,' Kennedy said, feeling the penny finally drop.

'The people who are making a career in CABS know and accept the system, and if you become a branch manager, there are various bonuses and what-have-you for every time they move you.'

'Tell me this, Miss Codona, was Harry Ford good at his job?' Kennedy asked.

'Harry . . . Mr Ford was absolutely brilliant at his job. As I said, under his management, Camden Town became the most successful branch of CABS, and that was entirely down to Mr Ford. He ran the office efficiently, he gave praise where praise was due and at the same time he showed he was capable of dealing with the McCracken type of characters. I'd have to say though . . .'

After too long a gap, Kennedy prompted, 'Yes?'

'Well, I was going to say that he wasn't exactly taxed running the branch. I always had the feeling he was capable of more.'

'Like being area manager?' Kennedy suggested.

'No, no,' Codona laughed out loud. 'No, not at all, all that running around, no, that's only for people who don't have a life. No, I meant something outside of being a building society branch manager. I always thought he'd have made a great doctor, or lawyer, or teacher, or something where his brain would have been more taxed and he'd have been a bit more . . .'

Again too long a pause and another nudge from Kennedy. 'Fulfilled?' he suggested, remembering his earlier conversation with Ford.

'Yes,' Codona replied, drawing the word out. 'Fulfilled. It's funny, in a way he was just like the rest of us. We become slaves to the old monthly salary, and whereas I bet 90 per cent of the people in here have ambitions elsewhere, the pay *is* good and the conditions are fine. It makes that part of the package hard to better and . . . well, it's always very difficult to go backwards to go forwards.'

'Yes,' Kennedy agreed. 'Particularly when you've got commitments.'

'Yes,' Codona began hesitantly. 'And Mr Ford had more than his share of commitments.'

'Like?'

'Oh, you know,' Miss Codona started and then appeared to think better about what she had intended to say. 'Running families is also a full-time job.'

Kennedy was convinced that she had backtracked, so he took one more shot at trying to return her to her original thought.

'Yes, but you'd have to imagine that Mr Ford was well off and wouldn't be hurting on that front.'

Then a strange thing happened. Jill Codona sighed a huge sigh. Kennedy was convinced it was a sign of disappointment. Like she'd dropped some clue for him and that he'd failed to pick up on it. He feared that the moment had passed, and although they talked around for a few more minutes, nothing else productive came out of the interview.

When Miss Jill Codona left the office, DC King closed the door behind her and said to her boss, 'She was obviously madly in love with Harry Ford.'

'Sorry?' Kennedy replied in a you've-got-to-be-joking kind of way.

'Okay, it's the new millennium; PA's rarely refer to their boss as "Mr" all the time. The couple of times she slipped and called him Harry, you could hear obvious affection in her voice. She went to great trouble, unsolicited mind you, to state that he wasn't her type and she wasn't his type. There was absolutely no reason for her to bring that to our attention. She handed us her chief suspect, Frazer McCracken, on a . . . a piece of paper. She was wearing Diptyque's Philosykos—'

'A perfume?'

'No, kind of, but not really, more of an eau de toilette, you know, a watered-down perfume. Full-blown perfume is considered somewhat offensive in certain circles these days, so some of the more hip companies such as Diptyque have come up with these milder scents, usually as a spray.'

'So, let me get this right, you think just because she was wearing perfume—sorry, eau de toilette—just because she was wearing eau de toilette, you maintain she was in love with her boss?' Kennedy enquired, more intrigued than confused.

'No. But Philosykos is *too* expensive to wear in the office; well, at least it is for me. I love it too, but I have to persuade my father to buy it for me for birthdays and Christmases, and then I have to ration it to make it last. So she was wearing her Philosykos, I would guess, for the benefit of Harry Ford. So, if you take all the evidence together, I would say we wouldn't be jumping to conclusions to consider she was in love with her boss.'

'Well, possibly,' Kennedy started. 'But you also have to consider the fact that she could have been wearing this Philosykos for someone else in, or out of, the office.'

'No, believe me, she was definitely in love with her boss,' King replied assertively. 'But, I fear, her love was unrequited.'

'Well, I would hope so; he was a happily married man, wasn't he? But I'm interested in why you think her love was unrequited?' Kennedy asked.

'Because Miss Jill Codona informed us that he was having an affair with someone else.'

'When, when exactly did this happen?' Kennedy asked, now thoroughly enjoying the exchange.

King consulted her notes before saying, 'Well, she said, "Mr Ford seemed to go for the more ethereal, intellectual, classic beauties." Why did she not say, "Oh he's only into his wife" or, at least, "He's only into his wife type of person"? And does "beauties" suggest there were more than one?'

'No, it's my suspicion there's not just the one,' Kennedy said.

'What?' King replied, now her turn to be shocked. 'You agree with me?'

'Of course, though for me the giveaway line was when Jill Codona said, "Running *families* is also a full-time job", thereby implying that Harry Ford had more than one family.'

Chapter Seventeen

ENNEDY LEFT KING to interview Denise Goldsmith and sent some of the constables to do the lunchtime run of sandwiches, Coca-Colas, health drinks, crisps and chocolate—mostly Kit Kats—for the staff of the building society. He himself returned to North Bridge House deep in thought over the information he and King had just learned.

The ever-reliable Desk Sergeant Timothy Flynn had two messages that he shoved in Kennedy's outstretched hand as it floated past the amused Flynn's nose.

The first message was timed twenty minutes earlier and advised Kennedy that Fr Vincent O'Connor had rung and requested that Kennedy return the favour. The second message, a mere two minutes old, was a request for Kennedy to ring Dr Leonard Taylor, at the detective's earliest convenience.

Kennedy suspected that the O'Connor call would be the longer of the two and so, the minute he entered his office, he lifted the phone and dialled Taylor's number and then tried, and achieved, the extremely difficult manoeuvre of keeping the phone to his ear while simultaneously removing his jacket.

Taylor claimed to have made a couple of amazing discoveries during the autopsy and stated that he would much prefer they did their business face to face. Kennedy hoped he would get the O'Connor call made during the time it took for Taylor to reach North Bridge House. O'Connor, however, also voiced a preference for a face-to-face meeting, and Kennedy happily scheduled the priest in for two o'clock.

Then, having a few unexpected seconds on hand, he started to feel guilty about not having advised ann rea of the morning's developments.

His call to the *Camden News Journal* was greeted only by ann rea's plaintive voice requesting the caller to leave a message, a time and a date.

Kennedy wondered why these standard messages did not also request a weather bulletin, not to mention to an update on the stock market.

Here he was, keen as mustard to get stuck into his case, and everyone was leaving him in a holding pattern. It was doubly frustrating because of the number of people he and his team still had to track down and talk to; but experience told him that patience had proved itself to be a virtue, not to mention a great help in solving a crime. He knew he would be better served collecting Taylor's information before proceeding. He felt also that it would be easier to interview both Neil Roberts and his sister Alice Cain after having had an opportunity to discuss both characters with the highly enlightening and enlightened Fr O'Connor.

'This is a weird one, Christy, I can tell you,' Taylor announced the minute he waddled into Kennedy's office.

Kennedy had been bringing his kettle to the boil over the previous few minutes in anticipation of making the perfect cup of tea for himself and the doctor.

The good doctor unbuttoned his jacket, flopped down in the leather armchair and opened his tattered tan briefcase, which looked so old that Kennedy was convinced Taylor and it had been inseparable since the doctor's college days. He produced a file with the same flourish a magician uses to *create* a bunch of flowers from fresh air. Meanwhile, Kennedy was involved in a different kind of magic, creating the perfect cup of tea.

'It's the combination that creates the perfection,' Taylor announced as he dunked and devoured a shortbread chocolate-chip cookie in one mouthful.

'No, for me the real secret is never to have a second cup of tea. I'm afraid that only serves to take away the taste of the first cup,' Kennedy started, following a dunk of his own. 'Harry Ford—what can you tell me?'

'Well, someone didn't like him, a lot,' Taylor began, rubbing his hands together furiously to remove any crumbs or sugar from them before opening his file. 'He was stabbed nine times.'

'Oh, yes, well, we already knew that, didn't we?' Kennedy replied, replacing his white bone-china cup on its matching saucer and looking somewhat disappointed.

'Oh, indeed,' Taylor replied. 'I can tell you're not on the edge of your seat, but look at these.'

Kennedy took the four photographs offered to him by Taylor.

The first, from a distance, jarred with him somewhat. Harry Ford was very clinically laid out on Taylor's stainless-steel table. His clothes had been removed and his body washed down. The stab wounds were represented by a series of nine uniform one-and-a-half-inch ridges of dry blood. The eyes were closed.

In death, Harry Ford did not look like he was sleeping. This thought sprang to Kennedy's mind at that moment only because it was the most commonly used refrain at wakes back home in Portrush. Visitors to the house, the night prior to the funeral, would always be shown the corpse, and they would invariably report to the relatives, 'Sure isn't he/she very peaceful, just like he/she is only sleeping.' Kennedy could never work out if this had been said as a comfort for themselves or for the relatives; but to his eyes, then, as now, nothing could have looked further from the truth.

Death, to Kennedy, was never peaceful.

For him, there certainly was sadness about the deceased: a sadness—maybe even a bitterness—that life had either been stolen or wrested from the deprived corpse. Even the word *deceased* suggested an unwilling termination. Now, particularly around the deaths Kennedy frequently came into contact with, he felt there was always an air of deep frustration about a dead body. For some reason he could never figure out, Kennedy preferred to see dead bodies clothed. Perhaps it was harder to concede that the most vital organ of the body no longer functioned when it was clothed. Even now as he looked at the photographs Taylor had given him, he knew it was impossible to detect life, but he was still uncomfortable seeing the corpse naked. It was as if the final indignity of mankind was to remove their clothes without their permission. It wasn't even as if they were going to be bothered; *they* no longer existed, so bother was never even an issue.

To Kennedy, the eyelids always looked so much heavier in death; but the biggest betrayers of the lack of life were the hands. Even when humans were comatose in sleep, they always did *something* with their hands. People would put their hands everywhere: on/under their cheek or between their knees as comfort; one hand up on the pillow with the other behind their back as if involved in a (very) slow jog; hand up to face with thumb in mouth; hand up on face and over ear as if to dispel hearing any evil; arm over head in protection; hand or hands covering, as in protecting, the solar plexus; hand or even hands over eyes to keep out the light; hands as part of the body form in any one of a thousand ballet-like poses frozen on the mattress, all unconscious but all inspiring in their own unique beauty. Yes,

Kennedy thought, even in slumber, hands looked alive: pointing; making fists; clasped as though in prayer; thumbs up in approval; cocked as if preparing to pitch a ball or even ready to accept a cup of water.

But in death hands were . . . well, evidently lifeless, flaccid, lacking in ability, power and authority. Death can occasionally be not so much hidden as disguised, but never ever when it comes to the hands.

It took him those few moments, moments which Taylor was gracious enough to afford the detective, to tune out of the signs of death and tune into the pieces of evidence before him.

The second photograph was taken from the left-hand side of the body, looking to the right just below shoulder level. The next was taken from the feet, looking up the torso, and the fourth from the head, looking back down the torso. Kennedy spotted what had obviously intrigued Taylor. He quickly flashed through the last three photographs, the way a gambler would examine the hand he had been dealt. The main difference was that, mostly, the card players kept studying the cards in the hope or maybe even dream that they would become something else. In this case, should these photographs have been cards, Kennedy would have been extremely happy with the hand he had been dealt. This particular hand showed—if nothing else—premeditation.

'I thought you'd see it,' Taylor said, ending Kennedy's thoughts.

'I've never seen anything like it in my life,' Kennedy replied.

'Nor I.'

'Surely, it's an impossibility?'

'Well, if you ran up to someone in an attempt to kill them this way, you'd have to . . . well, as you say, it would be an impossibility,' Taylor conceded.

Both men studied the photographs again.

Harry Ford's nine stab wounds symmetrically followed the shape of a cross.

The apex was just below the Adam's apple and the base was just above the naval. The wing stretched in a line that ran parallel to, and just north of, the nipples.

'The top wound is the most shallow and the centre one the deepest,' Taylor explained.

'Can you tell if all or any of the wounds are post-mortem?'

'From the bleeding we found, I'd say none of the incisions were made after death.'

'But surely there would have been a struggle,' Kennedy said. 'I mean, how could he have been restrained by one hand?'

He checked the photographs again.

'Perhaps there were three of them,' Taylor offered when Kennedy seemed unable to come up with something.

'There would need to have been a lot more than three to hold him still enough to carry this out. Ford was a fit man. Did you find anything in his bloodstream?'

'Some alcohol, I believe. The boys were still doing tests as I left. Do you know if he was on any prescription drugs?' Taylor asked.

'No, I don't, but I can find out for you,' Kennedy admitted as he crossed his desk to answer his phone. 'Okay, bring him straight up.'

Taylor took his cue. 'Right, I'll be off then. I just thought you'd want to see these. Give me a shout when you can about the drugs; it'll just make our work that wee bit quicker if we can rule out what we know. I'll get the full report to you by the end of the day.'

Dr Leonard Taylor and Fr Vincent O'Connor passed each other in the corridor just outside Kennedy's office. Both nodded silently and absent-mindedly to each other. Both men were preoccupied with their own thoughts about the death of Harry Ford.

Chapter Eighteen

JUST AS O'CONNOR was entering Kennedy's office, DS James Irvine and DC Dot King were driving to Hampstead in the specific direction of the address Ford's secretary, Jill Codona, had handed over to the police in her sweat-wet piece of folded paper.

Frazer McCracken lived on Prince Arthur Drive, close enough in London's famous *A to Z* to be considered part of Hampstead, but architecturally speaking a million miles away from the classic Hampstead houses.

'Wouldn't DI Kennedy normally interview McCracken himself?' King asked as they crossed the leafy borders of Belsize village and Hampstead.

'And what makes you say that?' Irvine inquired, smiling to himself.

'Well, he's the first person we've come across with a clear motive to murder Harry Ford,' King said, negotiating the small, tricky Hampstead streets.

'Ah now, you'd never get Kennedy to admit to that so early in a case. He likes to amass a lot more information before he starts to use terms like prime suspect. Secondly, he's a great believer in and supporter of his team. He long ago accepted the fact that neither he nor any other DI for that matter can do everything, so he's happy to let us get on with it.'

'Is he not afraid you'll steal his thunder?'

Irvine laughed but said nothing.

'What?' King persisted. 'What?'

'You'll see. Eventually you'll see,' was all Irvine would say.

'But from what I can see, it's mostly superintendents who run the cases these days, so you can't tell me he's happy to give all around him a pat on the back and a leg up the promotion ladder while he remains a DI?'

'As I said, eventually you'll see,' Irvine said with a larger smile on his face. He cut off further conversation in this area with, 'Oh, if I'm not mistaken, here we are.'

As it happened, King and Irvine met Frazer McCracken on his

doorstep. From the smell of Ford's former colleague's breath, Irvine guessed he'd enjoyed much too liquid a lunch.

Introductions over, McCracken said, 'So?'

'We'd like to ask you a few questions, sir,' King said.

'What if it's not convenient?'

'What if we bring you down to North Bridge House to answer our questions instead?' Irvine threatened, taking an instant dislike to the character.

Frazer McCracken was about five foot eight, slim but with the early signs of a beer gut evident. His black hair was oiled and spiked—as appeared to be a trend in the wannabe sector. He wore a white shirt—one day too many exiled from the laundry basket—a red tie, a dark blue, shiny, fashionable, well-creased suit and black slip-on shoes.

'What if I slam a writ on you for defamation of character?' McCracken replied, slurring his words but still betraying his Aylesbury roots.

Irvine laughed but knew it would be funnier if the guy wasn't being serious. He knew the FU generation used such threats successfully to keep one step above or beyond the law. He knew it probably wasn't a hollow threat, and equally he knew there was always a lawyer who'd be happy to represent McCracken and his mates.

'Have you something to hide then, Mr McCracken?' Irvine said, refusing to be intimidated.

'Look, should we just come in and have a chat, rather than all of this doorstep stuff?' King suggested.

'Hey, it's the good-cop, bad-cop routine,' Frazer replied, trying unsuccessfully to fake a laugh.

'No,' King continued. 'I was just thinking that we don't want to be embarrassing you in front of your neighbours.'

The young policewoman's words seemed to have an instantly sobering effect on McCracken, who looked up and down the street and immediately pulled out his keys, opened the door and shooed the police in.

He then led them up three flights of stairs to an apartment. If Irvine's first impression was that McCracken looked like the kind of person who would live in a shoebox just to have a Hampstead address on his consultant letterhead, he was way off base. McCracken enjoyed what estate agents would best describe as 'a unique space'. His rooms occupied the loft space of the three-storey house, and the lounge cum office he brought them into benefited greatly from wooden beams. To McCracken's credit, the room was incredibly tidy and clean. Yes, the Pamela Anderson posters were more than a little suspect, and Irvine was surprised to notice that they appeared to amuse rather than upset King. Apart from that, McCracken had an office corner with obligatory computer set up, and clean lines of shelves tidily packed with files and books; a dining corner with a white table and (four matching) chairs; and a den corner with lots of books, CDs, a flat screen television, a CD player, a coffee table and black leather chairs, three of which sank under the respective weights of Irvine, King and McCracken, the last to be seated.

'Okay, let's cut to the chase. What's this all about?'

'We're here investigating the death of a former work colleague of yours,' King replied, cutting to the chase, as per McCracken's request.

'Oh, I see,' McCracken interrupted. 'You mean Ford. Yeah, I heard something about that at lunchtime.'

'Yes, very sad,' Irvine began. 'Tell me, when was the last time you saw Harry Ford?'

'Oh,' McCracken began expansively. 'It would have been three months ago.'

'Would that have been at CABS?' King asked.

'Yes, that would have been at CABS.'

'Why are you so certain it was exactly three months ago?' Irvine pushed, just the slightest hint of frustration noticeable in his voice.

'Well, let's put it this way, Mr Ford and I would never have had any reason to meet up socially, so by a process of elimination and deduction, mate, the only place we would have met would have been the building society offices.'

'Is it true you were dismissed from CABS?' Irvine inquired.

'It's true that I was *suspended* from CABS pending an investigation,' McCracken replied indignantly. 'Let's just keep this accurate, please, shall we?'

'Oh, sorry, Mr McCracken. We were led to believe that your employment was terminated due to a serious transgression on your part,' Irvine replied diplomatically. In truth, he really want to say, *You were caught redhanded with your fingers in the till, mate!*

'Well, let's wait and see what comes out at the tribunal, shall we?'

'What exactly were you accused of?' Irvine continued.

'I don't believe my lawyer would want me to answer these questions. It's *sub judice* or something, isn't it?'

'Only if you're to be tried in a court of law, Mr McCracken,' King added immediately. 'That's not the case, is it?'

'Certainly not. Don't you think that if anything criminal had gone on, they would have fired me immediately and handed me over to the Old Bill . . . I mean, to you guys?' McCracken said.

Irvine was growing increasingly frustrated by McCracken's short replies. He hoped his frustration was not showing. Kennedy had taught him that you could learn as much from people's lies as you could learn from their truth, but *only* if you could get them to talk. It's much easier for a lie to go undetected in short answers. However, when you can get people to expand on their replies, the words are as precious as gold dust. Kennedy was always saying, 'Treasure them because the words, particularly the words surrounding lies, will always betray their author.'

'Okay,' Irvine continued, trying to perk up a bit. 'We've ascertained that this is not *sub judice,* so would you mind answering a few questions about why you were suspended?'

'Yes, I would mind. I wouldn't be comfortable doing that,' McCracken said through a smile. 'I'd have to take that under advisement.'

'We're not on *West Wing* or *Law and Order* here, you know . . .' Irvine started and immediately regretted it.

'Hey, we're not even on *The Bill,*' King quickly interrupted, trying to make light of Irvine's gaff, 'but we do need to find out what happened to Mr Ford. You were a colleague of Mr Ford's, and I'm sure you'll accept that from where we stand you're perfectly positioned to give us some information on the deceased.'

'I'm happy to tell you whatever I know, but without sanctioned input, I can't, and won't, go into the reasons for my suspension. You have to realise that I have a great job at CABS. I'm not prepared to walk away from all the hard work I have put into that branch. I don't have the time to start all over again from the bottom. So, it is my wish to do everything by the book with them so that I can resume my employment rather than jeopardise my position by infringing their rules. They have instructed me not to discuss this without counsel, and I'd like to honour that instruction, okay?'

'Okay,' King and Irvine said in unison, as Irvine thought, *Wow, he's only gone and broken through the one-line answer.*

Irvine continued, 'Did you work closely with Harry Ford?'

'Well, he was my immediate superior,' McCracken replied and stopped offering further information.

'Yes, and . . . ?' Irvine pushed.

'Well, of course I worked under my own devices and initiative, but I would . . . I would occasionally have to report to Harry Ford, or would have to attend meetings with him and, obviously, I would bump into him periodically around the office.'

'Did you get on well?' King asked.

'Not particularly.'

Drat, Irvine thought, *Back to the one-liners.* Not wanting to return to those, he rephrased his question: 'Did you not get on well?'

'Here, look, why don't we just cut to the chase?'

'Great,' Irvine responded involuntarily.

'I'd come from nowhere, Ford had been around a long time, and the office gossip was that I was after his job.'

'And was that the case?' King asked.

'I can honestly say no, I wasn't after his job.'

'Not even on the quiet?' Irvine asked.

'No, absolutely not,' McCracken replied. When he saw the look on Irvine and King's faces, he continued, 'I know you don't believe me, and I don't want to speak ill of the dead, but let's just say that Mr Ford wasn't really what you would call ambitious . . .'

'And?'

'Okay,' McCracken sighed. 'I'll spell it out for you. My ambitions went way beyond branch manager.'

'Oh,' Irvine said.

'Was Mr Ford aware of that?' King asked.

'We never had any discussions on that particular topic.'

'Tell me this, Frazer. If you had been up for promotion, would Mr Ford's recommendation have been required?' King asked. Irvine was impressed by the chat-like technique she used when interviewing; he was equally unimpressed by his own performance.

'We'd be naïve to think otherwise.'

'Do you think this incident—?' Irvine started.

He was interrupted by McCracken. 'I've already stated that I can't get into this.'

'No, no, we accept that,' Irvine replied. 'If we ignore for the moment what the incident was, what I was about to ask was whether you were of the impression that the allegations of the incident in question had come from Harry Ford?'

McCracken noticeably smiled and acknowledged the word 'allegations'.

'I couldn't possibly say, but I will admit that others had suggested as much.'

'For instance?' King asked.

'I'm sure if you ask around you'll find that particular suggestion surfacing.'

'Okay,' Irvine replied and considered his next approach before asking, 'Were you surprised when you heard Mr Ford had been murdered?'

McCracken looked taken back.

'I don't understand your question?'

As Irvine was about to qualify his question, McCracken continued, 'Oh, I see. Was that your way of asking if I knew of anyone who might want to murder Ford?'

'Yes,' Irvine replied.

McCracken turned his nose up at Irvine and pouted his lips slightly.

'And?' Irvine asked, following a few seconds' silence.

'Do you take me for a fool; of course, I'm not going to answer a question like that. If you don't mind me saying, it's a ridiculous question.'

'Well, from where I'm sitting, it's a pretty simple question. Either you do know someone you feel had a reason to murder Mr Ford, or you don't.'

'Well, of course I don't know of anyone who had a reason to kill him.'

'Good. At least that's an answer,' Irvine replied. 'Now, can you tell me what you were doing between the hours of six o'clock last night and two o'clock in the morning?'

McCracken seemed to have been expecting the question; in fact, he looked as if it was the only question he'd been expecting.

'Okay, yesterday afternoon I was here, working on the computer. I finished around six. I popped out for a bowl of spaghetti. I got back around eight o'clock and made a few calls to the States. I went out at nine o'clock to meet a few mates, but I had missed them, so I went to another bar, had a few drinks by myself, chatted up a girl, pulled, we had a few drinks too many, I went back to her place, we had a few more drinks, went to bed and I got up about 6.30 and came back here.'

King busily made notes.

'Could you tell us where you dined?' she inquired

'The Pasta Experience up by the Heath.'

'Did you spot anyone there you knew?' King asked.

'No.'

'What about the name of the pub you visited to meet your friends?' Irvine asked.

'I think I might have gone to the wrong one, because I was on time but they weren't there.'

'And which pub would that have been?' Irvine persisted.

'The one opposite West Hampstead tube station. It's a kind of club more than a pub.'

'Its name?' Irvine asked again.

'The Tinker's Well or something like that.'

'And the names of the friends you'd arranged to meet?' King asked.

'Oh,' McCracken drew out the word in obvious annoyance. 'You know, just a bunch of mates; we call ourselves the Stoli Gang. You'd be out on a vodka crawl and one would say, "See you in the Well on . . . blah blah, and then whoever of us was free would show up. I mean, there's no one at the door with a class register ticking you off as you enter.'

'One name will suffice,' King said politely.

'Ahhh,' McCracken replied in obvious annoyance and appearing to be wracking his brain. 'Shit, em, maybe JJ or the Music Man, or Broadband.'

'Eh, would any of these friends have real names?' King asked, pen poised over her notebook.

'Those are the handles they go by when we hang out,' McCracken sniggered. 'Shit, I'm embarrassed to admit this, but I don't really know their real names. They're just the Stoli Gang, you know.'

'Okay,' King said, concealing her impatience. 'How would we contact these people?'

'Well, agh, the Tinker's Well would be a good starting point. That's one of the three or four places we hang together.'

'But you missed them yesterday evening?' Irvine asked.

'Yeah, I must have been too hammered last time to pick up the details of the meet correctly.'

'Okay,' Irvine said, moving right along. 'You missed your mates, but you stayed on and had a few drinks by yourself . . .'

'No,' McCracken protested loudly and instantly. 'That's not what I said; I said I moved on to another bar. I don't particularly like to drink at the Well by myself; solo Stolichnaya is nowhere near the same fun as gang participation. So I moved on to another pub.'

'Which one?' This time it was Irvine's turn to interrupt.

'I've got to confess, I don't really know. I mean, apart from the Well, West Hampstead is not my patch. I came out of the Well and crossed the road. There's a pub there on the corner—it's too high street for me, so I went on down that road. I think it was on the right-hand side. I'm afraid I have no idea of the name of it.'

'Okay,' Irvine said. 'You went in there and had a drink . . .'

'Two . . .'

'You had two drinks and then a girl chatted you up?'

'For a cop, you don't really focus on detail too well, do you? I stated that *I* chatted *her* up.'

'Right, so you did,' Irvine apologised, noting that McCracken had picked up on all three fishing expeditions. 'So tell us about the girl.'

McCracken remained silent.

'Was she alone or with a bunch of mates?' King asked.

'When I saw her, she was by herself,' McCracken said. Following another pause he continued, 'She might have arrived with a gang, I don't know.'

'And her name?' King asked.

'She called herself Nicola.'

'Why did you say she called herself Nicola and not that her name was Nicola?' King asked.

Irvine was happy to step a backing role, letting King get on with the questioning.

'Well,' McCracken replied smugly, dissing the DC for the first time. '*Because* she wore a wig and falsies, so she obviously wanted to be someone else. I would surmise from that that quite possibly she'd also chosen a false name. I have to say she didn't look like a Nicola.'

'Yeah, I know what you mean—some people do look like their names and some don't. What was it particularly about her that made her not look like a Nicola.'

'Well, someone with a name like Nicola wouldn't look out of place on, say, *Coronation Street,* but this girl looked like she'd have been more at home in the cast of *Eastenders.*'

'Interesting,' King replied, looking like she was genuinely considering this hypothesis. 'I think I see what you mean. Anyway, if you can give us her address, we'll try not to land you in it over the name thing, you know. We'll be ever so discreet.'

'No can do, I'm afraid.'

'Sorry?' Irvine said.

'No can do.'

'You mean you're refusing to give us her address?' Irvine said. 'Is she married or something?'

'Or something, I don't know. As I said, by the time we left the pub, we'd both had a few and, well, I was quite drunk. We went back to her place, but I couldn't take you back there if my life depended on it.'

'Did you get a phone number?' King asked, just a wee bit too hopefully.

'Well no, not exactly,' McCracken replied and twitched his head to the right and downward. 'Like, ah, the words "one-night stand" spring to mind, and, on reflection, I'd have to say it was one night too many.'

'You realise, of course, that this means you don't exactly have a watertight alibi for yesterday evening?' King offered.

'Yes, of course,' McCracken said, raising the palms of his hand towards the ceiling in an apparent declaration of innocence. 'I'd say that puts me in with about 50 per cent of the population. I'm sure if I'd murdered someone though, I'd have been able to offer you a minute-by-minute account of yesterday, along with 100 per cent back-up, signed, sealed and delivered, and maybe even the odd video of corroborating evidence thrown in for good measure.'

'Yeah, we're going to need to have another little chat with Mr McCracken,' King said to Irvine about ten minutes later as they returned to North Bridge House.

'Yes, only next time I suspect it'll be at North Bridge House and he will be in the company of his solicitor and Madge.'

'Who on earth is Madge?'

'Oh,' Irvine replied, feigning surprise. 'You obviously haven't been introduced yet. Madge is our tape-recorder in interview room number one.'

'Why on earth Madge?'

'Well, it was Desk Sergeant Tim Flynn came up with that one. It stands for "Murderers Always Do Get Entangled",' Irvine replied with a chuckle. 'I think he meant on tape.'

'Yeah, I kinda got that,' King replied, rolling her eyes to emphasise the point.

Chapter Nineteen

FR VINCENT O'CONNOR strode into Kennedy's office just as the Ulster detective's phone rang. Kennedy nodded a greeting to the priest as he lifted the phone.

'Hello,' a female voice announced. 'It's Christine Riley here.'

'Hello,' Kennedy replied, feeling a little awkward because, firstly, he had no news on her missing father, and secondly, being even more brutally honest, due to the discovery of Harry Ford's body, he had not afforded her father a single thought that day.

'Oh,' was the only word Kennedy could find as he motioned O'Connor to take the comfy leather seat.

'Em, look, yesterday evening I received a telephone call.'

'Oh,' Kennedy replied, this time with a totally different emphasis on the two-letter word. 'Your dad?'

Kennedy wasn't sure, but he thought he noticed O'Connor's ears perk up at this question.

The priest mouthed the words, 'Christine Riley?' to Kennedy, who tightened his lips and moved his head backwards and forwards very gently.

'Yes,' Christine said, but then dampened the proceedings by qualifying her statement with, 'At least, I think it was.'

'You *think* it was,' Kennedy repeated for O'Connor's benefit. 'Did he sound too distressed or something for you not to be able to tell 100 per cent?'

'Well, not exactly,' Christine replied sheepishly down the phone line. 'You see, he didn't actually say anything.'

'He didn't say anything?' Kennedy asked in disbelief as O'Connor furrowed his eyebrows. 'How did you know it was him then?'

'You know, when you just have a feeling someone is there? They don't have to say anything, but you know they're there?'

'Hmmm,' Kennedy replied, unconvinced. 'But he didn't say a word?'

'No, but I could hear him breathing.'

'And did *you* say anything?' Kennedy continued, deciding to let that one pass for now.

'Well, I just said, "Is that you, Dad?" and there was no reply, just breathing. And then I said, "Okay, look, if it's you, we're all okay. Mum is a little worried, but she never believed you were dead." Then I just said, "Look, Dad, just tell me if it's you and everything will be okay." I said, "You can work this out in your own time, but please let me know that you're okay."'

'And?'

'And then I heard what I thought sounded like scratching, and then I said, "If you're Dad, don't hang up immediately; you know, wait a little time before you put the phone down." He didn't set the phone down immediately. It was about a minute or so later that the pips went and then the line went dead.'

'What time of day was this?' Kennedy asked.

'Oh about 5.30,' Christine replied after a moment's break. 'I'd just got in from work.'

'And could you hear anything in the background, like traffic, bells, people talking or anything like that?'

'No, I heard nothing like that. I did hear what sounded like a high-pitched whine or scream, but it could just as easily have been feedback on the line or something.'

'Did you try the 1471 service when he hung up?' Kennedy asked hopefully.

'Yes, and the service confirmed the call had been made from a pay phone. The number was 0207 722 5978. I tried the 1471 redial thingy, but there was no reply.'

Kennedy jotted down the number. He recognised the code as from the Primrose Hill area.

'Good,' Kennedy said into the mouthpiece, realising that Christine had now relayed her information. He was conscious of trying to find a way to work out the lesser of the two social evils: winding down the call too quickly or continuing to ignore his waiting visitor, the priest.

'But I have to tell you that I believe with all my heart that it was my dad ringing to tell me that he was okay,' Christine said, appearing keen to make a point.

'Good, good. If you believe that so strongly, then it's great news, but em . . .' Kennedy paused, struggling to try to find the right words—a balance between encouragement and realism. 'The only thing I'd like you to do is to keep an open mind on this. Okay?'

'I will, Inspector, if you will agree to do the same,' pleaded the voice of hope down the phone line.

'Okay. Agreed,' Kennedy replied, a smile evident in his voice. 'Look, please keep in touch and let me know if you receive any more calls.'

'I will do,' Christine Riley replied immediately. 'Oh, and Mr Kennedy, I'm not a nutter; I know it was my father. I could feel his presence.'

Chapter Twenty

KENNEDY FILLED O'CONNOR in on the missing half of the conversation.

O'Connor felt strongly that Christine's call *had* been from her father.

Kennedy felt that the priest was probably correct and quickly changed cases by asking, 'How's Lizabeth?'

'You know, I'd have to say she's not great. She keeps asking to see you,' O'Connor replied slowly, looking as though he wasn't exactly the best himself. 'Would you mind very much if we got out of here? I just can't be in a police station now.'

'Okay, that's fine. Let's go for a tea,' Kennedy suggested.

'No, I've got my car outside. Let's drive up to Primrose Hill, and we can go for a walk up there, and you can interrogate me there.'

'Okay.'

Kennedy was truly intrigued by this priest and the concept of his not believing in heaven, but he could not for the life of him find a way to introduce the topic into the conversation on the short trip to Primrose Hill. Apart from anything else, with the racket from the engine of O'Connor' VW Beetle, he had trouble hearing himself think, let alone broaching the question. The priest seemed to be trying to figure something out for the entire journey.

And so, ten minutes later, the priest who apparently didn't believe in heaven and the policeman who didn't down a bottle of whiskey a day were standing on the crown of Primrose Hill, looking down on the city currently slightly blurred by the heat haze. The hill was quite quiet with the early afternoon lull—dogs had been walked, people had traversed it in numerous directions on their way to work and back, and all that was left was a lone jogger, a mother with a pram, and two kids and six magpies. Kennedy tried to remember what six magpies signified.

The priest and the detective discussed religion in general and the fact that O'Connor didn't believe in heaven in particular. Eventually the conversation wound its way around to the pros and cons of the confessional box.

'I have to say, I have a major problem with allowing criminals to shelter behind the confessional boxes,' Kennedy offered.

'Well, initially there would have been nothing great or devious behind the confessional. It's pretty basic, and would have been a great help to people.'

'I'll accept that,' Kennedy said quickly.

'You see, people gain a lot from talking, from having a form of release; and a form of release works all the better when they know that what they confess is never going to go any further than their priest. People, if they are to benefit spiritually from confessing, need to feel confident that when they confess to their priest, they do so in complete trust and secrecy. Secrecy is the major element to the success of that particular therapy. And, as Oscar Wilde so succinctly put it, "It is the confession, not the priest that gives us absolution."'

'I agree in principle. Confession is fine and dandy, but it doesn't work so well when some people are allowed to use it to their advantage.'

'What can I tell you?' O'Connor laughed. 'Sue the Vatican.'

'That's all very well, Vincey, but think of the pain and suffering you could help prevent if you could just at least tip the police off . . .'

'Aye, like informing,' O'Connor offered indignantly. 'And that's another slippery slope on the road to persecution. I think it's possibly fine to reveal something that was said which would confirm the truth, but only after the fact, as it were. You know, to help corroborate.'

'But isn't that hypocritical?'

'No, not at all, Christy. Don't you see? If the offender in question has been caught out in a crime, so to speak, then there wasn't really any truth on their part in the confessional process in the first place.'

'So, in other words, you don't want to be the one to shop them, but if and when we catch them, you don't mind sticking the boot in as well.'

'Exactly!'

'Okay,' Kennedy said in a quieter voice. 'Tell me about the Four Musketeers?'

'Oh, that was good, that was very good,' O'Connor said in reply.

'Sorry?'

'That shift,' O'Connor replied, refusing to look Kennedy in the eye. 'If you hadn't changed into a quieter voice, I would never have noticed that we'd gone official.'

Kennedy just shrugged, in the hope that it would encourage the priest to continue. It did.

'Oh, well, the Musketeers, now there's a story,' O'Connor said with the beginnings of a large smile.

'I mean, we all ended up reading at Reading, and, you know, when you look back on it now, you wonder what brought us together. Mind you, in those first few days, we weren't thinking twice about it. We were all hoping that we'd make it to the next step on the academic ladder. The problem I had by that stage was that I knew the previous steps wouldn't count for much, even though when I was trying to achieve them—my leaving cert, for instance—they seemed like the biggest goal in the world. Now there we all were at university, trying to do what we needed just to stay afloat. The first thing one instinctively does is to look around and see if you can take some comfort by spotting anyone who looks as poor a swimmer as you feel you are. The three of them had already hooked up by the time I met them.'

O'Connor paused and acted like he was searching his memory bank.

'Yeah, that's it. Harry and Neil met up first in the Student's Union bar—surprise, surprise. They both admitted that they were on the lookout for girls. Well, we all were really, you know—first time away from home. Of course, we'd all been dreaming about such an opportunity since our hormones first kicked in.'

'Sorry,' Kennedy said unable to hide his surprise. 'I'm afraid I'm a bit confused now.'

'You mean, what was a young priest doing out looking for girls?'

'Well, something like that, yeah.'

'Well, the thing was, in those days, I'd no thoughts about being a priest. It wasn't, shall we say, my first career choice.'

'Oh,' was all Kennedy could find to say, adding an 'okay'.

'I'll be very honest with you here, Christy. I became a priest as part of a grand gesture . . . there was this girl, you see—'

'Back home in Ireland?' Kennedy asked, breaking the golden rule of never interrupting someone when they're on a roll. He took comfort from the fact that he was not questioning O'Connor professionally.

'No, in Reading University actually,' O'Connor continued. 'And we never really stood a chance. Well, if I'm being brutally honest, *I* never really stood a chance—'

'Was she the girl in the Musketeers?' Kennedy asked, remembering the photograph of Alice that was in Harry Ford's wallet.

The Ulster-born detective was slowing down O'Connor's flow once more. He wasn't sure if his uncharacteristic interruptions were because he didn't really want to hear this from a priest he didn't really know or because he was giving the priest ample opportunity to be sure that he did actually want to tell this story. They had already gone way beyond the limits of their freshly formed friendship. Equally, Kennedy understood that sometimes people want to talk, as much to hear themselves speak the words that pre-occupy their thoughts as to enjoy the experience and relief of being listened to.

'The very same girl,' O'Connor sighed. 'But I'll get to that presently. It's better if I tell you the story from the beginning.'

'Okay.'

'You have to realise here that, in spite of all my trepidations, it was all very exciting. A new country, a new town, new buildings, new people . . . You know, the thing that hit me most in those days was how different England smelled! It was full of aromas that were strangers to my nostrils. Like in Clonakilty in County Cork we had one takeaway, a fish and chip shop. Reading Town in those days was just bursting with takeaways; Chinese was a favourite with the students, but there were takeaways to accommodate every palate. The dorm carpets always smelled of yesterday's carry-in left-overs. When you'd been in your room for a few hours, you became accustomed to it, but when you just returned to your room from outside, there was always such an overpowering stale pong rising from the carpet. Never in a million years would my mother have allowed our house to smell like that, and, in truth, we would have been quite indignant if she had. But, as students, house proud we weren't. In our own digs we seemed quite happy to live in a pigsty. Getting back to the smells though, even the streets had a different smell, like a smell of newness, concrete pavements, cut grass and tarmacadam roads. On top of which, the English girls smelled different from Irish girls. Irish girls didn't have a noticeable smell to me; they smelled fresh and natural, whereas the English girls were scented and somewhat intoxicating. I'll accept that's a flaw on my part. But you take the overall combination of new and strange sensations, and it all felt like an adventure—a *big* adventure.

'So, let's backtrack here slightly. Harry and Neil met up in the Union bar. They shared some common interests—football and dances. I could never get the hang of dancing. George Bernard Shaw summed up dancing perfectly for me; he said, "Dancing is a perpendicular expression of a horizontal desire." In the Irish ballrooms though, it was always a case of "Slow, slow, quick, quick, no!" I could see what attracted them to dancing, but I could never share their excitement over football. Harry supported Man United, Neil supported Liverpool, and so they'd go into London whenever one of their teams was playing. On one of their trips—a famous clash between Man United and Chelsea—Neil brought his sister Alice along. She was also a Manchester United fan—well, more a George Best fan—so the three of them became so close you could hardly see the join for the best part of a term, and then, just before Christmas, I met up with Alice. She was being hassled by a few townies. We'd (separately) been to see Al Stewart play at the Town Hall. I'd spotted her; well, it would have been hard, if not impossible, not to. She was literally drop-dead gorgeous; she still is, in fact. The big thing about Alice though was that she was totally unaware of her beauty; she carried it naturally. I got the feeling that she instinctively knew that, as far as she was concerned, she might have been blessed with good looks, but she wanted—no, she *needed*—more.'

'So she wasn't,' Kennedy interrupted, 'like that girl in *Lying Eyes*, the Eagles song—you know, the girl who can open doors with a smile.'

'The detective knows his music,' O'Connor offered and paused again for the second time in seconds. He obviously had some vision in his mind, but this was something he *wasn't* sharing with Kennedy. 'Mind you, if she ever wanted to use it, Alice has a smile that could open all the doors at the new Wembley Stadium,' he offered, suggesting an edited version of his thoughts. 'Anyway, where were we? Oh yeah, once the townies saw that she wasn't going to be an easy target, they cleared off. Alice and I started to chat and realised that we were both from campus. So I walked her back, as you do, and we fell into a comfortable chat. The thing was that we chatted like we'd been friends all our lives. I think that just might have been part of our downfall—we because friends too easily—but I'll get back to that later.'

The tranquillity of Primrose Hill was disturbed somewhat by several students celebrating something or other. *Just the way students might*, Kennedy thought as the priest continued.

'When we reached the Student's Union, she told me she had promised to meet a couple of people for a drink before the bar closed. She also said that she'd love to buy me a drink. She introduced me as her knight in shinning armour. She might even have pronounced it *amour*, but I was so hopelessly intoxicated by her by that stage, I may have been putting words in her mouth. Anyway, they—Neil and Harry—were friendly enough to me. Neil was quite territorial about his sister. Like when we arrived together, Neil immediately moved into the space between us and put his arm around her shoulders—in fact, until Alice introduced us, I thought he might have been her boyfriend. It was a little strange, to be truthful; it wasn't like he was exactly over-affectionate. No, but I felt it was more perhaps as a sign for my benefit. Outwardly he wasn't at all hostile, and perhaps, on reflection, he was just reacting instinctively as the brother who has to see off numerous, potential would-be suitors of his beautiful sister. Harry was friendlier, more open; he'd no hidden agendas. I think they could both see right from that first night that I was totally smitten by her. Fortunately they didn't come right out and poke fun or anything similarly embarrassing at me. I think my saving grace was that we were all into old movies, although in those days it was hard to drag Neil and Harry out of the Union bar. All of us felt—and probably still feel to this day—that the old forties classics have yet to be bettered.

'In a way, I suppose, that first night in the Union, the four of us reached a major point in our lives, a point which, some might say, had been predetermined since our grandfathers met our grandmothers, or maybe even way before that, if you believe in that kind of a thing.

'For myself, I spent the next two terms trying to get closer to Alice. I succeeded in the proximity sense in that I moved into their spare room the following week. After that great initial start, I bumbled along, hoping against hope that I was getting somewhere. And when you are right there in the middle of it, living it as it were, and the object of your affections says something, anything—I'm talking about really basic stuff here, like how she liked the way I scrambled the eggs, for instance—then you tend to take such words as great encouragement. Yes, I'd take a lot of heart from her words. But later, when I looked back on it and examined the words as I often did . . . well, under closer examination . . . I'd realise and accept the fact that they were only words in a conversation.

'I suppose I'd have to admit I knew that a girl just positively has to have a boy she can call on as a friend and with whom she can have long, deep, meaningful conversations, mainly about other boys—now that's a cert. The fact that the same boy will use this closeness to try and get into the girl's bed is also guaranteed.

'My problem, Christy, was that she liked me and, I now have come to understand, she liked me a lot. BUT she didn't fancy me; she wasn't attracted to me in that way. That was my big mistake. I believed that I could turn our relationship around and move it up from friendship to romance just by a few carefully chosen words. I tried to talk my way into her affections, and on the several occasions when I'd ask her outright if I could kiss her, she'd say . . . she'd always say, "Let me think about it Vincent."

'I even took that as encouragement. Agh, I can see you smirk, but let me tell you, on those winter mornings, all crumbs are treasures to the birds of the air who seek them. I think that Selrahc said that. What I couldn't see at the time, of course, was that she was only trying to spare my feeling by refusing to use the "No!" word.

'We'd talk about very intimate stuff and, I suppose, as I mentioned, I was taking advantage of being her confessor. She was so comfortable with me in that role that she started to talk to me about Harry. I mean, I don't— to this day—know where it all came from or how it started. I do remember when I became aware of it though. I was walking to the flat one day. It was wintertime, snow had been falling all day, and I was aware of the footprints I was leaving in my wake and, all of a sudden, I thought, "Hang on a minute—when did this thing with Harry and Alice start?" I gave myself such a hard time about being preoccupied with my path through life, like the footprints in the snow, that I'd stopped considering the actual life I was meant to be leading. I realised that although I hadn't picked up on it, when she'd been talking to me, something had obviously happened between both of them. Here I was trying to talk my way into her life, and here he was nearly ignoring her, and yet something had started to happen between them. Explain that one to me, if you can.'

'I'm afraid I'm not the right person to ask on matters of the heart,' Kennedy admitted.

'Then she only goes and tells me about their first kiss! Do you think that a couple seals something with a first kiss? Does a kiss, particularly the first one, really move the relationship to another level?'

Kennedy blew a long breath through his tight lips before offering: 'They say the early kisses in a relationship are the best. I think it's got something to do with the fact that it's your first shared intimacy. That newness is an aphrodisiac.'

'I've never enjoyed that feeling; I've probably been too self-conscious. As I told you, I'd been asking her permission to kiss her at every available opportunity, and then Harry just goes ahead and seizes the moment and just kisses her! That was exactly when the daily bulletins stopped. Then I became aware of a little distance growing between us, between Alice and myself. Looking back on it afterwards, I could see why.

'They became very tight.' O'Connor paused and sighed as if trying to catch his breath.

Kennedy was amazed to hear this priest talking about an incident that had happened nearly thirty years ago and still hurting about it.

'They became very tight and started sleeping together. You know . . . they were each other's first lovers. That totally destroyed me. *I was de-vastated* That's a very special thing, you know. It means, apart from anything else, that they are going to remember each other for the rest of their lives.

'So, I did all I could do. I got stuck into my studies.

'Neil, for his part, seemed equally upset over their relationship. I remember not being able to quite figure that one out at the time. Harry was his best friend and Alice was his best—not to mention, only—sister, so you'd have to think he'd be happy about their liaison. But I'm not exactly sure he gave them his unconditional blessing. I couldn't ever work out if he was upset because his sister was stealing his best friend or he was upset because his best friend was stealing his sister.

'Either way, their love grew stronger, and pretty soon we all just accepted the fact that Harry and Alice were going to be together and live happily ever after. And that was that.'

'Except for Lizabeth,' Kennedy stated and asked, 'How did she come into the picture?'

'Patience, my boy, patience,' O'Connor chastised his audient before continuing: 'Then didn't Harry and Alice only go and beat all the predictions and odds by going and splitting up! The break-up was all down to a big misunderstanding really. Neil had a go at her in the flat one night; I believe it was for my benefit. He claimed that she'd lost all her personality since she took up with Harry. He liked Harry, he said, but he loved his sister. He hated to see her run around after Harry like a puppy, totally losing her own personality by becoming someone's "old lady". They lashed out at each other as only sister and brother can do. They were pretty tight as brother and sister, even though you'd never have guessed it for the venom they spat at each other on that particular evening. She claimed he was just jealous because, even though he was dating a lot, there was no one special in his life. He replied that he was not just jealous. He claimed she'd become a little lapdog.

'Each had an immediate and telling effect on the other. Neil sulked for about a week. Alice, determined to show that she still enjoyed a degree of independence, told Harry she was going out with a bunch of her female friends at least one night a week from then on. "Why go out with them?" he asked. "They're only going out because they're on the lookout for boys, and you already have a boy—me." "Boys aren't everything," she said. "Surely it's possible for us to go out and just have a bit of fun without looking for boys." "No," he said. And just like thousands had said before him and many thousands more would say after him, "We're either in a relationship or we're not. If you go out with them, then clearly we are no longer in a relationship with each other."

'It was quite an argument, and the problem Harry had was that it was three to one. Neil stamped his feet and got rather ugly, adamantly claiming he didn't want his sister settling down so early in her life and I . . . well, as you know, I had a vested interested in Harry and Alice not working this out.

'On top of which, Alice, it has to be said, is nothing if not headstrong. She went out with her mates as planned. Harry swore quite a bit, and he also went out, 'to get hammered', he claimed. Ten minutes after Harry's loud departure, Alice returned in tears and, through her sobs, told Neil and me that she didn't want herself and Harry to split up—she really loved him. He was, she claimed, the nicest human she'd ever met. She told us Harry was considerate, intelligent, funny, sexy, great looking and, unlike Neil and myself, could laugh at himself. I for my part had to agree with her on all counts. I still saw myself as Jimmy Stewart straight off the bus from Hicksville and about to make my mark on the world. I will admit to you that I truly felt I was going to make a big mark.

'Anyway, Alice continued with her tirade against us and how lovely Harry was. She kept repeating how lovely he was. She didn't care how much her brother objected to their relationship—now that she'd found her man, she was going to damn well stick to him like glue for the rest of their life, no matter what had happened in the past.

'Neil and I had to sit and listen to all of Harry's virtues, and . . . well, you've met him—everything she said was true. He was a straightahead guy with principles, and she was right—she would probably never meet a better guy in her life. She told Neil that his approach of sampling every apple on the tree only tended to make you feel sick and forget which one tasted best. She lectured that, unlike her brother, she had some backbone and confidence and, now that she'd found her man, she didn't need to play the field just to convince herself that she was right. She knew she was right. I think she might have peppered all of that with a few swear words. Neil at that stage was still semi-sulking and was very quiet and sheepish.

'Okay, at this stage there isn't a dry eye in the house, right?' O'Connor said, sweeping his right hand over Primrose Hill.

'Right,' Kennedy agreed.

'Okay,' O'Connor sighs, building himself up for something. 'Well, get out your Kleenex; it gets worse. Unfortunately, not only did Harry get hammered; he also got laid. *And* Alice found out. So now Harry and Alice aren't talking. Alice then used my shoulder to cry on. The only problem was that that particular shoulder was attached to my body, and my body was reclining in my bed at the time. Anyway, that particular little episode was a total disaster. Sure, I've never been able to work out what all this fuss of jumping each others' bones is all about. It's pretty basic really, isn't it? Come to think of it, it's not even pretty, really. I mean, we don't share any of our other toiletry functions with our friends, do we? So why that?'

Kennedy had to admit to himself that if you took love out of the equation, the priest certainly had a point.

'Either at the vital moment Alice had second thoughts, or my inexperience of the mechanics of the procedure, shall we say, and the resultant fumbling, turned my most cherished dream into a nightmare. She ran away, screaming at me about trying to take advantage of her at a time like that—you know, when she was so low and vulnerable—and that she never ever wanted to see or speak to me again.

'Which was all very fine for me, I grandstanded. We'd finished our studies, and right then and there, I shouted after her, "Okay, that's it. I've had enough of all this craziness and the affairs of the heart to last me a lifetime. I'm going to become a priest." "No big loss, believe you me," she shouted back at me.

'So that's what I did,' O'Connor concluded.

'And Harry met Lizzy?' Kennedy said, regretting flippancy the minute the last name had left his lips.

'And Alice met Robby,' O'Connor said, smiling and joining Kennedy's joke. 'Robert Cain, that is, and eventually Alice became Mrs Alice Cain.

Literally within months of each other, Alice and Harry had married separate partners, and again within months of each other, within the year later, they both celebrated the arrival of their respective first-born. It wasn't until several years later that the four of us—Alice, Neil, Harry and myself—all got together again. My ordination, in fact, was the miracle it took to get us all in a single room again.

'I see all of them from time to time, but mostly Harry. He and Lizabeth and Babe now seem to have adopted me as their token voice of good and evil.'

'Goodness,' O'Connor sighed, breathing in the gentle night breeze. 'Now, thanks to your good self, I can fully appreciate the power of the confessional for the first time in my own life. Believe it or not, that is the first time in my life I have ever told anyone *all* of those details. I have to admit that I feel as though a great weight has been lifted off my chest.'

I didn't really need to know all that, Kennedy thought. One thing the story did serve to do though was to show that when it came to relationships, Kennedy and ann rea were definitely still in the kindergarten.

'Do you mind if we go back to my office? I've a photo I'd like you to look at,' he said, walking down the hill again in the direction of his office. O'Connor nodded, skipping a couple of times to get into step with the detective.

Chapter Twenty-One

WHEN PEOPLE LOOK sad, they certainly look gentler, Kennedy reflected, stealing a glance at O'Connor as they left Primrose Hill, crossing Albert Terrace to get to Prince Albert Road. Take Fr Vincent O'Connor, for instance; he was certainly no oil painting, but he wore his sadness like a soft hue. Kennedy imagined that, in the priest's particular case, he had the accumulative sadness of a lifetime's disappointments. Inevitably all this disenchantment contributed to his moroseness, which rose to the surface when the dark clouds regrouped and descended upon his shoulders once more. The detective wondered just how difficult a life the priest had led.

He had certainly got off to a terrible start when, as a student, he had fallen in love with Alice Roberts. This 'unrequited affliction' (O'Connor's words) seemed to have been the catalyst that had driven the young O'Connor to priesthood.

Then, as a priest, how much sadness might he have been forced to absorb?

And now, one of his few friends, perhaps his only friend, had been murdered. Kennedy wondered if O'Connor had ever cried out in despair. Had the priest ever called out to his God in anger, 'How much is one man expected to take?'

But then again, O'Connor had admitted to Kennedy that he didn't believe in heaven. Did this mean that he *really* didn't believe in God either?

And if he didn't believe in God, was it God's way of proving the priest wrong by the amount of punishment he was able to fork out?

'Whom do priests go to when they need comforting?' Kennedy asked.

'What? Sorry?' O'Connor replied, appearing startled by the question.

'Well, we know who the Riley family and Lizabeth Ford go to for their comfort. But where will you go in your hour of need, Vincent?'

'Ah well, I'd love to be able to tell you that there is wise old silver-haired priest who knows all the answers and doesn't mind sharing his wisdom with me. But, sadly, there is no such person I know of. Harry and I would have talked to each other over the years when the need arose, and Alice . . . and sometimes even Neil in the early days. . . .'

'Never your parents?'

'No,' O'Connor replied with visible regret.

'And from what you've been telling me, you don't take much comfort from your religion either?' Kennedy asked but knew the answer.

'Well, actually, these are exactly the times I question my religion most. You know, why should Lizabeth and Babe be forced to go through this? They're good people. Why should good people continually be put through the wringer? And at the same time, someone like Harry's murderer appears to get away with using evil to further his own selfish desires—I mean, how big an advertisement is that for any religion or church?'

'So, who might have furthered their selfish desires by Harry's death?'

'Hmm,' O'Connor began, looking a wee bit too considered coming up with his reply. 'Am I my brother's keeper?'

'Sorry?' Kennedy asked, not sure he was picking up the priest's thread.

'Yes, Harry and I were close, but that's not to say that he would have told me absolutely everything that was going on in his life, nor I him for that matter.'

'Does that mean you believe that there might have been something going on in his life that caused his death?' Kennedy asked, wondering if O'Connor had just given himself an out without lying to the detective in the process. For some reason, Kennedy found himself changing tack at that precise moment from one of talking to a friend to questioning someone in a professional capacity. He now found himself wondering what exactly was going on in and around O'Connor's words.

Not for the first time, Kennedy also noticed that O'Connor had a very irritating habit of putting his fingers to his face: he'd draw them across his lips to signify that there was something he couldn't say; he'd cup his nose and mouth in his hand as if he wanted to check if his breath was socially acceptable; he'd place one—usually his forefinger—to his chin to demonstrate that he was deep in thought; he'd fiddle and pull upon his ear with his forefinger and thumb, signalling he wasn't sure of an answer; he'd pull upon his large nose in consideration; he'd mouth a silent 'O' and raise his middle three fingers to cover the offending aperture in high camp shock; he'd brush his cheek to check the growth of his five o'clock shadow when he felt he needed to be somewhere else. Pretty soon, Kennedy had started to realise that he could predict how the priest was going to respond, according to the various finger gestures.

Kennedy wondered if these mannerisms had grown over the years as a convenient way to disguise the priest's evident bad looks.

O'Connor brushed his hair through with his right hand in an uncomfortable, unconfident kind of way.

He said, 'No, Detective. What I am saying is that I didn't know of anything untoward that was going on in his life, and I'd qualify that by saying I would never have thought that a close friend would always have been the person perfectly positioned to be aware of such events.'

'Right, I think I follow you,' Kennedy sighed. He wondered whether he'd been expecting much more from a priest or whether he was feeling professionally let down by O'Connor's reaction. He knew, on closer examination, that ann rea would probably have accused him of being a little oversensitive.

He decided he should cut the priest some slack, if only because O'Connor had just lost, quite possibly, his oldest friend.

Kennedy continued, 'Tell me, have you ever heard of a chap called Frazer McCracken?'

'Yes, in fact I have,' O'Connor replied, seeming more comfortable. 'Yes, wasn't he the character Harry had to fire—the employee who was involved in that whole hoo-ha at CABS?'

'Yes, the very one,' Kennedy confirmed and continued, 'But I believe he was suspended not fired. Did Harry ever talk about him to you?'

'He did as a matter of a fact.'

Kennedy waited for a fuller explanation, but nothing seemed to be forthcoming.

'So, what can you tell me about him?' the detective inquired.

'Well, I don't know the nuts and bolts of the case, but I think the thing that shocked Harry most about the whole affair was the fact that here was someone, Mr McCracken, who was clearly great at his work, extremely ambitious and competent, perhaps even ruthless on the promotion front, and yet at the same time, he seemed, according to Harry, to have absolutely no qualms about embezzling incredibly large sums of money from the building society.'

'But you don't know anything about the mechanics of the embezzlement?'

'No, I don't,' O'Connor replied with a sigh. 'Harry didn't seem overly preoccupied with it. I suppose it was because Harry would have felt he was well capable of dealing with him on all matters concerning money. But he was, as I have said, enormously confused by the extremes in McCracken's personality.'

Kennedy stared at the priest.

'You don't mean to tell me McCracken is a suspect?' O'Connor continued, in a tone that suggested the priest wouldn't be at all surprised if this were the case.

'At this stage, all we're doing is checking out each and every lead,' Kennedy replied in what sounded, even to him, to be *too* official a tone. 'Let's talk a bit, if we may, about Neil and Alice Roberts.'

'Yes?' O'Connor replied quickly. 'Fire away.'

'Okay, I think I know about Alice and Harry and how it all went sour after the falling out, but was that it, or did they still stay in touch with each other?'

O'Connor smiled at Kennedy—nothing more, just a smile—and then, 'Remember I also told you how the four of us, the Four Musketeers, got together again at my ordination?'

'Oh, yes,' Kennedy replied. 'So you did.'

'Well, it was quite strained at first, as you can well imagine, but in the space of a few years, we'd all put the good old college days behind us and grown into mates again. Initially it seemed to be Neil and myself who did all the running to keep it together. At times, I have to say, it didn't seem like it was worth it, but in hindsight I'm glad we got there.'

'Did you communicate individually or only as a group?' Kennedy asked, not really sure why he was doing so.

'Well, as you know, I was probably closest to Harry, and Lizabeth, of course, but Neil and Harry still go to the gym together regularly—twice a week, I believe. I rarely see Alice outside of the group, but we talk occasionally on the telephone. And although officially I'm what you'd term Neil's priest, I don't really communicate with him so much as an individual; we speak on the phone—rarely, but well . . .'

Kennedy thought O'Connor was about to give him something important, so he allowed the space to hang between them.

'I suppose it does sound terribly old fashioned and the kind of short-sightedness I'd accuse other priests of, but in truth Neil is a wee bit too macho for me. You know, he considers himself to be a bit of a ladies' man, and I suppose when the four of us were together, he'd always manage to keep it in check—probably because of Alice. On top of which, I think he knows Harry would just laugh at him. Alice, for her part, can't abide this in men. Even with all of that, let's just say that sometimes he still manages to prance around a bit like he's Richard Gere in *The American Gigolo*. Seeing up close a man behave as one imagines a ladies' man should behave—well, it's not a pretty sight. It's laughable really; in fact, if it wasn't so funny, it would be sad. But when you examine it closely, you realise that his continued behaviour must be for some*one's* benefit.'

'I think I know what you mean,' Kennedy said with a laugh. 'But he's an okay guy underneath it all, right?'

'Ah, he's got the ability to surprise me,' O'Connor said flamboyantly. 'But wasn't it Shaw who said, "Nowadays every great man has his disciples, but it's always Judas who writes the biographies." I'm sorry to have to advise you that I'm not going to play Judas for you, Inspector.'

Kennedy shrugged his shoulders and said, 'And Harry and Alice?'

'You haven't really been listening, have you?' O'Connor replied with a hint of bitterness evident in his voice. 'You've still your big question tucked up your sleeve there waiting for the best moment to ask it, "And what about Harry and Alice?" with the emphasis on *"and"*.'

'Vincent, I hear what you're saying, but whether or not this is uncomfortable for you is hardly the point. The point is that there are questions I have to ask you.'

'Yeah, but I wasn't expecting *Daily Star* questions,' O'Connor snapped back angrily.

'Look, here's the thing. Harry Ford is dead. Right? Now, we have reason to believe that he was murdered,' Kennedy said, experiencing a sudden flash of nine stab wounds in the shape of a cross. He made no reference to this though as he continued, 'Now, I'm not for one moment suggesting that Harry Ford did anything wrong, *but* we have to assume that someone was severely pissed off, at the very least, with him. Okay?'

O'Connor nodded in reluctant agreement.

'Now,' Kennedy continued, as they climbed the steps of North Bridge House, 'you're in the unfortunate position of having known Harry Ford and, well, being best mates with him, so as far as we are concerned, you are one of the key people for us to gather information from. I'm sorry if I'm appearing insensitive about your friendship with Harry, but you have to realise that I'm here first and foremost as a policeman, and these are the questions I have to ask you.'

'I can't answer any questions that might compromise my duties as a priest.'

'Personally I don't see the conflict,' Kennedy replied, a little taken back, opening the door of his office for the priest.

'Perhaps you can't,' O'Connor replied, going straight to the seat in front of Kennedy's desk. After a few moments' apparent consideration, he continued, 'Sorry, look it's my fault.' He reached his hand over Kennedy's desk. Kennedy took the hand and shook it. The priest's skin felt dry and warm. O'Connor continued to hold Kennedy's hand, and when he eventually let it go, Kennedy experienced an overwhelming wave of loneliness from O'Connor.

'It's so silly—it's like I'm accusing myself of being Judas, and I haven't even kissed anyone yet,' O'Connor said, and added, low camp, 'But enough of my sex life.'

The priest gave at least the outward appearance that his moment had passed. He rubbed his hands together and said, 'Sorry, Christy. What was your question again?'

Without batting an eyelid, Kennedy replied, 'I was asking you if Harry and Alice had much direct communication.'

If O'Connor's moment had been created as a diversion from this particular line of questioning, his demeanour did not betray the slightest annoyance at the fact that Kennedy had not given up on it.

'So you were,' the priest replied. 'So you were. Well, the honest reply is that I was never party to any of their direct conversations; otherwise they wouldn't have been direct conversations, would they?'

'But at least one of them—say, for instance, Harry—could have taken you into his confidence, couldn't he?'

'That would surely be deemed hearsay, wouldn't it? And isn't hearsay circumstantial evidence?'

'Well, maybe more inadmissible than circumstantial evidence,' Kennedy replied, deciding to let it go for now.

Kennedy wondered what it was that O'Connor knew but was refusing to tell. It wasn't even as though he was trying to be subtle about it, nearly but not quite rubbing Kennedy's nose in the dust cloud he appeared to be intentionally beating up. He considered asking this question outright but on second thoughts chose not to.

Kennedy opened his top drawer and removed a small clear evidence bag. He showed the photo to O'Connor, who studied the 'A' on the back.

'Alice?'

'Yes, where did you find that?' O'Connor replied, with a slight crackle noticeable in his voice, his eyes focusing intently on the shot.

'DS Irvine found it,' Kennedy said, in effect giving absolutely nothing away. Before O'Connor had a chance at a follow-up, the detective continued with a sigh, 'Vincent, are you aware that Harry Ford was having an affair?'

'I'm also aware that he was a great family man and was totally devoted to Lizabeth.'

'Once again, Vincent, you're not answering my question,' Kennedy said, not so much in frustration as in bewilderment.

'I think the answer I gave you has more relevance than the one you sought.'

'Meaning?'

'Meaning that, at this point, Harry Ford is dead and nothing you can ask or I can answer is going to bring him back again. That situation is totally irreversible; we can, however, try to help the living—'

'By not dragging Harry's name through the mud in front of Lizabeth and Babe?' Kennedy suggested

'*Exactly!*'

'I can appreciate that, but I need you to accept that in doing so we will be, in a way, helping Harry's murderer get away with it.'

'That's where we differ, you and I, Christy. You're preoccupied with the dead; I'm preoccupied with the living.'

'Do you not think that by helping effect closure on this we will help Lizabeth come to terms with it?'

'Even if it means hurting her and Babe, not to mention others, in the process?'

'I've always found that people generally do need to know the truth about things, no matter how painful, before they can move on with their lives.'

'I have found that people are just as happy to bury their dog-do in their gardens. Apart from anything else, it makes the grass grow greener,' O'Connor replied, just short of a snap.

'I think the mistake you're making here is in not accepting the fact that most people are as resilient as they need to be. It's incredible what we can deal with when we have to—' Kennedy replied, deciding mid-sentence that it was time to end this preposterous game of ping-pong. 'Tell me, Vincent, what were you doing between the hours of six o'clock yesterday evening and three o'clock this morning?'

'Oh, let me see,' O'Connor replied, camping it up again. 'I do believe I was in my professional quarters during that period.'

Kennedy stood up, amused, confused—he wasn't sure which. He said something along the lines of needing to talk further, but at a later time. O'Connor replied that he'd make himself available as and when. They shook hands, and as the priest walked out, Kennedy wondered whether the man of the cloth was taking his claim of never telling lies a wee bit too far.

Kennedy thought of the one of the three wise monkeys of whom O'Connor reminded him most: 'See No Evil'.

Not for the first time in his life, the Ulster detective considered the fact that you can see people, look at them, even study them closely, but never ever be able to comprehend the amount of heartache they might privately be carrying.

Take Fr Vincent O'Connor, for instance. Up to the recent revelation, Kennedy had pegged him as a competent servant of God who certainly seemed to have been very effective in his ability to comfort Sally Riley about her missing husband. But back there, while standing atop Primrose Hill, he had confessed to a relative stranger (Kennedy) that he had become a priest only because he could not move his relationship with Alice Cain from a friendship up to a romance.

And then take Harry Ford, whom Kennedy had just met for the first time several weeks previously. Kennedy did not think he was wrong in having considered Ford to be a decent chap, a good egg. But there was even a distinct possibility, according to what O' Connor had told Kennedy, that Ford's marriage was based on the fact that he had been on the rebound from Alice Cain, quite possibly the love of his life.

While on the topic, Kennedy considered Lizabeth Ford. Surely, he thought, she must have known, or at least sensed, that a part of Harry Ford was still pining after someone else. Did that mean that Harry Ford was such a great catch, that she was so madly in love with him, that she was prepared to accept this and accept the potential role of playing second fiddle? Could she really have preferred the little she had of Harry to having no involvement, or relationship, with him at all? Was that why she'd had a child with him so quickly, to move their relationship to a different level? Harry Ford was not a selfish person. Kennedy could see when he was with his daughter how his eyes were alight. Even after eleven years, he still hung on her every word. Had Lizabeth known that Harry would be a great father and would put his children's lives before his own?

His thoughts hopped back to Alice Cain. He wondered if she spent every day of her life thinking that if only she had not gone out that night in Reading—even just for the vital few minutes she was out—she would still be with her true love. Maybe she didn't think about it every single day of her life, but even if she thought about it only one day a month, it was still a lot; it still meant there was something strong there between them. Did she wonder what it would have been like if Harry had been the father of her children? Did she ever wonder what it would have been like to be married to him and to live in his house as the mother of his children? That was, of course, assuming that she was in the slightest bit envious of Harry and Lizabeth's lifestyle. On the other hand, Kennedy thought, perhaps she felt, 'Goodness, that was too intense. What a lucky escape.' Would her life with Vincent have been a disaster? Perhaps she even considered her life with Robert Cain and their children to be just perfect. Perhaps she thanked her brother Neil for sowing the initial seeds of doubt.

Then he thought back to the unsatisfactory interview he had just concluded with the man who seemed to be at the centre of all of this domestic unrest. Kennedy was prepared to put the behaviour down to the fact that the priest had just lost a very good friend. However, he wasn't so sure he could be so forgiving if the farce were to continue the next time they met.

Chapter Twenty-Two

AT THE SAME time as Kennedy was concluding the interview with Fr Vincent O'Connor, DC Dot King and DS James Irvine were returning to North Bridge House following their interview with Neil Roberts.

'Sure, he just *luves* himself,' was King's first observation to Kennedy.

'From what we've gathered, maybe with good reason,' Irvine added.

'*Please* don't put the cart before the horse,' King pleaded—really pleaded.

Irvine chose only to smile.

Kennedy could not work out if it was a smile of agreement or a smile of pride as King continued her thumbnail sketch of Roberts.

'You'd have to admit that he's in great shape, for his age, which I would peg as being somewhere in his mid-forties. He dresses well, he's still got his own hair, but I doubt if it could really be that black without a little bit of help from a bottle. He dresses quite cool, but not loudly—black trousers, a dazzling white shirt, a black waistcoat and extremely comfortable-looking black canvas shoes. He's confident in a slightly forced way, if you know what I mean. For instance, he had a mental list of how to behave with a woman—open doors, no swearing, offer them a seat first, offer refreshments, treat evenly, all of which he did to me. But I always had the feeling that he was doing it all from his checklist rather than doing it because it came naturally to him. He's probably great on a first date, but I don't think there would ever be much beyond that. I mean, you could say that he possessed a certain charm, and I wouldn't disagree, but I would have to say that it's also easy to see that he doesn't really *like* women.'

She's perceptive, this one, isn't she? Kennedy thought but didn't say. He still found it quite marvellous that some people could be so clued in whatever their age. He thought Dot King was what songwriter Tanita Tikaram referred to as an ancient heart.

Irvine and the ancient heart then recalled, near enough verbatim, the contents of the interview they had just enjoyed with Neil Roberts.

The contents (verbatim) were:

Irvine: I . . . we . . .

Roberts: Let's make this easier for you. I know about Harry.

Irvine: Oh.

Roberts: Yes, Fr O'Connor rang me earlier; he was very distressed.

King: We're sorry for your loss.

Roberts: Thank you. Yes, the first of the Musketeers gone. We all talked about this, you know, thinking it was at least thirty years in the future, I hasten to add. But I suppose when one of your gang turns out to be a priest, some of your conversations do tend to find their way around to the maudlin in general and your mortality in particular. Anyway, during these conversations we would all wonder (aloud) which one of us would go first. I suppose if only because Harry and I went to the gym twice a week and didn't drink as much as Vincey—Fr O'Connor that is—we thought we'd be okay. At the same time, Alice, if she followed in our mother's footsteps, was also going to enjoy the fruits of a ripe old age. So, by a process of elimination and deduction, that always left poor old Vincey as the elected candidate. Mind you, he always claimed he was sure to be building up a few credit points with St Peter, if only for all the poor souls he was saving.

Irvine: When was the last time you saw Harry Ford, sir?

Roberts: Yesterday, as a matter of fact. Mondays and Thursdays were our gym nights. We usually met at the gym; you know the one behind Marks and Sparks? We'd arrive around six o'clock and leave shortly after seven. Then we'd either have a quick drink or a pizza.

Irvine: And last night what did you do?

Roberts: We just had time for a quick drink.

King: Where did you go for this quick drink, sir?

Roberts: Last night, we had it at the gym. If we were going to have more than one, we'd usually go up to the Spreadeagle. I don't really know why; possibly something to do with the fact that the crowd around there never seem as desperate as the crowd in the gym bar, if you know what I mean.

Irvine: So what time would you have split up?

Roberts: Oh, I'd say about 7.30 at the very latest.

King: And then?

Roberts: And then, I believe, he was off home for one of Lizabeth's famous family dinners.

King: And what did you do yourself, sir?

Roberts: And then this sad middle-aged bachelor went home to enjoy one of Marks and Spencer's famous oven-ready dinners for one.

Irvine: What kind of spirits was Mr Ford in, sir?

Roberts: Well, as was usually the case with Harry when he first arrived, he was still buzzing from his day in the office. He worked very long hours, you know. Anyway, once he got on the treadmill, he'd allow himself to work up a sweat, and that would always relax him up a bit. I have to say, a lot of people come to the gym only to hang out. That's the main reason I liked going with Harry—he really wasn't scared of using the gym correctly. It's always easier for me if I'm there with someone who'll go head to head with me on all the pieces of equipment I'd use. We'd usually start on the bike; we'd follow that with some floor exercises, the treadmill, some more exercises, some weights; and then we'd finish by returning to either the bike or the treadmill.

King: So you would say that he was in a pretty good mood?

Roberts: Sorry, yes. I'm afraid I lost the plot there a bit, didn't I? Yes, he seemed to be in an upbeat mood. I mean, at the same time, I have to tell you it would be a very rare occasion you would have described Harry as being down. He was a great cheerleader, if you know what I mean. He was always the one who would rally around when one of the troops was down.

Irvine: Like who—I mean, who would be down?

Roberts: Oh, like Vincey, for instance. I mean, obviously it has a lot to do with his chosen vocation, but even taking that into consideration, Fr O'Connor is always taking the world on his shoulders, isn't he? He did tend to lean on Harry and Lizabeth a lot. I mean, Vincey was both Harry's and my mate, so that's okay, isn't it? But he must be a bit of a chore for poor old Lizabeth.

Irvine: Did Harry ever discuss work with you?

Roberts: Not a lot. I didn't encourage it. You have to understand that to me work is mostly about the pay cheque—in fact, work is *all* about the pay cheque. I never, ever, take my work home with me, and I think that all people who do are bores.

King: Did Mr Ford ever mention a person by the name of Frazer McCracken to you?

Roberts: No, not directly to me, but I did hear Harry and Vincey discussing him heatedly on more than one occasion. It seems he was some upstart in CABS who'd been caught with his fingers in the till.

King: But you never discussed McCracken with Mr Ford yourself?

Roberts: I suppose I might have chipped in one or two morsels of useful advice into the conversation. I think I remember telling Harry that what he should do was just promote this bastard McCracken and let him run the company. It seemed to me from what they were saying about him—what with his abundance of ambition—he'd do a really good job of it. It takes a certain kind of person to run these companies, and that type of person is not always the type you'd want to have as your best friend.

Irvine: Have you any ideas about whom Harry Ford might have upset over the years?

Roberts: Harry didn't have . . . sorry; you know what I was about to say there? I was about to say that Harry didn't have an enemy in the world, but on consideration that's blatantly untrue, isn't it? He must have had at least one.

King: And you've no idea who that might be?

Roberts: You know what, I really haven't a clue. I mean, all this friend and enemy stuff—it's all so much easier when you're younger. Like, when we were all at college in Reading and . . . well, I don't know if you've been told this yet, but hey, I may as well tell you—you're going to find out anyway. You're probably going to find it all very harmless as it happens, but when we—Harry, Vincey, Alice and I—were all at college together, the truth of it is that Harry stole Alice from Vincey. I'm sure that's how Vincey saw it. However, from Alice's point of view, she claimed she'd always fancied Harry and she was never really interested in Vincey in that way, if you know what I mean. But Vincey was totally smitten by her. Now, I know she's my sister and all, but I could still totally understand why. Sadly, I'm sure you could count on one finger the number of times they went out on a proper date. So, when Harry started going out with Alice . . . well, now, if we were back in those days and you were interviewing me then, there would be only one real suspect. But I'm sure our Vincey wouldn't hurt a fly. Anyway, the main point I was trying to make was that in those days, it was easy to know your friends and enemies, but as we grow older and supposedly become adults, we never allow our true feelings to show through in the same way. No wonder all of our generation is confused. None of us really know where we stand with one another, do we?

Irvine: But you were one of his best mates. Surely if someone was mad enough with Harry to murder him, you'd have known all about it?

Roberts: Why do people murder other people? This is your area of expertise—you tell me. Eh? Is it for financial gain? Is it for romantic gain? Or could it be as an act of retribution? Or, in this instance, could Harry just have been killed by accident?

King: We're definitely ruling out an accident on this occasion, sir.

Roberts: Okay, let's look at the other possibilities, one by one. Financial gain—who would gain in monetary terms by Harry's demise? Let's see—his wife, his children of course. I haven't seen his will, but I'd imagine his immediate family would all be well taken care of. At the same time, I'm sure they would all be prepared to give it back ten times over for the chance to have their husband or father back again. Harry has no other living relatives, so there's no one else who might legally gain financially from his death. I'm absolutely sure he didn't leave either Vincey or myself a penny in his will, so that rules both of us out. Okay, seeing you're prepared to leave all this deduction to me, I'll continue. Next, I believe I mentioned romance. Now, who would gain romantically by Harry's death? Even if Vincey still held a grudge about losing my sister Alice to Harry all those years ago, I'm sure, if nothing else, his collar would rule his heart. On top of which, Harry was with Lizabeth and Alice was with Bob, so that rules out Vincey on that account. Then there's Harry's secretary. They usually come into the mix somewhere in these affairs, don't they? I have to admit I can't really see Jill Codona and Harry Ford as an item though, I really can't. So, I suppose, when you examine the case carefully, the only obvious suspect to raise his head would have to be the McCracken chap. In his case, two of the above prerequisites come into play—revenge and financial gain. Shallow pickings though really, aren't they? Shit, I'd hate to be in his shoes if you can't find anyone else.

King: Just to confirm again, sir. After your Marks and Sparks meal yesterday evening, you did say you stayed in all evening by yourself?

Roberts: Well, no, I didn't exactly say that.

King: Oh?

Roberts: What I said was that I ate alone.

King: And then?

Roberts: Ah.

King: No telephone calls?

Roberts: Just one from Alice.

King: What time would that have been, sir?

Roberts: Oh, let's see now, 7.20 gym, 7.40 home, 8.15 dinner, so I'd say around 8.40 or so. She rang just as I was finishing dinner.

Irvine: And then, sir?

Roberts: Well, I failed to resist the temptation of the flesh, as Vincey would so eloquently put it.

King: How so, sir?

Roberts: Well, actually, I had a girl over.

King: Oh, I see.

Irvine: And did she stay all night?

Roberts: No, not exactly. She's an actress, you see, and she had to leave at two o'clock or so in the morning to head back to her hotel. She had an early morning flight for a shoot.

King: And what time did this actress arrive at your place?

Roberts: I'd say around about nine o'clock.

King: So from around nine o'clock until about two o'clock, you were with this lady?

Roberts: Correct.

King: Is this an ongoing relationship?

Roberts: I wouldn't have said so. I mean, we're both single and we see each other from time to time.

King: And her name, sir?

Roberts: I'd rather not say, if you don't mind.

Irvine: I'm afraid we have to mind, sir.

Roberts: I'm sorry, I can't possibly—

Irvine: I have to remind you that this is a murder investigation, and I have to insist you furnish us with her name.

Roberts: Okay, I see, but I would ask you to treat this information with the utmost confidentially.

Irvine: I can assure you that leaks will do nothing but hinder our investigation.

Roberts: Okay, her name is Nealey Dean.

King: You don't mean the girl who played opposite Hugh Grant in *First of the True Believers?*

Roberts: Erm, yes, that's her, but could I please repeat my request that you be discreet with this piece of information?

Irvine: Yes, of course. Ah, in the meantime, could I trouble you for her phone number?

Roberts: Perfect! A policeman—that's what I should have been. Then all I'd need to do is to say to all the beautiful women, in my best Sean Connery accent of course, 'Ah, in the meantime, could I trouble you for your telephone number, miss?' I mean, is that a gift of a job or what? I'll give you her office's number, and they'll put you in touch. I know she's away until the weekend. But I'd respectfully request you don't contact her until I've spoken to her first. I don't want her thinking I've just dropped her in the smelly stuff without due consideration.

King: Well, I'm not altogether sure that would be eth—

Roberts: Oh, I see. You're worried I'd want to get her to lie for me, to be my alibi. Oh, come on, please. I'm sure I'm not so good that Nealey Dean is going to lie for me.

Irvine: Well, we'll check with our boss, sir. I can assure you, he's the master of discretion.

As King and Irvine finished their verbal report to Kennedy in his office, Irvine added, 'Now, that's some alibi, sir—you know, being wrapped up in bed with Nealey Dean at the time of the incident! How much more good luck and providence could one man enjoy?'

Chapter Twenty-Three

TWENTY MINUTES LATER, Kennedy and King were on their way to interview Neil Roberts's sister, Alice Cain, in her apartment within a mansion block in the trendier-by-the-week Marylebone spillage area. Parking was a problem, as ever—reaffirming, first hand, exactly how successful Mr Livingstone's initiative had been.

Kennedy insisted on staying with King until she found a parking space. This gesture would have put considerable strain on lesser mortals, but not King; she just acted like it was the most natural thing in the world and visibly relaxed, enjoying the company. He used some of the time to radio into Sgt Flynn at North Bridge House and had him put a few constables on to checking the Camden Town restaurants and cafés—particularly Café DeLancey—to see if they could locate a time and place for Harry Ford's after-gym meal. Twice DC King nearly found a parking spot only to be robbed of it at the final moment by flashier drivers who were always just a wee bit braver—or more desperate!

The Cain home was a three-bedroom apartment on the top (sixth) floor, which afforded them a spectacular south-facing view over central London and beyond. The views were not quite as awe-inspiring as those from atop Primrose Hill, but in a more urban kind of way, they were equally compelling.

A cleaner or a maid—Kennedy couldn't be sure which—let the two members of Camden Town CID in. Everything about the apartment and furnishing enjoyed the look of old-money wealth. The slight problem with the décor and furniture, as far as Kennedy was concerned, was that it looked a wee bit too much like a show flat, so when the Japanese maid (or cleaner) showed them into the sitting room and invited them to take a seat, Kennedy hesitated for ages, trying to decide which seat would interfere least with the overall concept. He pacified himself with the thought that the minute he and King left the apartment, the maid cum cleaner would be buzzing around puffing up the deflated cushions and smoothing out the creases they had left on the sofa's seats.

Incredibly there wasn't a single photograph of the Cain family— amongst the numerous wooden-framed shots on the mantelpiece or cupboard or adorning the walls—that was at an incorrect angle. Nor did there appear to be a single offending speck of dust on the coffee table or bookshelves. The desk and its chair were both polished to the point that each item could possibly have been a millimetre slimmer than on the day it had been purchased.

The centrepiece of the deceptively large L-shaped room was a large painting above the marble fireplace. The painting looked like the work of one of the old masters who had perhaps spent just a little bit too much time in the local tavern swilling liquid inspiration. Either that or he had lost his glasses while completing work on the out-of-focus mountainous scene.

Kennedy and King sat on a very comfortable dark blue sofa, which afforded them the perfect vantage point for the painting.

'It's a teensy bit too opulent in here for me,' King whispered.

'Yes,' Kennedy replied, also finding only a whisper from his own voice.

'It's like waiting for some bad news in a doctor's waiting room,' King said, self-consciously checking the soles of her shoes for dirt.

'Bad *and* expensive news,' Kennedy agreed.

Kennedy rose from the sofa, walked over to the main window and stood looking out over the streets of London. He experienced a strange sensation—somewhere out there roamed Harry Ford's murderer, or murderers. What were they thinking now, less than twenty-four hours after their fatal deed? Did they feel avenged? Did they feel relieved? Did they feel vindicated? Did they feel scared? Were they feeling panicky at that moment? Or, might they not have cared less? His thoughts were interrupted by a presence that positively swept into the room.

Alice Cain looked like a woman ill at ease about her natural beauty but unable to do anything about it. Kennedy was convinced that she had certainly gone to some lengths to try to detract from her looks. Perhaps, on reflection, Kennedy thought, her efforts had not only been in vain but had even have added to her serene beauty.

She had shorn her hair to within half an inch of her scalp. All that this served to do was to highlight her eyes and accentuate her full lips. Mrs Cain did not wear even a spec of make-up, but if she had, all that it would have served to do would have been to hide her clear, unblemished skin. She had even chosen to wear a lifeless, shapeless, knee-length dress, but as she moved across the room in Kennedy's direction, the dress caressed the contours of her perfectly shaped body like a second skin. Her presence was bottled-perfume free, but the absence of artificial scents served only to make her natural aromas all the more stimulating.

'Hello,' she said in a bass, heavy voice, and extended her right hand to Kennedy. 'I'm Alice Cain.'

It was only when she was arm's length from Kennedy that he realised she wasn't the teenager she had first appeared from the other side of the room. He also noticed that her blue eyes were heavy, red and sad from recent tears. Kennedy assessed that she had shed quite a few. Perhaps the confident air with which she positively attacked the room had been composed just the other side of the doorway in an attempt to brave herself for this encounter.

'Good afternoon, Mrs Cain, I'm Detective Inspector Christy Kennedy,' he said, diplomatically flashing his warrant card. 'And this is DC Dot King. She's new to Camden Town.'

Alice strode across to King with a purposeful gait and shook the constable's hand. Kennedy stared at the hands shaking, still feeling the coolness of Alice's soft skin on his own hand. Alice continued with the handshake and said to King, 'Well, if what I've heard of your boss is anything to go by, you're in very good hands.'

'Ah, you'll have been talking to Fr O'Connor then,' Kennedy replied modestly, moving back across the room and taking a seat on a different sofa from King this time. Alice Cain sat beside him.

'No, actually it was Harry who was telling me all about you and your stunning journalist friend.'

'Ah,' said Kennedy, visibly surprised. 'I didn't realise you and Harry were—'

'Still in contact?' Alice said, filling in the end of Kennedy's question. 'Why, of course we were still in touch. Listen, I'll tell you all about it. I won't have people talking about us behind our backs. I'd prefer you heard it all from me.'

Kennedy unbuttoned his jacket and crossed his legs.

'But look, let's get ourselves some tea, shall we? I hear you love a great cup of tea, Inspector,' Alice said as she disappeared from the room, leaving King and Kennedy bemused in her wake.

'Everyone seems to know about your passion for tea, sir,' King offered quietly.

'Well, you know . . .'

'No, sorry, I didn't mean it as a criticism, sir. Personally I think it's brilliant that in the year 2006 we have a policeman who favours tea over alcohol.'

'It's funny,' Kennedy said, not so much in reply but more as a method of changing subject, 'but I was just thinking that if things had worked out differently between Alice and Harry, we wouldn't be visiting Alice here.'

King looked at him inquisitively in the way she had a habit of doing when she didn't fully understand what someone was saying but hadn't worked out a way to ask the correct question to solve her dilemma. Kennedy liked this quality in that she would never get in the way of the proceedings, and she could, and would, always seek clarification when she needed to.

'Well, we come in here and see Alice's habitat, and I can't help wondering how much different it would have been if she'd remained with Harry.'

'Oh, I get you,' King said. 'So you were wondering if Alice would have pulled Harry Ford into this kind of environment or if Harry would have pulled her towards his?'

'That's a good question, DC—'

'Right,' Alice Cain announced less than three minutes after her departure, returning to the room with a tray bearing cups and saucers, a milk jug, a sugar bowl—all in white bone china—and some boring-looking digestive biscuits.

Well, I suppose she doesn't keep herself that trim by indulging in chocolate biccies, Kennedy thought.

'I assume we're all having tea?' Alice asked, looking only to King for confirmation, a confirmation which was duly returned.

'So,' Kennedy began, 'when was the last time you spoke to Harry?'

'It would have been yesterday, around lunchtime,' Alice replied in an eloquent tone. 'I would have though his PA, Jill, would have already mentioned Harry's and my frequent telephone conversations. She had instructions from Harry always to put me through. Poor girl, I think she was besotted with Harry.'

'She didn't say anything about frequent telephone calls,' Kennedy admitted. 'Tell me, did Harry seem in good spirits to you?'

'He seemed perfectly fine,' Alice admitted. 'He was due to meet my brother later in the day for one of their gym sessions, which he always enjoyed.'

'He didn't, by any chance, mention to you anything, or anyone for that matter, that was troubling him?' Kennedy asked as King discreetly opened her notebook and stared writing.

Alice eyed King's movements and moved her lips from side to side as though in consideration. She raised her right hand to toy with an absent curl of hair that was probably still somewhere on her hairdresser's floor.

'No. I mean, we had a quick chat about this and that,' Alice began, and stopped as she broke into a feeble smile. 'Actually, if you must know, we talked about you for a while, and we talked about how ridiculous *Coronation Street* has become—my observation, not his; Harry never watched soaps—and we talked about other mundane stuff. You know, you have a chat with someone, and when you set the phone down, you wonder if you should have spent your time more diligently elsewhere. But that applies to the majority of ones life, doesn't it? Most of our time could be better served doing something else, something more spiritual or superior. It's just that we never make the time to organise that, so we end up occupying ourselves with all of the mundane stuff.'

'Em,' Kennedy started hesitantly. 'I have to ask you Mrs . . . Cain—'

'Oh, for goodness sake, please call me Alice.'

'Okay, Alice. I have to ask you how close you and Harry were.'

'Inspector, we were mates—we'd been mates since college, Harry and Neil and Vincey and I. What can I tell you? He was my bestest friend; he was my first lover.'

King not only batted the proverbial eyelid, but her eyeballs nearly popped out at the same time.

Alice kept talking, some of the bass of her voice being lost in the acoustics of the room. 'We were all close, the four of us—as close as four people could be. Neil is my brother and he's always been more like a . . . like a big sister to me; you know, always counselling me, even when I don't particularly want to be counselled. Especially when I don't want to be counselled, in point of fact. He's been a great uncle to Robbie and Caroline. He's as strict with them as he is with me, but my children absolutely love him for it. I genuinely believe that they are as anxious to canvass his opinion on all the big issues in their lives as they are to canvass their father's. That's not a put-down of my husband, Bob. He absolutely dotes on them too, spoils them rotten—but because of his affection, he can never be objective about their lives. Now, Neil, on the other hand, will argue passionately over the children and their respective education, careers and lifestyle.'

Alice stopped talking in order to take a bite of her biscuit and a sip of her tea.

'Then there is Vincent O'Connor,' Alice said as she very subtly removed the crumbs of the biscuit from the corners of her mouth. 'Poor Vincent claims that my rejection of him sent him on his way to the priesthood. I always say I hope he gained more perception on life after he was ordained than he had beforehand. I mean, anyone could see I had eyes only for Harry. I imagine you've already heard why we spilt up in the first place?'

'Yes,' Kennedy replied, and continued *à la* Russell Harty, 'It was down to bad timing, was it not?'

'That's a very sweet thing for you to say, Inspector, but to be perfectly honest with you, I'm afraid I'd have to admit that it was more down to immaturity on both our parts. I know we're all bred to believe that it's a jungle out there and we should spend a considerable time scouting out the perfect mate. If you ask me, the main problem arises when, and if, you meet your perfect mate immediately. Well, that's what happened with Harry and me, but unfortunately neither of us had the maturity to deal with it.'

Alice looked as if she remembered something and then looked to both members of the police as though trying to ascertain if they would understand what she was about to say. She continued, seeming either to believe they would or to give them the benefit of the doubt, 'You know, Vincent, in one of his more generous moments—and he can afford to be generous in all of this, can't he?—anyway, he said it's only through original sin (such as Harry's and mine, or at least mine) that we gain wisdom. I believe, in his same lecture to me, he also advised that Eve was right to eat the apple. Adam and Eve just positively, according to Vincent, had to go through what they went through. According to our enlightened priest, you have to go through self-consciousness and embarrassment in order to be wise. His point was that if Harry and I hadn't split up when we did, we would never have realised exactly what we had. He understood how painful it was, but he insisted that we all had to lose our innocence in order to survive this world. The wise father insisted it would just be impossible to go through life with everything just being wonderful all the time. If he wasn't a priest,

I wonder how many women he would have been able to coax into bed with that chat-up line.'

Alice stopped talking and studied King, who was writing away furiously in her book.

'And here's something else to note in your little black book,' Alice said, addressing King directly. 'And this is from me, not from a grossly inexperienced priest. When you find your man, whenever you find your man, don't hang around waiting for a sign from on high—grab him and hang on to him for dear life. Tell me, Miss King, do you have a boyfriend?'

'Yes, I do, as a matter of fact,' King answered politely, looking up from her notebook. 'My Ashley and me are . . . well, he's always been the one for me, and we're planning to get married as soon as we can . . .'

'Well, that's just great,' Alice said with what sounded more like envy in her voice. 'I wish I'd been so decisive when I was your age, but unfortunately I was influenced by my mates. They were all saying, "Stop being boring; get out of the house and have a bit of fun." I listened to Neil and he was saying, "Stop this now or you'll regret it." I often wondered if that was a threat or just good advice.' Alice stopped and thought for a few seconds before continuing, 'Do you know Jackson Browne? Do you know his work?'

Kennedy, thanks to ann rea, did; King didn't.

'Well, he's got this great line in a song and it goes something like: "And I met the fools that a young fool meets . . ." I think it's such a great line because it really does say it all. I mean, I *really* couldn't put it better myself if I tried.'

Again she stopped talking. This time she closed her eyes and seemed to go somewhere. Kennedy couldn't work out if it was into Jackson Browne's very fine song or if it was to a time when she was a young fool chasing other fools.

It was DC King who interrupted the moment. She broke it by stopping writing. That was not a particularly spectacular thing to do; it was just that when the only movement in the room—her hand moving across her page—stopped, the balance of the room was disrupted.

Cain looked to King's pen and continued, 'But look, what can anyone do? My husband, my children, my brother, my friend Vincent, have all had to live with my mistake, and sometimes it's not enough that you get on with your lives. You can see in people's eyes when they look at you, you can see them think, *She's not with the one she loves.* But I refuse to be slowed down by such mental interference.

Kennedy flashed on to a Stephen Stills lyric:

If you can't be with the one you love,
Love the one you're with.

He felt that Alice most likely followed the sentiment of the words. He realised, of course, that they were probably just some glib words Mr Stills— the allegedly *difficult* member of Crosby, Stills and Nash—had put together to fit his song. Kennedy supposed that Stephen Stills never realised how much goodwill and love he brought into tepid relationships.

Love the one you're with.

How many other times might those words have pulled a couple through difficult times?

Kennedy was distracted by this thought. He supposed that Alice and Mr Stills' logic was perfectly fine for those who weren't with the ones they loved, but for those—the other partner in said relationships, where their sweethearts were emotionally elsewhere; say Mr Bob Cain for instance— well, life for him couldn't have been a picnic, could it?

'Take my husband for instance,' Alice said, as if reading Kennedy's mind. 'Now, he knew my heart was elsewhere when we met, but for some reason, God bless him, he persisted. He instinctively knew when not to push. And one day I woke up, and I must have been halfway through the day before I realised that I hadn't thought about Harry. I'd been preoccupied with thoughts of Bob instead. So the next time he asked me to marry him, I said yes. I suppose it helped somewhat, from his point of view, that I was carrying his child at the time. He's frightfully old-fashioned, you know, and he didn't want to be responsible for fathering an illegitimate child—his words, not mine. So, I can't really say I've had a hard life. I can't even say that I've had an unhappy life . . .'

Alice stopped as the tears that had so obviously been lurking just below the surface since the police had arrived now escaped and flowed at liberty down her cheeks.

Kennedy and King both looked and felt awkward until, a few moments later, Alice turned to Kennedy and said through her crying, 'Oh please, hold me, won't you?'

Kennedy did as he was bid and did it gracefully. After a short time, Alice said, more as a whisper, perhaps intended only for Kennedy, 'It's just that ever since I heard about Harry, I've been overcome with the feeling that it might somehow be my fault.'

Kennedy glanced towards King as if to say, *Don't worry, it's not a confession.* Eventually, after trying unsuccessfully to catch her breath several times through her crying, Alice blubbered, 'It's just that I keep thinking that if only I hadn't been a right pranny at university—you know, going out with my mates just to show them and Neil that I was still totally independent—well, then Harry and I would have stayed together and he mightn't have been involved in the set of circumstances which lead to his death. I know it's very stupid, but I have to tell you that I can't get that thought out of my head.'

'Well, Alice, you know that if you want to go down that line, then that's fine, but if you do, then, in fairness, you have to take into consideration all the other possibilities as well,' Kennedy offered, in the hope of providing some comfort.

'Yes, like he could have got knocked down by a bus,' King said, proving that she was hearing a little, if not all, of their whispers.

'Sorry?' Alice said as she sat away from Kennedy and took the Kleenex King had left for her on the coffee table. 'Did I hear you right? Did you say that he could have been run over by a bus?'

King grimaced, setting her face into an acceptable form of apology.

Alice started to laugh, quietly at first and then louder, until she had burst into an uncontrollable fit. Kennedy joined in, and eventually King's embarrassment passed and she joined in as well.

'Well, that's quite possibly the most elegant pick-me-up I've ever heard,' Alice said, still laughing, wiping the last of the tears from her eyes and face. 'I apologise for that—it was unforgivable of me to break down like this in front of you.'

'I'm the one who should be apologising,' King said.

'Absolutely not; you're the one who got me out of it. Anyway, you were questioning me. I'm fine now if you'd like to continue.'

'Well,' Kennedy replied, requiring no further prompting, 'you said just there that he wouldn't have been involved in the set of circumstances which resulted in his death . . .'

'Did I really say that?'

'Yes,' King confirmed immediately as Kennedy added, 'Does that mean you have an idea about what exactly those circumstances might have been?'

'No, sorry, not at all, I'm afraid. I just meant that if we'd stayed together, Harry and I would have had a very different lifestyle.'

Kennedy said, 'I see.'

'I think, in a way, Harry always felt his life to be unfulfilled. I don't mean just because he wasn't with me,' she said in disdain to emphasise the point. 'It's just that he never seemed . . . well, he seemed to have such ambition when I met him at university. I hope that doesn't seem snobby. It's just that although he always seemed to have enough money to pay the bills, he'd never have been in the financial position where he could have afforded to retire. I often wondered, if he hadn't had children, how different his life might have been. I'm quite sure he'd never have been working for a building society at this point. Do you know what I mean?'

'Yes,' Kennedy replied, seamlessly adding a question of his own. 'But do you think he would like to have retired?'

'An interesting question, Inspector,' Alice replied very positively. 'Let me put it to back to you. Would you like to retire?'

'No,' Kennedy replied immediately.

'I thought as much, but then you don't strike me as someone who's very impressed by money,' she said, glancing quickly around her own opulent room.

'Well, I think it's easy to say or feel that when you have, as you said about Harry, enough money to pay the bills. But do you really think he was unhappy with his lot?'

Kennedy realised he was now playing a bit of a game in that unusually he was prepared to give away a bit of his own personal information in return for as much as he could gather about Harry Ford.

At this juncture, Alice seemed unprepared to give away any more personal information about Harry, yet she was still pushing Kennedy for more.

'But you see—and this is the one point that Harry and Vincent both agreed on—you don't seem to be the kind of policeman who works so much for monetary gain as for the satisfaction you gain by solving the crime.'

'Well,' Kennedy replied, sparing King a quick glance, 'I think it's more a case of being in a position where I can help to solve the crime.'

'And you do see yourself continuing with this until you retire?' Alice asked, still in the driving seat of the interview.

'You know, I can honestly say that I don't think that much about it, but I imagine that for as long as the work continues to engage me as much as it does at present, I'll be only too happy to keep doing it. That is, of course, assuming they continue to let me do it. Tell me, was there something else you think Harry would prefer to have been doing? You know, rather than being a building society branch manager?'

'Well, it was hardly taxing for him, was it?'

'But by all accounts he was very good at it.'

'Harry was very good at everything he chose to do. I think he stayed there only because he was under pressure to look after the girls' education.'

'So what do you think he should have been doing?' Kennedy asked.

'I always thought he would have made a great teacher. He was always so good with kids.'

'But that was hardly going to fast-track him on to an early retirement either,' Kennedy said, and then added, 'I was wondering if you and Harry ever discussed this business about Frazer McCracken?'

'Quite a bit, yes,' Alice admitted.

'Was there anything he told you about the episode—McCracken's dirty dealings—which led you to believe that McCracken could be the one behind this sorry affair?'

'He told me he didn't like McCracken. He said the thing that upset him most about the embezzlement was that McCracken was totally and utterly without remorse. McCracken acted as though, as far as he was concerned, the only crime had been the crime of being found out. What disturbed Harry the most was that this Mr McCracken was by all accounts very good at his job, extremely competent and very ambitious—a CABS career person absolutely everyone predicted was on the way to the top. Perhaps McCracken is exactly the type of person it takes to run a large corporation these days.'

'Whereas Harry wasn't?' Kennedy asked.

'I'd have said not, wouldn't you? As far as I could see, and I believe this was Harry's perspective, he was so happy to be rid of McCracken mainly because Harry didn't want to be around to discover exactly what that nasty piece of work was really capable of. Now, I don't know if that suggests Harry thought the creep was capable of murder or not.'

'You seem to have communicated a lot, you and Harry. Does that mean you saw a lot of each other?' Kennedy asked.

'We did most of our communicating by telephone. I still yearned for the good old days when we'd meet for coffee and have a good old natter, or at the very least you'd write a letter and spray a little perfume on to the pages so that the reader would have a sense of you as he read your letter. But now it's all telephone, texting and ghastly emails, isn't it?'

'So you only ever really spoke on the phone?' Kennedy pushed. It was obvious that Alice and Harry communicated a lot, but the detective was discreetly trying to find out the essence or their relationship.

'Mostly,' Alice replied, appearing deep in consideration. 'Occasionally we'd meet up at events, but you know, with Neil, Vincent, Lizabeth and Bob around, chatting by phone seemed to be the best way to have a private one-to-one conversation.'

'And was privacy required?' Kennedy asked, thinking he couldn't possibly be subtler if he tried.

'Oh, you know, Detective,' Alice laughed. 'It's always better to be discreet when one is gossiping.'

Kennedy looked at Alice Cain. He studied her closely. Was she daring him to be indiscreet and come right out and ask the question, *Were you having an affair with Harry Ford?*

'Tell me, Mrs . . . sorry, I mean, tell me, Alice, did Harry and Bob get on okay?'

'Well, they weren't best buddies, if that's what you mean, and yes, of course, Bob knew all about Harry and myself, but, well, we both had our families and took security, I suppose, from that. Bob doesn't believe in confrontation. He believes that if you leave things alone, they will sort themselves out of their own accord, and if the situation doesn't go away of its own accord, then the person will just have to deal with that. You know, Inspector, I don't think there is anything either of us could throw at Bob that he couldn't deal with. His philosophy is, and always has been, that there's nothing that can happen to you that you should get too hung up about, because no matter the circumstances, we're still all going to wake up the next morning and we'll eat and we'll wash and go about our day. That's the fact of the matter. The rest—well, that's just an ever-changing set of fiction and you have to help rewrite it to fit in with your own story. He absolutely believes that, lives his life that way and rarely gets upset. Vincent thinks it's because Bob suffered some great loss or disappointment when he was younger and probably went through a very traumatic time getting over that. Vincent also thinks that when Bob managed to get over this big thing, whatever it was, everything else since is small potatoes.'

'So, Harry and your husband never argued?' Kennedy asked, feeling a door closing on him.

'Goodness no, never at all,' Alice laughed and then stopped laughing. 'I can't believe I'm laughing today, the same day Harry died.'

Her eyes started to well up again. She kept her sobbing in check this time as she said, 'Tell me, Christy Kennedy, please will you tell me . . .' she paused to find either her words, or the courage to ask her question. 'Would

Harry have suffered? All Vincent would say was that Harry was murdered. But what exactly does that mean? I've never known anyone who was murdered before. Was he shot? Was he stabbed? Was he poisoned? Was he drowned? Was he . . . was he hanged? Tell me, Christy, but please don't lie to me, because if you lie, you won't be half the man Harry told me you were, and I will never ever forgive you.'

'Alice, it is my understanding that Harry was probably unconscious when he was murdered. I can't tell you much more at this stage, but I will say that I don't believe he died what you would call a traumatic death.'

'Was his body . . .' Alice started her question and then bit down on her lip. 'Was his body . . .' she stopped talking again and shook her head furiously, apparently frustrated with herself for not being able to find an appropriate word. 'Was his body all mangled up and destroyed? I mean, he's dead and all that and why should it matter? It's just that it feels important.'

Kennedy fought away a vision of Ford on Taylor's table with nine stab wounds all neatly lined up in the shape of a cross.

'When I saw him,' Kennedy began, in his quiet, gentle and comforting voice, 'he looked like he might have been sleeping.'

Kennedy wasn't exactly lying; it was more that the truth was always a certain person's version of the facts.

Chapter Twenty-Four

AND THAT WAS the end of the first day on the Harry Ford case. King dropped Kennedy off at his house and returned to North Bridge House to start compiling a timetable for Ford's last day on this earth.

Tuesday, 30 August

07.00	*Rises*
07.30	*Breakfast at home*
07.45	*Arrives in office*
08.30	*Jill Codona arrives at office*
13.48	*Call to Alice Cain*
18.30	*Meets Neil Roberts at gym*
19.35	*Drink with Neil Roberts*
20.00–24.00	*Murdered*

31 August

06.30	*Discovered by 'George' in St Martin's Gardens*

Later that evening, Kennedy and ann rea—after a fleeting visit en route to Superintendent David Peters' leaving do up at Kentish Town—visited Harry Ford's home to pay their respects to his widow.

It was the third time Kennedy had been to Ford's house, but it was ann rea's first visit.

Lizabeth Ford, Babe Ford and Vincent O'Connor were there, as were Babe's two older sisters. At least, Kennedy immediately assumed they were the sisters because they all shared Ford and Babe's distinctive curved eyebrows.

'I'm sorry about earlier,' O'Connor said, for it was he who greeted ann rea and Kennedy at the door. 'I don't know what came over me. I just don't know what came over me. I think I just must have got my whatsits in a twist because you were *questioning* me. I seemed to come over all Noel

Coward and awkward for some strange reason. All I can do now is apologise and say that I'll make myself available to you for questioning tomorrow
morning.'

'It happens,' Kennedy conceded gracefully. 'It's more to do with the
fact that when someone from your circle of friends is murdered, no one
really knows how to deal with it or how to behave. People generally, and
I'm not referring to you here, but some people wonder how they should
behave in front of the police, if only to assure them they didn't commit the
terrible crime. Naturally enough, by behaving in this obviously strange way,
they give off the appearance of . . . well—'

'Being strange?' O'Connor added.

'Well, yes.'

'But a good chap like yourself takes all of the above into account?'
O'Connor continued.

'Well,' Kennedy replied as ann rea spotted Lizabeth across the room,
excused herself and went to offer her condolences. 'The next thing you
have to consider is the mind of the murderer. They are capable of reading
the above situation as not being strange, but being entirely natural, and
they endeavour to give off the appearance of innocence while looking
guilty.'

'The double bluff?' O'Connor said.

'More like the multi-layered bluff,' Kennedy replied, his mind now on
the other side of the room. He felt he should cross the room as soon as possible to Lizabeth and ann rea, before that developed into an awkward situation. Sometimes it's better just to go up to people in mourning and offer
your condolences immediately. In seeking a better time, all you usually do
is add to the awkwardness.

'So, how do you learn to see through it all?' O'Connor asked, his back
to ann rea and Lizabeth.

'You don't,' Kennedy said, close to a whisper.

'You don't?'

'No, it's a waste of time trying to second-guess suspects,' Kennedy
expanded, focusing back in on O'Connor again. 'Some people are just not
nice people, but that doesn't necessarily mean they are murderers or even
criminals for that matter. I've got to admit, I don't usually heed my natural instincts on people. I . . . I mean, the team and I just go out there and
dig up as many facts as possible and then let the facts and the evidence
speak rather than try to fathom the personalities involved. One of the

important things that people, even suspects, fail to realise is that, nine times out of ten, the police are questioning them *only* to gather information. Really that's primarily what we're after. From the other side though, the people we question are simply trying to show us that they are not guilty.'

'But what about your questions and, "What were you doing between the hours of 6 p.m. yesterday evening and 3 a.m. this morning?" You can't tell me you ask everybody that question, can you?'

'Not every person, no,' Kennedy said, with an apologetic smile. 'It's totally wrong to generalise, but the facts are that the majority of victims are murdered by someone they knew. Naturally enough, when we question people in the victim's circle of acquaintances, we ask that question more to rule them out of our investigation. For instance, a wife might have been staying overnight with her mother, brother or sister, or even something simpler like being at the hairdresser's, or dentist, or even at a dinner party at the time of the murder. Now, at all of the above locations, she will have been in the presence of one if not several witnesses at the exact time, not to mention an hour before and an hour after the murder. With an alibi like the ones mentioned, 99 times out of 100, you can say that the wife couldn't have done it. So you can rule her out of your investigation, and you save valuable investigation time by not having to check out her alibi further, and her motives, relationships etc., etc. In short, when you ask someone for their alibi, what you are doing is generally trying to rule them out of your investigation rather than counting them in.'

'Right,' O'Connor replied, looking a little relieved. 'So, what you're saying is that I've not been watching enough telly?'

'Well, sir,' Kennedy tried his hand (unsuccessfully) at affecting a stage voice. 'That all depends on what *time* you were watching the telly!'

By this point, ann rea and Lizabeth had made their way over to the priest and the policeman only to hear the priest declare, 'Oh, I much prefer to watch the mirror; it's infinitely more interesting.'

Kennedy extended his hand to Lizabeth, who took it but did no shake it. She just stood there in the room, holding Kennedy's right hand in both her hands.

'How are you doing?' Kennedy asked.

'Oh, mostly I'm living in a series of reflections. Like, I keep flashing back to the last time I saw Harry. My memories are of how normal everything was. You know, just another routine start to the day in our house with the three of us doing our thing, sometimes paying attention to each other and sometimes more preoccupied with our own chores. He looked cool. He always looked cool. I remember fixing his tie before he left the house and brushing some fluff from the jacket he'd just bought on Saturday.'

Lizabeth stopped talking and broke into a warm gentle smile before continuing, 'He was just like a boy heading off to school, proud of his new jacket. I remember thinking how similar in a lot of ways men and boys are. Whereas girls—or at least my three—are always keen to leave childish things behind them, men seem to be happy to remain boys all of their lives.'

'You've got it right there,' ann rea added, smoothing her hand up and down Kennedy's back.

Lizabeth sighed, as if she hadn't been listening to ann rea, before saying, 'I was thinking earlier that there must be something more. I keep waiting for this big shock to come along and hit me smack between the eyes. I feel like I'm walking into a strange room and I'm all tensed up in preparation for this big something—I know not what. I feel there is something lurking in one of the corners or behind a door, and it's like my body is sprung tight as a coil, waiting for this thing, person or animal to pounce on me, but it never appears. Tell me, Christy, when is it going to come? When will I collapse in a heap?'

'It's just your defence mechanism,' O'Connor answered. 'It's your body protecting you, Lizabeth. Gradually the enormity of this situation will hit you, but what your body is doing is delaying that reaction until you are able to cope with it.'

At which point they were joined by one of Ford's young daughters.

'Christy, this is Von, our eldest daughter. Von, this is Christy Kennedy. Your dad and I became friends with him over the last few months.'

Von attempted a polite greeting, even going as far as shaking Kennedy's hand, then she said something, more off-microphone than quiet.

'Sorry?' Kennedy said, fearing that his ears were deceiving him in the little he picked up.

'Well, as you've asked, what I said was that this is all so fucking civilised,' she barked, addressing all four of the grown-ups. Then she continued, 'My dad's dead. He's just been murdered, and all you lot are doing is standing around like you're at a fucking dinner party. Won't someone *please* do something about catching the fucker who did this to my father?'

'Darling,' Lizabeth protested.

'And you're the *biggest* offender,' Von spat at her mother. 'If you hadn't always been driving him to provide a bigger house, bigger cars, bigger holidays, you wouldn't have driven him into the arms of death.'

By this time, Babe and the third sister, Vycky, had rushed across, and they went to comfort their sister, completely ignoring their mother.

'Come on, Von,' Vycky said. 'This is neither the time nor the place.'

'But it's so fucking pathetic,' Von cried. 'Our father is dead and look at them all. What is this? Is this another of those regular appeals for Fr O'Connor's roof? I mean, just how many holes are in the fucking roof? Would it not just be cheaper to get a new one? Or is it a fundraiser for SOS? Is it a Tupperware party? Or is it perhaps the launch of a political career? Duh! No, it's none of the above; it's only our dead father's fucking wake. Doesn't someone care about our father? *Hello!* He's dead, you know! Someone murdered him . . . could—'

The rest of her outburst disappeared under a cloud of 'There, there' and 'Oh, poor Von' and 'Let's get you upstairs' from her two sisters.

Lizabeth started to apologise and make excuses on her daughter's behalf.

'I won't hear of this, Lizabeth. It's not your fault. I've told you before, "If you roll about in the dirt, you end up speaking filth." She needs her mouth washed out with soap and water, does that one. I've warned you, she needs to be taken in hand and shown the error of her ways. That was absolutely un-forgiv-able,' O'Connor said, pronouncing 'unforgivable' in three long syllables and with more venom than Von Ford had been able to muster with her swear words.

'Shush now, Vincent,' Lizabeth pleaded. 'Von has just lost her dad; they were all very close. Harry was very close to the three of them. They all doted on him, and they're very close to each other, which I suppose is a very good thing in times like these.'

'They'll need all their resolve to get though this,' Kennedy added in a quiet voice. It seemed no one but he had noticed that everyone's voice had risen considerably in volume since Von's outburst. 'What you have to realise is that her anger is not directed at you. She's hurting and lashing out at everything and everyone around her, that's all.'

'It's all my fault,' Lizabeth said in a much quieter voice than before. 'You just can't win. Either you're strong and keep it together to support your daughters in their time of need, or you're a wreck and go to pieces and people complain that you're not looking after your family properly. But I know, some day soon I'm going to suffer; you mark my words.'

'Listen,' ann rea said, patting Lizabeth's back. 'Christy's right. This has nothing to do with you. You need to know that. We should leave you in peace though; we'll go now. Will you be okay?'

'Yes, yes I'll be fine,' Lizabeth said. 'Will you stay, Vincent? I'm not sure I'm capable of a three to one at this stage.'

'Of course, I will, Lizabeth,' O'Connor said. 'Whatever you need, you know that I'm here for you, don't you?'

'Okay, we'll leave you to it,' Kennedy said as he shook both their hands and kissed Lizabeth on both cheeks. 'I'll see you both tomorrow.'

Chapter Twenty-Five

'WHAT DID YOU make of that?' ann rea asked as they fastened their seat belts in her maroon Ford Popular saloon. 'A bit of a domestic,' Kennedy began. 'I'm sure it was nothing more than that. Emotions are naturally running at a high and any and all baggage rises to the surface.'

'Didn't you find it weird that all the sisters comforted each other? None of them went to the defence or comfort of their mother?'

'I'd say they've had a few "three to ones"—as Lizabeth called them—before.'

They drove straight to their favourite Italian restaurant, the one on Parkway, where they enjoyed dinner and a glass of wine, and returned to Primrose Hill without once mentioning the politics of their romance. In truth, it was a wonderful relief for both of them not to mention the 'Us' factor.

She parked her car outside Kennedy's house at the foot of the hill, and they went for a walk up Primrose Hill, without talking, but obviously lost in their thoughts. Kennedy reflected that at the beginning of their relationship he would have been petrified about having so much silence between them. But the silence did not mean that they had nothing to say to each other for that particular time. The silence—or more the need not to be rid of silence—was a sign that they were now totally comfortable with each other. When Kennedy had first met ann rea, he could never describe how intoxicated he was with her, with her manner and with her beauty. He would quite literally count the time until their next meeting. In lighter moments, he kidded himself about dropping by *Camden News Journal* just to catch a glimpse of her. In darker moments, he was not sure how much of a joke that was.

Before Kennedy and ann rea had become 'something other than friends', he had so desperately wanted to make that connection. In the space before you make love for the first time, Kennedy felt, you had a mountain as big as the world to climb. He wasn't the type who needed to climb the mountain just because it was there. No, he felt with all of his heart and soul *and* being that making love with ann rea was the only thing in his life that mattered. The fact that at one point such an outcome had seemed so unlikely had made his heartache so unbearable that he realised that if he had had a taste for alcohol, he might just have turned to it as a medicine.

Then one night, several months into their relationship, they were in his house, and she took him by the hand and led him to his bedroom, and the most wonderful thing in the world happened between them.

And, yes, it had been all that he had expected and more.

But . . . yes, there is always a 'but', Kennedy thought, *but* making love with ann rea had not really sealed, concluded or begun anything.

No.

He was not even sure he had expected it to do so. But he had thought that it would, well . . . that was when he found out that being lovers did not really affect the love status of two people.

In hindsight, he had then begun to realise just how close he had been to making love with ann rea for the previous few months before they had chased the butterfly for the first time. He supposed the biggest thing that ann rea had taught him was that making love was not as much a sign of love, or show of emotion, as it was a pastime of enjoyment. Yes, perhaps the greater the love—fondness was her exact word—the greater the fondness of the two participants, the greater the enjoyment.

She had teased him over the fact that he had grown up believing that when two people fall in love, they live happily every after. He had claimed he did not feel so but knew that there was more than a little truth in her accusation. He also felt that if perhaps he had spent a little more time during his life addressing matters of the heart, then he might—just might—have been better equipped to deal with ann rea when he found her.

He wondered how one so natural, so intelligent and so beautiful could be so cynical. Her beauty never ceased to amaze him. Still, particularly after some time apart, she would take his breath away when he saw her again. When they made love, she gave him his missing breath back again.

And yet other times, like when they had visited the Ford house together, he felt totally at ease and at peace with her and was completely happy to do ordinary things—things like going for a walk on Primrose Hill. He was shocked at just how much enjoyment he received from just being with her. All the time, from the very first moment he had met her, he had always felt that ann rea knew something that he did not know. Sometimes she behaved as if this knowledge made her sad; other times Kennedy felt as if she were thinking, *Don't worry, you'll get there.*

'We rarely have a chance to speak together, these days,' ann rea said out of the blue. They were standing at the top of Primrose Hill, looking over the magnificence that was London's distinctive night lights.

Kennedy's first reaction was to agree and apologise, and then he realised that she was voicing not a criticism, but her own regret.

'I miss our chats, Christy,' she continued after a few moments' consideration. 'Just me and you and your amusing observations on life.'

'I do, too,' Kennedy admitted.

'Maybe it's just the Harry Ford thing brings it all home. I mean, if you prefer me not to talk about him as you're working on the case . . .'

'No, it's fine.'

'It's just that you used to say that the more detached you can make yourself from the victim, the better you can do your job,' ann rea said and took a seat on the grass.

Kennedy made an ah-you-know shrug of the shoulders.

'Well, I was just thinking, and I know I'd met him only once, but he seemed a really nice guy, in a world of relatively few good guys. Then he goes out one day and doesn't come home. Can you imagine that?'

Kennedy was walking around ann rea. There was no one else about; they had the crown of the hill to themselves.

'No,' was all he could say.

'I can't either,' ann rea said as she lay back into the grass and gazed at the stars. 'In a single day, a wife loses a husband and three daughters lose their father. Just think of all the plans we are all busy making, all the sacrifices we are all enduring for something, we know not what, down the line. And then there's . . . nothing.'

'But don't you think Lizabeth is quite strong?'

'Yes, I did think she seemed relatively stress-free, but I bet you that's all a front in order to protect her daughters. But you don't think . . . goodness, Kennedy, you've been a cop too long if you're actually suspecting Lizabeth Ford.'

'Well, no,' Kennedy started. 'I mean, I don't think she's *not* a suspect, and I don't think she *is* a suspect.'

'I know, I know,' ann rea said, sitting up, a smile finding a way on to her serious face. 'You've-got-to-wait-until-you-get-all-the-facts,' she sang in a rat-tat-tat. 'But surely to goodness, Christy, you've got a better suspect than his wife, the mother of his children?'

'ann rea, if only it were that simple. If only we could rule out wives, husbands and children, we would solve most cases and solve them in hours. But in actual fact, statistically speaking, in the majority of cases, the victim and the murderer know each other.'

'So, does she have an alibi?'

'Well, so far one of our suspects claims that they must be innocent just because they don't have an alibi,' Kennedy claimed, carefully refraining from allowing himself to be drawn too easily on facts of his current case.

'How so?'

'Well, they maintain—'

'I love it when you do that, Christy,' ann rea said, jumping up and playfully digging him in the ribs. 'Even to me and after all the stuff we've been through together.'

'What?'

'Don't pretend you don't know. Whenever you don't want me to know someone, like just there when you didn't want me to know if you were talking about a man or a woman, you said, "Well, *they* maintain." Go on anyway.'

'As I was about to say, this particular person maintains that if they had committed the murder, then they would have made sure they had an alibi.'

'Is that always the case?' ann rea asked.

'Well, if a murder is well planned, there's usually a great alibi. However, say for instance it's an accidental death—you know, where there was malice but perhaps no intent to take a life. Then the suspect is forced to think on the hoof, as it were, and come up with some kind of reason, cum excuse and/or alibi, all of which have to fit the circumstances.'

They walked over and sat down on one of the two wooden park benches which added another couple of feet to Primrose Hill's existing 212 feet (and 8 inches).

'Talking about not talking,' Kennedy began once they were comfortably snuggled up against each other. 'That night we had dinner with Harry and Lizabeth, you said something about being invited to do a book with Willie Henderson. You never told me about that before. That's brilliant, isn't it? You really like his work, don't you?'

'Well, I do as it happens, but I don't feel good about taking a ride on his coat-tails. Apart from anything else, I don't really know him. I mean, yes, we've worked on a few stories together and I do think he has a great eye—'

'If only we could find a photographer with two eyes, they'd be absolutely amazing.'

'Kennedy!'

'Oops, sorry.'

'So you will be. Where was I? Yes, I do think he's a great photographer. But he's a loner. I don't really know a lot about him, and so I'm worried that whatever I write won't exactly be insightful. On top of which, as I said at dinner that night, Nick Drake's voice and words were just made for Willie's photos.'

'Well, all I'll say is: don't say no too quickly.'

'Yes, yes, Christy,' she said too quickly, interrupting Kennedy mid-sentence. 'You know what would be nice, Christy? I'd love to go down to your house and listen to some of Nick Drake's music, maybe even Bryter Layter.'

What more could a man ask for? Kennedy thought twenty minutes later. He was in his living room, listening to one of the top ten albums ever made, drinking an energising cup of tea and enjoying the company of the most incredible woman he had ever met in his life.

For Kennedy, the secret of music was listening to it—actually allowing yourself to get totally lost in it. To clear the decks mentally and physically and allow yourself to go where the music took you. And there wasn't much finer music than Nick Drake's to take you on such a trip. The mood of the music soon took both of them over, and they surrendered to Drake's hypnotic voice, stunning melodies, flawless songs and arresting arrangements. Kennedy thought that no matter what baggage, history or words spoken, when two people shared such a powerful experience—such as listening to superb music together—a definite connection of their souls was made.

They did not discuss whether or not ann rea would stay over for the night, or whether or not they would sleep together. When the music finished, he took her hand, and they went to bed together as if it was the most natural thing in the world to do.

Kennedy lay awake for a while, a long while. It wasn't that he couldn't sleep; it was more that he didn't really want to go straight to sleep. He felt great in this woman's company. He felt good being back at work again. He felt bad that he should feel good in part due to someone's death. He wondered about all the new people he had met on this long day, all the way from his first encounter with George to his last encounter with Von, Vycky and Babe.

He turned around to look at ann rea only to find that she was contentedly lying on her side, staring at him.

She was smiling.

His eyes asked, *What?*

'I was just thinking that this might just be a form of love, and if it is, I was thinking that I was quite enjoying it—being in love in this unresolved kind of way. I suppose I've discovered that I'm happy being unhappy with things left unresolved.'

'Hmph, it's just that I never want to look at you and see a look of regret instead of a look of love,' Kennedy said quietly.

ann rea stretched out her hand and ran her fingers through Kennedy's thick black hair. She was always trying to get him to grow it longer, but just as it was starting to look great to her eyes, he would always get it trimmed.

'It's just that today, with Alice Cain,' Kennedy mused, 'I had this overwhelming feeling that she was unhappy with her lot. You know, I had this feeling that she felt that her husband was all she was going to get in her life and that fact was the biggest disappointment in her life. I found myself wondering whether when they were together he had ever seen the look I saw in her eyes today. You know, when she was talking about him, her head was just turned a little to one side and her eyebrows were tightening down over her eyes. Did he ever see this look? And you know what? Maybe he did; maybe he did see it but he was just so preoccupied with his own thoughts that it just didn't bother him.'

'Or maybe it's only something that a stranger can ever see,' she whispered.

Kennedy looked at ann rea as though searching for something.

Without saying another word, she leaned across and kissed him. It wasn't a goodnight kiss.

No, the goodnight kiss came twenty-eight minutes later.

Chapter Twenty-Six

IF KENNEDY HAD realised just how hectic Wednesday morning was going to be, he would have savoured his early morning walk over Primrose Hill just a wee bit more. Perhaps he would even have dallied just a tad longer to enjoy NW1's most famous patchwork quilt—a pure blue of the sky, the expansive greens of the hill and the hints of browns on the hill's one hundred and fifty-nine leafy grand masters—as the autumn started to declare its intentions.

But he didn't, as you don't. He certainly paused to spare a thought for the wondrous sights around him but saved most of his thought bank to concentrate on the Harry Ford case.

As he walked into the reception of North Bridge House, Desk Sergeant Tim Flynn greeted him.

'Good morning to you, Inspector.' Flynn paused and hoked around on his busy desk. 'Two things for you . . . here we are. First, it seems that Harry Ford didn't dine out after his trip to the gym with Mr Roberts— well, at least according to the staff of Café DeLancey, who recognised him and said he hadn't dined there in the last week. The lads checked all the regular eating establishments and drew a blank everywhere.'

Flynn crunched up the first piece of paper and expertly tossed it into the wastepaper basket behind him. He focused on the remaining piece of paper: 'It seems that Miss Christine Riley's mystery caller is a neighbour of yours.'

'Oh?'

'Yes, the trace on that number she gave us came through. The call was made from one of the two telephone boxes outside the Queen's on the corner of Primrose Hill Road and Regent's Park Road.'

'Oh, the twin guards of St George's Terrace?'

'I believe so. Anyway, the call was made from the one closest to the hill.'

'Interesting. Thanks for that,' Kennedy said half to himself as he continued on the journey to his office on the second floor.

The first telephone call he received was at 07.56. The caller was Dr Leonard Taylor.

'Yes, pretty standard stuff, I'm afraid,' Taylor began. 'Traces of Rohypnol—better known under its street name of Roofies, the date-rape drug—*were* present in Ford's blood stream. Obviously that was what our murderer used to keep him still while carrying out his precise execution.'

'Hmm,' Kennedy grunted as he wrote down some notes on his pad. 'And have you discovered whether the stab wounds were made before or after death?'

'From the amount of blood he lost, I'd say definitely before. But do you know what the most surprising thing about the stab wounds was?'

'Go on,' Kennedy replied, allowing Taylor a moment of his favoured theatrics.

'They were all straight wounds. The knife was at right angles to the body for each and every wound,' Taylor declared. He seemed, even down the phone line, to be surprised at this bit of news.

'Okay,' Kennedy began, drawing a wee matchstick man on the pad in front of him as he spoke down the phone. 'Let's assume Harry Ford would have been lying horizontal with the murderer perhaps even sitting on him . . .'

Mid-theory, Kennedy had another thought: 'Tell me, Leonard, Ford wasn't interfered with, was he?'

'Not in a sexual manner, no,' Taylor replied immediately.

'Okay, so our murderer is sitting on top of a comatose body and he's stabbing him,' Kennedy continued as he drew another wee matchstick man, this time sitting atop the first one and with a knife attached to his matchstick hand. 'Even then,' Kennedy said as he drew the trajectory of the knife hand, 'the knife is still going to enter the body at an angle. The only way to achieve 90-degree wounds is if the assailant knelt above the body and carefully stabbed him from above in the predetermined way.'

'Our cross?' Taylor qualified.

'Yes, our cross,' Kennedy continued. 'The murderer would have to position the knife with one hand and use that same hand to hold it in position while the other hand either forced, or hammered, the knife down into the body.'

'That would make sense,' the doctor replied in agreement.

'But why would our murderer go to all of that trouble?'

'Beats me,' Taylor conceded. 'But that's why you're the detective and

I'm the doctor. I have to give you all the information I can, and then you have to work out the facts.'

'It's like Harry was murdered by a robot,' Kennedy said, and then laughed at the absurdity of his statement.

'Maybe a robot who was also a religious fanatic,' Taylor offered.

Kennedy thought for a few seconds, hearing only the electronic static between himself and Taylor as the detective continued to doodle with his sketches. Eventually he said, 'Tell me, Leonard, have you come up with a more exact time of death yet?'

'Oh, I'd say no earlier that 10.30 and no later than 11.30.'

'Come on, Leonard. How do you always manage to make such accurate guesstimates?'

'By not being afraid of being wrong,' Taylor replied. 'When I closed Mr Ford's eyelids up at the scene, I noticed that rigor mortis was at an advanced stage. Further examination of his jaw and neck confirmed this for me and let me know that the rigor was at the blunt end of the twelve hours required. His core body temperature was 22 degrees C, which means he'd lost 15 degrees. A body loses approximately 1½ degrees per hour, so by the time I examined him at 08.00, he'd been dead for about ten hours. This was also confirmed by the advanced state of lividity—the draining of the body's blood to the lowest part of the body. Again, this is a process that requires approximately a twelve-hour cycle.

'And then we when carried out the autopsy, I checked the level of potassium in the eyes. When the eye is living, the potassium level is low, but the transparent jelly-like substance rises at a known rate after death. And into that you add—'

'Years of experience,' Kennedy interrupted before adding as an afterthought: 'What can you tell me about the last time he ate.'

'There was nothing left in his small intestines, and it takes around seven hours for that process, so I'd say his last meal was probably around lunchtime.'

They bid their telephonic goodbyes, and Kennedy dug out and amended the murder time on the schedule of Harry Ford's day that King had started to prepare the previous evening:

Tuesday, 30 August

07.00	*Rises*
07.30	*Breakfast at home*
07.45	*Arrives in office*

08.30	*Jill Codona arrives at office*
13.48	*Call to Alice Cain*
18.30	*Meets Neil Roberts at gym*
19.35	*Drink with Neil Roberts*
22.30–23.30	*Murdered*
31 August	
06.30	*Discovered by 'George' in St Martin's Gardens*

Kennedy studied the schedule and double-checked the times to ensure that there were no conflicts. He left to King the task of filling in as many gaps as possible.

He and Irvine then collected Lizabeth Ford to accompany her to formally identify the remains. Kennedy thought that the word 'remains' was strangely appropriate. The lifeless skin-bag of fat, bones, organs, muscles and congealing blood remained behind to rot on this earth, while the spirit and soul travelled to wherever, depending on the individual survivor's beliefs.

Kennedy leaned more towards the fodder-for-the-worms theory.

Lizabeth Ford was still poised and controlled and very apologetic for her daughters' behaviour the previous evening. For Kennedy, it was telling that the mother did not refer to her offspring in the singular.

Kennedy and Irvine were both amazed (they discussed it later) by Lizabeth's composure as she looked at the corpse of her husband, the father of her children. She simply said, 'Yes, that was he.'

Those were her exact words.

'Yes, that was he,' she said quietly and without any apparent anguish or pain, implying that she had totally accepted the passing of her husband.

Following the identification, she requested that Kennedy and she go somewhere for a cup of coffee. She refused his invitation to North Bridge House.

'I'm prepared to acknowledge, of course,' she said, qualifying herself, 'that you probably have the perfect cup of coffee on tap, but I would imagine you would be somewhat challenged in the cappuccino department.'

'I know the perfect place,' Kennedy replied, and he had Irvine drop them off in Primrose Hill village, where they took a table on the pavement outside Cacao and awaited the delivery of the cappuccino, tea and two almond croissants they had ordered the moment they arrived.

In the intervening time, they discovered that the talk of Regent's Park

Road was about how badly the local optician's hair had been cut. The punch line of the story was: 'And you'll never guess where the hairdresser in question bought his glasses.'

'This is good,' Lizabeth began when their order arrived. 'To be out in public—it means I need to keep it together. I know you think I'm callous, Christy.'

'I think no such thing.'

'It's just that I refuse to let this ruin our lives. Harry is dead. Tragically, that is a fact that none of us can change,' she paused as she bit her bottom lip. 'But I'm damned if my daughters and I are going to end up victims as well. Vincent has a theory that everyone knows they're going to die; it's just that we don't really believe it. He says, "Once we learn how to die, we learn how to live." He says that Harry had learned how to live. I'm not sure if he thought that was meant to make it easier for either my daughters or myself, but I can tell you this, Christy—I am not going to end up allowing my daughters or myself to become preoccupied with making someone pay for this. Harry was a great father and a considerate husband, but I don't need revenge, Christy. I don't want to live my life seeking revenge. I'll leave all of that to you and the authorities. I'll leave the well-being of Harry's soul in the equally capable hands of Vincent O'Connor, but *I'll* take responsibility for my daughters' lives and for my own life. We have to get beyond this, Christy. We must get beyond this!'

'Yes,' Kennedy agreed. 'But if I could just say that you also have to allow your daughters and yourself time to grieve the loss of Harry. You need to accept that that is equally important, Lizabeth.'

'Yes, it is, Christy, but if you don't mind, we'll save all of that for when we are strong enough to deal with it.'

'Of course,' Kennedy replied gracefully, marvelling at the strength and resolve of women, the backbone of the majority of families he had come into contact with.

'Now, Christy,' Lizabeth said with a sigh and brushed off some of the offending croissant-icing sugar which had fallen on to her black dress. 'You can ask me whatever you like. Out here in public will be fine, and then perhaps you can bring me up to date with how things are proceeding on the case from your side.'

'Well, we're still pretty much at the information-gathering stage, I'm afraid,' Kennedy replied as he suddenly had a vision of a *Stars Wars*-type robot stabbing Harry Ford nine times as it manoeuvred its way around his body. Kennedy knew not where the image had come from, but when it disappeared, he continued, 'Did you speak to Harry at all during that day?'

'Yes, we spoke once in the morning, around about a quarter past eleven, and then once in the afternoon around twenty past four.'

'What were the reasons for the calls?'

'Just normal husband and wife calls, no drama. We generally spoke two or three times a day. You know the type of things—just to compare notes, catch up on things and remind each other about chores, this and that really.'

'So nothing specific then?' Kennedy asked quickly.

'Let me think now,' Lizabeth replied, and then squinted her eyes tightly and stared across the road as if the information she (and Kennedy) were seeking would flash up on a television screen in the bookie's. 'In the morning, we discussed Babe's school fees for next year. We talked about him going to the gym that evening with Neil. He was just really reminding me that he didn't need catering for. Then, in the afternoon, I told him what I'd been doing most of the day, which was surfing the net trying to find a bargain week at some great hotel for Christmas. I tell you, when your youngest daughter asks you how many stars a hotel has, it shows you that kids these days take a lot to be impressed.'

'Did you come up with anything?' Kennedy asked, hoping that a prompt, any prompt, might throw up some useful information for him.

'Yes, I think I did,' Lizabeth said, then stopped and seemed to pick herself up mentally before continuing, 'Well, there'll be no more hotels for all of us, at least not for a good while.'

'Did he seem concerned about anything?'

'No, not really. I mean, of course now, because of what's happened, I have been examining and re-examining every single thing he said to me and how he said it—you know, to try and discover if there was some kind of clue, perhaps, and that I'd been too preoccupied with my own stuff to pick up on it at the time. But there was nothing. It was just a standard boring, friendly, telephone conversation like husbands and wives are having up and down the country each and every day of the year. Yes, that's it—I knew there was something else we discussed. My car.'

'Oh?'

'Yes, not so much my car as opposed to how difficult it was proving to get a car for me. You see, a friend of one of Harry's customers was meant to be delivering a VW Golf to Harry's office. It was meant to have been a run-around for me. But we were the ones getting the run-around. Harry had had the money—wouldn't you know it, but cash, of course—ready for the dealer for several days, and each day there would be a different excuse as to why the car wasn't ready or why the dealer couldn't deliver it.'

'Right,' Kennedy said, nodding his head knowingly. 'This car wouldn't have had a £2,000 price tag, would it?'

'Yes, in fact,' Lizabeth replied, completing another bit of the puzzle for Kennedy. 'I kept telling him he was foolish for running around Camden Town with all that cash on him, but Harry was so conscientious he didn't want to use the office safe just in case some of the staff saw him withdrawing the stash and got the wrong idea.'

'So you spoke to him again at 4.20—then what?' Kennedy asked.

'That was it; that was the last time I spoke to my husband, Christy. Can you believe that?'

Kennedy knew that the conversation could go one of two ways at this point. He chose to steer it away from the maudlin route.

'So, you knew he was going to the gym with Neil?'

'Correct.'

'And what was their standard routine for their regular night at the gym?'

'They'd go and work out for an hour or so and then, at the very least, have a drink, and occasionally they'd go and have a meal. On gym nights, we'd each look after our own eating arrangements.'

'Were they really good friends, Neil and Harry?'

'What, you think they weren't?' Lizabeth inquired, looking very interested.

'Well, I'm not sure. I suppose if they were still going to the gym together all these years later, there must have still been some kind of connection,' Kennedy replied.

'I suppose after all those years it's hard to know if they still hung out together out of habit or if they really liked each other. I think, from Harry's side, he liked to go the gym but he was too self-conscious to go by himself,' Lizabeth replied.

'And from Neil's side?' Kennedy pushed.

'Well, the honest answer is I don't really know. I certainly know that Neil is vain enough not to be worried about going to the gym by himself. I suspect, from Neil's point of view, it was better to be seen to have a long-standing friend than not, and Harry fitted that role perfectly. I've never really been able to get to know Neil well. I always seemed to make him nervous, for some reason.'

'Did Harry and Neil dine together the day before yesterday ?' Kennedy asked.

Lizabeth smiled at Kennedy before asking, 'You've already spoken to Neil, right?'

'Right, or at least some of my colleagues have,' Kennedy confirmed, trying hard not to look upset by her response.

'So therefore you know the answer to that question. You weren't trying to catch Neil or myself out, were you, *Detective Inspector?*'

'No, not at all, Lizabeth. I'm trying to ascertain the facts as you know them. So, do you know where Harry dined after the gym?'

'Right,' Lizabeth replied rather curtly. 'Well, the honest answer, as I know it, is they'd usually decided on the hoof as it were. You know, if Neil had a heavy date, as was often the case, Harry was just as happy to pop across the road to the Café DeLancey and enjoy supper and a couple of glasses of wine by himself. He'd read a book or read his paper.'

'We've checked and he didn't dine at the Café DeLancey,' Kennedy offered.

'I'm sorry. I just don't know what he did. He certainly didn't expect me to hang around to see what he and Neil were going to do before I made my plans for the evening.'

'Which were?'

Lizabeth smiled again. It seemed to take all of her energy to raise her smile. This one was a forgiving smile, and Kennedy returned it with an I've-got-to-ask shrug.

'Actually I went to the movies. I went to see *American Dreamz* at the 02 Centre, and afterwards I made it a bit of a theme night for myself by enjoying an American hamburger and milkshake experience just to the right of the cinema as you exit. I caught a cab home around twenty to eleven. Babe was on a sleepover with her best friend, Katie Toal. Harry wasn't here; I imagined they had enjoyed a few drinks and got into a chinwag about the old days—the Four Musketeers days at college—as is their wont. I went to bed, read for an hour or so and must have been asleep by midnight.'

Kennedy kept looking at her but didn't say anything, so she continued, 'Then I woke up yesterday morning. Harry wasn't to be seen anywhere, so I figured he'd either left early or he and Neil must have got wrecked and

Harry (also) had stayed out all night on a sleepover—just like Babe. I doubt if Katie Toal and my daughter were drinking anything other than milk though. I went about my morning, expecting a call from Harry, and the next thing there was a policeman knocking on my door and—'

'Have you spoken to Neil?'

'No, not yet, just Vincey.'

'Did you ring Fr O'Connor or did he ring you?'

'He rang me first. Vincey always rings everyone first. I do believe he lives on the telephone.'

'The modern vicar,' Kennedy added.

'Or even the modem vicar, as Harry often referred to him,' Lizabeth said, breaking into another laboured laugh. 'Perhaps he even takes confessions by telephone.'

'Sermons by email,' Kennedy said, trying to make her feel a little better.

'Can I ask you a favour, Christy?'

'Of course!'

'I was wondering if you'd mind accompanying me to the reading of Harry's will. Harry's solicitor, Leslie Russell, being the gentleman he is, has already been on to offer his condolences. Of course, being me, and trying to be as normal as possible, I asked him if there was anything I needed to be aware of, anything that needed addressing. He said that Harry had made a will last year and that when I was feeling better, he would go through it with me. I said I needed to do it sooner rather than later. I told him I would like to do it today, in fact. And, you know, I could ask Vincey, but he might be mentioned in it, and it could be a bit messy—do you know what I mean?'

'I think so.'

'So, would you come with me?'

'Yes, I'd be happy to accompany you if that's what you definitely want.'

'Yes, I feel I need to have someone there with me. Since I spoke to Leslie Russell, I have this dread that our affairs are in a mess and we don't have a penny and, you know, I can deal with that . . . eventually, but I need someone to be there for me and, as I say, everyone else I know might be involved, and I don't want our daughters being there in case it's as bad as I expect. So, thank you. That's actually taken a great load off my mind.'

They made arrangements to meet later on that day, just after lunchtime, at Leslie Russell's office.

When Kennedy returned to his office, there was a message waiting for him to ring Jill Codona, Harry Ford's secretary at CABS. Kennedy returned her call immediately.

When he introduced himself over the phone, she whispered down the line, 'Are you in your office?'

'Yes.'

'Okay, stay right there. I'll ring you back immediately.'

She was as good as her word, because forty seconds later Kennedy's phone rang.

'Have you heard what's happened?' she enquired. This time she was speaking in full voice, perhaps an octave higher to accommodate her excitement.

'No,' Kennedy replied, but he was hooked.

'CABS have only gone and brought forward the date of Frazer McCracken's tribunal.'

'To when?' Kennedy asked.

'To today!' she half-shouted down the phone. 'To second thing this morning, in fact, and it gets better. Listen to this. They've dropped the suspension. They're claiming that without Harry there are no charges for McCracken to answer. His solicitor has demanded that all accusations be dropped and that McCracken be reinstated immediately. CABS rolled over on all of the staff and on Harry's memory, and there's even talk of McCracken coming back into the office by the end of the week as branch manager, as part of some deal McCracken's solicitor and CABS worked out.'

'Unbelievable,' Kennedy said, because that's what he was thinking. 'Was there no documentary proof of McCracken's dealings?'

'Yes, there certainly was, but when I got in this morning, I discovered that CABS had already removed all of our files—that's all Harry's files that were in my filing cabinet. Your people took the other files from Harry's office yesterday. But the CABS head-office people cleared out my filing cabinets this morning. So I bet you they'll surely go and bury all of the evidence.'

'But why would they do that if McCracken were genuinely guilty?'

'Simple,' Jill Codona replied enthusiastically. 'See, if McCracken were found guilty and sacked, well what with us being a public company and all, it wouldn't look good, and on top of which there'd be disgruntled share holders. The share prices would plummet, with people on the board being asked to account for themselves. The manager of their most successful branch has died in mysterious circumstances. So, cosmetically speaking, when you think about it, this is the best result by far for CABS. They're now saying to the public and their shareholders that there was no crime to answer on the McCracken front. So, if there's no dirt, there are no red faces either! Look, someone is coming—I'll try to come and see you later.'

'Shall I come over?'

'No, for heaven's sake, don't dare,' she hissed. 'They mustn't know you know, and they must never know that I've told you anything. I'll contact you later. Bye.'

Chapter Twenty-Seven

NO SOONER HAD Kennedy returned his phone to the cradle than it started to ring again, the new vibration buzzing in the palm of his hand. Without even having let go of it, he picked up the handset and returned it to his right ear. The uncomfortable heat of the handset made him feel as if the skin of his ear had been burnt in the sun, one of Kennedy's least favourite sensations.

What Kennedy heard from his handset was an almighty racket, and through what sounded like a female fracas, he could make out the distinctive Ballymena tones of Desk Sergeant Tim Flynn.

Flynn advised Kennedy that the three Ford sisters were in reception and demanding to see Kennedy forthwith. 'Immediately would be preferable,' Flynn, the canny rock of North Bridge House, said, quoting the noisiest of the sisters.

Less than a minute later, the three sisters paraded into Kennedy's office in ascending order of height, but not age.

Kennedy knew that, at twelve years old, Babe was the youngest. She was the second tallest and was dressed as if she had come straight off the set of M*A*S*H. From his conversations with Harry, he also knew that inwardly she was screaming, fighting and in training with all of her might to become, and be accepted as, a teenager. Harry had predicted that over the next three years there would be lots of 'slamming doors, grunts, moodies, wobblers, spotted-Herberts following her around, studs, escalation in clothing allowance, loud music, intolerance of adults', adding, 'And that'll be on the good days.' He said that he and Lizabeth had been through it twice with their first two daughters and were not exactly looking forward to it again.

Kennedy offered his hand to Babe and said, 'Hello, Babe.'

'Her name is Bernadette,' the shortest one said. 'That's one of the first things we are determined to sort out. She's nearly a teenager, and everyone's still addressing her as a baby.'

'Yes, Von's right,' Babe added with a smile. 'I know you were introduced to me as Babe, and in a way it's my own fault for not correcting it years ago, but I do want to clear it up now.'

So the oldest is the shortest, Kennedy thought, and said, 'Sorry, Bernadette, you're 100 per cent right. The only way to effect the change is to advise people of your proper name and advise people to use it.'

Bernadette smiled a large smile as if her day's ambition had been achieved and, as directed, she took Kennedy's comfy leather chair.

Kennedy extended his hand to Von, who took it somewhat reluctantly. She was the smartest dressed of the three, wearing an orange high-collared shirt and a Blackwatch tartan kilt affair over black leggings, completing her ensemble with simple black Nike trainers. Von looked to be about to say something else but instead took the left of the two chairs in front of Kennedy's chair, as directed.

Kennedy then took and shook the third daughter's hand. For a split second he was going to say, 'And so, by a process of elimination and deduction, you must be Vycky.' But he resisted on the grounds that it might open an ugly can of worms vis-à-vis his progress on their father's case. Vycky was undistinguished in that she was the middle daughter in age and height. She had a fuller figure than her sisters and was the only one of them prepared to leave her legs bare to the summer air. She was wearing a blue micro mini and two T-shirts, the top one in light blue, sleeveless, with the four Led Zeppelin logos, and the under one white with long sleeves. Bizarrely, her outfit was completed with a pair of black (treacherously) high-heeled sandals. She was also the only sister to wear make-up. They all had similarly styled French bobs with fringes, although in different colours. (Vycky's was dark red, Von's was black and Bernadette's was platinum blonde.) They all definitely looked like sisters, with Harry Ford's facial features very present in all of them. Kennedy was surprised that the father's forehead, eyes, nose, mouth, chin and particularly eyebrows would betray hints of beauty when transposed to a female face.

'Right,' Von said immediately they were all settled. 'We came here today to find out what progress you're making with our father's murder.'

'We mean,' Bernadette added, a tad more diplomatically, 'we were wondering if you were making *any* progress.'

If looks could kill, the stares boring into Bernadette from either side would certainly have been lethal.

'Well, here's the thing,' Kennedy began, trying to avoid being patronised like a leper, and walking over to his tea cupboard as he offered them drinks while he continued talking. 'I like to start off real slow, you know, so that I don't miss anything. Because if I miss something vital in the early stages, I can find myself wasting several days going down the same blind alleys to pick up on my mistakes. So, although my approach might seem slow—'

Von let out a loud sigh of exasperation, which Kennedy allowed to evaporate into the empyrean before he continued: 'But in the long run, I assure you, my method is actually a lot faster, not to mention more efficient.'

'Are you confident you're going to catch the man—' Vycky started.

'Or woman,' Von interrupted.

'Or woman,' Vycky corrected herself and finished her question, 'who murdered our dad?'

As Kennedy walked back behind his desk, he gave Von and Bernadette a mineral water each (they both wanted bottles, not glasses). Vycky had requested a Coca-Cola (Kennedy's last one and served in a glass). He thought Vycky's question was a tricky one, particularly considering the mood of the lynch mob in front of him.

He took a sip of the tea he had poured himself several minutes previously. He knew that it would be cold and he positively hated cold tea, but the gesture of even allowing the vile liquid to moisten his lips gave him the time he needed to prepare his answer: 'Oh, I'd be a fool if I made a boast such as that.'

'Correct answer, man,' Von said immediately and visibly relaxing, but not for long. 'Is there anything at all we can do to help?'

'Well, quite a bit really. You can tell me about your father. Ba . . . sorry, Bernadette, you're the only one who lived at home, right?'

'Yes,' she replied.

'And had you noticed anything unusual about his behaviour around the house?'

Both sisters averted their gaze from Kennedy to Bernadette.

'Well, not really, no,' she began self consciously. 'I mean, no, not at all. He was always being my dad and always caring for me and making sure that my life was okay, but at the same time he never shared any of his problems with me. We grow up believing that our fathers are always okay.'

'Yes,' Kennedy said, reflecting on his own experiences with Harry Ford. He imagined Harry would have been the perfect father.

'He was always there when you needed him but disappeared into the air when he knew you needed some space,' Bernadette said.

'Tell me, Von, how often did you speak to your father?'

'He used to ring me twice a week,' she replied. Kennedy had been thinking about the girls' accents since they had sat down. They all spoke well, sounding well educated, but there were just slight differences between them all, and now he was picking up on what it was.

Von's time at Queen's University had effected a few tiny touches of Ulster-speak and twang; the more vulgar street sounds of Manchester were just starting to creep into Vycky's accent; while Bernadette's was an undiluted, uncontaminated version of her parents' speak.

Now that he had sussed that, Kennedy found it easier to tune into the girls' words.

'He always rang me on Sunday mornings,' Von continued and broke into a smile, the first she had displayed since entering Kennedy's office. 'He knew how much I loved my Sunday morning lie-ins, so he knew he'd always get me if he rang around 11.30 in the morning.

'And did you . . . did he say anything to you that aroused your suspicions?'

'Not really no, but like Bernadette said, he was always the one checking up on us, to see if we were okay. I would always be patronising to him—you know, "Dad, I'm okay. I know how to look after myself, you know." And he'd say, "You know, if there is ever anything you need to speak to me, or your mum, about, night or day, it doesn't matter, you can always ring us. We just need you to know that we're always here. There is nothing you can do that will ever disappoint us . . ."' Von stopped talking and crunched up her chin until her lips completely disappeared into her face. It was not a pretty sight, Kennedy thought, but it was enough to enable her to hold back her tears. She started talking again, wiping beneath her eyes with the front and back of the forefinger of her right hand. 'And I'd say, "Yes, Dad, okay, I gotta go now. Bye."'

Kennedy looked at Vycky as if to invite, 'And you?'

The look was all that was needed.

'No, nothing either. I think the last time I saw him was about a month ago, when my parents got back from holiday. We used to speak only about once a month. For some reason, my father and I aren't . . . I mean, weren't . . . particularly close. We never were, in fact. And it wasn't just with my father, but my mother as well. I don't really know why. It might have something to do with the fact that by the time I came along, the novelty of an only child (Von) was no longer the case, and then Babe popped along five years after

me and she was always the baby, which left me stuck right in the middle, like
a minister without a portfolio. At first I thought, well one's the oldest and
other's the youngest, so what does that make me? But I soon got over it. I
don't know—maybe they'd hoped I was going to be a boy or something.

'No, no, it's okay really,' Vycky protested over the wave of universal
sympathy greeting her. 'I mean, my father especially would feel particularly guilty about it and he'd give me some kind of treat. They got nothing
back from me either. When he'd ring me, he'd tell me off about not ringing them. I'd tell him I didn't ring because I didn't have anything to say.'

'*I'd* have those types of conversations with him as well,' Von admitted.
'You know, when I went to Queen's, I eventually found a group of my own
friends over there. Pretty soon, it was out of sight and out of mind, and
when I'd speak to him on my two calls a week, when *he* rang me, I'd say
that I hadn't rung because I'd nothing I needed to tell them, and he'd say,
"Look, you must make the effort." His theory was that our relationships
of the future, you know when we were married with our own families,
totally depended on the effort and energy we put into our family now.'

'Yes, yes,' Bernadette agreed. 'He would often say that to me as well.
Our father had all these little theories. That was one of them. He told me
that when I left home it would be a very important part of my development
as an individual and that it was the interaction I enjoyed with him and
Mum then, rather than when I was growing up, that was going to be the
basis for our relationship in later years. He kept saying that he and Mum
really liked us.' Bernadette turned and touched Vycky's arm before continuing, 'Liked all of us, as people, and yes as parents they were duty-bound
to love us, but that didn't mean they would have to *like* us too. Dad claimed
they really liked us as people He told me they were desperate to continue
to have a relationship with us into adulthood, you know, beyond the
parent–daughter things.'

'You're right, you know,' Von cut in enthusiastically. 'He said that to
me as well. He said you could pick your friends but you couldn't pick your
family, and that he and Mum had both agreed that if they hadn't been our
parents, they'd really have liked to be our friends. I mean, that was such a
wonderful thing to say, wasn't it?'

Kennedy agreed with Von. Vycky didn't appear uncomfortable; in fact
she even picked up on the theme of her father's theory and ran with it: 'You
know, I remember when we were young, he had this trick for getting rid
of a toothache.'

'Oh, yes,' Bernadette enthused.

'Oh, yeah,' Von said, drawing much longer on the 'Oh'. 'The Harry Ford 100-per-cent cure for a toothache.'

Kennedy was sure a look of amusement was creeping over his face, because two of the girls, Vycky and Bernadette, said in unison, 'It's true, and it really worked.'

'You're not going to tell me he taught the old whiskey trick to his children?'

'No, no, much better than that,' Von started and then hesitated. 'No. Vycky, you should tell him—you remembered it first.'

'Well,' Vycky started, sounding very much the proud daughter. 'From as long as I can remember, our father would use this with us. When we were suffering from a particularly bad case of toothache, he'd say, "Look, the secret here is to embrace the pain." He'd lecture us about not fighting the pain. That, he said, only served to make it much worse. He'd tell us not to try to make the pain disappear. Then he'd start off his rap with, "Okay Vycky, remember now for me the worst ever pain that you ever felt. Tell me what it was." And you'd remember something really bad, like the time Von broke her arm.'

'Twice,' Von chipped in and stopped.

'Oh, yes, I'd forgotten,' Vycky gushed. 'Once you fell off your chair when we were sitting at the dinner table, and the second time you fell in the garden. Em . . . Bernadette has always suffered for her sport—twisted ankles, pulled hamstrings. You'd lots of those injuries, didn't you?'

'Yes,' Bernadette agreed with a sigh. 'And for some strange reason, you decided you could fly, and you tried to jump down ten stairs at once, breaking your ankle and spraining your wrist.'

'It always seemed to work on the telly,' Vycky said, recalling her own pain. 'Anyway, back to our dad. He'd continue with, "Okay, the pain you are now feeling—is it the worst pain you've ever felt?" And you'd think, no, it's not; it's not half as bad as it was on such and such an occasion. So he'd say, "Okay, and you got through that, didn't you?" Of course, you'd have to agree with him. So he'd say, "Okay, now at least you know you're going to get through this. All you need to do is demand that whoever you think it is—the devil or whoever—throws their worst pain at you. And you say, 'I can handle this.'" He told us that when we take the pain straight on the chin—you know, when you adopted that confrontational approach—well, you could deal with it, couldn't you? Now, there certainly didn't seem to be a lot of logic to his reassuring approach, but the fact that you thought it would work, well, he really did manage to talk you through the pain.'

'And then, when you got older,' Von said, looking over to Bernadette, 'and you'd have your heart broken by a boy . . . I mean, it could have been anything; maybe he'd told his mates he'd kissed you, maybe the boy you fancied who you didn't have the courage to speak to went out with someone else, maybe even your best friend. Perhaps the boy of your dreams had just dumped you. Dad would know, he always knew, and he'd come to your aid with a similar rap, "Embrace the heartache. Know that it's never ever going to feel this bad again"—if it was your first time. He'd always tell you that, no matter how bad you felt, you were never going to feel quite so devastated again in your whole life. And that just as your heart had mended in the past, it would certainly mend in the future. He was absolutely brilliant because he would never belittle you or how you were feeling. You always got the impression he knew exactly how badly you were feeling and he'd try and work that to your advantage.'

'He used to tell me,' Vycky said next, 'that disappointments are only disappointments if you lead a boring, sad life. He'd say that if you bothered to fill your life full of stuff, then if you got knocked back on one thing, there were lots of other events in your life to feel good about, and pretty soon you'd forget about your disappointment.'

The sisters nodded positively at this.

'Bernadette was telling us last night about the happiest she'd ever seen our dad,' Vycky continued, staying with the flow. Kennedy was happy to let them reminisce on the grounds that it was obviously good for them. Moreover, you never knew what information they were going to throw up.

'Our Bernadette runs quite a bit,' Vycky was saying. 'She's very good actually Anyway, there was one special meeting at Highbury last October, and she was brilliant and won three silver medals—'

Bernadette gave an oh-please-don't-embarrass-me shrug before Von took up the story.

'And when Bernadette won the third medal, she took it straight to Dad and gave it to him.'

Then Bernadette took over the narration of her own story: 'At first, he refused to accept it, saying they were mine and I'd won them all, and then I persisted, saying that *maybe* I'd won the first one with speed, the second one with a bit of speed and a bit of luck, but I knew the third one had come my way because of my training, and I knew that without his patience and coaching, I'd never have won it. I told him I *really* wanted him to have it and equally that I really wanted people to know that I wanted him to have it. So he accepted it reluctantly. But I tell you, it was totally awesome the way Dad beamed when I gave him the medal, it was like a totally better feeling than winning the medals in the first place.'

'Inspector,' Von said grandly, as though drawing some kind of line under the conversation so far, 'can we talk about how our father died?'

Kennedy couldn't remember the last time a conversation had turned from light to dark so quickly.

'I'm not sure—' Kennedy started, only to be interrupted by Bernadette.

'No, Mr Kennedy. This is important to us.'

'There are a few things we need to resolve for ourselves,' Von said, taking over from her youngest sister.

'Oh,' Kennedy replied, concerned with where this might lead.

'Well, here's the thing. We don't want to feel bitter towards our father,' Von continued, choosing her words as carefully as Lennon and McCartney had always done.

'Right.'

'You know, we've found ourselves wondering if he put up much of a fight against his attacker. You know, surely there must have been a point when he felt that he'd nothing to lose. I hope I'm not being too morbid for you, but, you know, I was thinking that if there was a point he knew he was going to die, well then, what did he have to lose? We've all agreed if it came down to it, and the choice was either for him to be murdered or for us still to have him, even maimed, well, there'd be no competition.'

And all the sisters nodded agreement. Kennedy did not know what to say, so he said nothing.

Von did not need much encouragement to proceed: 'Say, for instance, he'd struggled and he'd been stabbed repeatedly in the hands and arms, you know, maybe even lost the power of his arms, well then, we could have lived with that, couldn't we?'

This time Von didn't wait. She ploughed on with, 'Say, heaven forbid, that he lost his eye in the fight, well again we would all have been okay with that, even he was only say half-fit, that would have been fine as well; we could all have looked after him. Do you see what I mean? I mean, I suppose . . . what I'm saying is: why didn't he just put up more of a fight? That's all.'

She started sobbing and her sisters came to comfort her.

'From the little I knew of your father,' Kennedy started, moved by Von's peculiar sentiment, 'if there had been a chance in a million that he could have survived this ordeal, he would have gone for it. You all meant more to him than life itself. I can't tell you yet exactly how and what happened to your father, but I promise you that one day I will sit down with all of you and explain to you exactly what happened. In the meantime, I can just tell you that your father was not in a position where he could have fought his way out of this situation. Neither his bravery nor his love for you came into question. There are few things in this world of which I am surer.'

'Thank you,' Vycky said. 'And we'll take you up on your offer.'

'Have you questioned Alice yet?' Von asked, revealing that she still had an agenda she was working on.

'Yes, I have, as a matter of a fact,' Kennedy replied, careful not to add anything in qualification.

'And?' Von pushed, seeking qualification.

'Nothing relevant so far.'

'What about the fact that Caroline, her daughter, is mentioned in our father's will?' Von said, a blast of silence descending on the office.

'Von!' Vycky hissed. 'We all agreed that we weren't going to bring this up here.'

'It seems to me,' Von replied in justification, 'that with nothing else appearing yet on the bleak horizon of this investigation, Inspector Kennedy needs all the help he can get.'

'How do you know about the will?' Kennedy asked, trying hard to appear matter of fact.

'Well, my mother and I went through our father's papers late yesterday evening, and we came across a copy of our father's will by accident. I can tell you it makes for very interesting reading—very interesting indeed.'

'How so?' Kennedy asked.

'Well, it would appear that the Cain family is to benefit from my father's death.'

'Von!' Bernadette hissed. 'We positively shouldn't be discussing this with the *police!*'

'In lieu of anything else, I'm prepared to risk the faux pas,' Von announced to her sisters and Kennedy.

When they left, Kennedy wondered why their mother had gone through the whole charade of inviting him to the reading of the will when it was obvious that she already knew the details. Why would she have done that? Was she leading him to a potential suspect and just hadn't figured on her tempestuous daughters' discussing the previous evening's discovery with him?

It wasn't even lunchtime on the second day of the case, Kennedy thought, and so far two suspects had been delivered to him. One more likely than the other, it had to be said.

Chapter Twenty-Eight

A REPORT ON John Riley made by a detective sergeant from the Finance Division was amongst the files and reports on Kennedy's desk. Kennedy spent half an hour or so going through the various pieces of paperwork, and when he felt he had done enough to keep on top of the mountain, he had DC King go and fetch a car to collect him from the front door of North Bridge House.

Kennedy spent the time it took her to negotiate the heavy traffic watching the endless stream of people making their way up Parkway towards the Zoo and Regent's Park—with attentive good children in tow; then the return pedestrian traffic—with tired, restless and disobedient kids on the way back down Parkway towards Camden Town tube station. Kennedy stood studying other people contentedly, getting on with their lives, all efficiently and happily chasing their goals and dreams. He thought of all those involved with Harry Ford, and how all of their rushing about, now so aimless, had been put on hold, albeit temporarily.

King had to hoot the horn of the Granada a couple of times before Kennedy realised that his carriage had arrived.

'Right, first a slight diversion,' he announced as he clicked himself into the passenger seat. 'Let's pay a quick visit to Mrs Sally Riley.'

And so they did.

'Is there any news?' Sally asked anxiously the minute she opened her front door. Kennedy had decided to leave King waiting in the car during this chat. Apart from anything else, she could fend off the overzealous traffic wardens during his absence.

'Actually, no,' Kennedy conceded immediately, and then, as he saw her shoulders slump in disappointment, quickly added, 'That also means there's no bad news either, which in a way is good news, don't you think?'

'I suppose in a way it is,' Sally Riley said and broke into a laugh—the first time Kennedy had ever witnessed her laughing. 'Either that, or you've joined Labour's team of overworked spin doctors. Come on in and join me for a cup of tea.'

As Kennedy entered the house, he noticed King settle further down into the seat of the car and start to study her notebook. He also enjoyed a quick flash of himself and Mrs Riley swimming about in a rather large cup of tea.

Kennedy and Sally Riley engaged in apparent small talk for a few minutes, although the bit about Fr Vincent O'Connor and his recent bereavement could never have been considered small talk, particularly from the priest's point of view.

'John is missing fifty-four days now,' Sally announced to her kitchen walls as she boiled up another kettle of water to make a second pot of tea, more for herself, it should be stated. 'Fifty-four days, and you know what's the most noticeable thing?'

'What's that?' Kennedy felt compelled to ask, even though he feared he knew the answer.

'It's that people, even your own family, no matter how concerned they all were initially, start to get on with their lives. Sure, they rang me up several times a day at the beginning, then that dropped to once a day in the second week, and then twice a week, and now it's mostly weekly calls of concern and infrequent visits, near enough the same as it was before John disappeared. But you know what hurts the most?'

Again Kennedy repeated the words she wanted to hear before she continued: 'I'll tell you what hurts most. Now when our children ring up, they don't even mention their father. Good God, it certainly lets me know how quickly I'm going to be forgotten when I die. Fr O'Connor says that a life going is like watching a stone being dropped in the pond. We are the stone and our life is the ripples. Then as the ripples start to fade after we've gone, our survivors try—for a time—to keep the ripples going. In time though, they realise that the pond has grown still again, as though nothing on this earth has changed.'

'It's probably more awkwardness on their part. They don't want to hurt you by mentioning his name every time,' Kennedy offered in genuine sympathy, and then dropped a couple of the questions which were his primary reason for visiting in the first place. 'But are you okay though, I mean physically, financially?'

'Yes and yes,' Sally Riley replied, as though both topics were the least of her concerns. 'I mean, our joint account is very healthy. On top of which, I have some savings of my own. We own our house outright, so there's no mortgage. I've got three rental investment properties, one in Richmond and two in Wimbledon. To be very honest, they were John's idea. When my father died—oh, it has to be some thirty years ago—he left me the family home in Richmond. With John's encouragement and support, I converted the house into three flats, and with the rental return I took out a mortgage on a dilapidated house in Wimbledon a couple of years later, and I converted that into four flats. Three years after that, the house next-door came up for sale at a very reasonable price, so I bought that as well. This was before the property boom when you could still find the odd bargain. When they started to hike the interest rates in the mid-eighties, I ploughed all the rental income into paying off the mortgages. This means, of course, the rentals are mostly clear profit, so I just sit back and watch my three (four, if you count here) properties grow in value, year in, year out.'

'John was obviously aware that all your rental investments were sound.'

'Oh, yes. I mean, he helped me when I needed help, but he always insisted that the properties stay in my name. He said that way it could always be entirely up to me what I did with the houses if and when I wanted to sell them or give them away to our kids.'

'Mrs Riley, the first day I came here, you mentioned to me that you and John had had an argument. I think that it's about time you told me what that argument was all about.'

'Why now?' Sally Riley demanded. 'Has something happened?'

'Well, no.'

'You don't sound too convincing,' Mrs Riley said as she wet the two teaspoons of tea lying lazily about the bottom of her red-flowered, white china teapot.

'Well, I suppose it's only fair to tell you that I believe Mr Riley's still alive.'

'There's been a sighting, hasn't there? You're just playing it down, aren't you?' Sally Riley asked, so beside herself with excitement that she missed the teapot and spilled the boiling water all over her draining board.

Luckily enough, she missed her own fingers and shooed Kennedy away as he tried to help.

'Okay,' Kennedy began, resolving to give her the bit of information he had picked up in the report he had read before he came out. 'In the 1980s and early 1990s, John was receiving substantial bonuses from work.'

'Yes?' Sally Riley said, implying that she already knew but wasn't sure of his point. She continued to dry her hands on a red-flowered, white tea towel.

Kennedy was trying to figure out if she meant, 'Yes' as in 'Yes, I know' or 'Yes' as in 'Yes, really, was he indeed?' He continued, 'Now, unlike his monthly salary which was paid straight into his bank account, these annual bonuses were paid into an account in the Isle of Man.'

'Really?' Mrs Riley said, this time very much emphasising a question.

'Yes, and the money was drawn from the Isle of Man bank once a year, always in cash.'

'*Really?*' Mrs Riley said, sitting down in obvious shock, her jaw in danger of hitting her recently washed, polished and shining terracotta ten-inch tiles.

'Obviously that's where we lost the paper trail,' Kennedy conceded.

'Have you any idea of the amounts of money?'

'Yes,' Kennedy replied, removing a notebook from inside his black jacket. 'From 1977 to 1983, bonuses totalling £983,560 were dealt with in this manner.'

'*A million quid!*'

'Give or take a few bob.'

'You realise that's probably a million and a half with interest over the years. Well, I'll be!' Sally said in a whisper. 'What about taxes?'

'Those figures are all after tax. Mr Riley declared and paid taxes on all his salary and bonuses,' Kennedy announced.

'Holy Christmas cake!' Sally said. Kennedy couldn't work out whether or not she had blasphemed—he would check it later with Vincent O'Connor. The stunned Mrs Riley and the Ulster detective both sat in silence for a minute or so. She was the first to end their moment of consideration.

'I've just realised. It all makes sense now, or at least part of it does.'

'Sorry?' Now it was Kennedy's turn to sound confused.

'When we were having our argument that morning, he kept telling me my properties would be worth about a million and a half quid to me after tax.'

'So he wanted to leave?' Kennedy said, managing to sneak *the* question in at last.

'He wanted a divorce,' Sally announced, staring blankly at the unblemished floor. 'Sixty-one years old and he wanted a divorce. Huh, men, you never do grow up, do you? Any of you?'

Kennedy hoped it was a rhetorical question and declined—on the mental grounds of the Fifth Amendment—to answer.

'He came to me, and he sat down at that table you're sitting at, and said, very matter of fact, that he wanted to retire, and just as I was about to say, "That'll be nice for us, dear; we can go to Italy a lot more," he added, "And I want a divorce." Of course I said, "We can't get a divorce—we're Catholic." He laughed and said he didn't need a religious divorce, a legal one would do.'

Kennedy sat listening to this woman acknowledge to him for the first time in two months that her marriage was over.

'I told him, no way,' she said. 'I said, "Not for as long as I can draw breath in my body." Then he said, very calmly mind you—he was good at that. When there was something he wanted to discuss with you, he'd always speak in real calm tones, and if I disagreed or shouted, he'd just sit quietly and wait until I stopped ranting, and then he'd continue. He said in a calm voice that what we'd had together wasn't a life for him. What was it he said? He said, "I don't call this, us together, a life." And here I was always thinking I was the one who'd drawn the short straw. He said we should leave this house to the children, to Christine, her sister and her brother. And that's when he said, "Your rental properties are worth over a million and a half after tax." He said he would take care of himself. He also informed me that he wasn't going to do this—"live this lie"—a day longer than he had to. He said our children were old enough now that we didn't need to stay together for them.'

Sally Riley stopped talking and broke into a strained laugh. 'I can see you're thinking, "The crafty old codger, he had another woman, didn't he?"'

'No, actually, I was thinking how sad it was that humans have such a capability and capacity to hurt one another.'

Mrs Sally Riley stopped laughing; she shrugged her shoulders and said, 'Well, I was having none of it. I told him, "No divorce." Who am I going to meet at this time in my life? I wasn't going to be pitied by my family and friends. I wasn't going to be thrown out of my own church. I'm sixty-three for heaven's sake—have I been making sacrifices all my life just to end up on the scrap heap? He bloody owed me! He owed me my life! Holy Christmas cake—he owed me his life! We were only waiting for this moment to arrive. The kids have fled the coop, he was about to retire, and we had our little nest egg. This was meant to be *our* time!'

On two counts, Kennedy was almost guilty of a careless laugh. Firstly, there was that 'Holy Christmas cake' again, and secondly, he had never ever heard of three million pounds being referred to as 'a *little* nest egg' before. Luckily enough, he composed himself just in time.

'What was I to do?' she pleaded, as if desperate for Kennedy to see her point of view. 'Was I meant to say, "Yes, of course, dear, you just run along there and enjoy the rest of your life." A marriage is a partnership for life, Detective Inspector. Yes, he might have managed to save up a million and a half quid for himself, but he wouldn't have been able to be in a position to earn any of that if I hadn't been there backing him and looking after him, his family and our home.'

Kennedy felt it would be inappropriate at that point to mention the three houses currently in Mrs Riley's name, which, in her own words, John Riley had helped her set up.

'But there was no other women?' was all Kennedy could find to say in the hope of offering the woman some comfort.

'Nobody he would admit to.'

'But from the little I've learned about the man, he doesn't seem the type.'

'I believe you're right,' she said, taking heart indeed from his words. 'On top of which, he swore to me that he'd never cheated on me. He told me he'd never even entertained the idea. But he said . . . there's always a "but" isn't there? *But,* he said, there was someone he felt he might be able to enjoy some happiness with and he felt he owed it to himself, and to her, to give it a try. I mean, what a joke! I tried to remind him that he wasn't a schoolboy or even a middle-aged man any more, for heaven's sake. I told him to admit to himself that he was almost an old-age pensioner and that perhaps he'd better wise up and accept his lot, because there was no way, no way in this world, that I was going to give him a divorce.'

'But what I can't work out is why he didn't just leave you. Why did he go to all the trouble of the big Houdini act?'

'To understand that, you'd need to know John a bit better, Detective; he just can't stand things to be messy. He can't abide turmoil. He always claimed that things like our sanity, the lack of chaos and so on, all hang together only by the weakest threads. He said the secret was that we should never ever test the strength of the thread. He hated confrontation. Why do you think he spent so much time in the garden? The plants can't talk back to him. As long as he gave them care and attention, they'd obediently do as they were told and all look good at the same time. John gets physically ill when any part of his life is in mayhem. That's why he ran. He was avoiding a messy situation. When he first disappeared, I was going to tell Christine and Fr O'Connor about the argument we'd had, but when it got down to it, I just felt I couldn't discuss the divorce issue with Fr O'Connor. I was just so ashamed, and I felt I would have been betraying Fr O'Connor by telling you, the police, what I couldn't tell my priest. Truth be told, I also expected John to come running home with his tail between his legs or for you to find him for me. I knew if he came back of his own accord, he'd be such a sheep for the rest of our days together, but if the police brought him home, he'd have been ill to his dying day. Sometimes I used to send myself to sleep wondering, you know, why he couldn't just have waited until death had separated us.'

That gloomy thought was the one with which Kennedy left the Glenilla Road household. He officially informed Mrs Riley that he could no longer classify John Riley as a missing person. Camden Town CID would close the file on her husband. He also left her some leaflets on the Missing Person Helpline, 0500 700 700, knowing that the sterling support work they did was second to none.

Chapter Twenty-Nine

ENNEDY AND KING resumed their journey to the Marylebone home of Alice Cain, nearly knocking down Barbara Windsor, one of the district's famous residents, in the process.

Kennedy had given King the two-minute version of the Riley story. King's only observation was: 'Well, I suppose it only goes to emphasise how important it is to choose the right person to share our lives with. I suppose my generation has less of an excuse for getting it wrong than you, the previous generation, had.'

The conversation they were about to have with Mrs Alice Cain would not contradict the young police officer's philosophy.

Alice Cain immediately greeted them, particularly Kennedy, with an oh-I've-been-expecting-you smile. She said, 'Oh, it's you,'

Kennedy seemed to recall similar phrasing on the unsigned photo found in Harry Ford's wallet.

Alice Cain's cup of tea was much superior to Mrs Riley's, Kennedy thought, as the very first sip passed his lips. A great cup of tea should be too hot to drink when you first receive it. Furthermore, their current interviewee had gone to the trouble of extending her sandwich preparation to accommodate the unscheduled lunchtime visitors.

'Well, I suppose you heard that Caroline, my daughter, has been mentioned in Harry's will? I suppose that does tend to let the cat out of the bag somewhat.'

'Only slightly,' Kennedy replied, trying hard not to sound judgemental.

'As they say in the movies,' Alice said warmly, 'I had better start at the beginning, hadn't I?'

'Yes, this time I think that would be advisable,' Kennedy offered, he hoped, as encouragement.

'I mean, it's not that any of us—Harry, Vincent or myself—told you any lies when we talked to you about our past. It's just that we didn't tell you all of the truth. If only the story had ended during our college days, maybe it would have been a happy tale and perhaps less complicated than it is about to become.' Alice Cain had the ability to address Kennedy as though he were the only one present.

DC Dot King, it should be noted, had the ability to know that she should not break this communication between Cain and Kennedy, but that she should simply chronicle the proceeding in full, in words fitting the master, Dr John Watson.

'So, I believe Vincent told you all about our college days: how me met; how Vincey fell for me—I'm quoting Fr O'Connor verbatim there of course; how Harry fell for me—Neil's words; how I fell for Harry—my words; and then how Harry and I, particularly I, listened and gave too much quarter to other people's words and therefore went off to seek comfort in the arms of others.'

'I believe I'm up-to-date with all of that,' Kennedy admitted as King raised her eyebrows slightly.

'Good,' Alice said, returning her cup of tea to the coffee table in front of them. Then she added, more voicing a thought than imparting further information, 'Goodness, as far as all the men are concerned—Harry, Vincey, Neil and Bob—my life has been a total disaster.'

Today she was wearing a sleeveless, dark blue-and-white striped top and slacks; the slacks were cream and very Jackie Kennedy.

'Well,' she continued, 'we all got on with our lives for a few years as Vincent turned to religion. He would claim—frequently and loudly—that he became a priest because I shunned him romantically. In my defence, I would claim I never had the feeling he was ever very attracted to girls.'

Alice laughed her throaty laugh at this point and decided to let them in on what was amusing her: 'That's not to suggest that he's attracted to men either, of course. No, I just don't think he finds himself attracted to people in the physical sense, and if you want to get analytical about it, it really is a pretty peculiar business, isn't it? I always find it to be so, except, of course, when you're in love, and then you don't even think about it—it's just the most natural thing in the world. So my theory, and I'm sticking to it, was that Vincey wasn't physically attracted to people, and so he found a profession which would disguise what he considered to be a major flaw. Vincey being Vincey, though, threw his heart and soul into becoming a priest, and goodness weren't we all only knocked for seven (it's closer to heaven) when we were invited to his ordination a few years later.

He said that the Musketeers were his only real family and he wanted us all there.

'By this point, I had a child, Robbie, with Robert, and Harry had Von with Lizabeth. I had a husband and Harry had a wife, so why not accept Vincent's invitation? Harry and I hadn't seen each other since we'd split up, and I thought in my very mature way, life goes on blah, blah, blah. I agreed to go. I was composed, aloof and totally over Harry to the point that I was quite looking forward to seeing him and letting him know that I was over him. Then I saw him and my legs turned to jelly and I was a schoolgirl again. He was more beautiful than ever. His boyish promise had matured perfectly into the strong character of a young man and—I'm being as frank here as I know how to be—I wanted him right there and then, priests or no priests. We talked in the company of others, and I managed to keep all my true feelings in check. Apart from anything else, Lizabeth looked stunning and radiant, and I suppose I got the feeling that he was over me, so I was adult about it, but I still hung on to the arm of my husband all day long, and the day came to an end and we bid our goodbyes and that was it. A few months passed, and soon I was staring to doubt the feelings I thought I'd experienced on Vincent's big day. I dismissed them as a schoolgirl's final whim and got on with my life.

'Trust Vincent not to let sleeping dogs lie, though. He thought the ordination get-together had gone so well that we should all get together for a reunion dinner. "Why not?" I said, and so we did, and it was a great get-together. That's when I realised that my true feelings for Harry were anything but schoolgirlish. You could see Vincent and Neil look occasionally from Harry to me and then back again, you know, seeing if we were okay being with each other. Towards the end of the evening, Neil disappeared to the toilet and Vincent discreetly went off in search of the bill, without telling us. Harry immediately took my hand under the table and said that he'd never stopped loving me, and I just blurted out about how much I still loved him and how sorry I was that I'd ruined both our lives.

'We chatted a bit, generally about university, and then he said, "Look, they'll be back soon, but I'd love to meet up with you some time, just the two of us." I asked him if he thought that was wise. He said, "Well, it's your call. I'd just love to see you, but I understand why you might prefer not to." He told me where he worked and said that he would leave it entirely up to me. If I wanted to see him, I was to give him a call at work. There was no awkward transferring of pieces of paper with telephone numbers written thereon or anything tacky like that. I fought with myself for about six weeks, and then I had to do it. I just had to ring him; I couldn't bear not to any longer. So I rang him and I suggested the safety of a lunchtime meeting. We met in a little café down on St Christopher's Place—very nice and very . . . um, shall we say, off the beaten path, literally.

'And, well, it was like we'd never been apart really. The hour and a half flew past, and he seemed to be fighting with it as much as I was, because he said he'd love to meet again. He reiterated once more that he'd leave it to me and, three months later, which was the day before Christmas Eve, we met again, and this time we made love.'

Alice stopped talking and seemed to be revisiting the memory herself.

'I had such mixed emotions. I knew he did as well. It's just wasn't in either of our natures to be deceitful. We didn't meet again until the following March, by which time I was three months pregnant with Caroline, and once I knew he wasn't being cavalier about us, I told him she was his baby. In spite of everything, I told him, because I felt that he, like me, had been trying to avoid "us" like the plague. He was convinced that it was outside our control. We were just in love; it was as simple or as difficult as that. It would have made both of our lives much easier if we hadn't been, but the simple fact was that we were in love and we had to deal with it. We agreed that we'd already messed up big time by blowing it at university. He said we shouldn't mess it up any longer by denying the fact that we were in love.

'Equally, neither of us wanted to ruin the lives of those around us, so we made a pact that we would find—someway, somehow—time for each other and deal with the relationship as sensibly as we could, without ruining the lives of the people around us. We agreed to have Caroline together, but that I would bring her up in my marriage. No one but Harry and I knew it. We avoided meeting publicly. We still met as part of the group; the others would have been suspicious if we'd avoided these little get-togethers of Vincent's. We were just so scared we would let something out. We knew if we were found out, it would be over—our covert rendezvous would be history—and that's why we were so careful. We wanted to continue this precious relationship. We agreed to be as considerate as was humanly possible with our spouses. We refused point blank even to discuss the possibility of leaving our spouses *or* each other. Whatever we had to do to succeed, we were committed to finding a way through this without splitting up any of the relationships. We would joke about trying to match-make Bob and Lizabeth so that we could all live happily ever after. Truth be told, Bob and Lizabeth are more suited to each other than either of them was to either of us. However, Bob thinks Lizabeth is an opportunist and she thinks he's a boring old man with too much to say for himself and too much money that he never earned himself. Lizabeth positively hates inherited wealth. Most people who didn't—inherit, that is—do, if you see what I mean.'

'Quite,' Kennedy said in agreement, but not really sure whether he agreed or not.

'Harry and I continued. We were never given anything on a plate, but over the years we even managed to enjoy a few holidays together. I think Harry and I were rarely in each other's company socially, so no one suspected a thing. That was the main reason we were able to steal our holiday time together. I mean, if we weren't both around at the same time, no one would imagine for a moment that we were off somewhere together. Harry even went as far as to take up golf, so golfing trips would be expected and accepted. He'd say he was flying to Spain on a golfing trip, while I'd say I was catching Eurostar to Paris to catch a fashion show. We'd both do exactly those things, and then one of us would fly to meet the other.

'We also agreed not to have any more children together. It was just too painful for Harry not to be able to be a real dad; you know, the sad thing is that he's such a great dad. I had no more children with Bob either, but Harry and Lizabeth had two more girls, as you know. For some strange reason, that never had an effect on me or, more importantly, on our relationship.

'And that was that, really,' Alice said in conclusion. However, before Kennedy had a chance to ask his pending question, she added, 'I mean, you still have your dreams and you store your regrets, knowing or hoping (but never saying) that one day you'll both outgrow or cast aside the chains of your commitments and that you'll simply do what you want to do, what you've always wanted to do. The biggest regret of my life is that I didn't get to spend it with Harry. He was always telling me that experience was what you were left with when you didn't get what you wanted. I had been saving all my credits so I could finally publicly be his one day, one day in the future, but now, don't you see, it's too late.' Alice paused and, on noting Kennedy's look of concern, added, 'Oh, don't be worrying about me. I don't intend to do anything stupid; I won't always feel this low. I'll get beyond this. But if you were forcing me to be brutally honest, I'd admit that there's nothing really left for me to live for.'

'Well, of course there are the children,' Kennedy said sympathetically.

'Of course there are the children,' Alice Cain agreed.

'Did you know about the will?' Kennedy asked.

'Yes, of course,' she replied immediately. 'Harry told me he was doing it. We discussed the various ways to do it. You know, with him giving something to each of the children so no one would feel upset for whatever reason. In the end, we figured that by the time the will would come into effect, at least twenty years down the road for instance, there was a chance that our circumstances might have changed and Caroline would have known Harry was her dad. We were both desperate for her to know. I suppose the will was our safety net to ensure she did find out *eventually.*'

'And Lizabeth and Bob never knew or suspected anything about this?' Kennedy asked, as intrigued by this story as he was sure DC King was.

'Oh, Harry and I talked about that a lot. We imagined that they might have had their suspicions, but luckily neither of them was the type to seek out confirmation. And, as I say, for all we knew, they were just totally oblivious to the facts. Besides which, as a husband or as a wife, neither Harry nor I ever made them feel upset, rejected or shunned.'

'But now this?'

'Yes, now the will is about to come out, and I will have to deal with the fact that everything about our liaison could possibly come out. Neil is going to go absolutely ballistic. And I don't even have Harry around to comfort me through it. You don't know how much I need him at this moment. You'll never know how much I miss him. I feel a continuous ache in my heart,' Alice said, her hand automatically moving to her chest. She grimaced and then smiled.

Kennedy said, 'I wonder why matters of the heart are centred on the most vital organ in our body. Surely our heart has more than enough work to do—what with continually pumping the blood throughout our body—without having to take responsibility for breaks and aches of another kind as well.'

Kennedy smiled at the image as he said the words; he hadn't thought about it before. At the same time, he thought how, as ever, humans—Alice Cain in this instance—talked themselves better, demonstrating perfectly the mending power of the mind.

Then Alice's question showed that there might still be a few obstacles left in her mending process. 'Will you have to question Bob?'

'I'm afraid so. I have to after this recent information,' Kennedy admitted. 'What are you going to tell him?'

'I'll tell him the truth, or at least a part of the truth. I'll say that Harry and I had an affair, but I'll have to lie to him about how long it lasted.'

'That's your decision, of course,' Kennedy said, hoping he wasn't sounding too judgemental.

Chapter Thirty

'OKAY,' KENNEDY BEGAN. He was sitting in his office, along with Irvine, King, Allaway and a few of the other constables working on the case. And Superintendent Thomas Castle was making his presence felt by discreetly positioning himself at the back of Kennedy's office. He was in attendance for 'observation purposes', not to mention being closest to the tea cupboard in the event that a tea-drinking opportunity arose. Kennedy continued, 'So, where are we? Let's summarise what we've learned so far:

'1. Murder Victim Harry Ford, forty-six years of age.

'2. Stabbed nine times.

'3. Stab wounds form the shape of a cross.

'4. Antagonised one of his colleagues, Frazer McCracken, at work.

'5. Fathered another man's—Bob Cain's—child.

'6. . . .'

Kennedy hesitated at this point.

'What about, six, stealing a priest's lover?' Irvine said, helping out.

'Well,' Kennedy began his qualification, 'firstly, Vincent O'Connor wasn't a priest at that time and, secondly, I'm still not entirely sure they were lovers.'

'Either way,' Irvine continued, 'the only real surprise on this case is that he lived as long as he did.'

'I'm not quite sure we've come across any evidence yet which would have led to his murder, though,' Kennedy replied, hoping that someone might pick up the point for debate.

'Well, you'd have to say that fathering a child with another man's wife couldn't be all that great for your health, not to mention your long-term prospects,' Irvine said, showing that he really had nowhere to go with this point.

'Okay, let's talk about this McCracken business for a minute,' Kennedy announced, ending the laughter Irvine had succeeding in rising.

'Yes, I have to admit, I was shocked by that one,' Castle interrupted. 'This dimwit must have a donkey for a solicitor. I mean, talk about not having any sense of timing—'

'You should watch *Pop Idol*,' Kennedy offered, to more laughter.

'Getting your client off the hook on an embezzlement charge,' Castle continued, choosing to ignore the wisecrack, 'and by so doing automatically moving him to the top of the list of suspects in a murder investigation.'

'Well, I've requested all Ford's papers, sir,' Kennedy said, proving to his team that all bosses have their own superiors to report to.

'Could we not just steam in there and get them?' Irvine asked no one in particular and everyone in general.

'Well, I doubt it would do any good at this stage. The fact that they staged their tribunal so quickly shows that they'd prefer the sweeping-under-the-carpet approach to a proper house-cleaning approach, so I doubt very much that they'll leave any incriminating evidence around.'

'They're a public company, Inspector,' Castle announced. 'They have to conduct all their dealings with total accountability, so if we suspect even the slightest irregularity, then I'll have great pleasure passing them over to the relevant people at Scotland Yard.'

'I'm off to their offices in Aylesbury immediately after this briefing to interview their managing director, Mr Errol McGuinn,' Kennedy announced by way of qualification.

'Okay,' Castle said. 'Keep me posted on how it goes. In the meantime, what do we do with this Neil Roberts character? Does he have any motive to be rid of Ford?'

'Well, he has a complicated relationship with his sister,' Kennedy replied.

'Complicated?' Castle replied, his attention noticeably tweaked. 'How so?'

'Unhealthy is the word which springs to mind,' Kennedy offered, turning the heads of most in the room.

'Suspected or proven?' Castle continued.

'Suspected,' Kennedy replied. 'And so, his sister enjoying a continued relationship with Ford—and having his child—'

'Yes, yes, I get the motive,' Castle said, writing something down in his file.

'However, he appears to have an alibi for the time of Harry Ford's murder,' Kennedy replied, aware that the gathering so far was turning out to be a personal briefing to Superintendent Castle.

'Yes, from what I hear too, erm, quite an impressive alibi by all accounts,' Castle announced for the benefit of the rest of the room. 'Has that particular alibi been checked out yet?'

'No.' This time it was Irvine's turn to reply, taking a little of the heat away from Kennedy. 'I've spoken to her agent, Mick Griffiths at the Asgard Agency, and he advised me that she's working abroad at the moment but is due back in the country tomorrow morning. I'll interview her then, sir.'

'Well, let's just be careful, shall we? The last thing we need is for her to be associated with Ford's murder. The red-top papers would be all over her, and then her studio would be all over us, suing us for damages. Let's make sure we protect her. Mrs Castle tells me she's a very fine actress.'

'I believe so, sir,' Irvine replied. 'I do believe so. Anyway, her agent has set it up so that I can interview her before rehearsals for a television show she's going to work on next.'

'And what show is that?' Castle asked.

'It's a sham, sir.'

'*It's a Sham*—I've never heard of that one. Who else is in it?'

'No, sir, I meant it's—' Irvine began awkwardly.

'Of course you did, DS. I was only fooling with you,' Castle said, raising a few eyebrows including those of DI Kennedy who, in turn, continued: 'Okay, so let's see how Roberts's alibi pans out, shall we? We need to talk to Mr Cain. He's obviously got a motive now as well.'

'Okay, I can see you're well into this one. I'll leave you to it.' Castle said, making his excuses and leaving.

As soon as he was gone, Irvine said, '"*It's a Sham*, I know, DS. I was only kidding with you." Wow!'

'Okay,' Kennedy said, interrupting the titters. 'Okay, but let's not forget the very important point the superintendent made as well. We need to do everything humanly possible to keep Roberts's girlfriend's name out of this and the papers. Now, Allaway, tell me, did the door-to-door on the houses around St Martin's Gardens turn up anything?'

'Not really, sir,' Allaway replied quickly. 'One old boy takes his dog for a walk and a number two each morning—that's for the dog, of course, sir—and he avoids the square itself, but he thought he saw two drunks carrying each other into the square. Like everyone else around there, he gives the drunks and druggies a wide berth. He did say that he thought one of the two drunks he came across was definitely in a lot worse shape than the other, because one of them seemed to be experiencing difficultly in walking.'

'What time was this?' Kennedy asked, as King and Irvine started up their own conversation.

Allaway checked his notes before he continued: 'Our dog-walker thinks it was after two o'clock in the morning.'

'How were they dressed?'

'He'd no recollection, sir, other than the fact that he assumed they were drunks'

'Both of them?' Kennedy pushed.

'Yes, but he did qualify it by saying he didn't really want to hang around and take a good look at them. He only saw them from the back, and briefly at that. He didn't want them hitting on him for money. Apparently some of the inhabitants of the gardens are not as polite in their begging tactics as the locals would like.'

'Okay, good, Allaway, well done,' Kennedy said. 'Oh, congrats on your promotion, by the way—you deserve it.'

A year previously, if you had asked Kennedy for the name of one constable on his team who was a cert to remain a constable for his entire career, Allaway's would have been the first name to pass his lips. However, for some reason known only to Allaway, he had pulled his socks up and started to apply himself to his work.

'Thank you, sir,' he beamed proudly. 'I've only two months to wait now before it's official.'

'Right, DS Irvine,' Kennedy continued. 'I think another wee trip to CABS in Camden Town might be appropriate at this time. People's memories may have been refreshed by a good night's sleep, and if they look like they haven't enjoyed a good night's sleep, try and find out what they're feeling guilty about, okay? Also, when you've set up your team down there, I'd quite like it if you could take a trip over to see Lizabeth Ford and have another wee chat with her to see how she's officially reacting to the news of her new stepdaughter being in Ford's will. Let's make no mention of the fact that we knew she knew in advance about the will. I was meant to go to the official reading of the will with her, but she shied off. I think she has her suspicions that her daughters spilled the beans on her. And then maybe you'd drop in and have a quick chat with Mr Bob Cain for me.'

Chapter Thirty-One

A S INSTRUCTED, DS JAMES Irvine took the DS elect, Allaway, to see the recently widowed Lizabeth Ford.

Bernadette (formerly Babe) Ford let them into the house and told them that her mother was in the kitchen with the Irish priest.

Fr Vincent O'Connor bade his goodbyes as Bernadette introduced PC Allaway, 'and a man whose name I forget but who sounds just like James Bond in the early movies'.

Lizabeth rose to greet them. 'No Detective Inspector Kennedy this time?'

'Oh, he's off on other inquiries at the moment,' Irvine replied, accepting her gesture of an offer of a cup of coffee.

'Goodness, Babe's right—you do sound just like Sean Connery,' Lizabeth said, as she also offered Allaway a cup of rich aromatic coffee. 'Other inquiries? Is that on another case or is he still working on my husband's murder?'

'He's definitely working on your husband's case at the moment, ma'am,' Irvine replied.

Milked and sugared up, Irvine and Allaway took two of the high seats on the opposite side of the wooden preparation counter to Lizabeth Ford. By this point, Bernadette and O'Connor had left the kitchen together. Irvine could hear the front door close in the distance.

'I wanted to talk to you about the fact that Caroline Cain is mentioned in your husband's will.'

'I know. Can you believe it? What do you make of that?' Lizabeth said, cleverly returning the question to Irvine.

'Actually we were a bit more interested in what *you* make of it,' Irvine pushed firmly as Allaway prepared to take notes.

'Well, let's call a spade a spade. I suppose it must suggest that Harry got Alice pregnant before they split up.'

'Well, not exactly,' Irvine said, starting off delicately. 'Caroline Cain is not the first-born. For your theory to work, Harry would have mentioned Robbie Cain in his will. Caroline Cain was born three years after Alice and Bob Cain married.'

By the look on Lizabeth Ford's face, Irvine assumed she was aware of this.

'Oh, that's even more intriguing then. I suppose that would suggest that Harry was cheating on us,' Lizabeth replied, a little deadpan.

Irvine was surprised by how matter of fact Lizabeth Ford was about her statement. The red surround of her eyes was the only telltale sign of what she must really be suffering. Irvine couldn't work out if it was charming, or clever, that Lizabeth claimed Harry was cheating on 'us'—obviously meaning that she felt Harry was cheating on her *and* their three daughters.

'So, you weren't aware of a relationship?' Irvine asked, joining in her game of pretending that this was all new to her.

'No, sir. I was not aware of any relationship,' Lizabeth spat back at the detective sergeant instantly. She softened her approach somewhat before she continued, 'I mean, I was well aware that Alice was my husband's ex, before Harry and I met and married. We saw each other with our respective spouses and usually Fr Vincent O'Connor, whom you just met on the way in, and Alice's brother Neil—that would be Neil Roberts; Roberts is Alice's maiden name.'

'I suppose it might help if we knew exactly what Caroline Cain had been left in your husband's will.'

She studied both of the police officers for a few moments before declaring, 'Well, I've certainly nothing to hide from you. I have a rough draft of it here, somewhere.'

Lizabeth Ford then spent several seconds rummaging around a pile of papers on the kitchen table before continuing, 'Yes, I knew it was here. Here you are.'

Irvine had a quick look through the papers and noted that:

O'Connor was to receive Ford's CD collection of classic Bach.

Lizabeth was to get the house, but should she marry again within five years, she in turn would have to pass the deeds on to her children.

Lizabeth also received the funds in the two deposit accounts Harry had maintained at CABS—the account numbers were listed, and the balances (as of two years ago) were £38,000 and £129,000 respectively.

Harry Ford had also set up trusts in the names of Yvonne Ford, Vycky Ford, Bernadette Ford and Caroline Cain. Each was to receive £50,000, plus interest accrued, on her twenty-first birthday.

The inclusion of Caroline Cain was obviously the contentious issue and the first evidence of betrayal.

'Not a lot for a life together!' Lizabeth said when it appeared Irvine had absorbed the relevant information.

Her timing was correct. Irvine had another quick look down the single page before he passed it over to Allaway so he could record the details.

'If we all knew when we were going to die,' Irvine said, enjoying a less charitable thought about Ford's widow, 'I'm sure we'd all make more considerate plans.'

'Can you believe I'm not to have the house if I remarry within five years?'

'I think it's quite common,' Allaway suggested. 'Should you remarry, the property would become jointly owned between you and your new husband. So your new husband could supersede your children as your natural heirs. Therefore that particular clause is inserted mainly to protect the children of the first marriage.'

'Oh,' Lizabeth replied in an oh-that's-certainly-put-me-in-my-place tone.

'How do your daughters feel about all of this?' Irvine asked, not sure how much information he was going to be able to pick up on this particular fishing expedition.

'Actually, they're very compassionate, considering the circumstances.'

'Perhaps they thought that like their . . . er . . .' Irvine began and then stumbled over a word.

'Sister, I suppose, or should it be half-sister,' Lizabeth added, helping Irvine out of his awkward moment.

'Well, what I was thinking was that, maybe, like their sister, this was all outside their control and they are all victims of circumstance.'

'Perhaps,' Lizabeth replied sharply. 'What about Caroline and Alice Cain? Have they any idea about all of this? Or even Bob Cain—what does he think about all of it? This is surely a slap on the face for him, too. Yes, I agree my husband might have cheated on me with another woman, but if we're to believe all of this, not only did Alice cheat on her husband, but she also bore another man's child while still inside her marriage. For goodness' sake, it was right there under his nose. Which must beg the question, is Caroline really Harry's child? You know, if Alice is up to deceiving her husband by being involved in an illicit affair, then perhaps she's not beyond deceiving the man she's having the affair with as well. If at any point she was trying to cling on to Harry, what better way to do so than to say that she was having his child.'

There were paternity tests which could be conducted, Irvine imagined, but did not say. He felt that for the man to have included provisions in his final will, he must have been pretty sure Caroline was his child.

Lizabeth Ford had been deep in thought for a few moments and then burst forth with, 'How could he do this to me? How can anyone live with someone for twenty years and hide a fact like this from them? Did my friends know about it? Were they laughing behind my back? Do you think there is a possibility that Fr O'Connor was aware of this all these years? No? It's not possible, is it? Surely no one knew, apart from her. And then, if it is true, what exactly is it that she had that I don't have?'

At this point, Mrs Ford seemed to be mentally strutting her stuff, as proud as a peacock.

Irvine played the vulnerability card.

'Was there ever a time that you suspected, even just a little?'

'In truth, rarely a day goes by when you're not either feeling guilty of taking your partner for granted *or* suspecting that they are seeing someone else. Now I'm trying to recall all my days of doubt, and you know, there was a time about five years ago when I thought he was getting ready to leave me. I remember it clearly. It was just before one of his golfing trips, and I was sure I was about to lose him. But then I rang his hotel in Spain and discovered he *was* there, playing golf. I never left any messages for him. I felt much too guilty for that. I just decided that when he came back, I would show him exactly what he could lose if he ever left me. I decided upon that action rather than the usual bitching, fighting and all that ugliness—which in my opinion serves only to drive a partner away.'

'But he stayed?' Irvine asked.

'Yes, he stayed, but now when I do think about it, I realise he was never *really* there for me through all of our marriage.'

'Do you think Neil Roberts was aware of his sister's infidelity?' Irvine asked.

'From what Harry has told me of Neil and Alice's relationship over the years, I'd doubt it.'

'Let's go back to Alice if we may. Are you close with her husband, Bob Cain?'

'Not particularly.'

'So, you've never discussed this with him?' Irvine asked.

'No. You see, until the reading of the will, I had no idea Harry and Alice had enjoyed anything beyond the original college fling. Apart from which, I've never felt I had very much in common with Mr Cain. If you ask me, I'd say he was always a bit of a snob, always looking down on us. It's funny how such clearly unattractive people can be so self-confident; has that something to do with money? I wonder how superior he feels now, knowing what my husband was doing with his wife on at *least* one occasion.'

'Okay.' Spotting but not knowing what to make of the lie, Irvine sighed, standing up.

Allaway followed suit by putting his pen and notebook away. 'I think that's all we need for now.'

As they drove back to North Bridge House, Allaway had but one observation to make to his senior: 'For a woman whose husband was murdered just a few short days ago, you'd have to say she is coping remarkably well.'

Chapter Thirty-Two

MEANWHILE, KENNEDY WAS being chauffeured at a speed bordering on the illegal in the general direction of Aylesbury in Buckinghamshire. He didn't mind. He could not drive, so he was never aware how much danger he might be in. King was a fast, confident and smooth driver. He convinced himself that, should the proverbial cup of tea on the bonnet have been one of his special brews, not a drop of the special liquid would have been spilled.

Kennedy had been in Aylesbury once before in his life, and on that particular occasion, a fellow Ulsterman—a Detective Inspector Stephen McCusker—had accompanied him to a concert venue in Aylesbury, called Friars, to see a Belfast band called Fruupp. Stephen McCusker's younger brother, Vince, played in this band, and although Fruupp weren't especially Kennedy's cup of prog-rock tea, he was mightily impressed by the reaction they enjoyed from the Friars Aylesbury crowd.

Friars in Aylesbury was, McCusker senior pointed out, a great breeding ground for the progressive groups of the mid to late1970s. Friars bands, as they were known, tended to end up doing very well nationally. Sadly, Fruupp had not followed the path of success enjoyed by other Friars favourites—such as Genesis, Steve Harley and Cockney Rebel, Queen, Focus and the Kinks—and, in fact, had turned out to be the exception that proved the rule.

Stephen McCusker went on to distinguish himself in New Scotland Yard circles for the sterling work he did on the Dennis Nilsen Case. McCusker was the arresting officer of the infamous mass murderer in the case that became known as the Killing for Company Murders in Muswell Hill in 1983. Kennedy spared Fruupp and Stephen McCusker a few moments' thought as they drove into the town that had changed completely beyond recognition. Aylesbury had lost the charm of its 1970 New Town appeal to the 2000 homogeneous blandness, with the interchangeable streets of Gap, Next, McDonald's, W.H. Smith, Waterstone's, Alliance and Leicester, Boots, Starbucks, Lloyds, Sainsbury, Virgin, Prêt-à-Manger and Marks and Spencer.

The Coalition and Aylesbury Building Society had not really helped matters with its concrete five-storey monument to vulgarity. Designed with as much imagination as goes into a TV dinner, this building was certainly not going to produce any encouragement of the much-needed local pride.

Kennedy and King were immediately shown through from the reception to Errol McGuinn's office on the top floor. The views from McGuinn's windows were as spectacular as the exposed face of a quarry, and quite similar in texture. The inside of the offices wasn't much better, and Kennedy was directed towards the conference table which bore flasks containing, according to their handwritten labels, Tea, Coffee, Hot Milk, Cold Milk, and H_2O. There were also two plates of doughnuts and Danish pastries wrapped in cellophane.

'I think we'll have sufficient here to see us through our meeting,' Errol McGuinn said as he greeted Kennedy.

Kennedy had to advise McGuinn that DC Dot King was to be an integral part of the meeting and was not to be kept waiting in the outer office.

McGuinn went to his desk, buzzed through to his secretary and mumbled into the speakerphone that the other police officer should be shown through. He also requested the presence of someone called Oliver Flynn.

'Flynn, our legal eagle,' McGuinn explained to Kennedy. 'He'll take the notes and keep us all on the right track. He's a great chap and won't interfere with the flow of our chat, I'm sure.'

McGuinn was a solid man, a big man, big-boned as opposed to excessively fat. He looked to be in his early fifties. His full head of black curly hair was greased and combed back, all strands centring on a point at the back of his neck. Some of the curls had escaped, giving the impression that he had just come out of the shower. He was wearing a black, pinstriped suit, a red-and-white-striped shirt and a daring Wallace and Gromit tie. He flamboyantly removed his jacket and threw it across his office, where it landed in a heap on the chair at the other side of his desk. Flynn picked up his senior's jacket and folded it neatly over the back of the chair.

Three minutes and a mouthful of stewed tea later, Flynn and McGuinn, in their Tony Blair and Bill Clinton, shirt-sleeves look, were ready to commence proceedings.

'Could you please advise us why Frazer McCracken was suspended?' Kennedy asked, starting off the proceedings.

'We discovered that Mr McCracken has no charge to answer,' McGuinn replied.

'Sorry, sir. You're jumping ahead of yourself there. I don't wish to discuss, just for the moment, what happened at yesterday's hastily arranged tribunal. I'd like to establish first of all why Mr McCracken was suspended in the first place.'

All Kennedy received in reply to his repeated question was a blank stare from Errol McGuinn, who was trying hard to effect a there's-nothing-to-worry-about moment with an inane smile.

'He *was* suspended, wasn't he?' Kennedy asked, staring directly into McGuinn's eyes, daring him to lie.

'Yes, he was.' McGuinn replied, looking around the room as if to say, *What's with this guy?*

'And was he suspended on full pay, half-pay or no pay.'

McGuinn made a fuss of checking his notes before offering, 'Frazer McCracken was suspended on no pay. However, at his tribunal—'

'We'll get to that presently, if you don't mind,' Kennedy interrupted McGuinn and immediately addressed Flynn, who looked like a man who wouldn't lie: 'And, correct me if I'm wrong, but it's usually quite serious when someone is suspended with no pay?'

'Yes, that would be correct,' came the reply from the Dubliner.

'Okay,' Kennedy continued. 'So far, we've ascertained that Mr McCracken was actually suspended on no pay. Now, could you please advise me why such a serious step was taken?'

'Erm,' McGuinn replied, gazing around the room again like a rooster who wished to check out the competition before he pecked at his lunch. 'I don't believe we have to go into that with you.'

'Well, let's put it this way, and hopefully your legal eagle will keep me on well-oiled tracks. I'm investigating the murder of one of your officers, Mr Harry Ford. Now, in our investigation, it has come to our attention that Mr Ford was responsible for raising suspicions relating to Mr McCracken's dealings, and so, sir, I don't think it would be incorrect to assume that Mr McCracken's actions, which led to his suspension, could be relevant to this case. Now, if you don't stop stonewalling me, I might just feel it necessary to charge you on three counts—obstruction and withholding evidence. In which instance, I would find it necessary to arrest you and take you back to Camden Town CID, where we can afford you all the time you need to come up with some answers to our questions.'

'That's not going to happen. I'm the managing director. You can't do that to me.'

A quick uncomfortable grimace to the contrary from Flynn advised McGuinn that the detective could. The continued glare across the table from Kennedy to McGuinn informed the building society boss that the detective would not only take such steps but would take a certain amount of pleasure in doing so.

'Okay,' Errol McGuinn sighed. 'There were unsubstantiated allegations that Mr McCracken was pilfering the dormant accounts.'

'And what exactly are "dormant accounts"?' King asked.

'They are accounts where the customer disappears, perhaps even dies, without having made the necessary arrangements about what should happen in the case of their untimely death,' Flynn replied as McGuinn rolled his eyes towards the polystyrene ceiling.

'Good, now we're finally getting somewhere,' Kennedy said enthusiastically. 'Thank you. Now, could you please explain to us how these dormant accounts are uncovered?'

'Okay, normally dormant accounts might be registered when the annual interest statements we send out are returned with a note saying, "no longer at this address", "gone away" or "deceased". We would then endeavour to find either a new address or we'd endeavour to unearth a relative cum heir of our customer. If, through these channels, we subsequently discover that the customer has died without any relatives or a will, we will then mark these accounts as "dormant".'

'Okay,' Kennedy continued, businesslike. 'Now, could you please advise me what, in the normal course of events, would happen to these accounts?'

'In England, the building societies generally continue to have the use, but now the ownership, of these funds. That is to say, we will continue to use their money to make money. The dormant account will still enjoy the addition of interest—the rate agreed at the inception of the account—and the principal will be untouched. In Ireland, however, I believe you'll find the government will confiscate these funds for their own use!'

'Really?' King said and looked about to take the conversation off on a tangent until Kennedy interrupted.

'Okay, and how would he . . . sorry, how would one, if one were so inclined, help oneself to those funds?'

McGuinn barked, 'That would be an impossibility.'

Meanwhile, Flynn said, 'I can't think of a single case where that has happened.'

'Okay,' Kennedy said, finding it difficult to imagine why people would go to such lengths. 'Was there anything else he was accused of?'

McGuinn looked first to Flynn, then replied quickly, 'No, not that I'm aware of . . .'

Kennedy did not believe him.

'Are you 100 per cent sure?' Kennedy pushed. He felt the question would not reveal anything new, but it would serve to let McGuinn know that he was not believed.

'I believe Harry Ford had other stuff he wanted to bring up with us, but that was to be presented at the tribunal.'

'So, what back-up information and proof did Mr Ford give you that convinced you that you ought to take the extreme action of suspending one of your rising stars?' Kennedy asked, desperately rattling another door.

'He advised us of his fears,' McGuinn replied. 'Mr Ford was well respected in this company, so we were prepared to take action based on his suspicions. Sadly, when Mr Ford died, we had no way of substantiating those allegations, so we had to drop all of them and reinstate Mr McCracken. It was either that or risk being sued by McCracken for defamation of character. We just couldn't risk exposing our shareholders to potential substantial losses, and we complied immediately. Apart from which, Mr McCracken had already proven himself to be a vital employee, and I, for one, didn't want to lose such a valuable asset to one of our competitors.'

'Do you have in your possession any correspondence from Mr Harry Ford pertaining to this matter?' Kennedy asked.

'No!'

'Did you remove any such files from Mr Ford's office?'

'No,' McGuinn replied. There were no protests, no complaints at such an accusation, merely a single unqualified, 'No'.

'Tell me, Mr McGuinn, did you do a deal with Mr McCracken?' Kennedy asked, noticing that King had stopped writing and was looking directly at McGuinn.

'No,' McGuinn replied, but continued, 'I'm trying to understand what kind of deal you might mean, though.'

'Oh, like you would drop the charges and in return he would agree not to reveal another matter of a sensitive nature?'

'Detective Inspector Kennedy, I would remind you that you are asking these questions in the presence of a witness who has legal experience,' McGuinn replied, swinging out his hand in the general direction of Flynn as though the legal rabbit had just been produced from a hat.

'Here's the thing, Mr McGuinn. A question is not an allegation. I am not stating or repeating a fact; I am asking you a question. It's now down to you to confirm if this was the case, or not.'

'I'd like to repeat my caution,' McGuinn said, amid serious huffing and puffing.

'Listen, Mr McGuinn,' Kennedy said, shaking his head from side to side. He always felt it important, while questioning, to let the relevant person know that, no matter what words were being spouted or about to be spouted, he knew that the speaker was lying. 'A man has been murdered here. A very fine man, if you ask me. His death may or may not have had something to do with work-related matters within the company you are responsible for. Now, I'd like to caution you and warn you, sir. I won't allow this to be swept under the carpet. I have to advise you that it is my very definite opinion that Mr Ford's fears with regard to the actions of one of his colleagues did warrant investigation. I also confirm that I shall push for the fraud squad to undertake an investigation irrespective of the results of my current investigation. In my opinion, you, as managing director of this company, are responsible for the actions of your company.'

Kennedy stopped talking, and McGuinn looked to Flynn. When he found Flynn looking as though he expected him to address Kennedy's issues, he looked away again, embarrassed.

'So, sir, I repeat my question,' Kennedy started back up again. 'Did you, or did you not, reach an agreement with Mr McCracken that you would destroy any evidence—in particular, Mr Harry Ford's evidence—in exchange for Mr McCracken promising not to disclose another matter about your company?'

McGuinn leaned over and whispered something in Flynn's ear, similar to the way counsel and defendants frequently do in American movies. Flynn replied to McGuinn, who seemed about to speak, but before he had a chance to go on record, Flynn grabbed him by the arm tightly and they huddled together again in conference.

'I have been told by my advisor that part of the negotiated settlement reached with Mr McCracken and his representative contains a confidentiality clause whereby neither party is permitted to disclose the details of the agreement.'

'Clever! Very clever, Mr McGuinn, but this is not over yet. I think we should see what your shareholders think about this secret settlement,' Kennedy said as he rose and left the room. He was so furious he did not trust himself to remain for a second longer.

King and Kennedy's trip back to London was a long (heavy traffic) and silent (dark mood) one.

By the time they reached Finchley High Road, King seemed to pick up enough courage to ask Kennedy a question—a question that seemed to have been troubling her for the previous sixty-seven miles.

'You mentioned to Mr McGuinn, sir, that if he didn't answer your original question, you would arrest him on three charges. The two you cited, sir—obstruction and withholding evidence—I agree with, but I'm damned if I could come up with a third charge I'd agree with.'

'Oh,' Kennedy replied, pulling himself back up in his seat. 'I wasn't expecting him to come quietly, so I thought I'd better throw in the extra one to accommodate the potential "resisting arrest" charge as well.'

Chapter Thirty-Three

M R ROBERT (BOB) McCain occupied the next apartment to Alice Cain. Alice had explained that her husband used it as his office and more. James Irvine thought there was probably a concealed adjoining door somewhere, but he couldn't quite figure out where it might be.

Irvine and Allaway were greeted by Cain's maid, who showed them straight through to Cain's study. Three of the four walls were lined with dark-wood shelves packed with leather-bound volumes. The third wall was taken up mostly by a large window and a mahogany desk. Irvine noticed that amongst the photographs on the wall to the left and right of the window was a strategically placed mirror to afford Cain (while seated at his desk) a view of the door behind him. As the detective walked into the deep-pile carpeted study, Cain swivelled around from his desk and invited the two policemen to take a seat in the intensely polished leather chairs.

Cain ordered coffee for all of them and rose to shake their hands, forcing the police to rise out of their seats again.

Irvine figured that Cain was trying so hard to make them feel comfortable that he was making them feel slightly uncomfortable. As the detective sergeant took his seat again, he thought that Cain looked every inch the successful American lawyer at home in his London residence.

Robert (Bob) Cain wore a blue shirt, green striped tie, tan trousers, hand-made dark brown leather shoes and a dark blue blazer. His face was sculpted with pleasant features rather than good looks, and he enjoyed a healthy glow, more weather-beaten than a year-round tan. His brown hair with its knife-edge parting looked as if his barber's efficient comb and scissors were exercised at least once a fortnight. If anything, he gave off the air of a middle-aged man desperate to acquire the looks of an older man.

Bob Cain starred in all of the photographs on the wall behind him, some with his family. Irvine was convinced, on close inspection, that the daughter in the photographs bore no resemblance to her father. In other photographs, Cain was portrayed as friend to the likes of Blair, Prescott, Straw and Co., each and every one of them trying to outshine the other in the white-teeth and big-smiles stakes.

'This is such a frightfully sensitive matter, isn't it?' Cain said, his baritone voice carrying successfully around to every corner of the study.

'Murder usually is, sir,' Irvine replied plaintively.

'Yes, sorry, of course I see what you mean. No, sorry. I was referring to my wife's earlier indiscretion.'

'And you'd no idea that any of this was going on, sir?' Irvine asked, happy that at least Cain was not in denial about the affair.

'Of course, I knew all about it, Sergeant. What kind of fool do you take me for?'

'Oh, sorry. I was under the impression—'

'Yes, exactly. That's part of the problem—my wife was under the same impression.'

'I'm sorry, sir,' Irvine said, feeling compelled to interrupt. 'Are you telling me you knew about your wife's relationship with Mr Ford, or are you telling me that you suspected that Mr Ford was possibly Caroline's father?'

'My wife is certainly guilty of injudiciousness, sir, but she dallied with only one other, Harry Ford, and Caroline is most certainly his child, although I brought her up as though she were my own.'

'And you and your wife never discussed this?'

'Detective Sergeant,' Cain announced flamboyantly, showing that he did know Irvine's title, 'I'm a realist. I haven't got where I am today with blinkers on. I met Alice when she was on the rebound from Harry Ford. She admitted this to me on our first-ever dinner date. I knew that if they hadn't both behaved like the childish fools they were, I'd never even have met her, let alone found myself out on a date with her.'

Cain paused. Irvine could not work out if it was because he was waiting for someone to confirm that he was a realist. No confirmation came, so Cain continued.

'But their misfortune was certainly my fortune. All they really needed to do was to sit down and work it out. I'm a negotiator, sir—that's what I do for a living—and I'll tell you, if I hadn't a vested interest myself, I could have sorted both of them out in ten minutes flat—talked a bit of sense into them. But I noted that Alice was a fine woman, a darned fine woman, and

I'm sorry to have to admit it, but I knew she'd produce great children, and I just gave her space and time and waited. I knew she was the type of woman who wouldn't respond well to a pressured approach, and so eventually we did come together, we clicked and we had a child.'

'So, how long after the marriage did she and Harry meet up again?' Irvine asked the question. He quite frankly felt a bit guilty about asking and wondered if he was feeling guilty because Cain had chosen to be so frank with them.

'Oh, I can tell you *exactly* when it happened,' Cain declared, appearing almost proud at his knowledge. 'We all met up at Fr O'Connor's ordination, and you could tell—I could tell—Harry and Alice both still had feelings for each other. In their defence, it has to be said that, at that stage, they were both reluctant participants. You have to realise that they hadn't seen one another since they'd split up, yet both of them were with their new spouses, and they didn't really know how to behave. Their perplexity was blatantly apparent to anyone who had eyes to see. This was their first implicit test, and I'm afraid to say they both failed it, and failed it miserably. I feared it was only a matter of time before they would meet up again and resume their relationship.'

Cain stopped talking again and, this time, with one hand on the back of his neck and the other on his chin, he turned his head, first left until it audibly cracked. Then he repeated the same exercise to the right.

Looking all the better for his brief workout, he continued: 'I don't think either of them meant there to be a resultant pregnancy. To be quite frank, I believe she was even meant to be on the pill. But then again, she was also meant to have been on the pill when she fell pregnant with Robbie, our first-born.'

'I was wondering, sir—well, you seem so sure that the child, Caroline, isn't yours,' Irvine asked.

'Well, for heaven's sake, man,' Cain said, swirling around in his chair again and turning his back to the policemen in the process. He rose, walked a single step to the wall by the window and removed a photograph from the wall. 'Let's play a game. It's called spot the odd one out—sorry, but you'll forgive me if there are no prizes.'

Irvine had already successfully played this game.

Cain took the photo back and stared at it unemotionally for a few seconds before returning it to the faded dust lines on the wall. It fitted perfectly, like the final missing piece of a jigsaw puzzle.

'Apart from which,' Cain said, lording it a bit, 'women seem to think they are the only ones who can successfully count to nine. No, I have absolutely no doubt on the matter. Caroline is Harry's daughter—either that or she's the second child to be born as a result of the Immaculate Conception.'

'Yes, quite,' Irvine replied, desperate as always to stay away from all topics religious, but surprised at the Cain would be guilty of making the popular mistake. 'And you never looked to Mrs Cain to verify your suspicions?'

'No. I mean, why should I?' Cain boasted. 'She always came home to me. The children were both born under my roof, and I would have to say that when it comes to motherhood, Alice is second to none; she's really unbelievable. Look, I'll admit something to you here, Detective Sergeant, mainly because there's really no need not to. When it comes down to all the lovey-dovey song and dance, you can count me out. I say, you really can. I can't abide all that clingy nonsense. A man needs a maid and a man needs a wife and a man needs a break. Do you know what I mean? We certainly need neither wife nor maid twenty four/seven. I quite like spending time with Alice, but our time is always considerably better if it's rationed. So I suppose what I'm saying is that Harry gave her something I couldn't or wouldn't give her, *but* at the end of the day, she was always mine. She was always first and foremost *my* wife; she always returned to *my* home. Do you get me?'

'And you were never scared of losing her?' Irvine asked, wondering how much of the above Mr Bob Cain would have shared with his wife.

'No. Don't you see? With both of us, Harry and me, giving Alice what she wanted, she had no reason to want to leave. At one point, about five years ago, yes, maybe I feared they were planning to elope together and set up home. But something happened—I'm not sure what. There were three or four months where she was behaving very strangely. I just left her alone, and whatever it was that was troubling her, or them, worked itself out.'

'How well did you know Harry Ford, sir?' Irvine asked.

'Well, for my little plan to be effective, it was important I didn't get to know him too well, but in different circumstances I'm sure we could have become great buddies. You know, Harry Ford was a certified good guy—of that there is no doubt.'

'What about Lizabeth?' Irvine inquired, running down his checklist.

'I always felt sorry for her. I mean, I was happy with the situation; she can't have been. But having said that, I never had the feeling she was deeply in love with Harry. She did want him to love her, though.'

'And finally, sir,' Irvine said, forcing a smile. 'Could you please tell us what you were doing from eight o'clock on Monday evening past until two o'clock on Tuesday morning?'

'Yes, that's easy,' Cain announced, returning the smile then turning around in his chair again so that he was facing his desk. He opened his diary, flicked a page or two and then announced, 'I left for Amsterdam on a business trip on Monday morning and returned home at lunchtime yesterday, Tuesday . . . yes Tuesday.'

'Well that was interesting, to say the least,' Allaway said as they exited Cain's mansion block. 'He could quite possibly be our main suspect if it weren't for the fact that he was in Holland at the time Ford was murdered.'

'Well, the trip itself doesn't necessarily rule him out. A quick check of the meetings and hotel reservations he was kind enough to give us will let us know whether or not it would have been possible for him to have booked a return ticket from Amsterdam to London, done his business and managed to get back to Amsterdam again to pick up his original ticket.'

'A lot of trouble to put yourself through though, DS, isn't it?'

'Murderers do, as a rule, tend to put themselves to a lot of trouble. You could say it goes with their territory.'

'Well, Alice Cain is as beautiful a woman as I've ever seen,' Allaway offered, Irvine imagined, in justification.

Chapter Thirty-Four

KENNEDY AND KING and Irvine and Allaway arrived back at North Bridge House at 17.30. Irvine accompanied Kennedy to the Ulsterman's office, apprising his superior of the knowledge he had gained since his interviews with Lizabeth Ford and Bob Cain.

Kennedy made a few additional notes, which he pinned to his notice board.

'So, you still don't think there is any connection between Riley's disappearance and Ford's death?' King asked as Kennedy prepared a brew-up for King, Irvine and himself.

Kennedy stopped mid-process and stared over at his notice board for a few minutes. There was an uncomfortable silence in his office.

'Well, the only connection I can see is that of Fr Vincent O'Connor, in that he knew both men,' Kennedy offered. Initially he had thought that perhaps there might have been some connection, but he had quickly dismissed that idea on the grounds that he was one of the few who were even aware of the Riley case in the first place.

'I think that might be a strong connection,' Irvine said hesitantly.

Kennedy, clearly enjoining the exchange, willed the water to complete boiling so that he could finish off the tea-making and get fully stuck into the conversation.

'Oh?' he said in encouragement to Irvine.

'Okay, please humour me here,' Irvine started, as King celebrated the end of her shift by removing her clip-on tie and opening the top button of her shirt. Halfway through the process, she became self-conscious about it, but Kennedy nodded that the gesture was fine.

Irvine rose and walked over to Kennedy's notice board. He focused his attention, for the benefit of King and Kennedy, on the photograph of the corpse of Harry Ford. He tapped on it a few times and said, 'You see, I don't think we're putting enough attention on the method of murder. All these stab wounds. . .' and he paused, talking as he drew in, with his fore-finger, the two straight lines which traversed Ford's chest, '. . .in the shape of a cross. Right?'

'Yes?' King replied, looking over her shoulder at Kennedy.

'Well, there is obviously some sort of religious connection which must put Fr O'Connor in the frame, at least to some degree,' Irvine said, appearing not quite as confident as he had been before putting his theory into words.

'And Riley?'

'Well, we haven't found Riley yet,' Irvine replied, picking up steam again. 'But maybe when we do, we'll find that he's also been murdered in some religious ritual.'

'And why would O'Connor pick both John Riley and Harry Ford?' Kennedy continued, happy now that his water had boiled.

'Well, from what I can gather, Fr O'Connor must have been pretty pissed off at Ford for stealing Alice Roberts—Roberts or Cain. I'm not exactly sure how I should refer to her as she's both.'

'Either will do,' Kennedy replied. 'Maybe, let's for the sake of this discussion, and to avoid confusion, refer to her only as Alice. Do you take sugar in your tea?'

'Yes, two, please, and milk,' King replied and continued. 'Okay, Alice shuns O'Connor in favour of Ford, and O'Connor decides to go off and become a priest.'

'Well, it's not really as simple as that,' Kennedy said as he brought King and Irvine their tea. He returned to the tea-making area and collected a plate of Robertson's chocolate-chip cookies and his own cup of tea, and as he was walking to his desk said, 'Shortly after Alice and Harry start their romance, they break up, and O'Connor and Alice still didn't get back together. Surely he would have been just as upset at Bob Cain as Harry Ford?'

'Well, again, it's not as simple as *that*,' King said. 'No matter what we think, O'Connor *claims* that he became a priest because Alice shunned him. Isn't that the case?'

'Yes,' Kennedy replied. 'But I do think you need to take into consideration how old they all were at the time.'

'Well, with the greatest of respect, sir, I imagine I'm much the same age now as they all would have been when they were at Reading University. I have to tell you that I'm so in love with my Ashley that if anything ever happened between us, I'd be absolutely devastated. My world would collapse around me, and I believe—I hope—it would be the same for him. Now, maybe it wasn't pure and simply the act of Alice betraying O'Connor for true romance elsewhere. That would have been one thing; but surely, for a priest, the fact that he discovered that, several years later, Alice and Ford are back together and carrying out an illicit affair. Couldn't that be the proverbial straw which broke the priest's back? Add to that the fact that Alice and Harry would have been cheating on two of his other friends, Lizabeth Ford and Bob Cain. I mean, you can't get much more toxic a relationship than that, can you?'

'And the fact that he's a *priest,* sir,' Irvine added, appearing fully into this theory. 'He's had twenty-five years of celibacy for these feelings to fester away behind. No matter what you say, that's not healthy; apart from which, celibacy is just not natural.'

'Okay, if we go down this route, how does Riley fit into all of this?' Kennedy asked.

'Well, O'Connor and Riley certainly knew each other, em . . . maybe Riley found out about O'Connor's plan to murder Ford? Hey, or maybe O'Connor and Riley were in cahoots with Ford, and they were the ones embezzling CABS, and they used the extremely ambitious McCracken as a scapegoat. And then, ah, yeah, O'Connor got greedy and got rid of his two partners,' Irvine offered.

'Did we find out where John Riley went to college or university?' King asked, looking like she'd found the way to solve both cases that very second.

'Yes, he went to York University and, apart from that, even if he had attended Reading, age-wise he would have been long gone by the time the Four Musketeers arrived.'

'Oh,' King replied, taking solace in another cookie.

'I agree that the stab wounds were meant as a sign to us,' Kennedy started, 'but I think they were left more as signs to incriminate O'Connor. Our murderer wasn't scared of depositing Harry Ford's body in a very public place, knowing that it would be found immediately. John Riley still hasn't turned up, and he's been missing several weeks. No, I'm sorry. I don't believe that there is any other connection to Riley and Ford other than the indirect connection through Fr O'Connor.'

'What about Alice then?' King suggested, showing that she wasn't scared of dumping one theory and looking straight at another.

'Yeah,' Irvine agreed. 'She's got the motive.'

'Well, let's say *a* motive,' Kennedy said. 'And the thing about the precise angle of the stab wounds, I'm not quite there yet how exactly the murder was carried out, but perhaps the method suggests it could have been a woman.'

'Surely if we're going to look in that direction,' Irvine said, staring at Kennedy's Guinness Is Good for You notice board once more, 'we still can't rule out Lizabeth Ford. What if O'Connor spilled the beans to her and told her that her husband and Alice were continuing the affair? You know, it is quite possible she just couldn't forgive him.'

'And then there's still Bob Cain, if we're going for the jealous angle. I'd put him in the frame as a jealous husband way ahead of Lizabeth as a jealous wife,' King offered, appearing tireless on the looking-for-suspects front. A lesser cop would be throwing up their hands in exhaustion at this stage, Kennedy thought.

'I'm not entirely sure if I would agree. Personally I'd reverse those on any suspect list of mine,' Kennedy said, as he considered how contented with his lifestyle Bob Cain appeared to be in all descriptions.

The three detectives seemed to consider his comments for a time.

'And then, Neil. Surely we can't rule out the jealous brother either,' Kennedy said, voicing the final of the leads on his notice board.

'Well, he certainly wouldn't get my vote—' Irvine said.

'Nor mine,' King interrupted.

'What—too much of a smoothie for you?' Irvine joked.

'No,' King replied and offered a neat return: 'It has more to do with the fact that he has a cast-iron alibi for the time of the murder. That's what did it for me, Detective Sergeant.'

'Yes, of course,' Irvine replied, perking up several degrees. 'And I've got the pleasure of checking out that alibi first thing in the morning. Here, you two, I'd better be off. I'll need my beauty sleep tonight to ensure I'm on top-notch form for Miss Nealey Dean.'

Chapter Thirty-Five

FOLLOWING KING AND Irvine's departure, Kennedy noticed a large brown envelope on top of the other files in the middle of his desk. Kennedy's name, minus his rank, was handwritten on the envelope.

Kennedy opened the envelope and removed about a dozen foolscap sheets of paper. He had a quick read through the pages and was soon shocked to discover that they were Harry Ford's missing files and a carbon copy of a letter addressed to a certain Mr Errol McGuinn, Managing Director, CABS.

Codona had obviously kept safety copies of her own files stashed away somewhere, and Kennedy felt that the disgust she had for the CABS tribunal had obviously resulted in her covertly ensuring that he received copies of Ford's evidence.

Harry Ford had conducted his research very thoroughly. His presentation of the facts was equally impressive, although some important back-up information seemed to be missing.

From what Kennedy could gather, Frazer McCracken had, on three separate occasions, helped himself to what amounted to 90 per cent of three dormant accounts. Kennedy jotted down separate notes to himself from Ford's notes to ensure that he understood the proceedings completely. Nine times out of ten, he was merely repeating Ford's finding, but by writing them down, he was forcing himself to understand completely what had gone on.

The first case Ford had presented to his managing director involved the dormant account of a Mr Samuel Watson of Flat 9, 117 Tottenham Court Road.

Watson had been saving with CABS for thirty-three years, saving anywhere from £100 to £500 monthly. On one singularly rare occasion, he had deposited £87,500. Ford assumed that these proceeds were from the sale of a property in West Hampstead, because the deposit was made at the same time he had filed a change of address, from NW6, for his account and passbook. Then suddenly, five years ago, the deposits had stopped, and there were no further transactions on the account until six months later when a certain Mr Frazer McCracken had authorised a swift transfer for an amount of £150,000 to an 'S. Watson' in Douglas, Isle of Man. Ford stated that £149,950 of this was then, in turn, transferred to an account in favour of Camden Redevelopment Town Properties Ltd.

Ford did not provide any back-up proof of how he knew that £149,950 had left the account in the Isle of Man and ended up in the CRTP Ltd account.

Kennedy stopped reading and writing to consider this. The obvious answer was that Ford had gone through McCracken's office in the dead of night. The counter-thought was that if McCracken had been clever enough to have done what Ford was suggesting, could he have been stupid enough to leave incriminating evidence around his office? Highly unlikely, Kennedy thought, but at the same time he had to admit that Ford had produced the evidence, and if CABS had passed this information over to the police, the police could have further investigated the allegations and either proved Ford's findings or found McCracken innocent. Kennedy wrote a note to himself to check the details of CRTP Ltd himself.

The next case, according to Ford, involved the dormant account of Mrs Ethel Greenaway of 263 Riverwalk, Putney. Mrs Greenaway had been saving with CABS for thirty-seven years, with a five-year break between 1978 and1982. Her savings totalled a more modest £97,000—£90,000 of which had been approved for transfer to E. Greenaway, again in an account in Douglas, and again, according to Ford, this account had been raided and all the funds, save £50, had been transferred to Camden Redevelopment Town Properties Ltd. Again, Ford had not outlined where he had obtained his information.

The final case in Ford's file involved the dormant account of Mr Bryan Batchelor of Market Street, Kingston-upon-Thames. Bachelor had saved with CABS for twenty-seven years. In the early years, he seemed to have been withdrawing as much as he was depositing, although he never actually went as far as clearing out his account entirely. Then, in the early 1990s, he had seemed to enjoy a few great years where his reserves grew to £220,873. In 1997, he, like Mr Samuel Watson, had seemed to downscale his house. At the same time as he changed his address from Chessington to Kingston, he had deposited a further £160,000. The following year, all transactions in his account had stopped, and that had been it until April this year, when McCracken had approved a transfer of £340,000 to B. Batchelor at the same Isle of Man bank. Once again, all but £50 was in turn transferred to Camden Redevelopment Town Properties Ltd.

On a separate page, Ford had noted that the shares for Camden Redevelopment Town Properties Ltd were held by:

Mr Frazer McCracken 98 shares
Mrs Joyce McCracken (Secretary) 1 share
Mr John Wallace 1 share

According to Ford, Wallace was the company solicitor and Joyce was Frazer's mother.

But it didn't end there.

Ford also included a mortgage application from a Mr Gary Millings for the sum of £93,000, to purchase the freehold interest in a retail and residential property on Chalk Farm Road. The value of the property was listed as £180,000.

Ford had shown that Millings was a regular CABS saver. The survey on the property was positive and, in Ford's own words, the property was 'a steal'.

CABS had turned down the mortgage request. None other than Mr Frazer McCracken had signed off on the paper work.

Two weeks after this date, the property had been sold for £175,000 to Camden Redevelopment Town Properties.

And, as Jimmy Cricket would say, 'Cum 'ere, cum 'ere—there's more, there's more.'

Another mortgage application had been submitted from Miss Tamsin Pearce for £65,000 to purchase a property in Kentish Town. The property was listed as being worth £120,000. In the same way as with the Millings request, Pearce's application for a mortgage had been rejected and the property had been purchased by Camden Redevelopment Town Properties Ltd for £121,000.

Same thing with Miss Patricia Armstrong. She had submitted her request for a £56,000 mortgage to purchase a flat in Kilburn High Street. McCracken had refused that request also. The flat was valued at £81,500, and a week after Miss Armstrong received her disappointing news, the property had been purchased by Camden Redevelopment Town Properties Ltd for £82,000.

Next up in Ford's file was a rejection to first-time buyers Mr and Mrs Jack Hill. They had wanted a £113,000 mortgage to purchase a £250,000 dilapidated house in Delancey Street. Their paperwork showed that they had intended to convert the house into three flats, saving the top one for themselves and using the rental income to pay off the mortgage. Five weeks later, McCracken's company had purchased the property for £235,000. *Did he need the extra four weeks to allow the owners to grow desperate?* Kennedy wondered.

Finally, Ford included paperwork to show that Frazer McCracken had turned down a mortgage request made by a Mr Cornelius Costello. Mr Costello had required £200,000 for a domestic and retail property, which was also on Chalk Farm Road and valued at £460,000. Three weeks later, Cornelius' loss had been CRTP Ltd's gain. The company's good fortune had been further extended six weeks after that when it sold the property on for £523,000. Ford noted that he doubted McCracken would have paid over any more than the initial 10 per cent deposit, netting himself a cool profit of £63,000.

Harry Ford, in the letter to his superior, stated that he felt there were further instances which would demonstrate McCracken's scheming, and, given time, he could produce the proof. His only worry was that he felt his own work was starting to suffer with the proportion of time he was dedicating to his investigation.

Kennedy closed the file. He bumped it up and down a few times on his desk, lining all the pages up neatly in the process, he hoped. This was all pretty damning stuff, he thought, particularly if he could take up Ford's threads and prove the money trail suggested. Was it, however, a motive for murder? In Kennedy's experience, people had murdered for a lot less than the money McCracken was believed to have amassed as a result of the several cases Harry Ford had uncovered.

He still had a few points he needed to clear up for himself on the mechanics of the fraud, and the one person he knew could help him was Miss Jill Codona. He was wondering how he could possibly contact her without compromising her position within CABS when his phone rang. It was North Bridge House's desk sergeant who had just picked up a message for Kennedy.

Miss Codona proved to be one step ahead of Kennedy and had left her mother's number with Desk Sergeant Flynn, with a message saying that if Kennedy needed clarification on Ford's damaging file, he should ring

Codona's mum, whose call to her daughter would not be suspected. Kennedy's first thought was that it was all a bit cloak and dagger, more John Buchan than Colin Dexter. On the other hand, CABS had shown that they were capable of going to great lengths to sweep this matter under the corporate carpet.

Twenty minutes later, Jill Codona and DI Christy Kennedy met up in the beautiful rose gardens of Regent's Park. Kennedy would have preferred to have met somewhere else simply because he frequently visited this location for pleasure. But needs must, and when he saw the agitated and nervous state of Miss Codona, he was happy he had agreed to her request.

So, as tourists ticked off another vital location; lovers acted as though they were the only two people alive on this earth; families rambled and shushed their children; office workers dallied on their way home; patrons for the open-air theatre picnicked as they waited for the doors to open for the evening performance; experts loudly exclaimed the complicated horticultural names before they were close enough to read the name tags; and a couple of dogs behaved better than many of the couples of lovers, Jill Codona, freshly spruced up with a couple of precious sprays of Philosyko—more in memory of Harry Ford than for Kennedy, though, the latter imagined—and Detective Inspector Christy Kennedy sat down in a quiet corner under a rope and rose-bush-covered bench.

'Were you able to make head or tail out of my own file copies of Harry's report?'

'I think so,' Kennedy began, thinking Miss Codona's eau de toilette blended perfectly with the scents of the various roses. 'I jotted down a few questions though.'

'I thought you might,' Jill replied, her big eyes focusing on the notebook Kennedy produced from his pocket.

'Okay,' Kennedy began. 'First off, how would he have discovered these accounts?'

'Before we get into that, I need to explain to you that I'm not normally into this cloak-and-dagger stuff. To tell you the truth, it's doing my nerves in. Neither am I usually into removing files from my office. But, you know, I thought this would all resolve itself when the tribunal found McCracken guilty. But when they didn't, I decided Harry would have wanted me to give you his evidence.'

'Yea, but I thought that CABS had taken your files this morning?'

'Yes, they did, but I'd made a safety copy of the McCracken paperwork and stashed it in a safe place. I mean, it's just too explosive to leave around the office, and so I made and hid my own copy.'

'Right,' Kennedy said and nodded.

'Okay, going back to your question. From what Harry could gather, McCracken's secret was in locating these, let's say, 'future dormant accounts', before they officially became registered as dormant accounts. The main reason banks and building societies register such accounts is to avoid fraud. You see, we send out our annual interest statements, and, well, if they fall into the wrong hands, they contain all the information needed for fraudulent embezzlers and identity thieves.'

Her cockney pronunciation of the word 'embezzlers' definitely made it sound like a word that described a person responsible for evil deeds. Kennedy thought she sounded as if she had just recently got her tongue around the word. He jotted the word down in his notebook, for no reason other than to appear to be listening. Jill continued, 'If we notice an account has been inactive for an extended period, we will write to the customer, asking them if they wish the account to remain open. If we don't hear anything back, we officially class the account as dormant and will cease correspondence.

'The money in the account will remain the property of the account holder or, if it transpires the account holder has died, their heirs will inherit it.'

'So, how would McCracken find out if a customer might have died?' Kennedy asked.

'Well, Harry reckoned McCracken was monitoring the accounts, and the minute he noted a lack of activity or response, he would just check the name with the register of births, marriages and deaths at the Town Hall.

'He obviously kept this information to himself and targeted these accounts. Harry figured he'd then open an account in this name in an Isle of Man Bank.'

'Why the Isle of Man?' Kennedy asked.

'Well, between you and me, when you want to open an account there, all you need is a certified copy of documentation. What that means is that all you need is a photocopy of your electricity bill, or library card, or similar, and to have it signed by someone of standing. I don't need to tell you how easy it is to forge things when you start using a photocopier.

'He'd then write a letter to CABS using this person's name and forging their signature. He'd use the type of letter we'd receive several times a week.

"Dear Sir, I've recently moved from so and so address. During the move I lost my passbook. Could you please send me a new one marked up with all interest accrued." He'd also request a withdrawal—usually 90 per cent to 95 per cent of the balance on the account—and he'd also include with his letter a forged signed copy of a lost passbook declaration form.'

'Yeah, I think I've got that part,' Kennedy said. 'But what address would he have used without being caught out?'

'Oh, yes, sorry,' Codona replied, laughing nervously. 'Harry found out that McCracken had rented a bedsit on Parkway using Bryan Batchelor's name.'

'One of the accounts he pillaged?' Kennedy prompted.

'Exactly.'

'How did Harry discover that?' Kennedy asked.

'I don't know,' Miss Codona admitted.

Kennedy thought he must have shown his disappointment because she continued, 'You have to realise here, Detective Inspector, Harry was obsessed with this. If I am being brutally honest, I'd also have admit that I think Harry must have been trailing McCracken, and with some of the information my boss turned up, I believe he must have broken into McCracken's home. I can think of no other way he could have uncovered all this information.'

'So, the letter comes in to CABS. Would there not be any security checks before sending out that amount of money?'

Again, another nervous laugh from Jill Codona.

'It's our core business, Mr Kennedy,' she said earnestly. 'We deal in money. We receive money and we pay money out. I imagine we probably deal with about two hundred pieces of mail a day. McCracken would have found it easy to get in first, search out his own items of mail, and deal with them, as his signatures proved he did. At the same time, should any of the CABS staff have come across the pertinent pieces of mail, McCracken would still have got away with his theft. If this had been the case, then none of the staff involved could have been held accountable for what happened to the accounts of Bryan Batchelor, Samuel Watson or Ethel Greenaway. They would have been conducting CABS business as per normal.'

Kennedy wondered at the ease with which Jill Codona recited these three names. Perhaps Ford was not the only member of the CABS staff who was obsessed with the McCracken affair.

Miss Jill Codona bade Kennedy goodbye and disappeared in a matter of seconds. Kennedy returned to North Bridge House, thinking that no matter how discreet they thought they may have been, there was still a good chance ann rea would greet him the next time they met with, 'And who was the slim, Spanish-looking daughter of Tony Curtis you were seen canoodling with in the rose garden on Wednesday evening?'

Chapter Thirty-Six

AND SO CONCLUDED Day 2 of the investigation into the murder of Harry Ford.

At least for the majority of the team—bar Kennedy, that was. Fr Vincent O'Connor called at North Bridge House at 7.40 and invited Kennedy to join him for a bowl of pasta at Trattoria Lucca.

'How's it going?' O'Connor asked as 10 per cent of his spaghetti disappeared with one complicated but chic and swift manoeuvre of his fork.

'Oh, one step forward to about five backward. Tell me, did you know about Harry being Caroline Cain's father?'

'How does one best answer your question?' O'Connor mused as he toyed with a forkful of the greenish pasta.

'Truthfully will be fine,' Kennedy suggested.

'In that case, the truthful answer is, no, I didn't know that Caroline was Harry's daughter. I did have my suspicions about the relationship between Alice and Harry though.'

'Oh?'

'Well, nothing you could put your finger on really, until about five years ago. Harry and I were out for a bit of a boys' night out, and we had more than our fair share of drinks. He asked me if I had any regrets in my life. So, I started to list my regrets. And when I noticed he was getting pretty bored with my reply, I guessed that maybe he'd brought the subject up because he had a major regret of his own.'

Kennedy laughed as much at the camp way O'Connor was recalling the incident as at the details.

'"Tell me, Harry," I said. "Just to prove that priests are perceptive humans—by any chance would you have any regrets of your own?"

'"Oh, you know," he began expansively. "At one point in your life, you think you know exactly what the right thing is to do. Then you grow a little older and you realise you were a complete fool, and the thing that hurts you most is not the damage you've done to yourself as much as the damage you've done to others, and that's what hurts most, you know? I'd spend everything I have just to turn back the clock.'"

'So, what did you say?' Kennedy asked.

'I was hoping you'd ask that,' O'Connor said. 'I quoted him a bit of Oscar Wilde. The great man is reported to have once said, "No man is rich enough to buy his past." This didn't seem to help, so I simply asked him who he'd hurt, who he'd hurt that he regretted it so, and he said, "Oh, you know, women, children, fathers." Now, I have to admit, at that stage he was more than a little incoherent in his speech, and I was equally incapable in the hearing department, but I plodded on: "So, can I take it you're referring to Alice?" "Oh, now," he replied. "If it were only just Alice and me, that would be easy."'

O'Connor had been twirling his fork around on his plate for a time now, and his food was in danger of growing cold. Some people didn't mind that, but Kennedy couldn't abide cold food himself, so he let the priest continue with his reminiscing as he continued with his own pasta.

'"Don't forget," I said. "Don't forget me. I was hurt as well in the little episode you're referring to."

'"Yes, yes, of course. Sorry, Vincey. You were hurt too," he agreed, but I could tell my pain was the furthest thing from his mind. He trudged on regardless though. "But you know what? Sometimes I think it's such a mess and will continue to be a mess, no matter what I do, so why don't I just do whatever it takes to make myself happier? As I say, it'll all still be a big bloody mess, but at least I'll be happier." So I asked him what he would need to make him happier. I wasn't really expecting him to answer me truthfully, or even to answer me at all, but he said, "Well, I know I'd upset Lizabeth. I also know I would certainly upset Neil, and I know I'd upset Bob Cain, and that means we'd all upset the kids, but what's the difference between that and what we have now? None of us has a perfect life. I think that's what I'll do," he said. "I think I'm going to do what we should have done twenty years ago. She's right—we should just do it, just turn our backs on the rest of it and do it."

'"Let me get this straight," I said. "You are going to leave Lizabeth and the kids, and Alice is going to leave Bob and the kids, and you're going to move in together?" And he looked me straight in the eye and replied, "Yep, it's about time!"'

O'Connor stopped speaking and indulged himself in a forkful of pasta and a swig of wine.

'So they had been planning to move in together?' Kennedy asked.

'Apparently so,' O'Connor replied.

'I have to say, that surprises me. You see, when I spoke with Alice, she said the reason why her relationship with Harry worked was purely and simply because neither she nor Harry put that kind of pressure on each other. She claimed that they were both content and happy with where they were together.'

'Well, she probably was content, and it was probably just the drink talking that night with Harry, because nothing ever came of his great plan. He never mentioned it again, and neither did I.'

'And you never discussed it with anyone else?'

'Well, I must admit I was a bit worried about the repercussions both of them might suffer, so I mentioned it to Neil to see if he was aware of anything,' O'Connor replied.

'And what did Neil say?'

'Well, I was a little taken aback at his reaction, too. I mean, in the university days, he was so anti their being together, but I suppose he'd mellowed. He didn't seem to care, to be truthful. He told me that Harry and I were nothing more than two old lushes and that I'd obviously been too drunk to realise exactly what was being said. He told me Alice was very happy. He said maybe that was what Harry was really depressed about— the fact that Alice and Bob were so happy.'

Kennedy took a drink of his wine, savouring it before speaking: 'The thing is, whatever was going on that was upsetting Harry five or so years ago seemed to have resolved itself. The questions we need answering now are: what has been happening in his life recently? What did Harry Ford get involved in recently that resulted in his being murdered?'

'Oh, I positively just love to play detective,' O'Connor gushed, and then lost his enthusiasm somewhat as he admitted, 'But in this case Harry was my best friend and this is not a game. Have you any indication yet as to whether the motive was domestic or professional? Is there any chance that Bob only recently discovered that Harry was Caroline's father?'

'He claims he knew immediately,' Kennedy replied, hoping he was not giving too much away. At the same time, he realised that the more he fed O'Connor, the more he was likely to reap in response.

'How did he find out?' O'Connor asked, perking up by at least seven degrees of jolliness.

'Mr Cain claimed his ability to be able to count up to nine was the only knowledge required.'

'Okay, okay. He could be lying, of course. If he knew about Caroline all those years ago, he wouldn't have waited all this time to murder Harry out of spite or revenge now, would he?'

'Well, he could be a very patient man,' Kennedy replied.

'Or unless, as you say, something else happened recently that drove him to murder,' O'Connor suggested.

'But what could he have found out recently? Maybe he discovered the truth about Caroline before Harry's will revealed it. What, other than that and the fact that his wife had been cheating on him for going on twenty years? What other than either of those two motives could have driven him to murder?' Kennedy asked, turning the tables slightly by putting O'Connor in the hot seat.

'Well, maybe he discovered that Harry and Alice were now actually planning to run off together. Maybe when it came to the crunch, Harry wouldn't actually run off with Alice, so she murdered him, eh? What about that? Maybe Lizabeth discovered Harry and Alice's affair and she murdered him. Maybe this guy McCracken murdered Harry in revenge for discovering his scheming. Maybe Neil murdered him because Harry beat him once again at press-ups in the gym.'

'I notice you've mentioned everyone bar yourself,' Kennedy said quietly and seriously, watching to see how the priest would react.

'Oh, yes, of course. Be sure you don't forget to put me down on your list as well,' O'Connor jested, appearing completely unfazed.

'And what would your motive be?'

'Oh, let's see now. How about I topped him because he stole my girl?' O'Connor said, a tad too quickly.

Kennedy was about to say something else when O'Connor continued, 'Aye, if only that were true, I'd have had a much happier twenty years. At least I'd have had someone to blame. But the truth is not quite so romantic. Alice just wasn't interested in me in that way, and if there'd been no Harry, or no one else knocking on her door for that matter, it wouldn't have changed things a fig; we didn't click—she didn't fancy me, so there ended the story. I don't think it was ever a case of me saying, "I'll never get over her." Boys and girls do make a song and dance over saying this about each other, don't they?'

'Well, there's certainly been a fair share of songs written on that particular subject over the years,' Kennedy said in agreement.

'But what was really the matter? Were the boys and girls in question ill? Surely it must all start with lust, a physical attraction. I've never really been able to get into all of that. I remember when I was young, looking at girls' bums and thinking *What's all the fuss about?* But some girls, like Alice, also possess an intellectual beauty, and that's what turned me on. She probably sensed that the other stuff, the physical stuff, was never high on my agenda. If only I'd been interested in her in that way, then maybe she would have viewed me differently, and we'd have clicked, and Harry would never have suffered his bitter end.'

Kennedy couldn't be sure if O'Connor was manipulating him and leading him away from the path of suspicion to emphasise that he had no reason to murder Harry. As Kennedy was considering this, O'Connor posed his next question:

'Tell me, Christy, does Bob Cain have a good alibi?'

Chapter Thirty-Seven

KENNEDY THOUGHT THAT even considering that DS James Irvine was usually well presented, he looked *particularly* well turned out that Thursday morning. In the same second, the detective inspector remembered that Irvine was off to interview Miss Nealey Dean, an up-and-coming new actress about town.

If Irvine was benefiting from an inch or two to his step that morning, Kennedy could certainly understand why. Nealey Dean possessed that rare combination of an ability to act and drop-dead gorgeousness. In ann rea's words, Miss Dean was the greatest actress the UK had produced since Julie Christie.

When he asked for the same Miss Nealey Dean at the front desk of the Landmark Hotel, Irvine was surprised when he was instructed by the receptionist to go straight to Miss Webb's room on the fifth floor.

That'll be a great one to tell DI Kennedy, Irvine thought, as the lift bolted through the floors, *I thought I was going to spend some time in Miss Dean's bedroom, but we ended up in a threesome in Miss Webb's room.* He brushed all such distractions from his mind as he knocked on the door.

Irvine was not prepared for the barefoot vision that greeted him a few seconds later.

'Oh, you must be Detective Sergeant James Irvine,' a girl said in a small but sweet voice, delivered with a smile large enough to light up the entire fifth floor hallway. 'Well, at least I hope you are Detective Sergeant Irvine. I'm Harriet Webb.'

Irvine, temporarily speechless, produced his warrant card. Then, oxygen gradually reaching his brain again, he remembered his selected task.

'Ah, I've come to chat to Miss Nealey Dean.'

'Yes, of course you have. I'm her as well. Nealey Dean is my stage name, if you see what I mean.'

'Oh,' was Irvine's only reply. It was a good word to use, if only because it allowed his mouth to remain in its chosen position while enjoying the vision before him.

'Yes, my agent persuaded me I'd never get anywhere as an actress called Harriet Webb, so eventually we settled on the more obvious Nealey Dean. Don't ask why.'

'Well, it certainly rolls off the tongue easier than Jonathan Ross's "w"s.'

Dean was dressed in a Hothouse Flowers sweatshirt, two sizes too big, and blue denim jeans rolled up to her calves. Her blonde hair was rolled into a makeshift bun, which, if Irvine was not mistaken, was caught and held in place by a pair of knickers.

'Oh, that'll do nicely,' she hammed up as she invited him into her room, nodding at the warrant card Irvine had been holding outstretched for a few minutes now.

If Irvine had been expecting piles of clothes, make-up and various girly things thrown all around the room in a big mess, he was in for a disappointment. The outer room of her suite had obviously been set up as her office, and she had a laptop on the desk. The television was turned on to Sky News, and the sound was turned down. The tidy remains of a solitary breakfast were on a tray in the door port.

'Would you like a tea or a coffee or something?'

'A coffee would be brilliant, ma'am,' Irvine replied.

'Oh-mi-god, was that for real, or are you taking the piss?'

'Sorry, ma'am?'

'Your accent. Is that for real?'

'It's my very own, ma'am. I'm afraid I canee do anything about it at this stage,' Irvine replied, aware that he was now unquestionably guilty of hamming it up, if only slightly.

'Nor should you ever. It's a wonderful accent, but it's just that it's so pure Sean,' she said.

Irvine noted she hadn't stopped smiling since she'd opened the door. It was a wonderful, warm, genuine smile. She also had something of a unique voice, herself. Her tones were distinctive in that when you heard her speak, in her non-girly voice, she brought a smile to your face, and yet, when you put the voice to the person, for some reason they matched perfectly. Irvine imagined that if Miss Dean were ever booked to dub a voice for a cartoon, she'd have the perfect voice for a bear cub.

'It's been said before, actually, ma'am,' Irvine replied, taking a seat on the deep luscious sofa. 'God, I'm gonna need a crane to get out of here.'

Nealey laughed a hearty laugh, 'You should meet my mum.'

'Goodness, that's surely a bad sign for me,' Irvine said in genuine disappointment. 'You know, ma'am, I meet a beautiful woman and she immediately invites me to meet her mother.'

'No,' Nealey gushed through fits of laughter. 'It's just that my mum is so in love with Sean Connery. I did a project with him recently, and she was just in heaven. My dad was nervous though. He'd heard Sean was a bit of a ladies' man. I just had to remind my father that at seventy-something, Sean is somewhat older than my grandad! I'm not sure he was convinced, but Sean—the real Sean that is—is a bit of a sweetheart. Excuse me a mo,' she said as she lifted the phone. 'Yes, hello, thank you. Could I order coffee for two and a couple of croissants, please? That'll be right up,' she said to Irvine as she jumped on to the sofa next to him, curled her feet under her and circled her arms around her knees.

Nealey caught sight of herself in a mirror on the wall behind Irvine.

'Oh-mi-god,' she shouted, quickly pulling the white material out of her hair. 'Bad habit I'm afraid, but I assure you, most girls do it.'

Irvine saw a small blush rise in her snow-white cheeks, and he noticed for the first time that although her hair appeared naturally blonde, her eyebrows were dark. It was this contrast, he figured, which resulted in her classically beautiful look.

She haphazardly straightened her hair using the mirror, but instead of getting down to business, she asked, 'So, why did you decide to become a policeman?'

'I didn't have the right accent for the Mounties,' Irvine said.

'You know, I think I could sit and listen to your voice all day long.'

'Oh, I think if your dad really was so worried about Mr Connery, he'd have something to say about that,' Irvine said, confusing even himself as to what he meant .

'You know, the reason fathers worry so much about their daughters going out with young lads . . .' she said, and then paused briefly. Irvine could not be sure but he thought he caught her stealing a glance at his hand. Was she searching for a wedding ring? Nealey raised her eyebrows and continued: '. . . is that they used to be young lads themselves.'

Irvine was wondering whether he was being considered in the 'fathers' bracket or in the 'young lads' class when there was a tap on the door.

As Nealey set about serving the coffee, Irvine explained that he had joined the police force because he had grown up with a romantic view of people who solved crimes. He told her that he remembered thinking it unbelievable that you could actually get paid money for doing something as enjoyable as solving crimes.

'On our current case, a man, Mr Harry Ford, has been murdered, right?'

Nealey, visibly excited, nodded back at Irvine immediately.

'Okay, so we then have to investigate Mr Ford's past life and the people associated with him during that life: his friends, his work colleagues, his wife, his ex-girlfriends. What we're looking for is a person or, perhaps, persons, who would benefit from Mr Ford's death. We're looking for a motive. And so, every person we come into contact with in our investigation leads us to several other people, who in turn lead us to more and on and on, all the time expanding our circle wider and wider.'

'And that's where Neil fits in, and consequently where I come in,' Nealey said as Irvine reached a natural stop.

'Exactly,' Irvine agreed and switched courses mid-stream. 'Mr Neil Roberts was a friend of Mr Harry Ford's, so our investigation naturally leads us to his door.'

'And Neil in turn gave me up?'

'Well, not exactly, but close.' Irvine smiled. 'In the majority of cases, a victim is murdered by someone they knew, so in our initial questioning we ask the immediate circle of friends and colleagues what they were doing at the time of the victim's death.'

'And to cut to the chase,' Nealey said, 'Neil said he was doing me.'

'Well, yes, but not exactly in those words.'

'And is Neil a worthy suspect?'

'Well,' Irvine started, sounding more like James Bond than he had ever imagined. 'It would appear that he was otherwise engaged at the time, ma'am.'

'Okay, I can confirm that Neil Roberts was with me on the night of Monday, 24 August. I didn't mean to tease you so. It's just that I thought our conversation might have ended there.'

'No, no, Nealey, that's where our conversation starts.'

'Oh, goodness, I just love the way you said "Nealey" there.'

'Okay, Nealey.' Irvine smiled again. 'Could you tell me how you met Neil Roberts?'

'Right, let's see. I met him in May of this year in Marks and Spencer's in Camden Town. He was the perfect gentleman and let me go ahead of him in the checkout queue. I'd only a few things and he had a trolley loaded to the top. I thought that was so nice. We continued to chat as the checkout girl totalled up my shopping. Then the penny finally dropped with me that he was trying to chat me up. He was trying to pull me right there in the queue at Marks and Spencer's.'

'Did he know who you were?'

'No, not at all, but as I later found out, it wouldn't have made any difference if he had. I mean, with Neil, I know it's a cliché and all, but he would literally chat up anything in a skirt.'

'I wouldn't have thought he . . . um, that he—'

'That he'd be my type?' she said, helping Irvine out.

'Well, yes, now you come to mention it.'

'And you're right, he wouldn't normally be, but for some reason he intrigued me, and I wanted to see what was behind all of his front. I mean, you'd have to admit, he looks clean, he's not married, he's always well presented—perhaps he does dress with too much of a man's eye—but I found myself wondering why he would be the way he was. Why would he think that he could chat me up? What exactly did a person like him think he could offer a girl like me? And if he pulled me, what did he have that he thought might keep me interested?'

'So, are you telling me you allowed him,' Irvine started slowly and looked over at her computer, 'to pull you for research purposes?'

'Hymm,' Nealey said, smiling again. 'I need to keep reminding myself you're a detective, but yes, in a way, I suppose you could say that.'

'And so, what happened next?' Irvine asked with a hint of, *I think I know what happened next, but am not going to like it.*

'Well, I waited for the hit line, and eventually it came. I was walking away from the checkout with my shopping, and he came running after me with a bunch of bananas, saying that he thought I'd forgotten them. Actually he was right. They were my bananas, but I don't think I'd forgotten them. I think when he was helping me with my stuff, he hid them. He told me it was okay—I didn't need to go back to the checkout, as he'd paid for them for me. And I offered to pay for them and he said, "No way", but he said I could buy him a cup of coffee in Café DeLancey, which was just around the corner from Marks and Spencer's. I smiled to myself as I agreed. We had a coffee there the following evening. His chat-up approach was fair; the conversation never lulled. He did talk about his sister Alice quite a bit. I got the distinct feeling she was the only person he was close to, maybe a wee bit too close to. He always seemed to be annoyed or frustrated by her though.'

'Did he ever mention Harry Ford?"

'Yes, a few times, but he never . . . well, he talked about him like he'd talk about the checkout lady at Marks and Spencer's. He was perfectly charming and polite to her, he made sure he gave her the time of day and all—mind you, she is brilliant: everyone wants to be in her line. But for Neil it was someone he frequently came into contact with because he had to, but not someone he was prepared to invest any emotion in, and I got the feeling Harry fitted in there somewhere as well. Maybe that's a wee bit harsh; maybe they were a wee bit closer or I was just hearing one side of a very competitive relationship. But there was none of that genuine warmth from Neil towards Harry Ford,' Nealey stated in a matter-of-fact tone.

He asked, 'What about Fr Vincent O'Connor?'

'Neil talked about him briefly, not a lot really. I think it was more a case that Neil thought it was cool to have a priest as a friend. He also believed that Vincent was a latent homosexual.'

'So, you're saying that you had coffee at DeLancey?' Irvine asked, not sure if he wanted the rest to be spelled out.

'Yes.'

'And then what?' he asked, thinking that she was really making him work at this.

'Well, we exchanged digits.' She stopped and laughed. 'I've always wanted to say that. It's so crass, don't you think? We exchanged telephone numbers, and he invited me to dinner at his place. I went over; he lives in a mews house near the foot of Primrose Hill. It was quite pleasant, and he invited me to stay the night. I said certainly not—I had certainly heard better chat-up lines in my time.'

'And then?' Irvine kept pushing, dreading where he knew this must end up.

'Well, then infrequently he'd invite me around for dinner or a drink. As a man, he was still giving nothing away, and I was still intrigued. He kept inviting me to bed, and I'd keep saying no. I have to say—in his defence, as a gentleman—he never pushed the matter. But you know, it always felt a bit like he was trying to *negotiate* me into his bed.'

'And?'

'And . . . that's it, Detective Sergeant. I hate to disappoint you, too, but I'm prepared to do dinner and drinks in pursuit of my research, but I'm certainly not prepared to sleep around for an insight into how people's mind's work.'

'Oh!'

'If I'm not greatly mistaken, James Irvine, you seem somewhat relieved.'

'Oh, you know . . . I mean . . . it's really none of my busin—'

'I think I know *exactly* what you mean,' she said kindly. 'And your first thoughts were correct—I'm *not* that kind of girl.'

'And what about Monday this week?' Irvine asked in a slightly more civil tone.

'Well, the previous Friday, Neil rang me to invite me round for dinner on Monday. He promised to whip up another of his specialities, à la Marks and Spencer. I advised him that I was shooting late and leaving early the following morning and that I'd prefer to leave it to another time. We'd seen each other about four times by that stage and we still hadn't even kissed. Now, for a man who had more front than Sainsbury's, I was more than a little surprised, to be honest. I kept expecting him to move into a different gear. He did seem a wee bit more desperate than usual when he rang on Friday, however.'

'How so?'

'Normally when I couldn't see him, for whatever reason, he'd just let it go, but on Friday, he politely kept up the pressure, saying out-of-character things like, "I really enjoy our chats" and "I'm really looking forward to seeing you again"—all of that stuff—and so I thought I'd wasted enough time on the great romancer, but I'd give him one final chance, and if there was no . . .' She paused and smiled a smile that melted Irvine's heart. Irvine wondered if she knew what she was doing or if it was just her natural charm. She continued, 'You know, James, if there was no research material, as you so eloquently put it, I would drop him, for once and for all. I always thought there must have been something else going on in his mind, but either I couldn't get it or he was someone who compartmentalises everything and not one of his friends gets it all. I was still intrigued to try one final time, so I told him I'd come around but that I'd be late. It was nearly ten by the time I got there. He did a few Indian starters with dips-type thingies for me—he knew I liked them. I brought a bottle of wine, and we went round in exactly the same circles as we had in the past.'

'He invited you to go to bed?'

'Yes, he asked as usual and I declined as usual. I decided that Neil's pulling secret was that he had no secret. I know there are probably girls who fall for his "I may be a playboy, but still I'm really cool around women" routine. What on earth's going on there, James?' she asked.

Irvine did not seem to have any answers, or if he had, he wasn't offering them.

It was Nealey Dean's turn to switch tack: 'Are you married? Do you have a girlfriend? Do you have a boyfriend?'

'In the order of your questions: I'm not, I don't and definitely not.'

'Does that mean you're not a good guy then?'

'Sorry?'

'Well, my girlfriend—that's a friend who's a girl by the way—says that all the good guys are either married or gay.'

'Maybe she meant to say that all the safe, good guys are either married or gay.'

'She also said that there are currently 50,000 more single girls in London that single men.'

Irvine wondered why he did not take any comfort from that particular statistic.

'Hmm,' Nealey mused. 'I've just thought of something, James. Do you think Neil Roberts might have wanted to see me on Monday night just so I could be his alibi?'

'No, definitely not,' Irvine replied immediately.

'How come you're so sure?'

'Elementary, my dear Nealey, elementary,' Irvine replied with a smile James Bond would have been proud of. 'That's why I asked you if Neil Roberts had invited you to bed. You see, if you'd said yes and accepted his invitation, I know for sure he just wouldn't have been able to resist, so this action, potentially—if you had accepted—would have foiled any other trick he had up his sleeve.'

'Flattery will get you . . . somewhere,' Nealey said, stealing a glance at her watch. 'Erm, look . . .'

'I'm sorry. I've been behaving like a married man by outstaying my welcome,' Irvine said, rising as quickly as a startled deer.

'Yes, I mean no. It's just I've got a rehearsal meeting with a director down in Soho Square in about twenty minutes . . .'

'I could drop you down if you like,' Irvine offered.

'Yes, I'd like that,' Nealey said, jumping up from her sofa and running around the room, sticking this and that and just about everything into her backpack. She disappeared into her bedroom and returned wearing a floppy red woollen jumper. She broke the world record for applying a coat of vibrant red lipstick. Just as she was breaking away from her image in the mirror, she brushed her forefinger along her lips and used the crimson-coloured finger to add a little blush to her cheeks. 'Just a handy trick of the trade—you must promise never to tell a soul.'

On the sixteen-minute journey down to Soho, they chatted away about everything under the sun. Just as Nealey Dean exited the car, she scribbled something on her yellow-paged notebook, tore out the page and pushed it into Irvine's hand.

'That's my mobile,' she said with a smile. 'Just in case you need any more information on Neil Roberts.'

Irvine did not feel the slightest bit self-conscious as he smelt the yellow page for her perfume, before carefully folding it up, with a smile, and placing it in the breast pocket of his tweed coat.

Chapter Thirty-Eight

KENNEDY WAS SURE there was some information he had missed during his previous meeting with Alice Cain. He had no idea what it was, and he did not believe that she had actually lied to him. He wondered, in the middle of a mess such as the one he was working on, what exactly was the difference between the lies and the truth. In a Flintstones flash, he remembered—it was his job to discover precisely that.

In his briefing with Irvine over the actress—who had made a mighty impression on the detective sergeant—one of Neil Roberts's lies had come to light. Or had it? Roberts had not actually claimed to be intimate with Miss Dean. He had never used the specific words, 'And we slept together.' But he had implied it, hadn't he? Why had he done that? From Roberts's point of view, the alibi still stood, whether or not he and Nealey Dean had had sex. On reflection, he also certainly could have been more discreet and said that he had spent the evening with a Miss Harriet Webb. He certainly could have spared the young actress some potential embarrassment with the use of her real name. She had been in his company during those vital hours—the hours when Harry Ford had lost his life—so what did it matter what they had been doing? From Roberts's point of view, did he consider that sleeping with a beautiful young actress made him a bigger, better man in other people's eyes? What did that tell Kennedy about the type of person Roberts was?

Kennedy had not been as quick as Irvine to dismiss Nealey's suggestion that perhaps Roberts had, to some extent, staged her presence as an alibi. But why would he want to do that? Why would he need an alibi? What motive could he have had?

Now, on the other hand, Frazer McCracken certainly had a motive, and, thanks to Jill Codona's file copy, Kennedy had proof that it was quite a big motive. Kennedy had sent Irvine and King off to pick up McCracken. 'Arrest him if necessary,' had been Kennedy's instruction.

Kennedy thought about McCracken. Surely someone whose star is so obviously on the ascent was not going to murder Harry Ford just for a couple of hundred grand. And if McCracken's star had been allowed to keep on rising to the top, what salary could he have been hoping to achieve? £150,000 perhaps; maybe even as much as £200,000? This was not really very much when you considered that Ford's report suggested that McCracken had illegally turned over nearly four, possibly five, times that amount. Ford had also intimated that McCracken was up to other scams as well.

Once again, Kennedy found himself returning to a recurring conundrum. For the sake of his thought, as he strolled though Regent's Park in the direction of Marylebone, he framed Frazer McCracken as the murderer and Harry Ford as the victim. Now, in that set of circumstances, why would McCracken feel that he had a right or a justification to murder Harry Ford? It was ludicrous to think that McCracken would feel exonerated just because his career prospects, not to mention his freedom, were in danger should Harry Ford continue to live.

If there was such a thing, a higher being, then surely a mitigating circumstance in this instance should have been the fact that Harry Ford was a family man?

How was it, or why was it, that in the big picture, a dishonest person, such as Frazer McCracken, would be allowed to live, just because, in his book, the end justified the means, while at the same time an honest person, such as Harry Ford, would be condemned to die, even though he would never consider committing such an act against a fellow man or woman?

Where was the logic in that?

Kennedy was not getting any further in his quest for an answer, and he certainly was not going to get any further on that particular Thursday morning, because, at that precise moment, he arrived at the home of Mrs Alice Cain.

'Oh, it's you,' Alice said in greeting as she opened the door. 'Goodness, you look like you were miles away.'

'Sorry,' Kennedy replied shakily. 'I was wracking my brain to try and find the solution to an age-old puzzle.'

'Oh, and what puzzle would that be?' Alice asked as she showed him straight through to the kitchen area.

So, Kennedy told her exactly what he had been thinking. He obviously removed McCracken and Ford's names from the equation.

By the time the superb tea was brewed, Alice had given Kennedy's problem her consideration.

'I think the easiest way to look at it is to believe that this instinct to prey and kill must have been inherited from our animal forefathers and mothers. We're all still living by the basic laws of the jungle, and when it comes down to it, those instincts quite simply take control of our actions.'

'Surely—' Kennedy started.

'No, I know what you're going to say, but please hear me out first,' Alice said, interrupting him as she passed him a plate loaded with home-made chocolate-chip cookies.

'There's no finer way to keep me quiet,' Kennedy replied as he tore into one, resisting the temptation to dunk, of course.

'I hope you don't mind, but I prefer to dunk mine,' she said. Then, following as expert a dunk as Kennedy had ever witnessed, she continued, 'My husband and I were watching a programme on the Discovery Channel, the other night. It was all about lions and how they hunt their prey. And I'll tell you something: after watching that, I know exactly where the murder instinct, if not justification, comes from.

'When you watch a lion in its attack, it is so natural, so uninhibited, in fact, it even seems so at one with nature. The lion, in its need to kill, shows neither care nor respect for the rest of the herd; spares not a single second's thought for the buffalo's family nor the orphans his rampage will surely leave.'

'Surely the main difference is that if the lion doesn't kill, then its family will starve,' Kennedy said as he polished off the last of the delicious cookies.

'Well, yes, I'd agree, and that's what I'm saying in a way,' Alice said, as if she were reliving the brutal scenes she had just described. 'That's certainly where it originally came from, from our need to survive, and although we've obviously, at least on the surface, grown a lot more sophisticated, deep down, those instincts are still there. So what we do when our family is being attacked is to revert to these primeval feelings. I'll admit to you here and now that I would commit murder if it meant protecting my children. I'd happily die doing so. If push comes to shove, and no matter our breeding, no matter our class, we'd all go at it hammer and tongs. We might not be as graceful or as cunning as the lion, but surely that's only because we don't have the experience of doing it every day of our lives any more?

'Take you and your work—surely there have been instances where a fight breaks out, and you've witnessed that rarely do people stop and think about the strength of the enemy. No, they just lash out and continue to do so until they know they are safe. Never will they stop and think, "Oh, I won't hit them on the chin too hard in case I break their jaw or drive their nose up into their brain and kill them." We're all driven by instinct; we kick, bite, punch and body charge until the enemy has been immobilised.

'So, let's take our case. Harry Ford's a good man, a family man, but someone obviously decided that he was a threat. Perhaps they even considered Harry, with his knowledge, a danger to their family, and so, for their peace of mind, Harry had to be terminated. Maybe he was just in the wrong place at the wrong time. We just don't know. Perhaps Harry, good and all as he was, did something wrong himself and just had to pay the price for it.'

Kennedy asked, 'In all the time you knew Harry, did you ever know him to do any wrong?'

'Hold on a minute. Let's slow way down here. Now, that's a big question, isn't it? I suppose that would all depend on from whose perspective you were looking, wouldn't it? I mean, let's be honest here, fathering a child with another man's wife in some circles is not considered to be a very nice thing to do. From Harry's and my point of view, though, Caroline is a symbol and result of our love for each other. From my husband's perspective, or from Lizabeth's perspective, for that matter, I'm not so sure they'd wish to be so liberal with their degrees of understanding. Do you see what I'm getting at here?'

'Yes, I do,' Kennedy replied. 'Erm, anything else? We were talking about if you were aware of Harry ever having done any wrong.'

'Well, our continued affair,' Alice said. 'Again, it was all fine and rosy from where we stood, but at the same time I will admit that if Lizabeth and Bob were the ones having the affair, I'm not so sure I'd have been able to turn a blind eye or even the other cheek. I'm not sure I would have been the forgiving member of the foursome.'

'Would you have forgiven him if he'd been having an affair with someone else?' Kennedy asked, thinking particularly at that moment about Jill Codona.

'Well, if he had several affairs, then perhaps I'd have justified his actions as being those of a typical man with lustful weaknesses. But being with one person, well that implies love, doesn't it?'

'And you and Harry were really in love?'

'Most definitely,' she replied confidently, appearing shocked that he would even entertain the thought that they were not, let alone seek clarification on it. 'Mostly I'd have to admit that as far as men in my life are concerned—mainly Neil, Vincey, Harry and Bob—my life has been a complete and unmitigated disaster. However, having said that, in Harry's case, I am totally convinced I loved him, and I know he loved me. Shall I tell you how I know; why I'm so confident?'

'Yes, please,' Kennedy said.

'Actually, now I come to it, I find myself embarrassed. I assure you that I've no reason to feel proud of my actions. I've never told anyone this before, and I suppose I'm telling you not simply to prove to you the power of Harry's love, but in the hope that the information may be of some help to you in your investigation.'

This might be interesting" Kennedy thought as he said, 'At this stage, Alice, we can't have enough information.'

'Okay. About four or five years ago, I persuaded Harry to leave Lizabeth,' Alice said, and then appeared to be studying Kennedy to see what he thought of her revelation. After a few seconds, she continued, 'Don't you want to know why?'

'Well, I would have thought the reason would be pretty obvious.'

'Okay, you tell me why,' Alice said.

'Well, you were both in love, and it seems to me it would have been something you both wanted.'

'I'm sorry to admit, it wasn't quite as noble as that. I persuaded him to leave Lizabeth to prove to myself, as much as anyone else, that I could make him leave her.'

She obviously saw the disappointment in Kennedy's eyes.

'Ah, come on, Christy. You must know by now, all love is not as untainted and chaste as you'd like to believe. You know, there really is no such a thing as living happily ever after. Even when the princess is awoken from her sleep by the magic kiss, she still has to go to the toilet because her bladder's bursting; the food still needs cooking; the dishes still need washing; and then when the children come, they still need to be attended to twenty-four hours a day. So, even in paradise, reality has to set in. I see someone—say, for the sake of our discussion, Harry Ford, for instance. We meet and we disrobe and we make love. Sometimes it's great and sometimes it's not. We share a glass of wine or two and we put our clothes on, we say goodbye and we go home. We do this week in, week out, month in and month out. Yes, and then that becomes year in and year out and, before you know it, half of our lives have passed by and, well, you know, perhaps that's when you realise how flawed you are and how maybe paradise is not all it was made out to be after all.'

'A bit like the line in one of Dylan's songs: 'and don't go mistaking paradise for that place across the road'?

'It's a lot like that, Christy. So, then you find yourself thinking, *Well, Harry hasn't really had to make much of a sacrifice, has he? He's been married and he's enjoyed his bit on the side*. A bit on the side, in point of fact, who was so considerate that she had never ever asked him to leave his wife. And, right there in that gem of a thought, the evil seed has been sown, and you watch helplessly as it blossoms into a fully grown whinge.

'And the whinge wouldn't go away. Eventually I heard a voice, my voice, say, "Enough of this, Harry. Either we have to move in together or we have to stop seeing each other." And immediately, he replies, "You're right." And I say, "It's okay for you; you don't have a lot to give up." I realise how I was being very immature, referring to lifestyle here, of course. And then I told Harry that before I would give up all of my life, I wanted proof that he would actually take the plunge and be with me. He said, "Okay, that's fair." And two weeks later, he rang me and said, "Right, I've done my bit. I've got a place and I've moved into it; now it's your turn."

'He kept saying it was my turn. I went round to see his new, clinical flat. God bless him, he hadn't a clue—it was a DIY Habitat heaven. I told him he'd passed the test; he could move back to his beautiful home with Lizabeth. He got all upset and asked if it was the flat. He said not to worry about it, that it was just temporary accommodation. I told him it wasn't the flat. I told him breaking up with Bob was not what I wanted to do with my life, and as I was explaining this to him, he just got up and walked out on me, and wouldn't speak to me for ages and ages. You know, if I'm honest with myself, and I try to be, it's never been the same between us since. Yes, we did get together again and resumed our weekly habits, but I suppose, in his eyes, I'd spoiled our love, and you know what? I probably had. But the real moral to the tale was that he hadn't told Lizabeth that he was leaving her for me. So, really, he'd proved nothing to me other than that he knew how to find a bedsit. So, that little episode surely said a little about both of us.'

'So, as far as you were concerned, Lizabeth knew nothing about you and Harry?'

'Absolutely nothing.'

'What about your husband?'

'The same, nothing,' Alice said, and then added as an afterthought, 'That is, of course, apart from the information I had to reveal to him about the will and all of that.'

'Then you'd be surprised if I told you that your husband was aware of the little tiff you and Harry had about five years ago?'

'No, never! Who told you that?'

'He did. He said that apart from that one time, he never felt that there was a risk of losing you.'

'I suppose he also told you he'd known about Harry and me from the beginning?'

'He did, as a matter of a fact,' Kennedy admitted.

'Yeah, well, that's Bob for you. He always has to give the impression that he knows absolutely everything that's going on and that he's the one in complete control of everything.'

'What about your brother? Did Neil know anything about Harry's and your plans?'

'Wow!' Alice blew a large sigh through her lips. He might have expected that such a gesture would have made her look ugly. But for some reason it didn't, though it certainly made her look slightly comical. Kennedy could not figure out if the sign came from exasperation at his continued questions or from frustration over her brother.

Kennedy was not prepared to let the question go, so he said nothing, merely continuing to look Alice in the eye.

Eventually she spoke again: 'Look, Harry and Neil weren't really each other's confidant. They were no longer the college friends of all those years ago. They'd clearly outgrown each other. For some strange reason, they both kept up a kind of relationship. I asked Harry why and he replied, 'Habit.' I suppose maybe the underlying thing between them was, from Harry's point of view, firstly we were in a relationship of sorts, and secondly Neil is my brother, so a certain amount of civility was called for. From Neil's point of view, it's harder to figure. Perhaps he sensed there was something unresolved between Harry and me, and he . . . well, come to think of it, Neil doesn't really seem to have any friends of his own and so maybe he held the relationship with Harry because of that. Hey, Christy, I don't know. I'm struggling here to find things for you.

'But enough about me,' Alice sighed, drawing a line of sorts under this story. 'What I'm intrigued about is how a respectable, seemingly intelligent detective inspector can be confused as to whether or not he's in a relationship.'

'Sorry?' Kennedy asked, badly wrong-footed.

'Well, I was asking Vincey O'Connor about you, and he was saying that you claimed that you didn't know if you were in a relationship or not.'

Kennedy was wondering how much of the ann rea story he would tell.

'Well, it's difficult, you see, she's . . . well, I suppose in a way she's still suffering from her previous—'

'Hang on, hang on a minute,' Alice said, slapping her hands down firmly on her thighs and cutting him off in his tracks. 'Over our two meetings, I've completely spilt my guts, enlightening you on chapter and verse of my life, and you seem to be working under the misapprehension that I'm going to permit you to fast forward even the edited highlights version of yours. No, no, no, Mr Kennedy. Let's go back to the sandy beaches of . . .' She paused to search her memory banks. 'I believe it was Portrush Harry told me you came from.'

'Yes,' Kennedy sighed largely. 'You know what? I'm afraid my student life wasn't as exciting as yours. I studied at the New University of Ulster in Coleraine, which is but a few miles away from my home, so I commuted. I'd a couple of mates; we'd go to the ballrooms to see the showbands. As Portrush is a seaside town, we had a big ballroom, the Arcadia, and all the main showbands played there, and none better than Billy Brown and the Freshmen. I think they were responsible for turning me on to music. I mean, the majority of people visited the ballrooms in order to meet a boy or a girl. For my own part, I went mostly to hear the music.

'Through bands like the Freshmen, who played mainly cover material, I got turned on to Ray Charles, Hank Williams, the Beatles, the Kinks, the Interns, Taste and Them. Through Them, I discovered Van Morrison. Through the Beatles, I got turned on to Dylan and American music. I mean, music literally stopped me in my tracks. I've never really been one to favour getting under the influence of alcohol, but I will admit to being under the influence of music lots of the time.'

'I hope this is leading somewhere, Detective Inspector,' Alice said with a smile. 'Are you trying to distract me just so that you can avoid telling me about your romantic life?'

'No, I mean, yes,' Kennedy stuttered, himself thrown off course by the unexpected interruption. 'I think because I was so into music at that stage, I neglected the romantic side of my life.'

'Or you used it as an excuse to avoid contact with the fairer sex?' she added.

'Perhaps . . .' Kennedy replied and paused, appearing to consider that as a possibility, for the first time. 'University over, I moved straight to London, joined the police force, and within a few weeks of moving to London, met and fell in love with a young girl.'

'Ah,' Alice sighed. 'Young love—this is precisely what we want to hear about.'

'Well, sadly there's not a lot to tell you about. I loved her; she didn't really love me although she liked me—'

'And where have we heard that tale before?' she asked, but continued before an answer was offered: 'At least you didn't run off and become a priest in protest. And her name?'

'I didn't really do anything quite so drastic. I wanted to become a policeman because I grew up loving to consider the puzzle of the crime. It always fascinated me, but I'd never even considered trying to make a living out of it until my father suggested it. Anyway, I'm in London, loving my work, and before I know it, I wake up one morning, it's twenty-plus years later, and I realise that I've totally ignored one side of my life. I mean, yes, again I will admit I've enjoyed a few relationships along the way but none that were ever due to become anything more than two people on their way somewhere else enjoying a little time together.'

They spent the time it took to drink a cup of tea talking about things other than the case.

Alice offered a refill. Kennedy refused, choosing that precise moment to continue what the visit was meant to be about, namely questioning Alice Roberts.

'Do you and your brother get on well, Alice?'

'Well, what a strange question,' Alice said and leaned back in her chair, affording Kennedy a new and perhaps more respectful look. 'Neil and I didn't have a bad relationship. Being candid with you, we had a lot of issues which we resolved just before we went to university.'

'Issues?' Kennedy asked, feeling the ice creak under him.

'Personal issues, Christy,' she replied very quietly. 'You know, where one becomes confused over emotional lines. When I met Harry, Neil's and my relationship changed. My brother is always there when I need him. He's certainly an amazing uncle to my children. It's a difficult one. Though I loved Harry, I couldn't really say I love Neil. Is that a bad thing to admit about your brother? I don't know.'

Kennedy did not know either; he had never had any brothers, or sisters, for that matter.

He left Alice Cain with her thoughts and wondered if there was anything else she was still holding from him. Could he dare assume what he felt she had been hinting at?

Kennedy took some time out to think about Harry Ford, Lizabeth Ford and Alice Cain.

He wondered how Harry felt being with Lizabeth when he really wanted to be with Alice. Did that feeling ever disappear? From Kennedy's perspective, Alice was everything Lizabeth was not: naturally beautiful, sensual, comfortable, relaxed, earnest, considerate. Equally he realised that this was his comparison and did not necessarily mean that Lizabeth was not beautiful, sensual, comfortable, relaxed, earnest and considerate. It just meant that when he compared Lizabeth to Alice, she was lacking, in those departments.

Similarly, for example, when Steve Ovett beat Sebastian Coe into second in a 400-metres race, Ovett was still the winner and poor Coe was beaten into second place. But surely the important thing to remember here was that Coe, even when beaten, was still the second-best runner in the whole fecking world!

Kennedy considered areas in which Lizabeth might have been superior to Alice. For instance, was there a faint possibility that Lizabeth was a better mother than Alice? Perhaps, was his conclusion, although he realised that he had not witnessed Alice around her children to say for sure. And then again, was Lizabeth the type of person who would put on a show with her children just for the effect?

For Kennedy, the thing about Alice Cain was that she was—*No, 'was' is not the correct word,* he thought. Perhaps it would be better to say that she 'appeared' to be a more intuitive woman. So, Harry Ford knew both of them and, you would have to assume, knew both well. Did he feel that Lizabeth was inferior to Alice? When Kennedy had been in Harry and Lizabeth's company, they had seemed genuinely affectionate, although there was always just that wee bit of . . . what was it? Kennedy tried to get a grasp on his thoughts, trying hard to articulate them properly, knowing that if he managed to catch them correctly, he might be on to something. He knew from experience that your subconscious can pick up on things your consciousness is rarely able to tune into.

So, what was it he would say about Lizabeth and how she reacted with her prime mate? Well, she seemed to be always holding something back in reserve. Whereas when Harry would genuinely want to condole with her— as on the occasion when Kennedy and O'Connor had been in the Ford house for supper—Lizabeth did not react naturally. She reacted as perhaps she felt someone should react when their partner wanted to cuddle with them in public.

Now, Kennedy knew that there were a few mitigating circumstances— mainly the fact that Lizabeth might have a preference for privacy in such intimate moments. Nevertheless, Kennedy still felt that Alice would have handled the situation differently.

Kennedy returned to his original thought about how Harry might feel about continually being with the wrong woman.

When he visited Alice on family occasions, did he think *This should be my home—I, and not Bob, should be staying here and going to bed with this woman?*

Would Bob Cain ever have picked up on this resentment?

Both men had made love with Alice Cain.

Would Bob Cain have resented that?

And, if he didn't resent the past, supposedly defunct, relationship, would he have resented the renewal of their affair shortly after Fr O'Connor's ordination?

And if he was a mature enough man to take that in his stride, surely knowing, as he claimed he did, that Harry had fathered Caroline, whom Bob had brought up as his daughter, would be quite simply too much to take. Was that the step too far that Harry had taken—the deed that had sealed his fate?

Had Bob Cain some kind of grudge against O'Connor which might make him want to land him in the frame by making the sign of the cross on Ford's torso?

Kennedy realised that he had veered away from his thought towards Bob Cain. He realised that he wanted to consider the difference between making love to Alice Cain and making love to Lizabeth Ford. Rather than be negative on Lizabeth's behalf, he preferred the more gracious route of concentrating on Alice's qualities. Her naturalness would have been the key quality.

But would her naturalness run through her other personal qualities—say, for instance, extending to forgiveness of Harry's continued intimacy with his wife?

Alice Cain worried Kennedy; instinctively he was not entirely comfortable with her as a suspect. His main concern was whether he would be so unsure of her as a suspect if she weren't so beautiful, sensual, relaxed, earnest and comfortable with herself.

However, Kennedy felt that, unlike the next person he was about to question, there was little or no chance that Alice Cain or his other suspect would be tempted to do a runner.

Chapter Thirty-Nine

RAZER MCCRACKEN REFUSED to say a word until his brief was present, and so he had to stew in his muggy cell in North Bridge House until Scottie Burns could firstly be located and secondly be persuaded to visit North Bridge House. The entire process took about two and a half hours, so it was just around lunchtime when McCracken, Burns, Irvine and Kennedy sat across the table from each other in the windowless interview room.

Scottie Burns subscribed to the DLD (dresses like dad) fashion school and was wearing inexpensive brown shoes, grey flannel trousers, a red button-down shirt, which clashed totally with his flush-red completion, and a brown corduroy jacket. He had boyish, unkempt black hair, which contrasted completely with his organised briefcase, which he placed on the table and opened, removing a note pad, a pen and pencil, a rubber and a ruler. All of the above he arranged in his space on the table. Kennedy thought Burns was behaving more like someone about to sit his GCE examination than someone about to give legal guidance to a client who quite possibly was guilty of murder.

McCracken, on the other hand, had probably spent a considerable amount of time raiding his wardrobe that morning. Kennedy was not altogether sure it was time well spent and wondered if it would have been considered appropriate dress code for his first day back in the office, although McCracken was prone to attitude statements. An opened Hawaiian shirt revealing a grey t-shirt, khaki jungle shorts with bulging pockets and black sandals (more like soles). With hindsight, it might not have been the best uniform to be caught wearing when the police picked one up.

Kennedy made the announcement for the benefit of Madge (tape recorder) and allowed a few moments for Burns and/or McCracken to say something. In Kennedy's less charitable view, both characters were cut from the same cloth in that they both gave off the air of people who felt the world owed them a living, and for whom the end always justified the means.

But would McCracken go so far as to murder someone to achieve his ends, and would Burns knowingly represent a murderer to further his ambitions?

Neither was currently giving anything away, so Kennedy took the first throw.

'Mr McCracken, I wanted to talk to you about your time at the Coalition and Aylesbury Building Society.'

'Look,' Burns immediately replied, setting the tone. 'We were under the impression this meeting was about Harry Ford's murder.'

'I know I certainly didn't give that impression,' Kennedy said and turned to Irvine. 'Detective Sergeant, did you give these two fine gentlemen any reason to believe that they were called in here to discuss the specific matter of Mr Ford's murder alone?'

'No, sir, not at all.'

'Okay, okay. Let's lose the Laurel and Hardy routine,' Burns interrupted again. 'Can I just say that the CABS affair has finally been put to rest. My client was reinstated in his rightful position this morning. And not only that, but I can now confirm, in the strictest confidence, of course, that his promotion to branch manager will be announced in the near future.'

'Which won't have been helped by the Camden Town flatfoots streaming into the offices this morning and arresting me,' McCracken said, and then addressed the tape recorder directly: 'I tell you now, if I lose this promotion, I'm going to hold you personally responsible.'

'Yes, yes,' Kennedy said dismissively. He wondered how McCracken and Burns had persuaded CABS to break their normal policy of not promoting people upwards in their current branch. He also wondered who'd lost their soul to the devil on that deal, as he announced guardedly, 'I wonder if, just for the record, your client would be prepared to provide us with a copy of his signature?'

'I would have no objection to that,' Burns announced on behalf of his client, giving the impression that he fully expected the proceeding to be over in minutes, if not seconds.

Frazer McCracken flamboyantly put his signature on a clean piece of paper that Kennedy had slid in front of him. Kennedy even offered McCracken the use of the standard issue Met biro. McCracken looked at him as if the detective had offered him cold potatoes for dessert. He produced his own monster-sized Mont Blanc. Kennedy asked for a repeat signature on a second clean sheet of paper. Again, Burns and McCracken were cooperative to a fault.

Kennedy gave one of the signatures to Irvine and kept the other for himself. Both police officers studied their respective pages for at least a minute while Burns quite literally clapped his hands.

'Yes,' Kennedy began. 'It looks familiar. Let me think, where did I see this signature last? Yes, I think I remember. James, could you please pass me the file?'

Kennedy could not be sure, but he thought he caught a slight flicker of betrayal in McCracken's eyes. Burns, on the other hand, seemed oblivious to the proceedings and was making a very good impression of someone who needed to go to the toilet.

Kennedy opened the file and said, 'Yes, I think I'm right. Just for the record, however, could you confirm that this is, in fact, your signature on this CABS withdrawal form?'

McCracken made the mistake of checking the signature before checking the details on the file.

'Yes, it's mine,' he announced impatiently.

Kennedy announced to the tape recorder, 'I've just shown Mr Frazer McCracken a CABS account withdrawal form, reference number "W1FE". He's just verified that this form includes his signature authorising a Swift Chaps transfer of £150,000 to be transferred from Mr Samuel Watson's savings account into an account at Mansell's Bank in the Isle of Man. The account holder there was S. Watson.'

McCracken had just turned bright red.

Kennedy continued, 'Sir, just for the record, would you mind reading out the date of the transaction?'

McCracken froze.

'Sorry, sir,' Kennedy said, now addressing Burns. 'Your client appears to have lost his tongue. Could you please advise the date on which your client approved this transaction?'

'March 17 this year,' Burns replied, with a can't-anybody-here-read?-shake of the head.

'Yes, that's what we saw, too,' Kennedy said. 'Now, can you please tell me, sir, how it could be possible for Samuel Watson to transfer funds out of his account into another account marked "S. Watson" when the same

Mr Watson, veteran of both wars and long-time saver with CABS, had died prior to the transaction?'

This time, Burns took the file and studied it more closely. Eventually, with no apparent enlightenment coming from his client, he said, 'These dates can't be right. There must be a typo or something.'

'So it would appear. But I have to tell you, they are correct. We've had the Fraud Squad working on them, and they've confirmed that all the dates are correct.'

'But you can't do anything about this. CABS have already had their tribunal, and they've decided there are no charges to answer. You certainly can't go digging this up again; apart from anything else, you've no jurisdiction. All of this is already done and dusted. Look, if you've nothing else, we're out of here,' McCracken semi-shouted as he stood up and pushed the table away from him in disgust. 'This is a travesty. We're out of here, Scottie.'

Irvine stood up and nodded to McCracken to sit down. He then repeated his request, this time verbally, for the benefit of the tape recorder.

'Look, Frazer,' Kennedy announced, breaking the stalemate. 'There are two of you on that side of the table, and there are at least fifty officers in the station. In short, there are a lot more of us than there are of you. So, just sit down.'

'I don't need to listen to this. CABS dropped their charges—can't you hear properly? Ring them yourself, and confirm it. Here,' he said, searching in his pocket. 'I'll even give you the money for the phone.' McCracken continued to search around in his pocket, appearing unable to find a coin. 'Damn it,' he grandstanded, pulling a wad of notes out of his back pocket. He peeled off a twenty-pound note which he flung at Kennedy in sheer unadulterated disgust. 'Take it out of this, asshole. You can keep the change!'

The major problem with throwing bank notes, notes of any denomination, is that their journey tends to take a lot longer than anyone, say an irritated embezzler for instance, would expect, and the effect of a twenty-pound note floating lifelessly down on to the floor bordered on pure Laurel and Hardy comedy.

Irvine stood up, put his hand on McCracken's shoulder, and bent at his hips and knees so that he squatted on the floor. His sheer strength contrasting with McCracken's feebleness and the shock resulted in McCracken's tumbling back into his chair. With his other hand, Irvine lifted the twenty-pound note from the floor and shoved it unceremoniously into McCracken's breast pocket.

'Listen, sir,' Irvine said, his accent and contempt managing to make the word 'sir' sound more dismissive than McCracken had managed with the word 'asshole' earlier, 'I'd keep that if I were you. I think it might come in handy for your defence.'

'Listen, you can't keep me here—'

'He's absolutely right,' Burns said, speaking for the first time since Kennedy's disclosure. 'You can't hold my client here indefinitely on some trumped-up charges just so you can try and pin the Harry Ford murder case on him.'

'No,' Kennedy said, hoping his mock sigh was not too transparent. 'You're right, of course. We can't hold your client indefinitely . . .'

McCracken and Burns celebrated this announcement by simultaneously breaking into large smiles.

'. . . that is, of course, unless we're going to charge your client,' Kennedy continued once McCracken and Burns had enjoyed their brief moment of relief. 'Detective Sergeant Irvine here and I—we felt that the appropriate thing to do would be to give you all of our evidence before we charge you. But make no mistake, sir, charge you we will, and we believe our colleagues in the Fraud Squad will have a lot more charges to lay at your feet as well.'

Kennedy then went through all the names and details contained in Harry Ford's valuable file. Names like the aforementioned Samuel Watson, not to mention Miss Ethel Greenaway and Mr Brian Batchelor. DC Dot King had spent a considerable amount of time putting characters and stories to the names. Then there were the likes of Gary Millings, Tamsin Pearce, Patricia Armstrong, Mr and Mrs Jack Hill and even the strangely named Cornelius Costello, all of whom had had their mortgage requests rejected by CABS representative, Mr Frazer McCracken, who then proceeded to make a killing on the properties they had taken the time and energy to research and find.

On and on, Kennedy read the details of Camden Redevelopment Town Properties Ltd, and how that company had acted as a front for McCracken to siphon off funds he had swindled out of the dormant accounts.

McCracken and his beetroot hues seemed to confirm this. He looked like someone who had been done up like a kipper.

Kennedy posed but one simple question at the end of his tirade of facts, figures and accusations: 'The thing I can't work out, Frazer, is why your friends at CABS were so lenient with you.'

'Perhaps,' McCracken replied, doing a perfect impression of Johnny Rotten, 'I wasn't the only one to be helping myself from that particularly well-stocked candy jar.'

'Before we formally bring these charges against you, there is another investigation we'd like to discuss with you, sir,' Kennedy began, as the vision of Errol McGuinn disappeared from his mind's eye. 'The death of Mr Harry Ford.'

Kennedy instilled in the name Harry Ford as much pride as it was possible to muster. He wanted—he needed—to get across the high esteem in which he held Harry Ford in contrast to the sheer contempt he had for McCracken.

Chapter Forty

'I'M AFRAID YOU'RE holding a turkey for a hand on that one,' McCracken boasted, with what Kennedy assessed to be a certain amount of pride.

'Well, let's just go back to the night in question, shall we? When we interviewed you on Tuesday, you told us that you'd gone out to meet your mates, who then didn't show up . . . ?'

'Yeah, it turns out I messed up. The West Hampstead meet was for the following night, the Tuesday night,' McCracken replied, proving that he had been doing a bit of checking himself.

'And,' Kennedy continued, 'we've been around to the Station pub on West End Lane—where you claimed you went to instead—and we took your photograph. No one remembered either you or the girl you said you met. We've done a house-to-house check on all of the streets around the area where you claimed this girl lived and, again, nothing. It would appear there is no such girl.'

'If only that were true,' McCracken said. He seemed happier now. Kennedy wondered if this had anything to do with the fact that, unlike the bulging file on him on the CABS case, the police did not seem to have any solid leads on the Ford murder front.

'Sorry?' Kennedy asked.

'Well, if only there were no such person,' McCracken said ungenerously, 'then I wouldn't have made the biggest mistake of my life.' He looked at the files in front of Kennedy before adding, 'Romantically speaking.'

'Come on, Frazer, up to ten minutes ago it appeared you'd got away on both the CABS matter and the Harry Ford case.'

'Correct, 'McCracken replied. 'But I didn't top him. I couldn't have. Tell me, how was I meant to have topped him?'

'Come on, don't try that old chestnut on us,' Irvine said with a laugh. 'Of course you know—you strangled him.'

'It couldn't have been me. I'd never have the strength to strangle a person, especially a geezer like Ford. He was in good shape, you know,' McCracken replied, blowing Irvine's little snare straight out of the water.

'That's what we thought,' Kennedy continued, trying to recover the lost ground. 'Which is why you stabbed him.'

'Strangled him, stabbed him—for goodness' sake, which way was it?' McCracken laughed in the direction of Burns, who had turned rather frosty towards his client since the CABS disclosure.

'Look, we know you stabbed him,' Irvine said, taking the lead and also trying to recover the gap. 'And we've got all day to go though this until we resolve it.'

And very nearly that's what they did—spent all day in the small interview room, breaking only for tea, coffee and sandwiches, which were the only enjoyable breaks for Kennedy and Irvine.

Kennedy thought about it afterwards and felt, from his perspective, that the experience was akin to being stuck in a multi-department store, knowing exactly where the exit points are but not being able, for the life of you, to find your way through the maze of clothes, shoes, perfume, food, cases, electrical equipment, bedding, furniture, jewellery, carpets, bathrooms, kitchens, and so on and so on, to get there. And every time you might think you're getting close to where you think the exit is, you find nothing but another wing of stores, and so off you go again in yet another direction, which also, eventually, proves fruitless.

In the end, they charged him with the embezzlement of CABS accounts, and he was handed over to Desk Sergeant Tim Flynn for further processing.

'You see,' Kennedy whispered to Irvine. 'I'm afraid I am guilty of breaking one of my key rules with Mr McCracken.'

'How so?' Irvine said, turning to face Kennedy.

'Well, McCracken looked a likely suspect—too likely a suspect really. So I tended to view his and his solicitor's reactions as being a bit bizarre, and I suppose, on reflection, that made me suspect him even more. You see, when McCracken's solicitor worked hard to orchestrate getting McCracken off the CABS charge, if anything his actions hinted even more at McCracken's need to get rid of Harry Ford, due to his knowledge. But the actual facts were that McCracken knew he hadn't killed Ford. No matter how big a criminal he was, he knew that fact. So, he wasn't really concerned about his alibi when we thought he should have been. We figured if he was innocent, he should have been trying to get CABS to drop their charges. But the important thing in all of this, and what we maybe should have understood better, was that he was behaving the way a man who was innocent of the murder charge would have behaved. Yes, he was an embezzler, but he saw a chance to get away with that and at the same time set his CABS ambitions back on the road again. And so he took it, regardless of what he knew we'd be thinking.'

'Yep,' Irvine sighed as they watched McCracken's shoulders dropped low. 'You're right.'

As Kennedy and Irvine were watching McCracken being led away on the first stage of his long (they hoped) incarceration, DC Dot King came up to them and announced, 'I've just been advised that Mr Bob Cain's Dutch alibi checks out, sir.'

'Same thing there, sir,' Irvine said in regret. 'He was just being indignant and pompous with us because he knew he was innocent.'

'Yep, and bang goes another suspect. Oh, well, as Holmes famously said, "when you have eliminated the impossible, whatever remains, however improbable, must be the truth," ' Kennedy muttered to no one in particular as he wandered off.

Chapter Forty-One

KENNEDY GATHERED ALL his team in his office shortly thereafter. 'Okay,' he said, and they all quietened down immediately. 'Let's work on another theory. You can't accumulate if you don't speculate. Let's pay a home visit to Mr Neil Roberts.'

'But we're wasting our time,' Irvine protested. 'He has a cast-iron alibi for the time Harry Ford was killed. I've spoken to the girl in question myself, and I would put my reputation on the line and state here and now that she is not the kind of girl who would lie for him.'

'Exactly,' Kennedy replied. 'And even taking into consideration that I'm prepared to believe Miss Nealey Dean without question, there's still something that doesn't quite fit. Sometimes it's better to examine the strongest alibis rather than the weaker ones. Apart from which, at this precise moment, we have absolutely nothing else to go on.'

Kennedy's statement drew a certain amount of laughter; the only problem, as far as Kennedy was concerned, however, was that he was speaking the absolute truth.

Either way, the end result was that at 8.47 that Thursday evening, DI Kennedy and his team of eleven of North Bridge House's finest knocked on the door of 99 St Mark's Mews, just off Regent's Park Road.

Neil Roberts had acquired two mews houses, the first one, it transpired, in 1988, and the second (nearly but not quite) adjoining one in 1996. He had spent a considerable amount of money converting and connecting the two houses into one home. For someone like Kennedy, it was too modern a house by far, but at the same time it was a property the likes of which *Elle Décor* would positively have wet themselves over.

Roberts had built a drive-in garage in the middle of the two properties and used the single-storey study above the garage as a means to cement the two houses together. He had completed the overall effect by pebble-dashing the entire frontage and painting it a distinctive terracotta colour.

Roberts looked shocked by the sight of the police on his doorstep and tried, unsuccessfully, to turn his surprise to nonchalance.

Kennedy said, 'Can we come in?'

'Of course,' Roberts replied, standing back into the narrow hallway.

'Do you mind if some of our colleagues come in as well for a look around?' Kennedy asked, knowing that Roberts could refuse and that, if he refused, by the time Kennedy had been able to get a search warrant, whatever it was that Kennedy was looking for would have been long gone.

'Is this still about Harry Ford?' Roberts asked.

'It's about Harry Ford,' Kennedy declared, knowing that any improprieties on his or his team's part at this stage would come back to haunt him.

'Well, you'd better come in then and for once and for ever get this over with,' Roberts replied. 'You know what I was doing at that time, don't you?'

'Yes,' Kennedy agreed, but waited until the majority of his team had crossed Roberts's threshold before adding, 'It's just that I wanted to examine more closely the time just before and just after your alibi period, if you don't mind.'

'Have you been speaking to Vincey or something?'

The question took Kennedy totally by surprise, but just in case there was some relevance to something Fr O'Connor might or might not have said, he replied, 'Let's just say, we're continuing a certain line of inquiry.'

The forensic team painstakingly examined every single square inch of Roberts's concrete garage floor and the adjoining workshop space. They did not, on close examination, find any hints of blood. They did find several empty plastic 2-litre mineral-water bottles, carpentry tools, some new unused wooden planks and boards, a newish-looking garden hose and a large wok lying on his otherwise tidy workbench. The officer who discovered it thought it was strange to keep a cooking utensil in the garage, and he showed Kennedy how it looked as if the carbon steel of the wok had been beaten in inch arcs in four locations on the rim, which could be considered the corners of a square. The officer bagged the wok for further examination back at the lab.

Just to show how efficient—or desperate, depending upon your standpoint—they were, the officers also took the contents of a dustbin which was positioned just under Roberts's workbench. The bin contained more empty plastic bottles; lots of used J-cloths; lots of used nails, from one to six-inch—some rusty; three empty Tate & Lyle 2 lb sugar packets; newspapers; a couple of empty biscuit packs; wood shavings; a steering-wheel glove; a cardboard box with what looked like the remnants of soil in the bottom; a single shoe; two used gaffer-tape cardboard spools; a discarded copy of a Tom Clancy paperback; a claw-hammerhead with a broken handle sticking out; various rusty washers; two leaky biro pens and several dead bulbs.

When the team had concluded its work in the garage, Kennedy, leaving Irvine with Roberts in the sitting room, took one of the stools from the kitchen and placed it in the centre of the garage floor space, then sat on it, studying the garage, turning slowly through 360 degrees. Unlike Ford, Roberts had not declared his passion for carpentry. Kennedy looked at the workbench with all the tools neatly racked within arm's reach. The detective noted that these tools were not purely for show—they had been used frequently and, more importantly, they had had good care taken of them.

What was it Kennedy's dad had frequently said to him while at work in his workshop? 'A bad workman blames his tools; a good workman cares for them.' The memory brought a smile to Kennedy's face. He remembered the hours he had enjoyed in his father's company as Kennedy senior had busied himself making some piece of furniture or, alternatively, working on repairing something. He remembered how he would question his dad about everything under the sun, and some things even over it. His father, with the patience of a saint, in his down-home kind of way, would explain things as he saw them. Most of those valuable snippets of wisdom had served Kennedy well all his life.

He continued to survey Neil Roberts's modern workshop.

Under the bench was a roll of plastic sheeting. He noticed a deep, clean Belfast sink to one corner of this bench. To the left of the sink was a worn car tyre. There were several grocer's weights lying on the floor beside the tyre. Kennedy wondered if Roberts used these for home training work. Was he the kind of person who would want an edge on his gym partner? At the opposite end of the bench was a Bunsen burner connected to a Calor gas cylinder underneath. There was a second spare cylinder next to it—perhaps empty.

Kennedy thought it was incredible what some people were prepared to accumulate and not be prepared to discard, no matter how useless and worn and no matter how much space such things took up. What would Roberts ever use the worn car tyre for again? For that matter, why was he holding on to a large wooden valve radio, a portable television, about four feet of a broken ladder, rolled-up window blinds and lampshades, all of which were heaped semi-neatly beside the tyre?

As Kennedy continued his examination, he was aware of two members of his team conducting a close inspection of Roberts's car, which was just outside the open garage door. It was a cool night and Kennedy thought the breeze quite pleasant. Every now and then, he would be distracted from his own search by one of the officers in the car carefully bagging something. Some of the time, Kennedy could not actually see what it was they were placing in their evidence bags. Kennedy thought that anyone watching them could be forgiven for thinking that they were confiscating invisible bits. Pretty soon, the car itself would be taken away for closer examination at the lab. All examinations were being videoed simultaneously, as back-up proof that nothing could have been planted.

By about 3.40 a.m. the following morning, the police had bagged, boxed and tagged all the stuff they believed might be relevant.

The truth was that when it came down to it, they did not really make any revolutionary discoveries which might have made Kennedy comfortable enough to read Roberts his rights and take him away for questioning. Instead, Kennedy had let his new chief suspect retire just after midnight when the team had done a thorough search of his bedroom and the adjoining bathroom.

But Kennedy was a patient man, and discovery on site was only a small part of the invaluable work the forensic team did.

At 11.30 that morning, he received his first call from the forensic team.

They had discovered that one of the J-cloths discovered in the dustbin contained traces of a water and sugar solution.

This turned out to be exactly the same solution and density as they had discovered on the arms of Harry Ford's new jacket and on the legs of his trousers.

At 12.15, Kennedy received the second call from the forensic team, whose officers were turning out to be front-line detectives on the Harry Ford murder case. This time, he was advised that the particles of fluff they had discovered on the passenger seat of Roberts's car matched neither the fabric from Ford's trousers nor that from his new jacket. However, several of the threads they had removed from the *back* seat of Roberts's car were definite matches to the fabric of Ford's jacket.

Irvine then entered Kennedy's office and said that he had checked with Dr Taylor one more time to see if he was absolutely convinced about the time of Ford's death. Irvine reported that Taylor had confirmed the time as being between 10.30 and 11.30.

Kennedy did not seem as disappointed with this news as Irvine was. The DI merely said: 'Okay, James, give me an hour, and then bring Neil Roberts in for questioning, will you?'

Chapter Forty-Two

FORTY-SEVEN MINUTES LATER, Kennedy received a weird telephone call—at least it was what he considered to be a weird telephone call.

'Hi, Christy. It's Vincent O'Connor.'

'Oh, hello, Father, how are you doing?'

'Fine, fine,' came the unusually taut reply. 'Tell me, is it true that you've just arrested Neil Roberts?'

Kennedy had been expecting it to take a little longer for the effective Camden Town bush telegraph to work its magic. To be truthful, he had been expecting the initial call to come from Alice Cain, with Fr O'Connor being the one lending the latter support.

'Well, actually, we're bringing him in for questioning as we speak.'

'Good,' came the short reply, just a mega-second before the priest hung up, leaving Kennedy with an earful not of the anticipated protests, but of pure white noise.

As Kennedy returned the phone to its cradle, he recalled O'Connor telling him that, in effect, he would never grass anyone up—even if the person in question had confessed to him professionally, so to speak. But if the suspect were caught by other means, perhaps the priest would be more cooperative. Was that what the telephone call had been about? The initial question was innocent enough, but the 'Good' was certainly judgemental enough for Kennedy.

Chapter Forty-Three

ON THE WAY to the interview room, Kennedy stopped by the forensic lab and was shown a virtual image of what had been done to the large wok with the aid, he was informed, of a Bunsen burner, a wooden hammer and an inch dowel rod. The result was what appeared to be like four small spouts coming from the wok.

Kennedy made his way down to the interview room where DS Irvine, Neil Roberts and his solicitor, Mr Harry Bryson, were waiting.

Bryson was very much the old-school solicitor and warmly greeted Kennedy as he arrived. The gesture drew only a look of concern from the client.

The minute DS Irvine turned on the tape recorder and announced the time, date and those present, Harry Bryson had moved into a different gear.

'Okay, I'd like to state here and now and on record,' he said, 'that for the precise time of the murder, my client has a watertight alibi. Furthermore, it's my understanding that you've already questioned a young lady, and it's my belief that she has corroborated my client's statement.'

With that, Bryson smiled a very smug smile and sank back into his hard chair.

'Okay, let's go through what we have here,' Kennedy began, sounding tired and weary.

Irvine sat forward in his seat, appearing as keen as those on the suspect's side of the table were to learn exactly what his superior had.

'First, we have to tell you that some of the thread fibres we removed from the back seat of your car have now been confirmed as having come from Mr Harry Ford's dark blue blazer.'

Roberts tittered. 'Oh, come on—we were good mates. I don't know how many times Harry was in my car. I was always dropping him off somewhere.'

'Accepted, but you did confirm to us earlier that you did not give him a lift in your car on Monday night.'

'Yes, that's right. He walked off into the night. I believe he was going to pick up a cab. That was the last time I saw him, in fact.' Roberts willingly repeated his earlier statement for the record and the tape recorder.

'You see,' Kennedy sighed, his tiredness miraculously lifting with all the theatrics of a Cape Canaveral launch. 'That's where I have my first problem.'

Kennedy stopped and left the words hanging between them, using the space to let Roberts mentally retrace his tracks. If he was doing so, his body language was not betraying him.

'Well, I'm afraid you're just going to have to take my word for it, in view of the fact that the only other interested party is deceased,' Roberts said defiantly.

'Not necessarily,' Kennedy replied, and then excused himself with, 'No, sorry if that seems a bit ambiguous. Of course, I didn't mean that Mr Ford was "not necessarily" deceased. No, what I meant was, we don't necessarily have to take your word for it.'

Kennedy paused again. He studied Roberts for a few seconds; still, the detective did not pick up on any pointers, so he continued: 'So, you claim that Harry Ford wasn't in your car on Monday evening?'

'That's correct.'

'And did you see Mr Ford on Saturday or Sunday?' Kennedy asked.

'No, I didn't.'

'So, he would not have been in your car on Saturday or Sunday.'

'Oh, please,' Roberts protested to his solicitor. 'Do I really have to put up with this? If I didn't see him on Saturday or Sunday, then Harry could certainly not have been in my car on either of those two days.'

Kennedy did a very bad impression of Colombo as he searched around in his pockets before eventually producing a folded foolscap piece of paper. He unfolded the paper slowly and passed it to Roberts, who looked at it and continued to study it. Kennedy allowed Roberts a few seconds to digest the information on the photocopy before he continued: 'Could you, just for the record, relay for us, if you please, the contents of this page?'

There was no reply at first, and then Roberts said, 'It's only a stupid receipt from a clothing store.'

'Just humour me, sir, if you would, and read out the date on the receipt,' Kennedy pushed, ever so politely.

'Okay, it's dated 27 August—that's Saturday just past,' Roberts said, eventually complying.

'And could you tell us which store the receipt is from?' Kennedy asked.

Roberts duly read: 'It's from GB Gentleman's Outfitters on Parkway in Camden Town.'

'And could you tell us what item or items are listed on the receipt?'

'There's only one item,' Roberts replied, apparently very much hoping Kennedy had made a mistake.

'I'm sorry. Of course, whatever you say. You've got the receipt. Could you tell us what the single item listed is?'

'It's a dark blue gentleman's blazer,' Roberts replied, still bewildered. 'What's this about? Are you trying to show us what a blazer costs these days? £59.50. Okay, I would have thought that was a little on the cheap side.'

'Perhaps, or perhaps just the kind of bargain the father of three grown-up children needed to seek out,' Kennedy announced. 'You see, Harry Ford bought a new blazer on Saturday. The first time he wore it, in fact, according to his wife, Lizabeth, was on Monday last. Furthermore, I have to advise you that it was the threads from this blazer which were found on the back seat of your car.'

The penny dropped first with Harry Bryson, then with Irvine, and, shortly thereafter, Roberts realised the direction of Kennedy's trail.

'So, we have proof that you did give Mr Ford a lift on Monday last, although I'm not entirely sure it's the kind of lift he would have wanted, given a choice. The other telling point here is that there wasn't a single fibre from Mr Ford's new blazer found in the front seat of the car, just on the back seat.'

Roberts was still giving off an unconcerned air—not so much cocky, as unconvinced.

'And then, the second thing which ties the murder of Mr Harry Ford directly to your doorstep, or should I say ties the murder of Mr Harry Ford directly to the dustbin in your garage, is three standard-size J-cloths.'

'If I'd known you were so desperate for J-cloths, Inspector, I could have given you a whole new fresh pack to save you from rummaging around in my dustbin.'

'Yes, but the used ones are of much more interest to us, Mr Roberts. You see, those particular J-cloths were soiled, and we've discovered exactly what it was they were soiled with,' Kennedy said, and then stopped.

He was beginning to think that he was grandstanding a tiny bit too much when Bryson said, 'Yes, Inspector, you've managed to get us all hooked with this one; we'd all love to know what exactly it was that you found on the J-cloths that apparently, if your dance is anything to go by, is so exceptionally interesting.'

'We found a sugar-and-water solution,' Kennedy replied, somewhat deflated.

'Goodness, is that all?' Bryson said. 'From the way you were going on, I thought you'd found a cure for the common cold.'

'Perhaps,' Kennedy said, gaining in confidence again, 'as far as the out-come of our case is concerned, our discovery will prove to be equally important, Mr Bryson. You see, we also found the same solution, 100 per cent identical, in fact, on the arms of Mr Ford's jacket and the legs of his trousers.'

For the first time since he had started the questioning, Kennedy thought he noticed a twitch of acknowledgment from Neil Roberts. Not so much a direct sign of guilt as perhaps the first drops of autumn rain. Your first thought invariably is, *No, it can't be,* and then a minute later you concede, *Yes, it is!*

'So,' Kennedy said, in apparent summary, 'we know that Mr Ford was in Mr Roberts's car on Monday night, even though Mr Roberts lied about this fact, and we know that Mr Ford was in Mr Roberts's garage on the same night, thanks to the fact that Mr Roberts tried to clean up after him using the J-cloths, which have now betrayed him.'

'Yes Detective Inspector,' Bryson said. 'I can see where you're trying to go with this, but none of this is at all relevant when you consider that we have a witness who has already gone on record saying she was with Mr Roberts at the time of the murder.'

'Okay. Fair point,' Kennedy graciously conceded. 'Let's discuss that issue in a moment or two, when I've shown you how Mr Roberts was able to murder Harry Ford, while at the same time being in the company of Miss Nealey Dean.'

Irvine shot Kennedy a look that suggested, *Yes, sir, I could be doing with the same explanation.*

'Okay,' Kennedy said, and took a rather long sigh. 'We know that from the early days of the Four Musketeers—you, your sister Alice, Vincent O'Connor and the aforementioned Harry Ford—you were very protective of your sister; perhaps some would say overly protective? We know that you were partially responsible for hijacking Alice and Harry's first attempts at romance, perhaps even driving her towards Vincent O'Connor in the process. You knew that O'Connor would never last the pace with someone like Alice.

'Your hijacking was successful because, as a result of that incident, Harry went off and married Lizabeth, and Alice went off and married Bob Cain. I believe that those who know about this type of infatuation of yours would suggest that you would not have seen the much older Mr Cain as a threat. In your eyes, he could never have replaced you in Alice's affections the way someone like Harry was capable of doing.

'Recently, I believe, you discovered three very important facts. First, that Harry and Alice had resumed and continued their affair over the past twenty-odd years. Second, that they had had a daughter together. And finally, you discovered that on at least one occasion in their relationship, they had both made plans to leave their respective spouses to live together.

'To you, this was unthinkable, even though all those years had passed—here was your original competitor charging back in on his white horse to steal your sister again. So, you decided to do something about it, just as you had done all those years ago at university, except that this time merely undermining Alice wasn't going to work. You were going to have to take much more drastic actions, make your solution permanent this time, as it were.

'So, you hatched a plan—a very cunning plan at that. You planned what you considered to be the perfect murder of your competitor.

'Now, I think it's safe to assume that, for you, the perfect murder was one where you would have the perfect alibi for the time of the murder.

'Come Monday night, you'd made all your plans. All your careful preparations were in place when you met Harry Ford, as usual on Mondays, in the gym.

'You invited him back to your place for a drink; you probably walked back from the gym which would account for no traces of Harry's new jacket being found in the front seat of your car. When you reached your home you spiked his drink with Rohypnol, more commonly known as Roofies, the date-rape drug.

'You moved Harry's comatose body from your living room to your garage. You had plastic sheets already stretched over the garage floor; you laid Harry's body down in the middle of the plastic-covered floor. Here's the clever bit—you obviously remembered that whenever a little water gets in a sugar bowl, if unattended, the sugar will eventually go rock hard. Yes? You prepared four pots with such sugar masses. We found three empty Tate & Lyle 2lb sugar bags in your dustbin—too much sugar for someone to use at once, no matter how sweet a tooth they have. So you strategically placed these four pots around Harry's body, one by each arm and one by each leg.

'And these pots were positioned so that the four legs of a coffee table would fit into them. It's an exact science, all of this—you had to work out how much shorter to cut the coffee-table legs for it to be effective. Just like you had to experiment with how much water you would need to add to the sugar pots to ensure the required rock-hard effect. Too much and the solution becomes a mush which will never solidify, and too little and no transformation takes place at all.

'Now, your coffee table—even apart from the shortened legs—was no ordinary coffee table. On the underside, you had hammered in nine six-inch nails, in the shape of a cross. Perhaps they were in the shape of a cross to draw attention to Fr O'Connor, or perhaps merely to satisfy your sense of the bizarre, I don't know—and, to be perfectly honest, I don't really care. Anyway, to each of these nine nails you had gaffer-taped the handle of a knife.

'With me so far?' Kennedy asked.

For different reasons, everyone was speechless, so Kennedy continued: 'Now, you had your coffee-table death contraption with legs resting in your four rock-sugar pots, with the blades of the knives pointing down towards the comatose Harry Ford. You then placed a large wok in the centre of the coffee table. You steadied the wok with several of the weights, which were also lying around your garage. Not only would the weights steady the wok, but they would also, later, help the knives to achieve their goal.'

Here Kennedy produced a copy of a print of the virtual wok as reconstructed by his forensic team.

'As you can see,' Kennedy continued, primarily addressing Bryson and Irvine, 'Mr Roberts created four spouts on the perimeter of the wok. To each spout he attached a tube and ran each tube to its corresponding rock-sugar pot.

'Next, you ran your new garden hose from the tap of your Belfast sink and over to the wok,' Kennedy said, now talking directly to Roberts again. 'I should say that it was the garden hose that first got me thinking. Why would you buy a new garden hose when you don't have a square inch of garden on your premises? I suppose you could claim it was to wash your

278 • PAUL CHARLES

car, couldn't you? But then our people discovered several car-wash receipts in amongst the receipts on the clipboard in the garage, all neatly done up with your petrol receipts ready for your accountant.

'Right, so you had the hose running from the tap above the sink. Again, in your research you'd have needed to work out how long the wok would have taken to fill with water, and how far to turn the tap on to achieve this timing.

'You set your tap to drip at the required speed, then you nipped upstairs to prepare yourself for Nealey Dean. She arrived around ten o'clock; you enjoyed a drink and some Indian snacks. Meanwhile, downstairs in the garage, the wok eventually overflowed, and the water then dripped down the tubes and into the sugar pots.

'This water would quite quickly dissolve the rock-hard sugar into a watery solution, and the legs of the lethal table, helped by the weights on top, would sink down into the pots, and the knives would sink fatally into Harry Ford's body. I can only hope that he never regained consciousness.

'After Miss Dean left your house, around 2 a.m., you went down to the garage. You removed your apparatus, cleaned up the sugar-water solution that had spilled out of the sugar pots and stained Harry's jacket and trousers. You used the incriminating J-cloths for this. You placed a plastic sheet over the back seat of your car and dumped Harry's dead body on top of it.

'You put on a long trench coat, drove up to St Martin's Gardens and pulled Harry out of the back seat. During the course of this awkward manoeuvre, several fibres and threads from his new blazer brushed against your car seat and remained there. You propped Harry up against the side of the car, slung his arm over your shoulder, and you stumbled into the centre of the square like two drunks the worse for wear.

'You dumped him in the centre of the gardens and returned to your home and continued with the cleaning-up, eventually dumping the majority of the incriminating material, but, alas, not all of it.'

Kennedy could not work out if Bryson and Irvine were more impressed with his powers of deduction or with Neil Roberts's ingenuity. He and Irvine left Neil Roberts and Harry Bryson and the relevant paperwork to Sergeant Tim Flynn.

Roberts went without an argument in the end, perhaps happy in the knowledge that he had done what he had set out to do—he had removed the competition for his sister's affections. He admitted the murder of Harry

Ford on the condition that his sister would not be called to testify to the details of their relationship.

'How the heck did you ever get your brain around that one?' Irvine asked, still sounding in denial.

'Well, it really was a team thing. I just put all the information together. Firstly, I remembered seeing an Italian gentleman up in the Honest Sausage café in Regent's Park load his coffee up with so much sugar that his plastic spoon stood straight up in it, unaided, as he opened even more sugar sachets. Then Dr Taylor drew my attention to the fact that the stab wounds were not usual stab wounds, in that they were too symmetrical in their lining-up in the shape of a cross, and that all wounds went into the body at a pure 90-degree angle. Then we had the sugar-solution stains on Harry's jacket and trousers—that was a new one on me. Then your Nealey Dean—Roberts made just too much of a fuss, staging her as his alibi. When forensics discovered Harry's jacket fibres in Roberts's car, I remembered Lizabeth telling me about Harry setting off to work in his new jacket. Then we discovered the plastic sheet, Tate & Lyle bags and empty gaffer-tape rolls, all conveniently left for us in Roberts's garage—you see, he obviously figured that we'd never bother him again after we questioned Nealey Dean, so—'

'Ah shit,' Irvine gasped, interrupting his senior.

'What?' Kennedy asked in genuine concern.

'Nealey, sir,' Irvine gushed. 'I've got to contact her and tip her off that the proverbial is just about to hit the fan, and I do mean big lumps, sir.'

'Of course,' Kennedy said. 'Off you go immediately!'

Chapter Forty-Four

I RVINE RETURNED TO his office as fast as his brogues would carry him and dialled the mobile telephone number written on her perfumed piece of paper.

Her mobile answering facility clicked in on the third ring, and Irvine left a message requesting her to ring him back as soon as possible. 'It's very urgent,' he added and immediately regretted it.

Ten seconds after he had returned his phone to its cradle, it started ringing.

'Hello, I was starting to think you'd never call,' the distinctive voice said.

'I've just rung you.'

'I know. I use that as a screening device,' she replied and paused. 'So, what took you so long?'

'Look, Nealey, this is official, I'm afraid.'

'Oh,' she said, the regret clear in her voice.

'We've just charged Neil Roberts with Harry Ford's murder . . .'

'But I thought he was with me at the time of the murder?'

'He was, but please believe me, he did it. You won't believe how. I'll explain it to you some time. I just wanted to warn you that when the press picks up on the facts of his case, and he starts to use your name—'

'Yes, I see. Thanks for that, James. I mean, thanks for thinking about my well-being.'

'Oh, no problem . . .' Irvine found himself running through things he thought he should say to her, but when he got down to it, all he could allow himself to say was, 'Ah, well, I suppose I'd better leave you to it.'

'Yes, erm . . .' Now it was her turn to struggle for words. 'Oh, thanks again, James.'

'Look, Nealey, this is bordering on being unprofessional, but if I were to maybe offer to invite you out to dinner, I mean—'

'Gosh, I was trying to find a way of asking you the same thing without appearing too forward or compromising you.'

'Right, and would such a dinner invitation be for social purposes or merely for research?' Irvine asked, relaxing into a more comfortable line of conversation.

'Well, why don't you invite me out, and then you might discover the answer to that question, assuming of course that you're any good as a detective.'

'Okay, when are you free? Shall we say next week?'

'I'm free tomorrow evening actually,' Nealey Dean reported enthusiastically.

Chapter Forty-Five

THAT FRIDAY NIGHT at around about eight o'clock, Kennedy sat in his office in North Bridge House, making telephone calls. First, he rang Lizabeth Ford and Alice Cain to give them the news.

'I'm not sure I could ever be shocked by the actions of any member of that family,' Lizabeth said quietly to conclude their conversation.

Alice already knew and admitted that perhaps the 'brother-and-sister issues' she and Neil had should have been addressed professionally earlier in their life. As if offering justification, she revealed: 'Don't get me wrong, though, Christy. We haven't been physical since just before we went to university.'

Kennedy wondered whether he would have paid more attention to Neil if he had had his suspicions spelt out so clearly by Alice earlier in the case. He filed it under water under the bridge and moved on without the anchors of regrets.

She also said that she had started to miss Harry.

'When someone you know dies, you don't miss them for a time,' she went on. 'This surprises you, but it shouldn't really. I've been thinking about it a lot, and I think it's because, in the course of a week, I would see Harry once, maybe twice, and speak to him on the phone several times, so you see he was still fresh in my memory. Now some time has passed and I'm starting to realise that he's missing from my daily life and, what's more and hardest to take . . .'—the phone line went quiet at this point for a minute or so—'. . . is that I'm starting to realise that I will never ever see him again and I don't know if I can bear that.'

He rang Fr Vincent O'Connor. Once Kennedy had assured the priest that Neil Roberts had indeed been charged with the murder of Harry Ford, O'Connor explained the reason for his bizarre telephone call earlier and his rather strange behaviour towards Kennedy earlier on in the investigation.

Reading between the lines—although it was still not blatantly admitted by Fr O'Connor—Kennedy gathered that Roberts had guessed in a conversation with O'Connor that the priest was suspicious that Roberts was involved in the murder. Roberts then confessed the murder to his priest (the very same O'Connor), who was therefore obliged to keep the information confidential. He did say that he had been trying to steer Kennedy in the right direction. He reminded Kennedy of the Judas conversation they had shared. Kennedy was not sure if that hadn't been another of those *All the President's Men* moments of confusion. O'Connor reiterated that whereas he could never betray the confession box, he would have been happy to try to confirm any facts presented to him.

Kennedy then rang ann rea and arranged to meet her at the top of Primrose Hill. She was amazed at how quickly Kennedy and his team had solved this particular case, which she promptly christened Sweetwater. She suggested that it might have had something to do with the fact that his mind had been clear and refreshed after his recuperating break.

Kennedy, as ever modest, suggested that it might have had more to do with the great police work of his team and more than a little luck.

Twenty minutes later, they were sitting watching one of the prettiest sights in London as the dusk gave way to the equally spectacular London night-lights.

As they sat together, totally content in each other's company for possibly the first time in their four-year relationship, they were oblivious to a bearded man sitting on the other bench enjoying the same sights and experiencing the same emotions, with a silver-haired lady similar in age to the man.

Both couples, although a generation apart, had a lot in common.

Kennedy and ann rea's relationship had nearly not made it for several reasons, but most of the reasons had been in their control, if only they had realised it. However, the couple opposite were probably destined to be together. The elderly couple had not been kept apart by doubts or degrees of immaturity. No, the single biggest hurdle for them had been the fact that neither of them had wanted to start a relationship which would have caused them to cheat on their spouses. In the end, though, they had both reached their conclusion that for the little time they had left on this earth, they, like Kennedy and ann rea, should do what they felt in their hearts.

There was one other connection between the couples who sat that September night atop Primrose Hill.

Kennedy caught the other man's eye for a split second. The detective was sure he remembered something familiar about the gentleman, but he could not quite figure out precisely what.

ann rea snuggled up cosily to Kennedy, suggesting that they had reached some level of contentment of their own.

Eventually the detective and his friend stood up, and a contented John Riley and his companion watched the couple walk, arm in arm, back down Primrose Hill.

JACK BARRY
Miss Katie Regrets

From Dublin's criminal underbelly comes a gripping story of guns, drugs, prostitution and corruption. At the centre of a spider's web of intrigue sits the enigmatic figure of Miss Katie, a crabby transvestite who will, under pressure, kiss and tell. And, perhaps, kill.

ISBN 0 86322 354 0; paperback original

SAM MILLAR
The Redemption Factory

"While most writers sit in their study and make it up, Sam Millar has lived it and every sentence... evokes a searing truth about men, their dark past, and the code by which they live. Great title, great read. Disturbingly brutal. I enjoyed it immensely." Cyrus Nowrasteh

ISBN 0 86322 339 7; paperback original

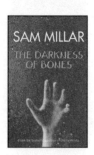

SAM MILLAR
The Darkness of Bones

In a derelict orphanage, a tramp discovers the mutilated and decapitated corpse of its former head warden. Millar's second crime novel is a tense tale of murder, betrayal, sexual abuse and revenge, and the corruption at the heart of the respectable establishment.

ISBN 0 86322 350 8; paperback original

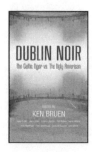

KEN BRUEN (ED)
Dublin Noir

Brand new stories by Ray Banks, James O. Born, Ken Bruen, Reed Farrell Coleman, Eoin Colfer, Jim Fusilli, Patrick J. Lambe, Laura Lippman, Craig McDonald, Pat Mullan, Gary Phillips, John Rickards, Peter Spiegelman, Jason Starr, Olen Steinhauer, Charlie Stella, Duane Swierczynski, Sarah Weinman and Kevin Wignall.

ISBN 0 86322 353 2; paperback original

KEN BRUEN

WINNER OF THE SHAMUS AWARD FOR BEST NOVEL,
FINALIST FOR THE EDGAR, BARRY AND MACAVITY AWARDS

The Guards
"Bleak, amoral and disturbing, *The Guards* breaks new
ground in the Irish thriller genre, replacing furious
fantasy action with acute observation of human frailty."
Irish Independent
"With Jack Taylor, Bruen has created a true original."
Sunday Tribune

ISBN 0 86322 281 1; paperback

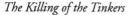

The Killing of the Tinkers
"Jack Taylor is back in town, weighed down with
wisecracks and cocaine ... Somebody is murdering
young male travellers and Taylor, with his reputation as
an outsider, is the man they want to get to the root of
things ...Compulsive ... rapid fire ... entertaining."
Sunday Tribune

ISBN 0 86322 294 3; paperback

The Magdalen Martyrs
"Exhibits Ken Bruen's all-encompassing ability to
depict the underbelly of the criminal world and still
imbue it with a torrid fascination... carrying an
adrenalin charge for those who like their thrillers
rough, tough, mean and dirty." *The Irish Times*

ISBN 0 86322 302 8; paperback

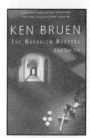

The Dramatist
"Collectively, the Jack Taylor novels are Bruen's
masterwork, and *The Dramatist* is the darkest and most
profound installment of the series to date... Readers
who dare the journey will be days shaking this most
haunting book out of their heads."
This Week

ISBN 0 86322 319 2; paperback original

KITTY FITZGERALD
Small Acts of Treachery

"Mystery and politics, a forbidden sexual attraction that turns into romance; Kitty Fitzgerald takes the reader on a gripping roller coaster through the recent past. This is a story you can't stop reading, with an undertow which will give you cause to reflect." Sheila Rowbotham

ISBN 086322 297 8; paperback

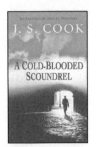

J.S. COOK
A Cold-Blooded Scoundrel

An Inspector Devlin Mystery
In London, at a time when Jack the Ripper is still fresh in the memory, a well-known male prostitute is brutally murdered, the head neatly severed, and the body set on fire.

ISBN 0 86322 336 2; paperback original

EVELYN CONLON
Skin of Dreams

"A courageous, intensely imagined and tightly focused book that asks powerful questions of authority... this is the kind of Irish novel that is all too rare." Joseph O'Connor

ISBN 0 86322 306 0; paperback original

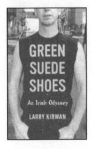

LARRY KIRWAN
Green Suede Shoes

"Lively and always readable. He has wrought a refined tale of a raw existence, filled with colorful characters and vivid accounts." *Publishers Weekly*

ISBN 086322 343 5; paperback original

FICTION   Charles, Paul.
Charles
           Sweetwater.